Fade to Black

a novel by

Josh Pryor

RED HEN PRESS | *Pasadena, CA*

Fade to Black
Copyright © 2011 by Josh Pryor
All rights reserved

Book layout and design by Andrew Mendez

Library of Congress Cataloging-in-Publication Data

Pryor, Josh.
  Fade to black : a novel / by Josh Pryor. —1st ed.
    p. cm.
  ISBN 978-1-59709-125-1
  I. Title.
  PS3616.R97F33 2011
  813'.6—dc22

                         2011011752

The Los Angeles County Arts Commission, the National Endowment for the Arts, the California Arts Council and Los Angeles Department of Cultural Affairs partially support Red Hen Press.

First Edition

Published by Red Hen Press
Pasadena, CA
www.redhen.org

*This book is dedicated to the memory
of my grandfather, Gene dePrado . . .
I advise the zip*

Fade to Black

And the earth was without form, and void; and darkness was upon the face of the deep.
—Genesis 1:2

Ross Sea: Antarctica
Longitude/Latitude: 80° 30' 17" S, 175°00' W
July 1981

Surfacing less than a kilometer from the disintegrating edge of the Ross Ice Shelf was insane in the best of conditions. Today, in conditions such as these when the wind howled across the gray-green sea like a pack of frothing wolves and the seasonal landmass was sheering apart beneath the onslaught of nearly four months of perpetual daylight, it was fucking suicide. A fool's errand. Monoliths of ice as big as the Politburo building in Moscow crashed into the churning abyss as the shelf contracted toward the southern pole laying waste to the mighty ramparts and battlements the perpetual darkness of Antarctic winter had built over the previous months. The largest of these—many weighing in excess of 1,000 tons—broke free with screeching thunderclaps that seemed to herald the end of the world. Only a lunatic would not have been terrified. But there was no chance of that—no chance that Senior Lieutenant Rodya Keldysh was *choknútyy* despite what his wife, Akilina, told him each time he shipped out. He was trembling too badly, his heart filled with too much dread he would admit shamelessly the next time he held Aki's soft, warm body in his arms. What he would give to be at home in bed with her now, her worried eyes prying at his impenetrable wall of reassurance, desperately wanting to understand him, though she knew better for he was too practiced at it, even as she carried a living piece of him inside her. They had talked about names, but nothing had been decided. A boy—he wanted a boy.

Keldysh had been above deck scarcely over a minute and already the pencil-thin cable tethering him to the conning tower had sprouted jagged teeth of ice that gnawed at his gloves. It was -45 degrees Celsius, a glorious summer day. One wrong twist, a move too sudden and the frozen umbilical would snap, severing his only tie to life but for the dream of it. Metal fatigue, the chief engineer had warned him—in temperatures so far below freezing the very physics of things was altered. The world was not the world we knew. A gust of Antarctic wind could instantly char the skin black as if by fire. Each time a swell smashed into the *Vaslav Annenkov's* hull, Keldysh was peppered with frozen pellets of spray that peppered him like buckshot. Poor little crab clinging to a rock in a raging sea. Hold on for dear life, little crab, or go swimming. Straight to the bottom, little limbs knitting uselessly against the oncoming deep. The cumbersome dry-suit promised to protect him from the glacial waters was a luxurious lie, a tuxedo on a dead man. If the cold of the sea didn't kill him almost instantly, Keldysh would be pulverized in the collapsed ruins of the White Kingdom crumbling into oblivion all around him.

It was taking them too fucking long. A coordinated rendezvous in this place, here and now—Christ Himself couldn't work miracles in cold like this. But neither did Christ take orders from the KGB. Given the choice of being tethered to the *Vaslav* in this mess or remaining nailed to the Cross for all eternity, Keldysh was sure that the Son of God would have chosen the Cross. At least it was not a cold death. A chance encounter with one of the 1,000-ton rogues bobbing in the sea about them could gut the *Vaslav* from stem to stern and render it a frozen tomb.

No more apparent than the dull buzz of an insect, came the labored growl of an outboard motor guiding a small craft through the shifting labyrinth of ice. The puny vessel, an ancient whale-boat, pierced the clinging mist, its high painted bow flaking and splintered to reveal patches of bare wood. Three men in dry-suits similar to his own—the helmsman wrestling with the outboard, another braced in the prow with an old wooden mooring pole he used to deflect the oncoming blocks of ice, and a third hunkered deep in the belly—comprised the miserable crew. Keldysh, officer that he was, suddenly found his own safety to be of secondary concern. How these three fools had made it this far was anyone's guess? Each heaving swell presented the whale-boat with a treacherous mountain to climb, each trough a frozen pit out of which to dig itself. If the helmsman misjudged the timing of his arrival by a fraction of a second, he would slam the deep-keeled whale-boat down hard atop the *Vaslav's* deck so that it would splinter apart and cast all three into the swirling abyss. That he might be crushed to death himself was Keldysh's only consolation. He'd never lost a man at sea; this despite all he had witnessed in nearly a decade as a submariner is why he slept like a baby each and every night. One way or another, he would allow nothing to change that. But with an impressive display of seamanship, the helmsman spared Keldysh his nightmares, timing the whale-boat's arrival atop a swell so that it scarcely kissed the *Vaslav's* starboard flank as the man in the bow snagged the one of the deck grates with the mooring pole and held them as steady as could be reasonably expected.

The man hunkered in the belly of the whale-boat—the poor soul tasked with the safe arrival of their cargo—heaved onto his knees and braced his chest against the gunwale scraping back and forth against the *Vaslav*. His face was muffled against the biting cold, but the thin crescents of his exposed cheekbones were badly frostbitten. Fringed in ice, his dark scared eyes had withdrawn deep into his skull as if huddling near the embers of his brain, his iced lashes wreathing the sunken hollows like the hoary blooms of first frost.

"Get on with it!" the helmsman barked. "I can't feel my prick inside my pants!"

The man with the dark ice-encrusted eyes carefully retrieved something from the bottom of the boat—a fairly large package wrapped in a drab wool blanket—and extended it out over the gunwale to Keldysh who was experiencing the early stages of hypothermia. His arms were impossibly heavy, weakened by the loss of blood that had since migrated into his core to nourish his vital organs. He dropped to his knees so he would be closer to the water, but felt closer to God than made him comfortable. The deck was enameled with ice but he managed the wrestle the parcel onto his lap without falling overboard. He estimated the wind at 30–35 knots.

The whale-boat had taken on water during its brief passage through the turbulent soup, and the helmsman bailed mechanically with a large coffee can to keep her from swamping. Still, she was riding dangerously low, low enough to be at risk of capsizing on the return trip. They wouldn't make it back to shore alive. Although he would catch hell from the captain, Keldysh urged the three of them to ditch the floundering craft and board the *Vaslav* where it was safe. "You're sinking!" he shouted into the face of the wind. "You'll die if you go back now!"

"*Udachi!*" blurted the man with the mooring pole, pushing off with all the force he could muster as the helmsman gunned the outboard and stabbed them back into the bobbing labyrinth of ice. But it wasn't Keldysh who needed good luck. He could hardly watch as the ludicrous craft clawed its way up the wind-shattered face of a three-meter swell and sledded into the gaping trough waiting to swallow them whole on the other side.

Although prayer was strictly forbidden onboard Soviet military vessels—an act of petty treason—Keldysh muttered one under his breath before passing the horrible parcel to a shrouded figure waiting in the conning tower. "*Holy God, Holy Mighty, Holy Immortal One, have mercy on us.*"

The select few on hand to witness the arrival of the mysterious cargo muttered to one another in disgust. For this, they had journeyed thousands of miles to the frozen asshole of the earth! To them, the creature occupying the Plexiglas cage the captain held before him like a lighted birthday cake was stew meat, a pair of cheap women's gloves at best. None could fathom an equation in which a small white rabbit with darting pink eyes and ugly yellow-gray incisors was worth dying for. Of course, Keldysh saw what they could not possibly see, what only he, the captain and a handful of others knew. Far deadlier than any bomb in the Soviet nuclear arsenal, Ivan the Terrible lurked behind those darting pink eyes. Who could've imagined that doomsday could appear so harmless?

They were just underway and preparing to dive when the *Vaslav* collided with an iceberg, taking the brunt of the impact aft of the port stabilizer and glancing sharply starboard. A grating metallic shriek reverberated down the length of the sub's sleek titanium hull. Keldysh knew what such a sound could mean and it turned his blood to ice water. As one of the only officers onboard experienced with polar navigation, he had warned the chief sonar man of the perils of nomadic ice. Subsurface clutter could wreak havoc on the echoes the *Vaslav* relied on to guide her safely through the water. If Keldysh were to hazard a guess, a phantom signal had led the sonar man to misjudge the relative position of the object they had struck. Armed with faulty information, the helmsman had steered directly into it. But now was not the time for guessing. Now was not the time for blame.

Although probably not severe enough to sink them, the collision had knocked the *Vaslav's* primary operational systems offline. This was a standard safety feature of all VM-4 pressurized water reactors, and under ordinary circumstances Keldysh would have been grateful. These, however, were not ordinary circumstances. At the moment of impact the captain instinctively threw out his arms for balance, sending the cage crashing into the deck. One of the six transparent panels it comprised split away from the others, setting Ivan free. Now it was out in the open, scampering about for a place to hide in the thin blood red glow of the auxiliary lights, fueled by adrenaline and instinct and only the devil-knows-what. In an instant, the crew, trained to act rather than react, gave chase through the listing bridge. None seemed to care that the *Vaslav's* primary systems had automatically gone offline to conserve power. They were having too much fun laughing and cursing at one another as the rabbit, aided by the slow circular rocking of the boat, darted through wide open legs and scrambled out of the reach of grasping hands, its claws scratching furiously over the steel deck plates in its futile bid for life. For a drawn-out moment, even the urgent calls from the chief engineer, a frantic voice on the intercom, went unheeded. Maybe the three on the whale-boat knew what they were doing—risking death on the water rather than death unknown.

And then it was over.

One of Keldysh's men cried out triumphantly as he scooped the rabbit from the deck and held it kicking wildly at arm's length. *"Ayyy!"* he cried, clutching the elusive creature by the roll of loose skin at the base of its skull. Twin pinpricks of blood marked the back of the crew member's left hand where he'd been bitten. The rabbit, for all its inherent menace, went immediately limp, a slow fixed gaze overtaking its once darting pink eyes. There it remained suspended in the devilish light, intermittently twitching its little pink nose, a model of utter docility.

"Hold on tight, Vidchenko!" one of the crew members chided. "We may have to scuttle the lifeboats if he gets loose again!"

The others laughed. All but Keldysh and the captain.

Seaman Vidchenko was with Military Unit 2 and had been on deck to oversee the exchange in case anything went wrong. Standard protocol. Vidchenko was a good man—all of the men onboard the *Vaslav* were good men, handpicked by the captain himself. All, of course, but Vidchenko. He belonged to Keldysh. Keldysh had pushed hard for Vidchenko. Not because his service record was exemplary, which it was, but because Vidchenko was Akilina's baby brother. Family. Serving on the *Vaslav* meant rapid promotion, better pay, and a distinguished military career. It meant a good life for Vidchenko's wife, Elizaveta, and Keldysh's two young nieces, Anastasiya and Nadina, the cousins of his own child-to-be. In Aki's own words, it meant that Keldysh could "keep Andrej out of trouble . . ." How was he going to explain this to her? Aki would never forgive him. But right now, Keldysh could not second-guess himself. He had tried to convince Aki that another vessel, any vessel—a crab boat in the Bering Sea for the love of St. Peter—would have been a better choice. But she would have nothing of it, and now her baby brother was dead. Vidchenko was still armed—an AK-47 slung over his shoulder—and there were four dozen other men and their families to think about. Right now, Keldysh's only responsibility was to the uninfected members of the crew. The living. Anastasiya and Nadina—Keldysh could help raise his two nieces himself if need be. But he could not raise the dead.

"Good work, Andrej," said Keldysh. It was the only time he had ever called his brother-in-law by his given name onboard the *Vaslav*.

Vidchenko smiled broadly in the fiery red shadows, Ivan cycling his legs idly in a half-hearted attempt at flight.

Keldysh smiled calmly. "Show me where you were bitten."

The captain and Keldysh exchanged glances before the captain excused himself.

"It's nothing," explained Vidchenko. "Just a scratch."

"Please, Andrej . . ."

Vidchenko held out his right hand. Gravity had stretched the twin droplets of blood into parallel exclamation points, reminding Keldysh of just how fucked he was.

After a brief moment, the captain returned. "I've contacted the doctor," he explained. "He should be up shortly."

"The doctor?" Vidchenko scoffed. "Captain, I'm fine. Like I said, it's just a scratch."

Keldysh's voice was now sterner, imbued with the authority of rank and no small amount of frustration with himself. He'd known having his brother-in-law onboard was a stupid fucking idea. "Remember to whom you're speaking Seaman Vidchenko!"

Vidchenko came to attention, the rabbit dangling comically at his side. "Yes, Senior Lieutenant!"

"At ease, seaman," the captain reassured, his tone conveying nothing in the way of alarm, simply concern. "You're bleeding. Permit me the decency of tending to one of my crew."

Shortly, two crew members emerged from below deck: the doctor and one of the reactor engineers, a man wearing a lead apron and monstrous lead-lined gloves. Keldysh recognized him as Seaman Bochkaiy, a thick, brutish man of Hungarian descent famous among the crew for his tolerance to vodka and radiation.

"Give Comrade Bochkaiy the rabbit," Keldysh ordered.

"It's just a scratch," Vidchenko echoed. "I don't understand."

Without expression, Bochkaiy received the rabbit from Vidchenko and disappeared with it at arm's length. A plodding Frankenstein dumbly anticipating supper.

"Stop being a baby and give me your arm" said the doctor. From a small metal case, he produced a hypodermic no bigger than his little finger.

Doubt now crept into Vidchenko's eyes. He withdrew his arm as if it was a poisonous snake the doctor held. "What is this, Rodya?"

"Seaman!" Keldysh's voice cracked slightly, but he quickly regained his edge. Keldysh could hardly forget the timetables the army doctors had outlined. The incubation period took anywhere from twenty-four to ninety-six hours depending on the individual and a variety of secondary factors, most notably body temperature. If an infected subject could be kept "profoundly" hypothermic—that is, hovering just below 20 °C—it was possible to stretch the timeline. The problem was keeping the organism cold enough to delay its lifecycle enough without killing the host. Ivan burned hot; the freezer would have to be cranked all the way down just to compete with his infernal nature. But why anyone would want to prolong the inevitable was beyond comprehension. Ivan the Terrible was a death decree. This man with whom Keldysh had shared countless holidays and family occasions, this man whose infant daughters he had rocked to sleep—*"Djadja Rody"* to them—this man who made Aki belly laugh—his "little brother" Andrej—was a danger to him now, to every man onboard. Keldysh knew what had to be done; the KGB had imprinted the ghoulish contingency protocol on his soul. Keldysh had never thought of himself as a fool, but in this instance he had somehow lacked the foresight, enough simple imagination to see that such misfortune as this wasn't so much coincidence, yet rather the natural consequence of his own stupidity. *"The wise man's eyes are in his head, but the fool walks in darkness. . . . And yet I know that one fate befalls them both."* He recited the familiar verse in his head, its words, he found, like so many of those borrowed from the Bible, as inevitable as was the sudden turn his destiny had taken. He now understood the bloody Rorschach marking Andrej's hand: it was the face of doom.

"The doctor needs to give you antibiotics so the wound doesn't become infected," Keldysh urged him with a lying serpent's grin. "Eli would cut off my balls if I brought you home foaming at the mouth lie a rabid dog."

"It's true," said the doctor. He was a thin man with watery eyes and breath that smelled vaguely of diesel fuel. Keldysh believed him to be an alcoholic, or worse, and did not trust him either.

"Why wouldn't it be?" Vidchenko's warm blue eyes were perplexed. He gently massaged his hand where he'd been bitten, smearing the blood into a pale pink Rorschach that he studied mutely, contemplating its hidden meaning. Keldysh saw the horror taking shape in his brother-in-law's mind, a wisp of smoke coalescing in advance of a raging fire that would lay waste to everything it touched.

The doctor clucked his tongue nervously and looked to the captain for instructions.

"Look," Keldysh reminded him forcefully. "I stuck my out neck to get you on the *Vaslav*. Don't make this into issue we'll both regret."

"My girls," Vidchenko whispered, as if it was they the bloody Rorschach had revealed.

"If it will make you feel better, I'll give you the injection myself." Keldysh fixated on the AK-47. If Vidchenko went mad now, icebergs would be the least of their worries. All he could think of was the grainy black and white photographs the army doctors had shown him. Oil rig workers murdered savagely and strung up by their intestines from the rafters of a small nondescript barracks somewhere on the ice. Accompanying the gore was an official framed portrait of Khrushchev hung on one of the walls. It was an old and faded photograph, and someone had penned in a long beard and bushy eyebrows so that he vaguely resembled Tolstoy.

"Enough!" the captain barked, his demeanor undergoing a profound and instantaneous transformation. "The clock is ticking."

Vidchenko looked up to find the captain leveling a Makarov 9mm squarely between his eyes.

The doctor stopped mid-cluck, paling. "Captain," he warned. "His blood—"

"Now," the captain instructed Vidchenko coldly, "or I tell your wife we had you shot for treason."

The *Vaslav* listed badly to one side, but no one seemed to notice. Keldysh's heart thudded in his ears; his mouth was dry. Vidchenko complied, slowly extending his arm. His eyes locked onto Keldysh's own and would not let go until the powerful sedative rendered him all but dead.

"Get him into the freezer before he wakes up," the captain ordered. He squatted and studied the small wound on the back of Vidchenko's hand. "Doesn't look like much."

❖ ❖ ❖

Fifty-two hours had elapsed since the collision in the Ross Sea and the *Vaslav* was limping back to Vidyaevo as fast as her damaged stabilizer would allow. A wounded duck. Despite a direct order from Senior Lieutenant Keldysh to stay away from the freezer, Seaman Kalinin, the cook, could not resist the temptation. He had never seen a man frozen solid before. And although the entire crew could have easily survived on their dried and canned stores for the remainder of the voyage, he saw no reason to deprive himself of real food. This had nothing to do with disrespecting the dead as the lieutenant suggested when issuing the order; this was about eight double-cut lamb chops hidden in a package marked CHICKEN LIVERS. Kalinin had traded a pair of real American Levi's for the delicacy and he wasn't going to let the beautifully marbled meat go to waste. The *Vaslav* would have to undergo extensive repairs when they returned to port and you could bet that one ministry or another would be watching her like a hawk. The only way he would ever get the lamb chops off the damaged vessel was in his gut. He had been thinking about them for days.

It was no accident that he was now too fat to wear the pants that had not long ago been the pride of his wardrobe. Comrade Vidchenko would understand; he, too, had been a born carnivore with an appetite for meat nearly as prodigious as Kalinin's own. Of course no one had told him that Vidchenko wasn't actually dead when they had locked him in the freezer . . . Heart attack—sudden, instantaneous death—was the official word being circulated around the *Vaslav*. And the rumors . . . Ridiculous ghost stories no more credible than the tales of sea monsters prowling the deep ocean trenches recounted by scared little tadpoles wetting their gills their first time out of port. As far as Kalinin was concerned, half of what you heard on a submarine was pure bullshit, and the other half was lies.

Aside from the obvious, his freezer was a mess. You would have thought the clumsy oafs who had stuck Vidchenko here had been grappling with a live gorilla and not a dead man. Much of what had been arranged neatly on the shelves—an assortment of vacuum-packed vegetables and brown paper-wrapped packages of meat—lay strewn about the floor. Fortunately, Kalinin had labeled each himself for ready identification. But it was Vidchenko's corpse that now interested him.

This was not at all what he expected. First, there was Vidchenko's position. Kalinin had expected him to be laid out flat on his back—like Lenin perhaps—a model of dignified repose. Not bunched up in the corner with his knees drawn tightly into his chest and his free arm wrapped about them in an icy hug. There was also the matter of the handcuffs. He couldn't possibly fathom why anyone would go to the trouble of chaining down a dead man. If they were aboard a ship and contending with waves such precautions were common sense. On a surface vessel, as had been made eminently clear to him during their brief ascent from the abyss, anything that wasn't secured was bound to end up in your lap. But down here. . . . He didn't see the point.

Locating his beloved CHICKEN LIVERS was not going to be easy. Nothing was where he had put it. Days of meticulous organization had been undone in less than thirty minutes dancing with the waves. And now with Vidchenko's corpse occupying a good two-thirds of the floor space, there was scarcely enough room for Kalinin to bend over let alone conduct a thorough search. He cursed the idiots responsible and began sifting through the mess.

It was cold and his fingers ached and he became more frustrated with each moment his prize did not turn up. At first, he had returned the packages neatly to the shelves, however before long he was stuffing them anywhere they would fit. By the time he reached the bottom of the pile, unearthing Vidchenko's half-buried legs in the process, Kalinin was ready to pull out his hair.

"Gahhh!"

And then he saw them—six or seven packages jammed beneath the bottom shelf behind Vidchenko. Until now he had done his best to show the deceased proper respect, but respect was no longer an option. Lamb, not the stringy impossible-to-chew mutton the butcher near his home peddled to the unwary, but juicy melt-in-your-mouth lamb . . .] Vidchenko wouldn't dream of denying him the pleasure. Too fat to be delicate, Kalinin wedged himself alongside Vidchenko and managed to coax one of the brown packages from the awkward niche: PORK LOIN. He grabbed another: SAUSAGE. The third package was further back—he had a good feeling about this one—so it was necessary for him to reposition himself. He was now practically sitting in Vidchenko's lap, his ear mere inches from the dead man's blue lips as he groped blindly for his prize.

It was faint, virtually imperceptible—a hoarse scraping emanating from somewhere deep within Vidchenko's throat—but he had definitely heard it: a whisper. Kalinin shivered but not from the cold. It was as if an insect had scurried out of the dead man's mouth and into his ear. It was now loose inside his head and he could not get rid of it. He nearly wrenched his arm out of the socket trying to escape. Terrified, he had crabbed backwards into the freezer door, and remained there crouching on his heels in disbelief, pain stabbing at his shoulder.

"Vidchenko, you fucking bastard! You scared the shit out of me!"

But there was nothing. No response, not even a twitch. Vidchenko just sat there, knees drawn into his chest, no less dead-looking than before.

"Vidchenko . . . If you're alive, say something! I'll get the doctor." Kalinin's warm breath encircled his head like a ghost.

Still, there was no reply. Maybe he had imagined it after all. Maybe the months of isolation beneath the waves were finally starting to take a toll. A day was an awfully long time to spend locked in a freezer. By now, Vidchenko's heart was probably harder than a diamond and about as useful when it came to pumping blood through his veins. One more chance—that's all Kalinin would give him.

"You'd better say something or I'm going to close the door and forget about you," he warned. "I'll let you die in here!"

Vidchenko responded as if he had been zapped with a defibrillator. A nervous jolt rattled him from head to toe, jump-starting his brain. One eye was frozen shut, but the other snapped open—luminous and milky white—and settled on Kalinin. Vidchenko tried to speak but the words stuck in his throat like dead leaves, used up and well on their way to becoming dust. After a moment of just sitting there—his one turbid eye staring blankly into space—he attempted to straighten out his legs. At first they were unresponsive. Slowly, however, his mind tapped into the proper nerve impulses, and with incomprehensible effort he uncoiled himself from his semi-fetal position at the rear of the freezer. Pain underscored every movement. The herky-jerky pantomime that ensued was both pathetic and terrifying. He flopped around lamely like a marionette in the hands of a rank amateur, straining toward Kalinin with all his strength. He tired quickly though, and gave up when he noticed that he was chained to the shelf.

"I'll get the doctor," Kalinin stammered, crossing himself. "Everything's going to be all right. Hang on!" He was propping open the freezer door with a large frozen roast when Vidchenko stopped him in his tracks.

"Please . . ." he rasped, rattling the handcuff and breathing the same frantic insect back into Kalinin's ear. "Get this off of me . . . I'll die in here."

Vidchenko was quaking with cold. Kalinin could hardly look at him. No man should have to suffer this way. He felt as if it was he who was somehow to blame.

"I don't have the key!" Kalinin shouted. He grabbed his heaviest apron, the one he used for butchering meat, from its hook near the freezer door and covered Vidchenko with it as best he could.

"You don't understand . . ." Vidchenko rambled on deliriously. "They want to kill me—that's why they put me in here!"

"You had a heart attack—they thought you were dead!"

"That's a lie!" Vidchenko wailed feebly. "The rabbit bit me . . . I'll show you . . . *Look*— look at my hand!" He tried to raise his right arm but the handcuff stopped him short and he sank back, defeated. *"Ple-e-e-ease . . ."* he whimpered, *"Please don't leave me . . ."*

Rabbit? There were no rabbits onboard. Vidchenko had obviously been in the cold too long; his brain was freezer-burned and there was nothing in the world anyone could do to fix it. But at least Kalinin could offer him peace of mind.

He kept a large cleaver in the kitchen that came in especially handy when he prepared oxtails for the crew. If he could hack through bone with it, there was a chance he could hack through a thin steel chain. After several whacks at it, though, he gave up. The blade simply wasn't sharp enough to sever the high tensile steel. The stale icy air scorched his lungs. Panicking, he pressed the cleaver into Vidchenko's frozen left hand and bent his comrade's rigid fingers into the shape of a fist around the handle. It was a miracle none snapped off in the process.

"There. You keep trying," said Kalinin, starting out the freezer door. "If I'm not back in a minute," he called over his shoulder, "you can cut out my heart." He heard the ring of the steel blade strike the chain as he bolted down the companionway toward the tube that would take him to the bridge.

Less than two minutes later, Kalinin returned with Senior Lieutenant Keldysh and an armed security detail breathing down his neck. Kalinin had never seen the crew in such a heightened state of alert. Not even when they played deadly games of cat and mouse hundreds of feet beneath the ocean's surface with their American counterparts was their tension so apparent. Fear unsettled the thin veneer of courage and self-control each man onboard wore as if it was no less a requirement of the uniform than rank insignia.

"What in God's name have you done, *cook!*" Senior Lieutenant Keldysh roared at Kalinin with malicious disdain as they arrived at the open freezer. "If any of us make it off of this boat alive, I will personally lead your firing squad!"

As for Vidchenko . . . Only bits and pieces remained. Butcher scraps. A partial fingertip, a few frozen hunks of flesh and bone splintered about the bottom of the freezer like wood chips. Nearby lay a severed hand hacked off at the wrist oozing blood as thick as tree sap. Two small puncture wounds marked the back of it. The cleaver was nowhere to be seen.

"Radio Moscow," Keldysh muttered to no one in particular, though he was looking at—*through*, rather—Kalinin. Despite the hell bent sprint from the bridge to get here, the blood had left his face and he was now the color of congealed bacon fat. "Tell them we're a ghost ship."

Antarctica: Approximately 150 Miles from the South Pole
GPS Coordinates: –89.23321, –19.6875
February 27, 2010

It was absolutely surreal, a nightmare, like one of the PCP-induced bad trips he'd been warned about as a kid growing up in the drug-addled afterglow of the disco era. *This can't be happening*, he thought, *no fucking way. I, Alan Whitehurst, a life-long science geek who didn't get laid until my second year in college and even then had to beg for it, am going to die on this godforsaken chunk of ice in the middle of nowhere.* Still, he had to appreciate the irony. Shakespeare himself couldn't have dreamed up a more improbable death for the Huntington Beach native who had never even been snow skiing, preferring instead the feel of the hot sand under his feet and the scalding summer sun beating down on his red shoulders. *Of all the places to die, you had to pick the only unheated structure on the ice field . . . Leonelli was right to question who the crazy one really was. If only he could've seen your mad dash through the snow in boxer shorts and bare feet!*

❖ ❖ ❖

Huddled like ice fishermen inside the small prefabricated hut they aptly called the Meat Locker, it had taken Alan and the team more than five-hundred hours, 24/7 for nearly a month at Igor's controls—feeding cable, siphoning off thousands of gallons of meltwater—to breach the subglacial lake a half-mile beneath the unyielding surface of this frozen waste. If the hole in the ice were allowed to freeze shut because they were too cold and miserable to hack it, all of their work would go to waste. *Suck it up and keep plugging away . . . You never know when you're going to hook the big one.* If Hell actually existed, they had discovered it in the last place anyone would think to look.

It seemed funny to Alan now that all of their troubles had started with a simple case of food poisoning. For weeks, Art Leonelli, the forty-three year-old hydrologist and aspiring gourmet from the University of Washington—affable, easy-going, a virtuo-so in the kitchen—had been going on about the poor quality of chow at the research station. Canned this, just-add-water that—they may as well have been dying from a rare disease with a name they couldn't pronounce, so flavorless and uninspired were their daily meals. Of course Leonelli wasn't the only one who thought so. They were all tired of eating like astronauts. If Alan never tasted another foil-sealed packet of dehydrated beef stroganoff it would be too soon. Another day or two of hunger like this and he, a staunch supporter of both PETA and Greenpeace, would have gladly taken up hunting if it meant putting fresh meat in his belly. He'd read the nutrition-al information on the packaging and was convinced that the manufacturer's claims were downright lies. The reconstituted scraps smothered in flavorless brown gravy left him feeling shiftless and weak.

Each night at dinner they made a game of comparing the food on the table before them with some of the most undesirable meals in human history. And although they came up with the notorious cannibal cuisine of such ill-fated groups as the Donner Party and the Brazilian soccer team whose plane had crashed high in the Andes, none could think of anything worse than the single-serving entrées of lumpy brown ooze and badly shriveled mystery meat on which they had and would subsist until Ethan Hatcher, a close friend of Alan's since grad school and the one in charge of the expedition, told them that their work here was complete.

Adding to their culinary despair was the fact that in nearly four weeks of tedious exploration, Igor, the remote-operated vehicle (ROV) they used to explore the light-less depths beneath them, had revealed nothing of particular interest: a dense layer of silt two-hundred feet thick in some places, and a sweeping expanse of darkness as impenetrable as the lake's virgin water was pure. It was not that what they'd found wasn't important; in fact, they had opened a window into earth's ancient past and the climatological forces that had been at work when man was little more than an evolutionary aberration in the primate line. Already this window had provided them with rare and invaluable insight into a rapidly changing global climate that many believed heralded the end of life on earth as they knew it. Much of what the team had learned so far was encouraging—that earth was no stranger to climatic upheaval, that large-scale atmospheric disruptions were nothing more than the natural grow-ing pains of a planet experiencing the cosmic equivalent of puberty.

They had also made less encouraging discoveries, dire predictions based on computer models assembled from data collected in the field. No two ways about it, their happy little home was heating up. In another 100,000 years anyone who planned on spending a significant amount of time outdoors had better be armed with a sunblock boasting an SPF of 1,000. *But why go all the way to the bottom of the world,* Alan wanted to know, *when one only had to look at the shrinking ice caps to draw the same conclusions about the warming trend that had concerned scientists for decades?* Once blanketed by ice and snow, polar regions that hadn't seen the light of day since well before the last Ice Age now lay bare and exposed. Alan appreciated the significance of their findings, however, he had hoped for something a little more dramatic, a little less apocalyptic. A new species of plant or animal, something not quite so passive as the acre upon acre of featureless abyssal plain Igor traversed much like a deep space probe.

It didn't help boost morale any that Ethan had been deliberately vague about what exactly it was he hoped to find. Whatever it was, Alan had never seen his friend push so hard, work with such single-minded purpose. For a change, Ethan was behaving like a man on a mission. They often worked eighteen and twenty-hour days. When they weren't sleeping or eating, they were alternating shifts in the drilling room—four on, four off. 'On' meant that you were freezing your ass off while Igor dutifully tracked a set of grid coordinates. These were plotted by Hamsun, a Norwegian undersea navigation expert who relied on coordinates plotted with the aid of an atomic clock to ensure they weren't going in circles. 'Off' meant that you were back in the lab compiling and analyzing data that had been collected during the course of your shift. It was scientific grunt work mostly—something to show the expedition's financial backers when it came time to account for the millions of dollars being spent. It was the first time in all the years Alan had known him that Ethan seemed determined to do things strictly by the book.

Despite the disappointment of their ongoing search, Ethan hadn't let up. The less they found, the harder he pushed. It wasn't like him. Alan had accompanied his friend on other expeditions. Usually, he was more interested in soaking up the local color, particularly if it came clad in a bikini or was served on the rocks with a splash of fruit juice. But this time was different. He'd been pressing—was more tightly wrapped than usual. They could all see it. Strictly business. Whatever the reason, Alan suspected the others were every bit as relieved as he when the Air National Guard V22 Osprey arrived to whisk Ethan back to McMurdo Station. He would then hop a C–130 charter to Christchurch International Airport in New Zealand where he'd catch a commercial flight to LAX. Apparently it all had something to do with business, an urgent matter that required his personal attention.

"Why don't you tell me what we're looking for?" Alan shouted above the roar of the Osprey's powerful twin tilt-rotors.

With the temperature hovering well below zero it was standard procedure for aircraft to keep the engines running. To do otherwise was to expose the vehicle to a host of problems, including congealed hydraulic fluid and pistons that cooled so quickly they ran the risk of cracking. Alan used his arm to shield his eyes from a blizzard of ice crystals kicked up by the Osprey's whirling rotor blades.

Ethan smiled uneasily from his seat behind the co-pilot. "You're in charge," he shouted. "I'll be back in a week." He then gave the thumbs-up to the pilot and off they soared.

Alan stood and watched as the unusual aircraft shrank from view—an olive drab speck vanishing over the horizon. *Lucky bastard.* He wished it was him and not Ethan leaving behind the bloodless chill of Antarctica for the blissful warmth of southern California and real food. The possibility that they might make a break-through discovery in Ethan's absence was little consolation. But it was something, and he was a scientist, and Ethan had had the forethought before making his getaway to remind Alan and the others that the great ones always suffered for their work.

Alan couldn't help it; he was losing interest in the expedition. He could fake it for the others so as not to further undermine morale, but he couldn't lie to himself. They had been out here fifty-eight days, two-thirds of which had been spent peering at a video monitor broadcasting images of a barren world they could only know vicari-ously. The cold, the isolation, the brief hours of daylight and interminable stretches of night were getting to him. Much more of this and he'd go nuts—start reciting the alphabet backwards, combing his eyelashes for dust mites, arguing with himself in the mirror. For months, they had been going through the motions like good little scientists—taking readings, recording their observations, checking their findings against established databases—but they hadn't come across anything that set their work here apart from previous, less grueling expeditions to Antarctica.

Okay, so Leonelli was having a whale of a time analyzing his ice cores and water samples, and Hamsun and Northcutt were getting pretty good at poker, and Ellis was convinced the ice cap was melting more rapidly than anyone previously believed—none of it fueled Alan's imagination the way Ethan had intimated the expedition would.

And what about Ethan? He was being so damn cryptic about it all. He hadn't given them anything to go on which wasn't like him considering he was typically all too anxious to hype his most recent quest. Equal parts showman and scientist, Ethan lived for the spotlight. He was described by many of his detractors as the P.T. Bar-num of the scientific community. But this time he was all go and no show. He was being guarded with information, deliberately obtuse, his agenda as ill-defined and impossible to fathom as the three chimps they had toted to the ass end of the world and had been caring for ever since. According to Ethan the chimps were nothing—he was simply making good on a favor he owed a buddy of his, a guy from UMASS Boston he'd once worked with. Ethan insisted that any day now a group of scientists would arrive to claim the ill-fated trinity of experimentees. Alan hadn't the faintest idea what anyone could want with chimps way the hell out here; however, he was of the impression that whatever their fate they were better off not knowing.

Alan was frustrated and a little pissed off that Ethan wasn't being more up front with him, but he had faith that his friend knew what he was doing. And as much as he resented the chimps their rowdy odor and occasional simian nattering—the shrill howls that every now and then reverberated within the walls of the station like pri-mal declarations of angst—he was sure that he and his human companions weren't faring much better in the personal hygiene department. Bathing wasn't exactly top priority in a region where every ounce of water had to be obtained by melting chunks of the surrounding ice. It was cold, miserable work that required a considerable expenditure of fuel better reserved for electricity and warmth.

Face it, without the chimps things would have been even worse. The personable knuckle-draggers were an antidote for the boredom that plagued them all. One in particular, the juvenile male Hamsun had named after his younger brother, Sven, had offered them a diversion when the nights seemed especially long. Now that Ethan was gone Hamsun insisted that Sven be permitted to roam freely about the station as long as he behaved himself. Alan and the others agreed, grateful for the comedy relief.

They weren't exactly model parents—Northcutt had taught Sven to brandish his middle finger like an enraged commuter on the 405—but they kept the kitchen knives locked up and had instructed him semi-successfully in the use of the chemical toilet in the rear of the station. Alan was going to miss Sven when his rightful owners arrived to claim him and do god knows what to him in the name of science.

Ethan had only been gone a few days when the team finally made the sort of discovery Alan had spent his entire professional life dreaming about. During a routine grid sweep, Igor happened upon a region of the lake bottom that was unlike anything any of them had ever seen before. For the time being, they were simply referring to it as an anomaly—at least until they better understood what exactly it was they were looking at. Much of their surprise was owed to the fact they had been searching the general vicinity for nearly a month—using every inch of the ROV's mile-long tether—without any luck. Why they had not spotted it earlier they could only attribute to the limited nature of the search protocol. Based upon some simple calculations, Hamsun had divided the lake bottom into a precise grid. Five-hundred square feet at a time, quadrangle after quadrangle, they plodded through the list of coordinates. They had passed within a hundred feet of the anomaly nearly a week ago, but had continued blindly with their sweep of the adjacent grid without ever knowing it. And then suddenly their prayers were answered.

Northcutt and Leonelli were at the controls when the discovery was made, but soon all of them were huddled together in the Meat Locker, eyes glued to the monitor. The first pass was like something out of a dream. The featureless abyssal plain gave way to a geologic hot zone about twice the size of a tennis court. A network of hydrothermal vents—deep fractures in the earth's crust—belched out a smoky mix of superheated water and toxic hydrogen sulfide gas. Stout, monolithic mineral deposits—each between five and six feet tall—proliferated along the edges of the vents like giant toadstools.

At well over +400°F the water in and around the vents was hot enough to boil lead. At such great depth however, the usual laws didn't apply. The tremendous pressure kept the typically raucous hydrogen molecules in check, and but for a slightly hazy tincture the vent region appeared more or less undisturbed. Decades of exploration had turned up a limited number of similar sites located primarily along tectonic hot zones at staggering depths in virtually every ocean on the planet. To the best of Alan's knowledge, though, no one had ever discovered a hydrothermal vent in a body of fresh water. Nor had anyone documented the presence of anything like the enormous stone toadstools studding the landscape of the watery inferno. The team was thrilled. From the way they jumped around cheering and laughing their heads off, you would've sworn that they had discovered a king's ransom in sunken treasure. But this was better. What they were looking at may have constituted the basis of all life on earth. A living Eden.

Igor's second pass—this time to within an arm's length of the bizarre colonnade—ignited an otherworldly fireworks of bioluminescent activity. Much like coral, the toadstools apparently comprised the skeletal remains of colonies of microbial life. The unusual formations closely resembled stromatolites—ancient deposits of calcium carbonate located in the hypersaline shallows of Hamelin Pool on Australia's west coast. Perhaps it was Igor's running lights, or the disturbance in the water generated by his passing—whatever the case, it was suddenly like the Fourth of July. Rapid pulses of ethereal blue-green light rippled over the surface of the phallic domes as Igor glided silently through the eternal night. Before long every one of the hundred or so stromatolites was flashing wildly. The lake bottom was transformed into an eerily beautiful light show. Their raucous cheers gave way to awestruck silence. No one moved, no one spoke. About the only thing Alan could hear was the doleful passage of the wind and the rapid drumming of his heart.

Acting as beacons, the stromatolites summoned an unexpected guest. Like snowflakes, frail and elegant, the first schools of shrimp descended on the fiery display. Ghostly transparent, their graceful passage through the water was hypnotic. With each passing moment their numbers increased. In less than a minute, thousands had swarmed out of the illimitable darkness to cling to the pulsating monoliths. There, congregating in a fervent crush like disciples before an arcane deity, thousands of crystalline decapods, each about four inches long basked in the ambient heat of the smoking vents. Whether predator or prey, their relationship to the colonies of bioluminescing microbes was unclear. The deluge of shrimp continued until it was as if a plague had been unleashed. Soon, it was difficult to make out the stromatolites at all within the swirling blizzard of shrimp. With the bioluminescent display all but totally obscured, the shrimp turned their attention to Igor and his high-intensity LED running lights. By the time Northcutt got over the spectacle of the amorous assault it was too late. Igor was dead in the water.

It took them nearly twenty-seven hours to retrieve the disabled ROV foundering at the end of five-thousand feet of Kevlar-wrapped fiber optic cable. It was cold, tedious work. Even with the aid of an electric winch, recovering Igor was no easy task.

It required an inordinate amount of hands-on attention and gentle coaxing to get him back to the surface where they could make the necessary repairs.

None of them had known exactly what to expect, but when they pulled Igor from the hole in the ice the source of his malfunction was abundantly clear. The ROV, once every bit as sleek as a Ferrari, looked like an entry in the World Series of sushi. The glassy little shrimp covered every inch of the five-foot long probe, clogging the prop and jamming the stabilizers. Virtually every last one of them, dozens in all, was still alive. Alan was astounded that they had survived the journey intact. The atmospheric pressure on the lake bottom could have easily compressed a school bus into a cube of scrap metal no bigger than a can of Budweiser. On the surface where the atmospheric pressure was relatively nonexistent, the shrimp should have been doing just the opposite and exploding like popcorn. The shrimp, however, continued picking over Igor's polished titanium housing, a writhing tangle of articulating legs and probing antennae.

"Tenacious little bastards," commented Northcutt. "Look at 'em trampling each other—they're like soccer hooligans."

"They're still fresh," said Leonelli. He was practically licking his lips.

"I don't know if that's such a good idea," said Alan. "We don't know anything about them. They could be poisonous."

"We don't know anything about the crap we've been eating for the past month," Leonelli observed wryly. "But it hasn't killed us—*not yet*. I can fry up a couple dozen in a little butter and garlic . . ."

Alan looked at Ellis. "What do you think?" he asked. "Would it be terribly irresponsible of us?"

A polar geologist with the USGS, Ellis was the most level-headed among them. A pragmatist through and through, he was not the sort to let the novelty of a good-tasting meal override his sense of the expedition's objectives.

"Absolutely," Ellis replied without hesitation. "Not to mention unprofessional, risky, and frivolous. We're scientists, not cooks."

Ellis was right. They all knew it. But it didn't make the verdict any easier to swallow. Alan looked around. Every last one of them was crestfallen—like children who'd had their Halloween candy stolen by bullies.

"With that said . . ." Ellis continued. "Why the hell not? It's not as if we deliberately went after them. They came to us, right? Think of it as divine providence."

Leonelli brightened. "They mobbed poor little Igor like he was a rock star. They were practically begging to be eaten."

"Groupie shrimp," said Northcutt. "Sounds naughty."

"I say we go for it," said Ellis. "Some real food will do us good. Besides, it'll be something to tell our grandchildren about when we're all rich and famous."

Schmidt, a climatologist from Oklahoma City, could scarcely contain himself. *"National Geographic*, here we come!" he shouted, his concern for the ailing ice caps momentarily dulled by the prospect of real food.

"Forget *National Geographic*," said Leonelli. "This will make the cover of *Bon Apétit*."

"Fucking shit!" said Hamsun. Because of his limited facility with English, he relied on a rich, though nonsensical, array of expletives to get his points across. Sven clung to Hamsun's side, bundled against the cold in a borrowed parka that fit him like a dress.

"Come on," Leonelli pleaded with Alan. "I'll whip us up a meal that'll knock your socks off. Shrimp *á la* Jules Verne. We can include the recipe with the *National Geographic* piece. I've got a bottle of wine I brought for just such an occasion. It's a Napa Valley cabernet . . . A bit heavy for seafood, but it beats the crap out of purple Kool-Aid. Look, there must be close to a hundred of the little bastards. I'll put half aside so we can study them later. And we can always get more if we need 'em."

Lim—the marine biologist on loan from the People's Republic of China as part of an international goodwill exchange program (his American counterpart was off in a balmy bamboo forest somewhere observing the courtship rituals of giant pandas)—didn't seem to have the faintest idea what was happening. In his neck of the woods scientists didn't use state-of-the-art technology to pick up groceries. He simply absorbed the mysterious debate and smiled.

"Let's ask Sven," suggested Leonelli. "He's got a good head on his shoulders. If Sven says no, then I won't say another word about it. Sven," he said, upping the pitch of his voice for the excitable ape. "What do you think—how does a gourmet meal strike you? That sound good, buddy? Yummy?"

Sven bobbed his head and curled back his lips exposing his formidable teeth. Hamsun and the others egged him on, encouraging the chimp from every direction at once like little league parents reacting to an infield blooper. Sven's movements became more anxious and demonstrative until a series of excited whoops escaped his mouth. When the noise died down they all turned to Alan.

"When do we eat?" he relented at last, the others clapping him on the back heartily. Ethan was probably sitting down to a gourmet meal at this very moment—Patina or Spago, if Alan were to take a guess. It was only fair that they all be allowed to enjoy the fruits of their labor. Particularly now with something worth celebrating.

An hour later the six of them, including Sven, sat down to a tantalizing concoction of shrimp sautéed in garlic-butter on a bed of instant Imperial Ramen noodles masquerading as linguine *al dente*. The pointed aroma of garlic filled the station. They each expressed their thanks and admiration for Leonelli's skill in the kitchen, toasted Igor's newfound vocation as a world-class shrimper, and tore into the food on their plates.

For a time no one spoke as they devoured the meal, the clink of utensils and chewing noises rising above the distant drone of the generator that powered the station and kept them from freezing to death in the sub-zero forge at the bottom of the world. Alan, their resident videographer, recorded the historic meal. It probably wasn't the sort of footage Ethan had in mind when he had assigned Alan camcorder duty, but what the hell. . . . In the interest of posterity.

"What do you think?" Leonelli asked expectantly. "Not bad, eh?"

"If you're this good in the sack," said Schmidt, "I may have found myself the perfect little wife."

Leonelli sized him up and smiled. "I'd give you a heart attack before you could get your shoes off, you fat bastard."

"World class grub," said Northcutt. "You really outdid yourself."

"What about you, Lim?" asked Leonelli. "Italian rub you right?"

Typically reserved, Lim smiled. "Very good."

Leonelli turned to Hamsun who was shoveling the food into his mouth with his bare hands. "Guess I don't have to ask you."

"Fucking good!" Hamsun replied robustly between heaping mouthfuls, his wild blond beard streaked with grease. He plucked a shrimp from the plate with his fingers and fed it to Sven, who occupied Ethan's seat at the head of the cafeteria-style folding table.

Sven gulped down the shrimp and reached for another. Jealously guarding his lion's share of the meal, Hamsun slapped the assertive chimp on the wrist. Sven let out a frustrated shriek and cuffed Hamsun on the side of the head. The table was momentarily quiet. Wind rattled the walls of the station. Hamsun, they imagined, was not the sort of man who responded well to physical abuse, especially from a precocious chimp he outweighed by two-hundred pounds. He was too big, too strong, too imposing to readily acquiesce to a show of force. The rest of them watched, expecting the worst. Leonelli collected his plate and scooted back from the table so as not to jeopardize a single shrimp in the event of a melee. Hamsun, though, merely shrugged and admonished Sven to use a fork.

What do you know?" said Ellis, letting go of the tension they all felt with a chuckle. "Hamsun's baby bro' eats meat."

"If a single drop of that cabernet crosses his gums," Leonelli warned Hamsun, "I'll cut out your tongue."

"I always thought monkeys were vegetarians," said Northcutt. "Like hairy little hippies minus the marijuana and incense."

"Don't you watch the *Discovery Channel*?" asked Schmidt. "The little savages will eat each other when the mood strikes them. Or when other sources of food get scarce enough. It's the law of the jungle. Natural born omnivores." He turned to Sven. "No offense, partner, but it's true."

Sven was too occupied picking over Hamsun's dinner to give these perplexing creatures a second thought. They were always chattering about something or other. He only tolerated them because it was better than being locked up in a cage. Every now and then he'd feign interest in their goings-on to ingratiate himself to the group. Otherwise, they were a nuisance and smelled bad.

Leonelli fixed Schmidt with a look of disbelief. "*And we won't?* Man is the animal kingdom's ultimate survivalist. The average human would rather eat his own mother than risk losing a few pounds to starvation."

"Is that right?" Schmidt replied, an amused look on his face. He and Leonelli were always wrangling with one another about something. "Of course you're speaking from personal experience."

"If the situation demanded it, I'd do what had to be done," Leonelli confirmed matter-of-factly.

"So it's toss Mom in the frying pan and pass the salt?"

"Like I said, if the situation demanded it . . ." Leonelli paused and took a small sip of the cabernet he had distributed evenly among the six of them. "Think about it. How else would a relatively weak primate with no natural defenses have survived the past two million years?"

"Intelligence?" said Northcutt.

"Attrition—" Leonelli continued. "It's in our genes. Pure fucking I'll-do-whatever-it-takes desire. Tooth and nail. *Homo erectus* didn't make his way to the top of the corporate ladder by blowing every Neanderthal with a stiffy." Leonelli downed the last of his wine and smacked his lips. "He did it in the trenches. With grit. The *real* dirty work. He ate bugs and fucked his own sister when times were lean."

"You're crazy, Leonelli," said Northcutt. "You can cook, but you don't know the first thing about human nature."

"Like hell I don't," countered Leonelli. "We're here of our own free will, aren't we? What do you call that? I'll tell you what—masochism. We're here because we're a bunch of goddamned masochists. We get off on being miserable. Shit, Jesus probably enjoyed it when they nailed him to the cross—at least the part of him that was human."

"Easy there," said Alan. He stopped recording and set aside the camcorder. "No point upsetting the flock."

"What are you gonna do?" Leonelli asked irreverently. "Try me for heresy? I'm a scientist, it's what I do."

Hamsun ignored Leonelli's earlier warning and offered Sven his wine. The chimp took one whiff of the contents of the plastic cup and turned up his nose.

"I'll be damned," said Schmidt. "A monkey wine snob. Looks like you've got yourself a friend, Leonelli."

"Ha-ha-ha," Leonelli crowed. "Go fuck yourself."

Hamsun's lessons had paid off. On cue, Sven's middle finger went up. They all laughed.

Alan changed the subject before things got out of control. They were a good bunch of guys but fuses had been running a little short lately. "What are you gonna cook for an encore?" he asked. "Now that we've been spoiled like this, you're going to have to come up with something really special to wow us."

Leonelli thought it over and flashed Alan a knowing smile. "Turn off the lights."

Alan didn't know what to think.

"You asked for an encore—" said Leonelli. "Get the lights, and I'll give you one."

Alan stood and flipped off the lights. There, glowing blue-green in the dark on each of their plates like malformed question marks, lay all the shrimp yet to be eaten. *It's an omen of some sort*, thought Alan. *It has to be*. But he was a scientist and didn't believe in omens. He believed in pathways, connections, cause and effect. The shrimp had been feeding on the bioluminescing microbes, and now he and his team were feeding on the shrimp. It was a simple case of *you are what you eat*. Just another link in the food chain. Their green, glowing smiles told them all they needed to know.

Leonelli was cataloguing ice core samples less than twenty-four hours later when he developed a fever. Despite being thousands of miles from the nearest urban center in a climate not exactly conducive to the propagation of viral organisms, Alan and the rest of the team dismissed it as a case of the flu, nothing a few days of bed rest and plenty of Tang couldn't fix. But then Leonelli's temperature had soared to +109°F and he had started hallucinating and muttering incomprehensibly.

They were prepared to medivac Leonelli to the nearest hospital—all they had to do was keep him alive until the sun came up in a little less than seventeen hours and McMurdo could dispatch the Air National Guard—when his fever broke just as suddenly as it had come on. He was exhausted and dehydrated, but seemingly intact and thinking rationally. Leonelli had begged Alan and the others to call off the medivac. They all knew that research opportunities like this came along once in a lifetime and that to send Leonelli home now because he couldn't hack it in the harsh conditions would almost certainly negate his inclusion in future expeditions to the white continent. If anything it was Leonelli's voracious appetite upon first rejoining the ranks of the living that convinced them he was well on the road to recovery. Already he was getting his strength back. Obviously, the thermometer hadn't been working right—a fever that high would've peeled the paint off the walls in Leonelli's cramped quarters. Nothing ever worked quite right down here. Malfunctions were the norm.

Then, one after another, each came down with the same blistering fever that had soft-boiled Leonelli's brain. Although they were too ripe with madness to see it, the fever's onset roughly corresponded with their shifts in the Meat Locker. Cold was, of course, the one common denominator shared by all, the obvious reason for the difference in the amount of time elapsed from infection to the fever's onset in each of them. But then again, reason to a madman is like prayer to an atheist—fool's gold. They had all gobbled down the shrimp together like one big happy family, but they took turns "walking the dog," Northcutt's colorful way of describing the regimented tedium that was part and parcel of overseeing Igor's sweeps of the not-so-lifeless abyss. The more time they'd spent in the bitter cold of the Meat Locker, the lower their core temperatures had remained and the longer it had taken this "flu" of theirs to incubate. Even dressed as they were in the warmest polar gear available, at −30°F hypothermia was always knocking at the door. The reason Leonelli's symptoms had progressed more rapidly than the others' should have been routine to a group of scientists who'd spent their professional lives answering complex questions.

As a way of expressing their gratitude for the gourmet meal, the team had volunteered to cover Leonelli's next shift, the hiatus from the Meat Locker allowing him to concoct a glow-in-the-dark gumbo they'd enjoyed the following day, even as he laid moaning and writhing in his miserable sweat-soaked cot engulfed in a blaze of fevered delirium. Of course Leonelli becoming bedridden (even after he was seemingly on the mend they wanted to give him a few days' rest before subjecting him to the harsh conditions) meant longer shifts and more of them for the able-bodied members of the team, Alan included. Getting warm was next to impossible after you'd spent four-plus hours shivering yourself silly in an unheated rattle-trap hut designed to protect the instruments from the blasting wind but not much else. It could take hours considering the temperature inside the station usually hovered around +55°F. By the time they got "warm" between shifts—what they naively mistook for warmth was undoubtedly the organism asserting its will—it was back to the Meat Locker at which point the unforgiving cold, to a limited extent, actually worked as their ally. But it was only four days from the time they had first eaten the contaminated shrimp that Alan and the others would realize, if only distantly, that they had made a terrible and ultimately fatal mistake.

That it may have been something in the shrimp they had foolishly eaten and not a particularly nasty strain of Antarctic flu that had laid siege to the station occurred to them much as everything else had in the wake of their fateful feast—vaguely and without the empirical connections men of science are trained to discern.

About the time they had all started coming down with the fever, Leonelli was well on his way to total and irrevocable madness. In less than a week they would all undergo the same cycle—fever, delirium, the rapid onset of a hunger-driven madness—but they would be too far gone to see it. No one mentioned the strange after effects—the horrible dreams, the alien out-of-bodiness, the taut lucidity of ideas once unthinkable to civilized, rational men.

Beneath the soft layering of flesh and blood now existed something larger and more vital, deeper and more absolute than mere words could ever hope to express. They had gone about their work collecting specimens and analyzing conditions at the hydrothermal vent but this somehow seemed remote and unimportant to them now. A new directive lived behind their eyes—or a very old one—summoned from an epoch unknown to men when all things living competed with one another for an evolutionary niche.

❖ ❖ ❖

Alan had felt it; he could feel it now. A primal current slithered through his bloodstream, amassing energy, each cell host to an unwelcome hitchhiker—slowly, almost imperceptibly subordinating his will, redirecting the flow of information, urging him toward a rendezvous with a side of himself from which there was no return.

Already he was contemplating a course of action he would have never dared consider only moments earlier. Sure, it was suicide—removing the fifty-five gallon fuel drum with which he had barricaded the door—but he was sick to death of Hamsun's maniacal rants, his stupid fucking *Berlitz* English, his pathetic howls echoing through the moribund station like the call of a brokenhearted coyote. Alan wanted to push aside the drum of fuel, fling open the door, wrest the ice axe from Hamsun's massive hands and use it to hack the dumb oaf into little pieces. And had it not been for the agony in his feet—a vicious all-consuming cold that seemed to gnaw at the bare flesh, cut deep into the bone—he may have done just that.

For the moment however he was forced back inside of himself. Hamsun's relentless assault with the ice axe against the thin steel door once again awakened Alan to his plight. Each blow was like the dull sky-rending rumble of distant thunder, the mean edge of the blade dimpling the metallic skin but failing to penetrate completely. Alan shut out the pain in his feet and continued to brace his shoulder against the drum of fuel keeping Hamsun at bay. Then, as unexpectedly as it had all started, the axe blows ceased. Alan held his ground for a minute perhaps, expecting Hamsun to resume his assault with renewed vigor, but the quiet only deepened.

"Hamsun, you still out there?"

There was no reply.

"Listen to me," Alan pleaded earnestly. "You need help. You're sick—we all are . . ." he continued, suddenly possessed by a voice not his own. "Leave me alone, you fucking freak or I'll kill you!" he roared.

Before he knew it the words were out, hanging in the static air. "I didn't mean that," Alan apologized, slipping back inside himself, and then out again just as quickly. "Like hell, I didn't. I'll chop you into little fucking pieces and eat your heart!" he shouted, battering the door with his frozen fists.

Thank god there was still no reply, Alan thought to himself as he regained his grip on his tenuous self-control. No point pissing off Hamsun any more than he already was. Nonetheless, Alan was not about to stick his head out and take a peek. *Just sit tight, help is on the way.*

Lim had escaped in the midst of the chaos. With a little luck he would make it to the Russian weather station at the opposite end of the ice field and return with the cavalry. But there was a problem: six hours of darkness and more than a mile of perilous terrain stood between the diminutive zooplankton expert and possible rescue. Not to mention the fact that Lim's brains were hopelessly scrambled. Nor could Alan have known that no sooner had their last hope lost sight of the single guiding light at his back then he had become disoriented and fallen into a jagged crevasse camouflaged by a thin crust of ice, breaking his arm and snuffing out any chance of rescue. Alan would never have the opportunity to consider why Lim had neglected to use the tundra buggy; he was simply too preoccupied trying to save his own skin to worry about that now.

Just because Alan was now and then beset upon by fits of murderous rage did not mean that he had lost the will to live. Strangely, his own survival seemed more vital to him than ever before. Although he couldn't explain it, he was certain that his newfound violent streak was simply a manifestation of a more aggressive approach to self-preservation—proactive, ambitious, indomitable. But he could think about all that later. *Now,* he decided, *is the time to sweeten my insurance policy, put a little more mass between me and Hamsun.*

Alan tried to move, but what little heat remained in his body had melted a thin layer of the ice beneath his feet only to freeze hard again as his core temperature dipped dangerously into the realm of hypothermia. Now he was stuck, his bare feet fused to the frozen slab. He clawed at the ice with his fingertips but it was hard like iron. *This is going to hurt,* he thought, marshalling his strength and heaving his legs upward, one after the other. After several attempts, he managed to wrench himself free, leaving behind bits of graying frostbitten flesh and congealed blood in his icy footprints. Fortunately, his feet were too numb to feel the pain that would surely register if and when he ever got warm again.

With considerable effort he was able to move the first of the half-dozen remaining fuel drums and belly it up to the one currently barricading the door so that the red diamond-shaped FLAMMABLE label was facing him. *Better,* he decided, *but not enough.* Hamsun was a big, powerful man—six-five, two-seventy maybe—riding an adrenaline high that had imbued him with superhuman strength. That he hadn't managed to breach the makeshift barricade was really just a matter of luck and pure life or death determination on Alan's part. If he could just get one more drum in front of the door, the additional weight would be enough to keep out a grizzly. He couldn't be too safe.

He began pushing a third drum across the floor, but the uneven surface, the poor footing and his waning energy made it nearly impossible. Exhausted, he collapsed where he stood and reclined against the drum, defeated. Deranged laughter wracked his body. That twenty minutes could change his life so dramatically seemed somehow funny to him, if not absolutely hysterical. It had all happened so fast that he hadn't had time to think about the sinister mood that had laid claim to them all over the past few days. And what about the bizarre turn of events that had left him bare-footed and freezing to death in a room fit for a side of beef at the edge of nowhere? It was amazing how much had changed in so short a time. When he finally returned, Ethan would be in for the surprise of his life.

Well on the road to recovery, or so they'd deluded themselves into believing, Leonelli had volunteered to accompany Ellis on a day trip to a dry rift valley on the other side of the mountains at their back. In a region dominated by sweeping expanses of unmitigated flatness and mountainous peaks, the geographic anomaly was irresist-ible to Ellis in the way that the golden city of Eldorado had fired the imagination of the legendary Spanish conquistador, Francisco Pizarro. Although they all agreed that exploring the valley was particularly dangerous given its limited accessibility and hazardous landscape, they couldn't exactly say no to him. After all, Ellis wasn't technically a member of their team, but rather a last-minute addendum insisted upon by the government agency that both signed his paycheck and had provided the $400,000 tundra buggy he and Leonelli would use to ferry them to their proposed destination. Ellis had promised that they would simply collect a few soil specimens, record a few elevations and return well before nightfall. It was late February and the sun wouldn't give its last hurrah for a few weeks. They packed an enormous lunch—enough for days—and headed out.

Leonelli flashed them all a sinister smile on his way out the door. "Be good," he said. "Don't do anything I wouldn't do."

Just as Ellis had promised, the tundra buggy trundled into view shortly before dark. From Alan's vantage at the station's only window, an ice-encrusted port no bigger than a dinner plate, the silly-looking vehicle resembled a large insect as it slowly made its way across the massive ice field that was now the color of zinc in the anemic Ant-arctic dusk. Preceded by the low growl of its powerful diesel engine and the squeaky revolutions of its all-terrain treads, it pulled into their encampment on the ice al-most fifteen minutes later. Because the external temperature hovered at $-72°F$ Alan and the others awaited the return of their colleagues in the common room. This is where the team ate, relaxed and commiserated about the cold when they weren't busy working. Since the fever's outbreak they had set the thermostat at a tropical $+85°F$, well above the prescribed maximum of $+55°F$. At the current rate, they would burn through their precious heating fuel long before the re-supply plane arrived from Mc-Murdo, but no one was talking about freezing to death. It simply wasn't tops on their list of concerns. Their sudden need for heat and the fact that they had been gorging themselves on everything edible were just two more reasons among many less clear to them why they were lying about in a hypnotic stupor when Leonelli burst through the door covered in blood and clutching the ice axe Hamsun had since appropriated.

Roused from their somnambulant state, Alan and the others gathered near the entrance. The bloodied hydrologist stood framed in the slate-gray rectangle of the open door, ice axe in hand like a character from a cautionary tale about the effects of hypoxic dementia on mountaineers. He was barely recognizable beneath the mask of blood that obscured his face, the viscous runoff of an open flap of skin still gushing just below his hairline. His eyes were impossibly wide and his chest heaved with the force of an overworked bellows. They tried to talk to him, to calm him down so they could figure out what the hell had happened, but Leonelli was incoherent, rambling.

"Where's Ellis?" asked Alan. Instinctively, he'd grabbed the camcorder when he had heard the tundra buggy pull up. He'd been filming since Leonelli had thrown open the door. Northcutt shouted something at him, but Alan wasn't listening. He didn't dare take his eyes off Leonelli who stared into the camcorder as if possessed.

For what seemed like an eternity they tried to convince Leonelli to put down the ice axe and allow them to dress the wound on his forehead. Although he was alert, he was unresponsive, his eyes bulging in their sockets. The stream of gibberish spilling from his mouth was driven by the same fever-pitched momentum that had been incubating in each of them and would soon boil to the surface in them all. His parka, the front of which was spattered with dark crimson constellations, was torn just above his left bicep, the blood-soaked lining revealing yet another gash worthy of medical attention.

Though there was no reason to suspect foul play, there was an unmistakable aura of distrust in the way they regarded their wounded colleague. Something—maybe it was his refusal to relinquish the ice axe—had awakened in them a base survival instinct. With each passing moment the standoff became tenser, a current of animosity, paranoia and rage spooling through their edgy minds as if they were psychopaths wired to the same faulty circuit.

Alan now realized how strange it was that no one, himself included, had probed Leonelli regarding Ellis's whereabouts. It was as if they already knew or at least had some idea of the terrible truth shrouded beneath Leonelli's blood mask. They knew what had happened in the dry rift valley—not the specifics per se but enough of the outcome that any questions they might have asked the resident gourmet would've been pointless. He knew; they knew; he knew they knew. And nothing anyone did was going to bring Ellis back. All any of them really wanted was to get warm again, for the inside temperature to return to the oozy tropical bluster in which they had basked like iguanas before Leonelli had opened the goddamned door and allowed their prized heat to escape into the very cold night. They didn't want answers—they didn't care. They wanted *Jamaica, man . . . No problem!*

Hours after Leonelli's return from the dry valley, Alan awoke in a deep sweat, his clothing and bed sheets knotted about him. The forced air spewing out of the vent in the wall of the tiny sleeping quarters he and Lim shared was as warm and dry as a Saharan wind. The entire room was awash in crisp ultraviolet light, one of the many tricks the scientists used to stave off the onset of seasonal affective disorder in a region where natural sunlight could be as elusive as warmth. The muffled shouts and curses he had at first dismissed as a component of the nightmare that had awakened him with a start, cut through the fog of his half-asleep mind and forced him to his feet. Socks, he needed a pair of socks. Like the rest of him, they were soaked entirely through with sweat. He couldn't go around in wet socks and not expect to catch a cold. He'd seen a pair somewhere in this mess not too long ago . . . Couldn't have gone far unless Sven had gotten his thieving little hands on them. And why the fuck not? The hairy little klepto had been wearing Ethan's precious Kirk Gibson jersey all over the station. *Fucking primates—can't trust any of them.*

As Alan rummaged through piles of dirty laundry and other junk camouflaging the floor the cramped quarters that reminded him of his college dorm—he had found one sock but had yet to track down its twin—he was distracted by a series of resounding thuds that rocked the floor and traveled up into his bare feet. There was more shouting, a savage exchange that passed easily through the thin walls compartmentalizing the station—Schmidt, he thought, possibly Northcutt—but this was cut short by a brisk wet whack. He shook off the torpor that had plagued him since first coming down with the mysterious fever, fitted the camcorder over his right hand and ambled into the common room.

Like the night of the big shrimp feast, the air was filled with the intoxicating odor of garlic and butter, a moist bank of aromatic steam originating from a frying pan sizzling on the small propane cooktop in front of Leonelli. This room was also awash in wan UV light, imbuing the skilled chef with a ghoulish purple tint. A trickle of blood seeped from the swath of crude blue stitches that traversed his gashed forehead like railroad tracks. It was a peculiar time to be cooking dinner. But then arose the insatiable hunger that had been nagging at Alan for the past couple of days and he understood perfectly.

Although he'd torn the storage room apart looking he hadn't found a single scrap of meat, dehydrated or otherwise, on one of his all too frequent daily raids—Kool-Aid, instant oatmeal, a dozen foil pouches of freeze-dried Neapolitan ice cream (*someone's idea of a sick joke!*), all of which lacked what he craved—but the rich succulent odor of seared flesh was unmistakable, intoxicating. But was it chicken? Pork? Beef? Fuck, for all he cared it could've been his neighbor's golden retriever twisting on a spit. So what was it sizzling away on the stove, the oily fats and precious juices wasted on the air? Did it really fucking matter? Leonelli had been holding out. A private stash in a time of famine—it was criminal and he needed to be dealt with accordingly. Desperate times called for desperate measures. One way or another Alan would have his pound of flesh.

"What's cookin'?" Alan asked casually, jockeying for an angle of Leonelli's latest creation. He had no idea why he still bothered recording their daily activities only that some small vestige of who he once had been was compelling him to do so. Posterity no longer factored into the equation. Perhaps he was gathering evidence. Of what, exactly—he hadn't the faintest clue. "Smells like meat . . ."

Leonelli smiled narrowly and shook his head, his eyes as hard and black as obsidian. "Can I help you?" He hunkered over the frying pan jealously, shielding Alan's view of its contents.

"I thought we were out of meat . . . You're not holding out on us?" Alan was sick of eating nothing but ramen noodles and dehydrated ice cream. Problem was, they'd already eaten everything else. Even now, his stomach was grumbling to be fed.

"Meat meat meat," Leonelli echoed mockingly. "Is that all you ever think about?"

Alan was no mind reader, but he didn't have to be to get the message. Leonelli wasn't about to share whatever it was that smelled so damn good. First things first . . . He was still practically naked, not to mention Leonelli was using Ellis's ice axe as if it were a spatula. No surprise really, considering he hadn't let go of it since returning from the dry valley the other day. One thing was certain; when the time was right Alan wouldn't have to look very far to find Leonelli. Neither of them was going anywhere. No bus stops down here. No time off for good behavior. "Socks," Alan replied distantly. "Mine are wet."

"Why don't you ask one of them?"

Had it not been for a low moan emanating from across the room, Alan would've thought the guy was seeing ghosts, a trick of the weird lavender light. But there it was again—the same low, almost imperceptible keening coming from behind the workstation where Northcutt had spent five hours straight earlier that day staring into an empty coffee mug.

Cautiously, Alan crossed the room to investigate. Northcutt and Schmidt lay entangled in one another's grasp as if locked in a life or death struggle, though only the latter was still breathing, each forced inhalation like the sound small pebbles being poured from a paper cup. Alan had never seen so much blood—smears and droplets and bold broad strokes of it painted about the site of the struggle by desperate flailing limbs. Mingled with the smell of garlic, the raw bouquet was both nauseating and inviting. The faces of both men were transfigured by bruises and swelling and assorted wounds so that the helter-skelter composition, particularly their hands—even Leonardo da Vinci cited the difficulty of accurately depicting hands—evoked the sort of visceral reality that only the most brilliant species of cruelty is capable of rendering. A masterpiece of human savagery. There were teeth marks—a near-perfect impression of both uppers and lowers—penetrating deep into the flesh of Northcutt's left cheek. Alan captured it all on flash memory.

"What did you do to their hands?" he asked. Schmidt grasped—if, in fact, it was possible to grasp *sans* fingers—for Alan's pant leg but only succeeded in smearing blood on Alan's bare feet. Irritated, Alan kicked Schmidt's ruined hand away.

"I've been thinking . . ." Leonelli mused dangerously. "We're something like 85% water, right? But what's the point? You'd have an easier time squeezing water from a rock. But if you really think about it, we're more meat than anything else . . . And it's right there for the picking."

"You're demented."

"I thought you came in here looking for socks?" Leonelli called back, annoyed.

"Schmidt's still—"

"Alive?" Leonelli finished. "How much you want to bet he doesn't last another minute? Hell, I *guarantee* you, he won't make it another thirty seconds."

"*Bet?* I—" Alan's voice was almost drowned out by the angry sizzle of the frying pan.

"For fuck's sake!" Leonelli gruffed, abandoning the cooktop and striding purposefully toward where Schmidt was still twitching and moaning. "Twenty-nine, twenty-eight, twenty-seven . . ." he counted down as he crossed the room. "Twenty-six, twenty-five . . ." At the count of twenty-four, he reached Schmidt, glowering over him; at twenty-three, he raised the ice axe high over his head; at twenty-two, he brought it down full force in a long whistling arc and buried the pointed end in the crown of Schmidt's balding skull. "Twenty-one . . . *Blackjack!*"

No doubt about it, Schmidt was dead in less than the thirty seconds Leonelli had guaranteed.

"You owe me big, partner," he informed Alan before returning to the predatory hiss of the frying pan.

"You killed him," said Alan, unsure how he felt about what he had just witnessed. If he had any sense of right and wrong it now existed in an abandoned corner of his mind, an arbitrary concept that had outlived its usefulness.

"Don't give me that look like I'm the whacko," Leonelli was incredulous. "It's fifty below outside and you're the one walking around in your underwear without any socks on."

Alan wanted to fly across the room and bash in Leonelli's skull with the camcorder. *"He's dead!"*

"Yeah, well, meat is murder . . ." Leonelli remarked dryly. "Isn't that what all the bleeding heart vegetarians say?" He popped something from the pan into his mouth, moved it around with his tongue until the heat had dissipated and crunched it down with a self-congratulatory grin. "God, I can cook!"

Alan was considering making a grab for the ice axe—*Leonelli can't be trusted*—when Hamsun and Lim emerged from another area of the station amid a raucous spectacle of giddy-ups and war whoops. Hamsun straddled Lim like a professional bull rider as the two of them galloped and bucked around the common room. Sven trundled along behind them shrieking with delight, waving his arms and beating his chest. Although

Lim was a willing participant in the bizarre exhibition, his body told a different story. He made it to the center of the common room and collapsed, his ribs snapping like dry twigs beneath Hamsun's crushing bulk. Hamsun exhorted his broken steed to get up, but the stunned marine biologist groaned in protest, the sudden influx of pain momentarily sobering him to the mad folly of their equine waltz.

"Hamsun, looks like your horsie's ready for the glue factory," Alan chuckled, zooming in on his face.

"YOU!" Hamsun thundered. He kicked aside Lim and plodded after Alan. "Now you be horsie-horsie!"

For the first time since he'd been awakened, Alan was . . . Not scared, exactly, but guarded, the old caution creeping back into him with new prominence. While the temperature of the air inside the station hovered somewhere in the range of an equatorial low pressure front, Alan's body temperature, although still well above normal, had been dropping since first stripping off his wet clothes. He and Lim were the only ones in the room not dressed as if for an assault on the summit of Mount Everest. Hamsun, Leonelli, Lim—even Schmidt and Northcutt (*wake up you fool, they're dead!*)—were bundled inside their parkas. Suddenly, he felt very exposed standing there wearing nothing but a pair of boxer shorts and an imaginary saddle only Hamsun could see.

Buoyed by an evolving awareness, Alan tossed the camcorder to Leonelli and retreated from Hamsun's groping arms. He circled behind the television where a short time earlier the erstwhile cowboy had watched Clint Eastwood gun down stubble-faced adversaries with cold, clinical precision. Leonelli laughed riotously, continuing with the documentary where Alan had left off. Alan's nerves twanged like banjo strings tuned well beyond the breaking point. It was as if something in the depleted UV light was corrupting their senses and aligning every member of the team with a wavelength at the wrong end of the spectrum. Hamsun overturned one of the workstations, sending thousands of dollars of lab equipment crashing to the floor. Leonelli laughed even harder, the manic cascade of shrill hoots taking flight like the warning cry of an imperiled spider monkey—primitive, lean, a baseline response to a threat older and more dangerous than snakes.

Dimly, Alan wondered what had happened to Ellis in the dry valley—not the outcome, that was obvious. But the trigger, the spark that had ignited Leonelli's rage. Ellis was dead somewhere out there, penguins congregating over his frozen corpse in pagan worship. Had a disagreement taken a wrong turn, aimed them toward a literal dead-end? Or was it a mood gone septic? Bad blood in the air. Whatever the case, they had finally succumbed to Antarctica's terrible desolation. Somewhere along the line the paradigm had shifted and they—himself—were no longer the same men they had once been. The old rules no longer applied. But the new rules? At this rate, they'd all be dead before anyone figured them out. Why, when he was running a malaria-grade fever, did Alan feel so unbearably cold, the brassy ache in his head and extremities deeper than Siberian permafrost? Over the past several days they'd all been sick at one time or another—aching, shivering, lapsing in and out of awful delirium. But this, too, seemed like the murky residue of a dream, a memory of a past life. But not here, not now.

Not me. Not like this.

And then Alan was shouting at Lim where he lay groaning on the floor, clutching his broken ribs. He screamed at him to get help, to go to the Russian weather station on the other side of the ice field and tell them what was happening. "Tell Shurik that we're killing each other! Have him call McMurdo for help!"

But Lim just squirmed and giggled.

"Snap out of it!" Alan bellowed fiercely. "Go, or we're all dead!"

Lim lurched to his feet in a rush of nervous laughter and scampered out the door, his mind coiled tightly about a message he interpreted as a component in a strange and exciting game. But Alan couldn't think about that now—whether or not Lim would make it and return with help . . . Couldn't think about it because there was nowhere to run from Hamsun, and because Leonelli was psychotic, possibly worse. Much worse. And mostly because he couldn't awaken from a nightmare that possessed them all.

Alan was beginning to think that Hamsun had called it quits, but this momentary lapse of optimism was almost immediately shattered by the heavy footfall that accompanied the Norwegian giant everywhere he went. The lumbering goon wasn't exactly cut out for *Dancing with the Stars—look who's talking, you'll be lucky if this little escapade doesn't cause you to drop two shoe sizes!*—but Hamsun was a natural for those World's Strongest Man competitions that dominated *ESPN 2*'s late night lineup. Alan forced himself back onto his feet, blue-veined and white as marble. Fortunately they were so numb with frostbite that he couldn't feel the pain he knew was there. In fact, he couldn't feel anything below the knee. Nothing. There was merely a pronounced absence atop which he teetered precariously as Antarctica's merciless cold traveled up his legs, ravaging the cells within. It was no surprise, really. His comical half-naked scamper from the research station to the Meat Locker—forty yards at best—was alone enough to make a double amputee out of him. *Finish barricading the door . . . You can worry about your feet later. If by some stroke of pure dumb luck you manage to keep your toes (wishful thinking), there will be plenty of time for pain and suffering.* The tiny beads of perspiration that had accumulated as a result of his earlier efforts had given way to a crystalline layer of frost covering every inch of his exposed torso. The skin beneath had acquired a waxy texture and bluish-gray cast that reminded him of the worn naugehyde upholstery of the 1966 Ford Mustang he had slammed into the side of the mountain on Mulholland one night during his first semester at USC. He had loved that car despite her uncanny knack of breaking down at precisely the wrong moment. From her broken heater and streaky wipers to her fickle starter and the extra quart of burnt oil she contributed to global warming each month. . . . Just like every other female in his life, she was a struggle, but well worth every headache and heartbreak. Her fickleness was no one's fault but his. He had the same deft hand with women. He hadn't been able to give her what she needed, what she deserved. By his own reckoning, he was never good enough. His lack of hands-on mechanical expertise—not to mention how utterly buried he was in student loans—was on display over every inch of her, but especially in the pair of rusty vise-grips he'd used to replace her broken passenger side window crank. But that was part of her charm, her mystique. She was a wondrous pain in the ass, and even after all these years he still had it bad for her.

The cold was killing him quickly—another twenty minutes and he would lose considerably more than his frostbitten fingers and toes to the sub-zero freeze—but he was urged on by a will to survive that surpassed all logic. It would have been a thousand times easier to close his eyes, surrender to the cold and allow himself to slip into the tranquil oblivion of a hypothermic coma—the deep white sleep of death Antarctic style—but the will behind his eyes rejected the notion, weakened though it had become in the absence of warmth.

I'm living for two, Alan thought ironically.

During those brief moments of inactivity in which he had sat around recollecting the series of events that had landed him here, Alan's joints had stiffened to the point that it was nearly impossible for him to move. Even so, he found himself, shoulder to the fuel drum, pushing with all his remaining strength so that he might keep Hamsun out until the Russians came to his rescue. Frustrated by the fact that his feet were slipping on the ice, and failing to budge the drum of fuel a single inch, Alan backed off a few paces and threw himself at it, directing all the force he could muster into a single push. Frozen as he was, he half-expected the impact to shatter him like glass. Instead, he was rewarded with an outcome not the least bit reminiscent of success. The drum moved, but only inches before it caught a rolled steel lip on the uneven scab of ice beneath it and pitched onto its side with a resonant metallic *oooomph!* Made brittle by the cold, the weld seam circling the lid of the drum cracked open. The damaged drum disgorged a bright pink cataract of fuel that spread quickly over the floor going *glurg-glurg-glurg* until Alan was standing in the midst of a small ecological disaster.

He was overcome by a wave of nausea as gasoline fumes filled the Meat Locker. And if this wasn't bad enough, things got immeasurably worse when he realized the reason behind Hamsun's earlier departure. He recognized the abrupt ripping sound of the chainsaw's starter cord from the dozens of occasions he, himself, had used it to carve blocks of ice for drinking water from the frozen reservoir all around them. On the fourth or fifth pull, the motor caught, roaring to life like a swarm of provoked insects. Hamsun triggered the throttle a few times and engaged the blade. Desperate,

Alan attempted reasoning with him, but either the crazy Norwegian was deafened by the violent growl of the motor, or he was simply too far gone to give a damn. The wall began to vibrate as the spinning toothed blade tore into the composite wood paneling comprising the station, and with zero resistance, sliced downward along the edge of the heavy insulated steel door, spewing popcorn-ish bits of yellow foam insulation into the Meat Locker.

"Hamsun!" he shouted, hammering on the wall with his fists. "You'll kill us both! I'm standing in a lake of gasoline. The entire station's gonna go up like a match if you don't stop. HAMSUN!"

But it was too late. A moment later the blade caught the lip of one of the fuel drums and let out a metallic screech. A spray of sparks ignited the saturated ice around Alan's feet. The fire spread quickly, flames engulfing the lower half of his body, his feet and legs wrapped in a ravenous shroud of blue-orange light. *So much for freezing to death,* he thought as he danced clear of the rippling conflagration playing out over the frozen ground beneath, and beat out the fire that had licked the hair from his legs and crisped his flesh in a matter of seconds. His feet were blackened to the ankles, but had been numbed to such an extent by the cold that they may as well have belonged to someone else. His nerve endings were simply too far gone to register pain.

He knew as only a doomed man can know that there was no escape. Short of jumping into the hole in the ice that gaped before him like an open mouth, his only way out was irretrievably lost to him, barricaded behind a wall of fire. Resigned to his fate and strangely comforted by the heat amassing dangerously around the drums of fuel—acquiring purpose as is the nature of fire to comfort, consume and destroy—Alan edged closer to the blaze. He was unfazed now by Hamsun's continued assault with the chainsaw. He simply wanted to be warm again, to not feel so torn between what he had once been and what he had become, to remember if only briefly what it was like to bask in the penetrating Huntington Beach sun and know nothing of the twists of destiny that would land him here.

If anyone ever asked him what was good on the menu, he would warn them to stay away from the Shrimp *á la* Jules Verne . . . Have the pepper steak, the Buckaroo Burger, the rack of lamb for two, *anything but the shrimp!* He had delivered this warning to Ethan via satellite phone—a rambling semi-intelligible rant—as he had announced their discovery of the hydrothermal vent community at the bottom of the lake. But this was days ago, and he had already been infected with whatever it was that had driven them all mad, and was far from thinking straight. He couldn't remember exactly how the conversation with Ethan had ended only that the signal had been weak and that his friend's voice had seemed hopelessly distant. It was as if it had originated from a point in time and space that no longer existed—a place no more accessible to Alan than the memory of the warm Pacific shore that was obliterated with the rest of him as the drums of fuel exploded and a massive fireball roared upward into the pale Antarctic twilight.

Marina Del Rey, California
GPS Coordinates: –118.4517449, 33.9802893
March 12, 2010

Ethan had spoken with Alan via satellite phone a few short hours after the team had discovered the hydrothermal vent community at the bottom of the lake. It was a weak signal, and the two men scarcely had time to congratulate one another before atmospheric interference had crippled the transmission. Forty-eight hours later, the solar flares had subsided and they were able to speak again. This time Alan's mind had seemed to wander, and he was vague and unresponsive when Ethan questioned him about the vent and the team's findings. When Ethan had expressed concern, Alan explained that he was just getting over a bad cold that had kicked the crap out of the entire team. *Nothing to worry about*, he'd said. *We're back on our feet and it's business as usual*. As evidence of their well being, he'd mentioned a geologic survey Leonelli and Schmidt were off somewhere conducting that very moment. Ethan couldn't say why exactly—it was just a feeling—but even though he'd popped a couple of Xanax to take the edge off it had been nearly impossible for him to sleep that night.

Maybe it was because he'd begun to believe in the existence of the organism his contact at the Department of Defense had strong-armed him to isolate. The golden goose of the DOD's covert biological weapons research program was beginning to look like the real thing. True, there was no way of knowing with any degree of certainty that what Alan had dismissed as a case of the flu was not simply just that, but Ethan had a hunch. First, there was Alan's shaky description of the stromatolite forest, the details of which he had communicated with an awe bordering on psychedelic rapture. Then there was the mystery illness. Although the symptoms Alan described were consistent with at least one stage of virtually every form of viral infection known to man, there was the troubling question of *how*.

Antarctica was fraught with innumerable dangers—hypothermia, pulmonary edema, frostbite, snowblindness—but catching a cold wasn't one of them. Viruses needed carriers to thrive, spread and propagate, and the bottom of the world was conspicuously devoid of such. Maybe his contact at the DOD wasn't totally crazy after all. Who knows, there might even be a shred of truth to his apocalyptic soothsaying.

Although infectious disease wasn't his forte, Ethan knew how to run an expedition and was in too deep with the IRS to turn his back on Okum's "offer." Uncle Sam's generosity was tempered with the knowledge that they had enough evidence to prosecute him on no less than ten felony counts involving tax-evasion, fraud and gross misuse of federal and state funds. The judicial system was cracking down on white-collar crime. This wasn't about a slap on the wrist. If convicted, he could expect a lengthy stay in the federal country club. His cushy career in academia would be wrecked.

So what if he had been living beyond his means, skimming a little extra off the top here and there, using grant money to make ends meet, billing the university for personal expenses—dinners at Campanile, the lease payments on his Mercedes . . . There wasn't a full professor in the department who hadn't at one time or another tweaked his code of ethics to supplement what could hardly be considered a living wage. The only difference between Ethan and the rest of them was that he had gotten caught. He would've been wise to keep a lower profile, steer clear of the spotlight like his less ambitious colleagues. But he enjoyed his modest celebrity so damn much that he probably would've done it the same way all over again if given the chance.

At least he wasn't a card-carrying drunk like so many of them. Nor did he comport himself with the social graces of a Tibetan yak. He was a functioning member of society, the department's golden boy, and not some tired old recluse holed up in a dusty little cave of an office dying of cirrhosis and chronic dandruff. Sure, he was guilty of minor indiscretions every now and then, but not the sort of thing that hurt anyone. If there was one thing he could've done a better job with, it was managing his libido.

Throughout high school and college—and with, of course, the exception of Claire—he'd never come close to notching the caliber of ass that regularly enrolled in his classes. He had been an okay-looking kid, but never very athletic or socially outgoing. He was a science geek, and had garnered his fair share of beatings from what had seemed like every Neanderthal in Orange County. Rather than concentrating on the awkward teenager who would never fit in, he had dedicated himself to developing the man he would one day become, the man he now was. A winner. These days his grading policy was as loose and legendary as was his proclivity for firm young tits and ass. He often boasted to his friends outside the teaching profession that everything was "negotiable" and that he "graded on curves." Of course he had learned to be charming—grant committees routinely favored personality above ability—but he knew that it was his position, the infinitely wise professor proselytizing from his gilded soap box, the taboo such a union entailed that lured the vampish young coeds into his bed.

Although not technically forbidden, the administration frowned upon student-teacher relations. He'd been reminded on more than one occasion that such faculty indiscretions were the stuff of scandal and sexual harassment suits. Recently, Ethan had made a conscious effort to only ride the thoroughbreds, and not go slip-slidin' around every wet spot that crossed his path. Be selective, discrete. So he wasn't a goddamned saint. Christ, he was making up for twenty years of sexually-frustrated youth. He'd managed to work the system all these years without any trouble. With a little fine-tuning, he could continue to do so. He hadn't come all this way so that he could retire on a scrawny pension and spend the remainder of his days kicking himself in the ass for all the missed opportunities, sexual or otherwise. The townhouse in Westwood didn't come cheap. And he'd had his eye on a little villa in the hills of Ravello for some time—nothing fancy, just old world Italian charm, a few grape vines, and the sparkling waters of the Tyrrhenian Sea stretching out over the horizon.

Ethan hadn't planned on Alan dying—that wasn't the plan at all. Alan was his friend, one of the few people Ethan felt had ever trusted him. But the fact remained. Nothing was going to bring Alan back, not all the remorse and tears in the world. Ethan could go on with his life and finish the job, or he could curl up into the fetal position and let the IRS bleed him dry. In a way, he almost envied Alan—no more treading water in a world teeming with sharks. Sharks and vampires. Bloodsuckers, every last one of them. Sure, Ethan could have been more honest with him about the nature of their work in Antarctica, but that would have exposed him and the others to greater danger than Ivan itself. In fact, Ethan had never truly believed in the existence of the deadly pathogen the military had assured him was very real. Most of their information was strictly anecdotal—Cold War fairy tales pieced together from intercepted Soviet satellite transmissions and the farfetched testimony of former Russian naval personnel. Not exactly what you'd call hard data.

Ethan's contact was a retired Foreign Service something-or-other who went by the name of Wayne Okum. He hadn't been at all what Ethan had expected. This was not the slick shadowy character you saw in movies and read about in Tom Clancy novels. This was the affable-looking guy you saw cruising the interstate behind the wheel of one of those massive RV's that populate every rest stop along the way. He had thick reddish blonde hair, the youthful luster of which had given way to a silver-gray burnish, and the uptight posture of someone who didn't get enough fiber in his diet. He wore a khaki polo-style knockoff tucked into a pair of crisp blue jeans and secured with a shiny black belt. Ethan guessed that he was somewhere between fifty and fifty-five years old, the inevitable consequences of which were a sagging neck, face and triceps. Drip-dry flesh. He drove a forest green minivan.

"Let me get this straight," said Ethan. "You want me to go all the way to Antarctica and find this really fucking deadly organism—"

"Ivan the Terrible," Okum interjected.

"Right, Ivan the Terrible . . . that killed a shitload of people and that no one's caught a whiff of since 1979?"

Okum dumped seven packets of Splenda into his iced tea and smiled. "You catch on fast, Dr. Hatcher."

"How do you know any of this is even real? Why not an elaborate hoax—something to keep you guys looking the other way while the Russians smuggled nukes into Cuba. Forgive me if I seem skeptical—but a bunny rabbit single-handedly wiping out the crew of a nuclear submarine?"

"What was *inside* the bunny rabbit," Okum clarified.

"Even so—"

"We have sources."

"You mean spies?"

"You say tomato . . ." Okum replied glibly, stirring his iced tea with a fork.

"You said everyone on the sub died a horrible death."

Okum nodded. "There was one—the only survivor. I think he was the cook or something. A Russian search and rescue team found him adrift in the sub's escape pod. They debriefed him on a closed frequency and then blew him out of the water."

Ethan chewed on his mixed baby greens and Szechwan-style grilled chicken breast. "Just like that?"

"Guess they'd heard enough."

"Let me ask again . . . You want me to go all the way to the South Pole to find this really fucking deadly organism because of what a whacked-out cook told some Russian sailors thirty years ago?"

Okum studied him over the rim of his glass and lowered his voice. "Any of this gets out and I'll make sure the IRS crawls so far up your ass that you'll have civil servants swinging from your tonsils. Copy?"

"Relax, I'm only trying to understand."

"One of our own subs was in the area keeping tabs. High stakes surveillance. Cold War chess. Anyway, she starts picking up these noises coming from the Russian boat."

"What kind of noises?"

"Voices mostly. Nothing out of the ordinary, except when you consider that each one of these subs is a mobile nuclear arsenal and that remaining hidden is priority one."

"Voices?"

"Nonsense—routine chatter. Guys mixing it up. Then things started getting weird. It sounded as if they were having a party in there—banging on pipes, smashing things, laughter, calling each other names. Raising hell. Remember, this stuff wasn't coming over the radio. It was traveling through the water—sound vibrations. The quality wasn't exactly hi-fi, but it was clear enough. Anyway, things went from bad to worse and pretty soon it was goddamned pandemonium."

"Mass hysteria? I'd go crazy too if I was cooped up in a submarine."

"At first, that's what we thought. Some sort of problem with the re-breathers—too much nitrogen in the air. Guys were beginning to hallucinate. But wait, it gets better. Out of the blue the Russian captain dials up Moscow and starts rambling on about the dancing bears he watched perform in Red Square when he was a kid. He nearly pisses himself laughing about it. The guy sounds drunk, like he's been in bed with a bottle of vodka for a week."

"What about the nitrogen?"

"Maybe."

"So why didn't they just pack it in and head home?" Ethan asked.

"I guess they couldn't or wouldn't. In the middle of the chat with Moscow someone cuts in on the captain: shouting, gunshots, some guy starts singing into the horn like he's Boris fuckin' Sinatra. After this, it's Chinese New Year for two days straight. *Brrrr!*" Okum shivered for effect. "Shit'll make your skin crawl. And then nothing. The Russian sub's dead in the water—a true-to-life ghost ship. No one knows what's happened. If anyone onboard is still alive, no one's talking. The cook blows the escape pod and here we are."

"What happened to the sub?" Hatcher asked.

"Russians scuttled their own boat. Sent her to the bottom right there. Four-thousand feet straight down."

". . . to get rid of Ivan."

"You catch on fast."

"Why the name? Why Ivan the Terrible?"

"Months before any of this a crew of Russian geologists was drilling for oil near the South Pole. But instead of oil they discovered millions upon millions of gallons of good ol' H_2O half a mile down. Hasn't seen the light of day since our ancestors had pubic hair to their knees. A week later every last one of them is dead, so Moscow sends in a team of military scientists to poke around. No one in Russia has seen anything this bad since the reign of Ivan the Terrible: guys with their eyes gouged out, bite marks covering their bodies, sodomy, limbs missing, walls inside the rig dripping with blood. Autopsies at the site reveal that the oil crew had been eating each other. In some cases, eating themselves."

Okum had gone on to explain that the autopsies had revealed an absence of drugs, but that other more enigmatic anomalies had been discovered. For starters, every last drop of blood examined by the team contained residual traces of what appeared to be an unidentified organism. Either it was some sort of here today-gone tomorrow mutation—a relative new kid on the block that would outlive its usefulness before coming into its own—or something infinitely older and more firmly embedded in the hierarchy of natural selection. Unfortunately, the drill rig had long since frozen over and despite their best efforts the team of scientists had been unable to procure a single living specimen by which to determine the course and consequence of its pathogenesis. Rather than simply give up, however, the scientists were ordered to hold tight for the arrival of a second drilling team.

When extensive analysis of the surface environment turned up nothing, the team concluded that whatever had infected the first group of drillers had come out of the ice thousands of feet down. The Kremlin was intrigued. The possibility of isolating such an organism for military applications was too valuable to ignore. After several weeks, the new team found what they had been looking for, some sort of microorganism living on the lake bottom.

It didn't take long for the Russian scientists to conclude that the pathogen slipped into a semi-dormant state once the temperature of its host fell below a certain point. It was possible for Ivan to revive, however the window of opportunity was somewhere in the range of forty-eight to seventy-two hours. After that its life functions ceased entirely. The military infected a rabbit, turned it over to the sub, disposed of the second team of roughnecks, and then lost interest in the project when the organism was . . .

". . . deemed too dangerous to fuck with," Okum concluded indelicately.

"Why a rabbit?" asked Ethan.

"Easier to transport a pissed-off bunny than a pissed-off man."

"Why me? Why not someone from the CDC, someone who has experience with this sort of thing. Surely, you have people on the company payroll."

"*The CDC* . . ." Okum scoffed. "News travels faster through that place than a case of syphilis at the Mustang Ranch. If we're not careful, we could lose the project to China or the North Koreans." Okum eyed Ethan meaningfully. "Besides, you're our guy—a mediocre, law-breaking scientist who's always on some kind of wild goose chase. Our interest in you is actually quite simple when you think about it. Someone who's dedicated his life to tracking down werewolves and sea monsters won't exactly arouse suspicion. Plausible deniability is the name of the game nowadays. Anyone asks, you tell them you're hunting the Abominable Snowman."

"Why now?" asked Ethan. He had to choke down an urge to tell Okum to go fuck himself. "Why wait so long to go back?"

"Administrations change. Policy changes. The war in Afghanistan got the man in the Oval Office thinking. Why risk our troops when there might be a way to encourage the enemy to kill each other? Hell of a way to keep the UN off our back. Show the rest of the world what a bunch of nuts Osama and his boys really are."

"Nice," said Ethan. "That's very humanitarian of you."

"Think of all the money it will save taxpayers like yourself . . ." Okum caught himself and shrugged. "Bad example, but you get the idea."

"If Ivan can't survive without a host, how am I supposed to keep it alive?"

"Gotcha covered," Okum assured him with a slippery grin. "You any good with monkeys?"

❖ ❖ ❖

In all probability Alan and the others never knew what hit them. They had been as oblivious of the organism thriving within their blood as the chimps had been of the purpose Okum had envisioned for the unsuspecting primates. Who was the bigger dupe, Ethan wondered, the hairy knuckle draggers or him?

He shouldn't have kept Alan in the dark about the true nature of their expedition, but what choice did he have? Okum was very clear about concealing the mission objective until the last possible moment. If anyone found out what the United States was doing in Antarctica, the UN would have had a field day raking the current administration over the coals of international scrutiny.

From the very beginning Ethan had thought the plan was more than a little myopic. Too much had been assumed. Too much had been left to chance. He couldn't imagine Alan and the others agreeing to infect the chimps with a deadly pathogen, especially given the fact that they themselves had been laboring under false pretenses. Okum's assurance that they would gladly slit their own mothers' throats when they learned of the enormous sums of money they were going to receive for their complicity didn't exactly hold water. To Ethan it was beginning to look more and more as if he, too, had been set up.

In the wake of the explosion he did a little digging. Alan was the only team member that had a family to speak of, and he had been Ethan's choice. In fact Ethan had insisted that Alan accompany him, a decision that now kept him awake at night. And of course there was Lim about whom Ethan couldn't learn anything, although he had gotten the distinct feeling from the civil servant with whom he had spoken long-distance that the Chinese government was none too fond of the marine biologist. Ethan was given the impression that Lim was something of a dissenter, a thorn in the Party's side, though admired and well-respected among his colleagues. He imagined an arrangement between clandestine sectors of the Chinese and American governments to get rid of Lim, make it look like an accident . . . But this was merely speculation—paranoia, he had to admit, that was undoubtedly nurtured by his own fear of ending up dead like the others.

Ethan would have dismissed all of it as simple coincidence had he selected the team himself. However the fact that Okum had given him a list of candidates from which to choose now struck Ethan as reasonably suspicious. No one on Okum's list had family, save perhaps a distant second cousin living in some backwater town on the outskirts of nowhere. Ethan now believed that the chimps were merely a smokescreen, decoys to put the true lab animals at ease.

Los Angeles, California
GPS Coordinates: −118.2436849, 34.0522342
March 12, 2010

By the time Claire Matthews had finished writing her doctoral dissertation she was regarded by many of her colleagues to be one of the world's most promising young contributors to the emerging field of cryptozoology. For this, she had an unusual pot-bellied herbivore to thank. Although no bigger than a common goat, the Ha Tinh pygmy rhinoceros, as it was now known the world over, had promised to get Claire in the door of an elitist community of male scientists that every now and then toler-ated a Madame Curie in their ranks. Claire had been a lead member of the research team who had confirmed the existence of the pygmy rhinoceros, a taciturn creature whose most prominent features were a pair of vestigial horns on its snout and zebra stripes about its rump. However, the discovery that should have rocketed her to rela-tive stardom fizzled mightily, and her career had more or less blown up on the launch pad nearly five years ago.

Admittedly, tracking down species thought to be extinct or merely rumored to exist was not going to make a celebrity out of her, but there was something inherently noble and gratifying about opening the eyes of the world to the mystery and diversity of fauna that had populated the planet long before there were humans to level forests for toilet paper. She also liked proving the skeptics wrong. They were men mostly, burnt-out practitioners of hard data and established facts, who regarded her passion for the unknown with the same scorn many of Copernicus's contemporaries had regarded the renegade astronomer's heretical model of earth's solar system.

For decades, people in the remote mountain villages of Laos and Vietnam had reported sightings of a reclusive mammal unclassified in modern taxonomy, but no one had paid any serious attention. That is until Claire had produced credible evi-dence of the Ha Tinh's existence in the form of badly decomposed remains. She had received the parcel via overnight mail by secret arrangement with an anonymous zoo acquisitionist operating without a permit in the balmy highlands of Ha Tinh province. In actuality, there was no zoo acquisitionist and the decomposed remains had belonged to a stillborn hippopotamus, but the ruse had been enough to convince the Los Angeles Museum of Natural History where she had been interning to fund a modest expedition. It was a big gamble. Claire knew that failure would've meant exposure as a fraud and the end of a career in its infancy; however, she was absolutely certain that something, if not the rumored pygmy rhinoceros, was out there waiting to be discovered. Once upon a time she had been an incurable optimist. Besides, she was not going to make it in a man's world playing by the rules. She had to take chances, make her own way. She had learned early on that her survival depended on her ability to adapt, eke out a niche in a field saturated with testosterone. Her hunch had paid off and after only three leech-infested weeks in the jungle she and the other members of the team had documented two adult and one juvenile Ha Tinh pygmy rhinoceros. It was the most significant addition to the Class Mammalia since biologists had confirmed the existence of the Vu Quang ox in 1992.

Despite her early notoriety she now lived with the distinct possibility that she was never going to be able to match the success of her first expedition, a triumph eclipsed by an over-inflated controversy that haunted her to this day. Already there were those who described her, in addition to less flattering appellations, as a "one hit wonder." Mostly, these were the same aging armchair scientists who had doubted her from the beginning, envious hemorrhoid sufferers who ruled university Natural Science departments and the professional journals with an arrogant dedication to rehashing what was already known. But the label bothered her anyway. Claire had known all along that her chosen field was with few exceptions little more than a bastion of male ego. Still, she had done nothing to deserve this.

Teaching general biology at Los Caminos Community College, an under funded, overcrowded haven for anyone who could afford the twenty-five dollars per unit enrollment fee was nothing short of a slap in the face. The gloomy little college was equidistant from every third-rate inner-city high-school in the area, and spitting distance from UCLA, and her alma mater, USC, powerhouses of scientific inquiry.

The majority of her students, most of whom were more interested in getting high and having sex than getting an education, couldn't have told the difference between an Arabian Oryx and a single-celled protozoan. But for the occasional outburst of a rabid creationist asserting that dinosaur fossils were nothing more than a hoax perpetrated by Satan to ensnare the faithless, her classes were painfully tedious and life-draining. Worse yet was the fact that funding at the community college level was harder to come by than inspiration. Claire had drafted countless grant proposals, any of which if approved would have helped to resurrect Los Caminos from the ashes of academic obscurity. All, however, had been summarily rejected in favor of more pressing needs—specifically the college's perennially lackluster athletics program.

Although it was poison to her system Claire couldn't help following the "work" of Dr. Ethan Hatcher. Hatcher had more or less stolen the position she had earned at USC and was now up to his armpits in honoraria and grant money. He had been a fellow grad student, museum intern, and team member of the Ha Tinh expedition back in 1999. The unscrupulous bastard was also the one primarily responsible for her ongoing exile in the wastelands of academic purgatory.

Hatcher had convinced Ellington Nosworthy, Ph.D., a self-styled intellectual and great glob of a man in charge of acquisitions at the Museum of Natural History, that it was foolish and a waste of time to go all the way to Southeast Asia without procuring a living specimen of the creature they intended to catalogue and study. With the exception of a few regrettable months in the summer before the expedition, Claire had seen Hatcher for what he was: a petty, unremarkable ghoul who believed the only way to truly understand something was to kill it. Okay, maybe she was exaggerating the facts a bit. Face it, she resented the knowledge that Hatcher was living the life of which she'd always dreamed.

From the moment Claire had been informed of the plan to return to Los Angeles with a living specimen of the pygmy rhino she was determined to make sure that it never happened. The fact that a creature yet undocumented were in all probability endangered, if not poised on the brink of extinction, didn't seem to bother Hatcher and Nosworthy. To the thoughtless pair, the Ha Tinh rhino was a living, breathing opportunity to advance their careers, no matter the cost. Claire had gently reminded them of the fate of Benjamin, the Tasmanian Tiger—the last of its kind dying alone in a cage at the Hobart Zoo in 1936—but she had known better than to press the issue. If she didn't have the stomach for "hard science" Nosworthy had reminded her with the artless condescension of a homicide detective, there were others who would be grateful to take her place.

In spite of a few logistical problems, Claire had known that deceiving Hatcher would be a snap. She had fooled him once already with the faked Ha Tinh remains, his powers of perception, as was his eye for empirical data, notoriously indiscriminate. As part of a ploy to demonstrate team spirit she had admitted her earlier lapse in judgment and had, herself, selected the container they would use to air freight the specimen back to Los Angeles in the event such a "golden" opportunity presented itself. With the exception of a few small breathing holes the portable enclosure was entirely sealed, offering scant visibility of the cargo within. Claire had little difficulty convincing her self-involved colleagues that it would be best to shelter the creature from any unnecessary stimuli. Emotional trauma, she explained, could drastically reduce the value of their investment, both scientifically and financially. After all, they wanted a specimen that would be responsive to their poking and prodding, not a wide-eyed, defecating beast on the verge of cardiac arrest.

After landing in Hanoi, Claire, Hatcher and the three other members of the expedition traveled overland into the dense montane forests of the Annamite mountains. They spent twenty-six kidney-jarring hours bouncing over unpaved roads in a U.S. Army supply truck that had been captured by the Vietcong during the war. While

Claire and the others reviewed the data on the purported whereabouts and living habits of the pygmy rhinoceros, Hatcher familiarized himself with the operation and feel of the tranquilizer gun the museum had provided. He spent the majority of the drive with the loaded weapon resting carelessly across his lap, eyes narrowed into cagey slits as if he was Ernest Hemingway on the trail of Cape buffalo.

"Careful, Ethan," Claire had warned. "You're going to put somebody to sleep if that thing accidentally goes off."

Everyone laughed but Hatcher. "You're a great girl," he apologized sadistically, "but I've moved on. Maybe you should think about doing the same. Our work here is too important to let our personal differences interfere with it."

Truth be told, it was Claire who had dumped Hatcher. Once they had started dating it hadn't taken her long to realize that he was a blue ribbon asshole, plain and simple. Unfortunately, the lesson came a little too late. A few short weeks before they'd broken up Claire had come down with a case of strep throat. She had taken the antibiotics and gone about the business of her life which she now dreaded to admit included having sex with Hatcher. She didn't understand how exactly but the antibiotics had somehow reacted with her birth control pills, rendering her only measure of protection temporarily ineffective. Hatcher was adamant that Claire have an abortion. He said that they didn't have time for distractions. A baby would only get in the way. Until then Claire hadn't seriously considered keeping the baby. She had no intention of staying with Hatcher and hoped that if and when she had a child that she would also have a husband she loved by her side. However, Hatcher's blasé attitude about the whole thing had nearly compelled her to make the worst decision of her life. At one point she had actually threatened to keep the baby if only to prove that she had a say in it. Hatcher freaked out. She had an abortion. And the rest was emotional baggage. Guilt mostly, but also wonder.

By the time they arrived in Vietnam, Claire had more or less gotten over the worst of it. That is until Hatcher had stirred things up with his vindictive rebuff. It was this exchange that Claire played over in her mind three weeks later as she released Hatcher's prize Ha Tinh specimen, a young female, while he and the others slept in a village hut nearby. By the time they had awakened the following morning Claire had replaced the emancipated rhinoceros with a pig of the same approximate weight and dimensions she had secretly purchased from a sympathetic local.

Hatcher's rage upon seeing that he had returned from halfway around the world with eighty-five kilos of bacon was only outdone by his shame at having to explain to Nosworthy how he had been duped by a *woman*. While Claire had managed to spare the Ha Tinh the indignity of becoming a lab animal, she had not fared equally well. Though Nosworthy could not prove that she had been responsible for the switch, the spiteful son of a bitch had made it his lifelong mission to see that she languish in professional obscurity—that she, like the species she so desperately desired to catalogue, remain undiscovered.

Claire had to hand it to old Nosworthy. The greasy blowhard was more influential than she had given him credit for. More than a decade had passed since the expedition to Vietnam and subsequent scandal, and other than an occasional sniff from some out-of-the-way foreign studies academy in Haiti or the United Arab Emirates she had been effectively shut out of the university hiring pool. Had Nosworthy's quest to avenge his bruised ego ended there, Claire might have been able to live with it. However, the fact that he had expended an equal amount of energy in furthering Hatcher's career had caused her no end of grief.

While the self-aggrandizing publicity hound headed lavishly-funded expeditions to the primeval forests of Borneo and the frigid waters of Loch Ness in search of creatures whose existence only the tabloids took seriously, Claire was stuck grading papers whose careless, uninspired responses assured her in no uncertain terms that her life was helplessly futile. No two ways about it, she had died and gone to hell.

This was Ethan's second meeting with Okum. Same location, same subject, same lousy food. But with one important twist. The first time they had met everything had been in place: the team, the station, the objectives. Now there was nothing left but a bombed-out crater, a handful of dead scientists, and a shitload of unanswered questions. Ethan wasn't exactly looking forward to their lunch date. He had no idea what to expect, but had gotten the distinct impression that he was now in deeper than ever. Okum had mentioned something about switching to Plan B, but wouldn't give him any details over the phone. In the past forty-eight hours Ethan had developed a profound distrust of the second letter of the alphabet.

"Have a seat," said Okum, scowling benevolently over the top of a menu smeared with greasy fingerprints. "The lemonade's for you. Drink up."

Ethan eyed the glass sweating on the table in front of him. The ice was half-melted and the contents looked like watered-down piss. Frozen concentrate. "Thanks."

"You hungry? I was thinking about having the steak sandwich, but I don't know about the sauce they put on it. What in the name of Saint Peter is a-oh-lee?"

"Aioli is garlic-mayonnaise. It's good."

Okum folded the menu and laid it on the table. "You were right about us sending in specialists to do this. Ivan may have been just a bit too hot for you and your guys to handle." He shrugged. "Live and learn, right?"

Easy now. There's no point losing your temper. "Can we make this quick? I've got a class to teach in forty-five minutes."

Okum steepled his hands as if he were about to pray and looked searchingly at Ethan. "I've gotta say we're a bit concerned with what happened down there."

Ethan couldn't help it. He was furious. *"Concerned?"* he echoed. "My best friend is dead."

"We don't know that for sure," Okum answered calmly.

"Are you telling me Alan might still be alive? We had a memorial service for him. His parents cried their eyes out!"

Okum's face hardened. "Well, boo fucking hoo. Your friend might be involved in something. Shit, for all anyone knows he's sipping mai-tais on a beach somewhere while we reminisce about what a swell guy he was."

"You make it sound as if Alan was a spy or something?" Ethan couldn't believe what he was hearing. "Are you insane? He rode a bicycle to work because cars leave too big a carbon footprint on the environment."

"Sure, and he used corn cobs to wipe his ass," Okum added dryly. He blotted the sweat from his forehead with a paper napkin. "Until we're sure that every member of your team died in the explosion there's the possibility that one of them—not your friend necessarily—destroyed the station to cover his tracks."

"You're joking?"

"I leave the jokes to the politicians," said Okum. "Something like Ivan turns up in a Middle Eastern weapons bazaar and every rogue nation, terrorist, and civil servant with a grudge will want a taste."

"I'm here and I'm alive. Shouldn't I be your number one suspect?"

"We're looking into that." Okum massaged his jaw. "In the meantime, we've put together another team. We'd like you to serve as a field consultant."

"What kind of team?"

"A military forensics unit. JPAC. Top notch. Give 'em a nose hair and they can tell you who it belonged to, cause of death, and how he liked his eggs done."

"Now you want me to play Sherlock Holmes?"

"You spent some time there," said Okum. "You know what to expect. I don't care if you end up serving coffee and donuts as long as this gets done. If and when our team identifies and accounts for the remains of every member of your team . . . Well then, case closed. *Via con Dios* and fuck-you very much."

"And that's it?" Ethan felt sick to his stomach. Alan had died for nothing. Worse than nothing. He had died because Ethan had fudged on his taxes. "What about Ivan?"

"Between what happened to the Russians once upon a time, and now this . . . Let's just say that strike three isn't worth the risk. We've decided to go in another direction. Call me fickle, but Ivan's just not right for us at this time."

"This isn't a blind date."

"Love 'em and leave 'em." Okum spread his arms and flashed a shit-eating grin. "Which reminds me . . ." He dug something out of his pocket and passed it across the table to Ethan. It was a photograph. "I understand you two know each other."

"Who gave you this?" said Ethan. Five years had gone by, but he remembered the moment well. In fact, it was Alan who had snapped the picture in a little village high in the mountains of Ha Tinh province.

"My sources tell me she's got some pretty interesting ideas about Ivan."

Ethan was tongue-tied.

"Don't look so surprised," said Okum. "Actually, Dr. Matthews was our first choice. But we couldn't dig up any dirt on her so we settled on you. I guess we should have dug a little deeper. Her expertise might have saved your buddy's life." Okum fingered the picture beneath his nose. He was practically drooling over Claire's long tanned muscular legs. "Tell me about her. I hear you two knocked boots once upon a time."

If there had been any doubt of Claire's current locale, it was promptly laid to rest that afternoon when Ethan Hatcher, the devil himself, unexpectedly appeared in her office. Although it had been years since they had been alone together, they had exchanged words on more than one occasion, heated Q&A sessions presided over by the rancor each felt for one another. The last time such an exchange had taken place was at the National Conference on Specialized Biology, a forum Hatcher had exploited to drum up financial backing for an expedition to Puerto Rico. That was nearly a year ago. It wasn't fair that she be subjected to him again so soon.

"Knock-knock!" said Hatcher, drawing closed the door behind him.

Clad in a pair of camouflage cargo shorts and a fitted jersey bearing the logo of some Podunk lacrosse team, he looked as if he had wandered out of the pages of the Abercrombie & Fitch fall catalog. No one in their right mind would've have taken him for a full professor of biology at USC. Not half bad for thirty-five considering this was the man who'd ruined her life.

"It's customary to knock *before* entering," Claire informed him coolly. "But since we're doing things in reverse order, let me begin by saying goodbye."

"Is that any way to treat a colleague?" he asked, extending his hand.

Claire remained seated at her desk, hands planted firmly on the stack of essays she had been grading. "Thanks to you and your buddy, Nosworthy, I don't have any colleagues."

"Look, Claire," he said, softening his tone, "I didn't come here to spar with you. I need a favor."

Why did he have to be so damn good-looking? It would have been a hell of a lot easier telling him to go fuck himself if he had begun to fall apart like other men his age. She was normally above the trivial ill-will that was the spurned woman's MO, but she couldn't help being a little disappointed that Hatcher's hair was still intact and more luxuriant than ever. Dark and unruly, it was the envy of much younger men, and had the irritating knack of looking styled no matter how unkempt it happened to be.

"*So* . . . You look good," she relented stubbornly. "Sharp teeth, good thick coat, clear eyes. Life at the top of the food chain must be treating you well, Ethan."

"Come to Antarctica with me."

"*Excuse me?*"

"I'm serious," he said in his deep flinty voice. "I need you."

"Don't make me call Campus Police."

"This is big, a chance to do some real fieldwork on someone else's dime."

"I'm dialing." Claire picked up her phone, index finger poised at the ready.

"I'm offering you a chance to save yourself from . . . From this." Grimly, he surveyed Claire's office. Professional journals, textbooks and her own research filled to capacity the 'L'-configured bookcase jammed in the corner near her beat-up wood desk (circa 1959, the year the school began serving the community) and not-matching blue poly-fiber Office Depot chair that was a Jackson Pollack of mystery stains bequeathed her by its previous long-term occupant. "What's going on here?" Hatcher went on jokingly. "You auditioning for a spot on that sickening show about human packrats, or something? *Hoarders*, that's it! They've got people on who bury themselves alive beneath mountains of pizza boxes and junk mail."

Claire squirmed inside her skin but masked it behind a cool chuckle. "You know I've never been the Susie Homemaker-type."

"I know I liked playing house with you," Hatcher breathed in that deliberately creepy-playful way of his she used to think was sexy. He finished her off with a classic Hollywood smile, a little whiter than she remembered, though every bit as attractive.

"Please, I've managed to block most of it out." Claire hung up the phone.

Still smiling and without skipping a beat, Hatcher remarked, "It stinks in here."

He wasn't being mean-spirited and Claire couldn't argue with him. Her office was a crime scene. Between the poor ventilation, the moldering stacks of books, and the fact that she was one floor below the Faculty Men's room—not to mention the advanced age of every permanent fixture, coat of lead-based paint and asbestos fiber acoustic ceiling tile—the crypt-like little room was certainly guilty of the smell of death. Though it might simply have been her dead career. "It's a little musty," she responded, "but it adds character."

Hatcher noticed the stacks of yet-to-be-graded papers occupying nearly every square inch of her desktop. "These are almost two months old," Hatcher commented, amusement evident in his voice.

"Evolution's a slow process, or were you out with a hangover the day they covered that in class?"

"Just an observation." He held up his hands in a peace-keeping gesture. "You're better than this place, that's all. It's a compliment—take it."

"Thanks for the backhanded vote of confidence, you arrogant prick!" She was too disturbed by the truth to give Hatcher the satisfaction of admitting to it. "I love it here!" she declared perhaps too vehemently. "The classes I teach are so low-level that I could do it in my sleep, I have next to nil in the way of committee responsibilities, total autonomy, and here there's zero pressure to publish." She delivered her lines convincingly, but the words left a bad taste in her mouth.

"It seems like every time I turn around you've published something new. You belong up the road with us in scenic South Central. In fact," Hatcher went on, "there's going to be a vacancy in the department this fall. Sam Russell's finally hanging it up."

"Not Sam . . ."

"The man's seventy-one years-old . . . I guess fieldwork isn't sexy forever, even to a man like Sam." Hatcher reflected soberly. "Our body only gives us so much time, then it's off to the glue factory."

Sam Russell—*Dr. Russell* as Claire had known him back when, had served on Claire's doctoral committee. He was a brilliant man, one of her most influential mentors, and had conducted more fieldwork than any biologist she knew of. His were some big shoes to fill, but it was an exciting notion. "Why on earth are you telling me this?"

"I can't make you any guarantees, but I'm chairing the hiring committee . . ."

Claire reached for the phone again.

"Stop," said Hatcher. "I'm serious. I want you to interview with us."

"The catch?"

"No catch. Just give me five minutes to pitch the expedition. If you're still not begging me to go after you see what I have in my pocket—no problem. The offer to interview stands, and I swear I'll do everything in my power to see that your name is on the short-list."

"I've already seen what's in your pocket, and I've gotta say I wasn't very impressed."

Hatcher ignored her, the sudden downshift in his tone and facial expression conveying the somberness of the situation. "You remember Alan Whitehurst?"

"Of course, Alan's a sweetie. I should've dated *him* instead of you."

Claire had always liked Alan regardless of the fact that he and Hatcher were close friends. Alan was very much like her, a dedicated scientist who put the planet and its ecological health first. She had always suspected that he had secretly applauded her switch of the Ha Tinh rhino. Although he hadn't come out and said so—Alan was too practical to risk openly allying himself with a black sheep—he had kept in touch with her over the years, offering his friendship and encouragement when times were tough.

"Alan's dead."

"That's not funny," said Claire, fighting back a chill.

Hatcher's expression flatlined. For the first time Claire noticed how exhausted he looked. Dark crescents underscored his gray granite-flecked eyes.

"Alan died two weeks ago in an explosion," Hatcher went on. "He wasn't the only one. There were five others—*my team*—all of them dead."

Although Claire hadn't spoken with Alan in close to a year it seemed just like yesterday that the two of them had sat in her office laughing about the horrified look on Nosworthy's face when the pig had trotted out of the shipping container. She wanted to say something—to mark the moment so that she could leave it behind—but she simply couldn't find the words.

"He and the others were at our research station near the South Pole. Apparently the fuel we used to run the generator ignited. I haven't been back to see the damage for myself, but I hear it's not pretty."

Claire was close to losing it. She could feel the hot sting of salt in her eyes. *Don't you dare! You're not a child.* And with that she forced back the tears. "I don't believe you."

"I couldn't get him on the satellite phone for a few days so I asked one of the Air National Guard supply pilots at McMurdo fly out to pay them a visit. When he got there, half the station was completely gone, wiped off the proverbial map. He said it looked as if a bomb had gone off."

Instinctively, Claire abandoned her refuge behind her desk and walked over to where Ethan was recalling the nightmare blankly. She hugged him. What else could she do? He was in pain; a mutual friend had died. The idea of not hugging him seemed callous to her.

"We held a small service last week," Ethan continued. He did not react to the hug, but stood there incanting the words emotionlessly. "I would've invited you, but my mind wasn't—*isn't*—working right. It still doesn't seem real to me. I don't know—maybe I'm better off," he said, pulling away from Claire absently. "I'm not ready to face the facts."

Claire's face was numb. Alan was only thirty-three, two years older than her. And now he was dead. Ethan was right; it didn't seem real. "The facts?"

Ethan took a deep breath. Were those actually the beginnings of tears in his eyes? "I should've been there," he blurted. Suddenly Claire was the recipient of a hug. Ethan drew her into him and held her there pressed to his chest. "But I wasn't and now Alan's dead."

"Listen to you!" she admonished him reassuringly. She held his face in her hands and forced eye contact. "You weren't even there when it happened. How on earth could it have been your fault?"

"Don't tell me there's nothing I could've done." He shot back at her with a tortured look. Their noses were practically touching. She could feel his breath on her face, hot and gusty. In ordinary circumstances she would've have mistaken it for sexual energy. But not this time; Ethan was hurting. "You don't know that!" he ranted and pulled away from her so forcefully that it startled her.

"Survivor's guilt," Claire observed after taking a moment to gather her wits. "You got it bad."

"So what if I do? I owe it to Alan and the others to see that we finish what we started. It's too important; too much has already been lost for us to let it all go to shit now." Ethan pinned her with his eyes. "You can help me make sure it doesn't."

"I'm listening."

"The article you published on spongiform encephalopathies in the *New England Review of Natural Science* . . . I'm still a little skeptical about all that cowboys and Indians stuff way back when, but I think we may have found a living colony."

For the second time in the last five minutes Claire was too stunned to speak. She hadn't written a word on cryptozoology for nearly four years. Instead, she'd taken up a professional and personal interest in the science of evolutionary biology, prions in particular. The switch was a natural. Cryptozoology was fine for an idealistic grad student who believed that anything was possible. However, in the wake of the pygmy rhinoceros scandal and her subsequent black-balling, she'd had to reinvent herself to survive. The transformation from Claire Matthews, shooting star, to Claire Matthews, schoolmarm, had engendered in her a bittersweet appreciation of adaptability in all its forms. Classifiable as neither plant nor animal, these simple but deadly organisms comprised a kingdom of one. In fact no one could say for certain if prions were living or dead. As far as conventional science was concerned they were neither, lacking the very essence of life on earth as we know it. Then came the discovery of deep ocean hydrothermal vent communities and the diverse array of organisms that populated them. An entirely new class of life that depended on the process of chemosynthesis for survival forced the scientific community to rethink many of its most basic doctrines. If complex organisms could survive in a total absence of sunlight, then why must nucleic acid—one of the so-called building blocks of life conspicuously lacked by prions—be present to count them among the living?

In the past three years, Claire had published a handful of articles championing the misunderstood prion and its place in evolutionary biology. The journal of Father Augustín Terrero, a promising medical student turned Catholic priest who oversaw Arizona's *Nuestra Señora de la Candelaria* Mission from 1863–1871 served as a lynchpin for much of her research. At this point it was still mostly theoretical, but Father Terrero's graphic account of a band of renegade Iroquois braves who conducted a string of horrific raids on settlers and US troops alike was too compelling, too clinically precise to be overlooked without serious consideration. The deeper Claire dug, the more convinced she became that prion encephalitis was the source of the carnage the Iroquois war party had reportedly left in its wake. Eyewitnesses to the unprecedented savagery described the killing spree as nothing less than demoniac. In nine weeks, forty-odd Iroquois men cut a three-thousand-mile swath of death and destruction from the northeast territory through the heart of the American Midwest and into what is present day Arizona. Not a single life was spared until they mysteriously turned on each other. If Father Terrero's grisly yarn had not been corroborated in a half-dozen newspapers Claire would have dismissed it as just that—a revved up morality tale documenting the perils awaiting the unsaved soul in this world and the next.

But there it was, a seemingly random bite of information the internet had regurgitated as she cross-referenced and conducted keyword queries into the pathogenesis of Mad Cow, Creutzfeldt-Jakob disease, and Kuru. By the time Claire was able to will herself away from the horrific page-turner and return to her work, she had begun to see the connection. The onset, symptoms and rapid mental degeneration were distinctly prion—right down to the telltale rod-shaped particles Father Terrero had identified in samples of brain tissue taken post-mortem from the slaughtered Iroquois braves. It was not long after his discovery that Father Terrero ordered that *Mission Nuestra Señora de la Candelaria* and everything in it be burned to the ground to prevent the risk of further infection. Decades earlier, smallpox had dealt a crippling blow to the Spanish Mission system. Father Terrero was not about to take any chances this time around.

Claire had published a number of related treatises under a pseudonym, the irony of which was that this was simply a form of adaptive behavior designed to camouflage her against Nosworthy's vindictive eye. Evolutionary biology at work. She was like the *Moma alpium*, a scarce species of moth commonly known as the *Merveille du Jour* that patterns its wings after lichens to conceal itself from predators. A scared little *Moma alpium*. And now she was exposed.

"I don't know what you're talking about," she said.

"*Dr. Clarence Shelby* . . . Come on, Claire. You could've done better than that. Shelby was your father's last name. You only started going by your mother's maiden name, Matthews, after . . ."

"You bastard," Claire uttered calmly. "You stole my ideas and now you want me to help you cash in. You're out of your mind."

"I know it looks bad. And I swear you'll get equal credit for the discovery."

"Like for the Ha Tinh—that kind of equal credit?" She was seething. "You're an asshole, Ethan. *And* a thief. Go fuck yourself!"

"Listen, we think that whatever Alan and the others found may have somehow been responsible for their deaths."

"*We?* . . . *Who?* . . . What are you talking about? That's ridiculous!"

"They want to poison the entire lake, Claire. Just to be sure."

"The lake? *What lake?*"

"It doesn't have a name. We burned a hole through the ice and—" Ethan lowered his voice. "The point is they're afraid of something getting out and infecting the planet."

Antarctica constituted 70 percent of Earth's fresh water. Although most of it existed in the form of ice, a significant amount remained liquid in dozens, perhaps even hundreds of subglacial lakes sealed thousands of feet beneath the frozen crust. Undisturbed for eons, and older than many of the species on the planet, Claire believed that such lakes could hold the key to unlocking Earth's evolutionary past. And now someone wanted to celebrate the discovery of the century by pumping it full of poison to kill whatever may or may not be down there.

"Who is '*they?*'" she asked, making no attempt to conceal her disgust. "Who's afraid?"

"The CDC. They're pretty worked up about the whole thing. They're worried we may have released some sort of super virus into the world."

"*S. iroqouisii* isn't a virus."

"You know what I meant."

"Well, did you?"

Ethan shook his head wearily. "Like I said, I wasn't there." Stressed, he raked his fingers through his thick, dark hair. "I wish I knew."

Claire was trying to make the pieces fit. So far Ethan hadn't given her much. "You said that Alan and the others died in an explosion."

"Yes, but—"

"But what?" she pressed, trying not to let her emotions get the better of her.

"There's a possibility that the explosion was the effect, and not the cause as we'd originally thought."

"What is that supposed to mean?"

"Nothing yet. It's still just a theory."

For a moment, Ethan actually looked his age, older even. He wasn't acting—the last couple of weeks had been rough on him. It showed in the slump of his shoulders, in the hollow tone of his voice, in the way he stared dimly into space.

"What do you need me for?" asked Claire. "For better or worse, it sounds like you already got what you were after."

"Confirmation," he offered simply. "We want you to tell us whether or not—what did you call it?"

There was no point pretending. Ethan had her dead to rights. "*S. iroquoisii.*"

"Right . . . That *S. iroquoisii*, or one of its cousins, was to blame for all of this."

"It's not that simple."

"That's why we need you—you're the best in the business."

"*We?*"

"You, me—the rest of the team," said Ethan. "JPAC."

"What's JPAC?"

"Joint POW/MIA Accounting Command."

"How long did it take you to memorize that?"

"*Very funny* . . . It's the military agency responsible for locating and identifying the remains of American servicemen lost in battle."

"What's the military got to do with this?"

"Nothing. They just happen to be perfectly equipped to handle this sort of thing. JPAC specializes in recovering human remains in extreme conditions. The CDC set it up—easier to control the flow of information this way . . . Keep it all in-house so people don't freak out."

"You mean they want to keep it a secret."

"This isn't Hollywood. This is real. No conspiracies. No secret government plots. Just good, clean science and damage control."

"Still, working with the military—I don't like it."

"It's a military agency, but they're not all military. They've got civilians on the payroll. Besides, it's not like they're green berets or something. These guys spend all of their time in the lab, not on some battlefield. Nothing shady, I promise. You should take a look at some of their résumés . . . Pretty impressive bunch of scientists, if you ask me."

"I guess everything's relative," Claire replied blithely.

Ethan smiled and folded his hands over his heart, wounded. "You just don't let up."

"What if I say yes?" Claire couldn't believe she was actually considering his offer.

"We leave in five days. We could be gone as long as a month. It all depends on what we find . . . Or don't."

"It's the middle of the semester. I can't just take off."

"Resign. This is an opportunity to do some real good. If we can prove that Alan's death was simply an accident, we can save the lake and whatever he discovered down there. That's why I—Correction, that's why *we* have to go back. This could be the most important discovery in the history of humankind . . . Think about it, a common denominator to every species on the planet. What did you call it? Evolution's Rosetta Stone. We can't let it be destroyed because some pencil pusher gets cold feet."

Claire shook her head. She was crazy to even be considering it.

"Look," continued Ethan. "If the science doesn't interest you, do it for Alan's parents. They want their son's remains back in Orange County, not blowing around some windswept patch of ice on the ass-end of nowhere. Even if it's only DNA. Come on, we owe them that. JPAC needs us there in case something pops up they haven't seen before. These guys are forensics experts, not biologists. And who do you think is covering the bill? If Uncle Sam wasn't in the mix, we could never afford to go back. We need them just as much as they need us."

Claire was no longer listening. She was too excited at the prospect of getting her life back on track to think clearly. She didn't care that she'd be freezing her butt off, that she'd be forfeiting any chance of tenure she may have had at Los Caminos, that Ethan was almost certainly using her to advance his own unscrupulous career. It was fieldwork, and it was somewhere other than here. And of course there was Alan to consider. Too often scientists toiled for years, pouring themselves into their life's work, only to die in relative obscurity. Claire, herself, had all the makings of an excellent case in point. If Alan had made an important discovery he deserved better than to be acknowledged in a lame footnote in some inconsequential science journal.

"Alan gets equal credit for whatever we find down there," Claire announced decisively. "The others, too. I want us all to be famous together."

"I'll leave myself out entirely," Ethan replied earnestly, "if it'll convince you to come."

Credit! That's the last thing in the world Ethan wanted if Alan and the others had in fact stumbled across Ivan the Terrible in that cold miserable godless place. *Poor bastards.* It would have been like taking credit for the Holocaust or the assassination of JFK. Only a psychopath wanted that kind of fame. Of course Claire couldn't have known any of what was really going on, but this didn't keep him from chuckling to himself as he dropped the top on his Mercedes SL65 AMG and started the engine.

She was hopelessly good. Altruism had been, and always would be her Achilles' heel. He checked himself in the rearview mirror and crept out of the Los Caminos parking lot, slowing to flash his laser-whitened smile at a hot little Latina who was eyeing him on her way to class. Tight body, but she was no Claire.

As he joined the bumper-to-bumper stream of cars on the 405 northbound, Ethan wondered if his ex was still the same horny bitch she'd been in college. Climbing into bed with Claire had been like stepping into the ring with Mike Tyson. You never knew if she was going to be satisfied rattling your teeth loose, or if she was going to take it a step further and bite off a piece of your ear. *Those were the days.* He didn't know if it was her long toned runner's legs, the fact that she was a hell of a lot smarter than him, or the knowledge that she despised him so goddamned much, but no one had even come close to turning him on the way she had.

"Dial, Dickhead," he commanded in a loud clear voice. The SL65's Bluetooth voice-recognition system responded immediately to the customized prompt and dialed the specified number. A few seconds later he had Okum on the line.

"Yeah, I got her," Ethan informed him casually. "She's the best scientist I know ... As long as Alan gets credit for ... *Alan Whitehurst* ... My best friend ... He died in the ex—"

The dial tone blared out of the speakers in digital stereo, a baseline reminder of who really sat atop the food chain. In this jungle, Okum was king.

Claire hadn't been this excited in years. Although Hatcher's spiel about *S. iroquoisii* was probably nothing more than a sales pitch, Antarctica was one of the last great wildernesses on earth. Here was an unspoiled living laboratory that until recently had existed outside the destructive influence of man. Although opinions within the scientific community varied, she was not the only who had speculated that the subglacial waters might harbor primitive ecological communities that could provide clues to the humble beginnings of all other life on earth. Many saw the hostile environment—a lightless world of extreme cold and unimaginable pressure—as a model for how extraterrestrial organisms might eke out an existence on celestial bodies that had long been regarded as incapable of sustaining life. As for Claire, the mere idea that she was being given the opportunity to explore a realm few human beings had ever seen, no less studied, had rekindled hopes that her life wasn't going to be a total waste. There was now the possibility, however slight, that her next great contribution to humanity wouldn't be spelled out on the organ donor card affixed to the back of her driver's license.

Why then did she have this awful feeling in the pit of her stomach? Resigning mid-semester wasn't going to be easy, but that wasn't it. Saying goodbye to Los Caminos would be good for her. She hated grading the papers. She hated the slack-jawed disinterest that was epidemic among the ranks of high-school holdovers. She hated the absence of accountability, drive and dedication that characterized the average community college student. Most of all, though, she hated herself for not being a better teacher, for the feelings of hopelessness and futility she experienced because she could not touch the lives of her students the way she knew she ought to. She was the problem, not them. They deserved better, someone whose heart was in the job. And just like that the reason for the uneasiness she was feeling struck her.

Claire had met Eric at one of the mandatory Natural Science Department meetings held each month during the course of the semester. He was an anomaly and a godsend. An anomaly because he was above the petty bickering that part and parcel of the meetings. A godsend because he had replaced a member of Los Caminos' old guard, Kate Madden, a frown-stricken professor of chemistry who never had a nice thing to say about anyone or anything. Eric had appealed to Claire as both a fellow scientist and as a human being. He was kind, good-looking, enthusiastic, and most importantly, intelligent. He liked his job at the college and made no secret that he found working with young people both challenging and gratifying. Claire admired his selfless dedication to the education and well-being of others whether or not they, themselves, appreciated it. It was Eric's example, among numerous others, that had convinced her she wasn't cut out to be an educator—at least not at the undergraduate level.

She and Eric had been friends for nearly a year but they had only been dating a little over a month. Still, it was the longest Claire had been intimately involved with anyone since the debacle with Hatcher. She attributed the success of their relationship to the fact that Eric treated her as his equal in every respect, never once succumbing to the gender stereotypes that governed the behavior of most men. When they ran the stairs in Santa Monica and Claire beat him to the top, he was always quick to give her a high-five. It didn't matter to him if she was first, last, or somewhere in between. They were both fueled by the same competitive spirit and respected each others' capabilities in every arena, be it physical or intellectual. The conversation was good, the sex better, and the fact that Eric had never once mentioned the possibility of marriage best of all. From the day they'd met he'd taken his time with her, never pushing, letting things progress fluidly, naturally. Things were unbelievably good between them and Claire was sure he wouldn't have a problem waiting. Still, it was going to be difficult explaining to him that she was ducking out for a month, possibly longer, just when things were really starting to click.

It was after seven o'clock that evening when Claire arrived at Eric's house in El Segundo. Built in the early 1940s, the beautifully restored craftsman's bungalow was nestled in an unassuming middle-class neighborhood just a half mile from the beach. Although parking spaces could be hard to come by, she lucked out and pulled into a spot right in front that had been vacated moments earlier by a forest green minivan. The heady perfume of roses mingled with the cool coastal air as she strode briskly up the brick walkway in the lavender dusk.

Eric was meticulous about his garden. The grass was neatly trimmed and edged, the flower beds devoid of weeds, the plants thriving without the aid of chemical pesticides and inorganic fertilizers. Fastidiousness was a trait echoed virtually every-where in his life. Claire, who was herself something of a slob, admired his attention to detail. Eric folded his laundry and stowed it neatly in dresser drawers. Claire's laundry accumulated in haphazard piles around her apartment, or as was more often the case, went straight from the dryer to her body. Eric paid his bills on time and regularly balanced his checkbook. Claire's budget included a monthly allowance for late fees, and her check register resembled the diary of an escaped mental patient. She called him Mr. OCD. He called her Flakey.

She entered without knocking—Eric never bothered to lock his front door—and found him in the kitchen. He was standing in front of the stove amid a sweet-smell-ing fog of sautéed garlic and olive oil. She could not imagine a situation in which the tantalizing aroma would fail to excite her taste buds. You could cook just about anything in garlic and be assured that it would taste wonderful.

"What's for dinner?" asked Claire. She approached him from behind, entwined her arms about his waist and kissed him on the cheek.

"Capellini with bay scallops in a garlic-basil sauce," said Eric. He added the scal-lops to the pan and reduced the flame. "And there's a spinach salad in the fridge."

"When do we eat?"

"You've got an appetite, huh?"

Claire lowered her voice to a whisper so that her breath prickled the tiny hairs on the back of Eric's neck. "You could say that."

She undid the top button of his shorts and slipped her hand down inside his box-ers. She ran her palm over the shaft of his penis until it began to swell.

Eric breathed deeply. "If I leave the pasta in the water too much longer," he ex-plained, "it won't be *al dente*."

She squeezed his penis and continued stroking it until it was completely hard. "Could've fooled me."

Eric was the only man Claire had ever slept with who'd had a vasectomy. At first she thought it was strange, him being so young and *normal*. But he'd explained that he was once engaged to be married, and that he and his fiancée, Nicole, had decided against children early on. Not because they didn't want kids but because Nicole was burdened with a medical condition that would have been grievously aggravated by pregnancy. They decided adoption was the best and safest solution. Claire was moved by Eric's commitment and self-sacrifice. But what had touched her most of all was his honesty and humility. Three weeks before the wedding, Nicole had left him for another man. Most guys in Eric's shoes would have rather died than admit to being dumped at the altar. But Eric wasn't most men. Claire was almost ashamed to take comfort in the fact that he could not get her pregnant. At least she didn't have to risk birth control. IUD's were scary, condoms for teenagers and the pill didn't agree with her. Honestly, if Eric had been able to knock her up, she would have freaked out being this late for her period. Eight days, but who was counting? It's just that the experience with Hatcher had left a bitter taste in her mouth. Like always, Eric had known exactly how to handle her, to make her see the light of her own folly. Just yesterday, Claire had suffered a mini-meltdown of sorts while the two of them were on their way to have lunch at a small Sushi bar near Los Caminos. Without a word, Eric had swung into a nearby Rite-Aid parking lot, ducked inside and emerged a few minutes later with a home pregnancy test in hand. "Here," he offered understandingly. "It's a two-pack. We'll do it together as long as you promise to marry me if I'm pregnant."

Eric abruptly killed the flame under the pan and turned to face her. He drew her in close to him so that their pelvises were pressed up against one another and slipped her top—a white and powder blue Adidas jog bra—off over her head. He then forced her breasts up and together and attacked her nipples with his mouth. Desire coiled uncontrollably inside of her like a spring that would break if wound any tighter. She grabbed Eric's shirt by the hem and yanked it off over his head. Simultaneously, he kicked off his shoes and shorts, nearly toppling the two of them in the process. But even this didn't slow them down. They couldn't strip fast enough, their breath coming in quick hot gusts.

It was now dark outside. Claire could see their reflection in the French doors that opened onto the tiny backyard. Although Eric was not a gym junkie like herself, he was rangy and lean, and had a swimmer's broad shoulders. His skin was smooth and always had a mild soapy scent as if he had just gotten out of the shower. Claire was turned on by the possibility that they were being watched going at it in the bright light of the kitchen like a couple of horny teenagers. She'd been wearing a pair of matching Adidas short-shorts that showed off her legs. She'd hoped the sexy little outfit would interest Eric more than the details of the expedition. It was best to keep things simple. The less involved Eric was the better. *So far, so good.* The shorts now lay twisted with her panties inside-out on the floor.

"Fuck me," she breathed, pulling him into her as he lifted her off the ground and pinned her between the refrigerator and the island in the center of the small kitchen. With each thrust, the rubber soles of her running shoes squeaked in protest as she struggled for traction on the wood cabinet face.

For the first time in months, Claire felt absolutely free. Shortly after Hatcher had left her office, she had gone straight to the department chair's office and resigned. Like burning a corset, the act was not only symbolic; it served the interest of promoting her emotional and physical well-being. She could breathe again. *And . . . ! And . . . !* And now she was somewhere else, and had about as little interest in the mechanisms of her symbolic liberation as in the physical processes that left her raw, quivering and breathless.

"All that squeaking rubber . . ." Eric remarked when they had both come and it was over. "It was like basketball practice."

They put their clothes back on and sat down to dinner a short time later. Claire was famished, although her appetite was buffered by an uneasy feeling. She didn't want Eric to feel as though she was abandoning him. He was good to her and the thought that she might hurt him, even a little bit, made her feel like a jerk.

"Imagine how good the sex will be when I get back," she said, squeezing his leg under the table.

"Stop apologizing," he said sincerely. "You need this."

"You sure?"

"A month is nothing," he assured her. "You'll be back before the sun comes up."

It was nothing more than a casual observation—a coincidentally bad figure of speech—but Claire felt as if she had been blindsided by a speeding truck. Her heart skipped a beat and hung in the center of her chest like a hunk of lead. She was up and out of her chair by the time it had resumed pumping blood.

"Where are you going?" Eric called after her.

She was headed for the second bedroom he used as an office. "I've got to check something on the internet."

She had the website bookmarked—timeanddate.com. Logging on was something of a daily ritual. The times of sunrise and sunset were as integral to her planning of each day as were horoscopes for the superstitious. Every shrink she'd ever seen had warned her away from this sort of hypervigilance, but she couldn't help herself. In a matter of minutes she was back at the table with Eric, a nondescript printout dangling from her hand.

"I'm not going," she explained simply. Her head was swimming. Her throat was tight and dry. "I can plead temporary insanity—tell the chair I was possessed—he'll give me my job back."

"Calm down and tell me what this is about."

"He knew all along." Claire responded weakly. She was an idiot not to have thought of it earlier. The excitement—she had been overwhelmed.

"Claire, I can't help you if I don't know what's going on." Eric explained patiently. "*Who* knew *what*?"

"Hatcher." Claire handed Eric the printout. "On March 24 the sun sets at 9:01 AM."

Eric glanced at the crowded columns of numbers but wasn't immediately sure what to make of it. "Okay?"

"Don't you see?" said Claire, reigning in her emotions. "The sun sets on March 24 but doesn't come up again until September 21. Six months of total darkness! The bastard knew I wouldn't be able to do it, that's why he offered it to me."

"Do you really think—"

"I *know*."

Claire was up and dialing Hatcher's cellular number before Eric could stop her. The deceitful prick answered on the second ring—a nonchalant "Yeah? . . ." There was music playing in the background.

"I changed my mind," said Claire. "I'm not coming."

"Claire? You'll have to talk louder. I'm in my car."

"You knew it was going to be dark, you sick fuck. That's why you asked me."

"You're not still sleeping with the lights on, are you?"

"Get someone else."

There was a moment of silence. "You never asked me about the money," said Hatcher. "Aren't you curious to know how much you'll be getting paid?"

"Are you deaf?"

"Twenty-five thousand dollars."

"I don't care about the money. Find someone else."

"What about Alan?" asked Hatcher.

"He'd understand."

"Are you near a computer?"

"I don't see how—"

"Don't cancel your reservations just yet," said Hatcher. "I'll be home in fifteen minutes. I want to email you some pictures."

Twenty minutes later, Claire and Eric sat glued to the computer monitor. Hatcher's email included an attachment of a dozen digital stills snapped by a remote operated vehicle several days before the research station, and Alan along with it, had blown up. Hatcher had gotten his hands on them only recently—inexplicably delayed by a glitch in the satellite uplink Alan had used to transmit the data. The images weren't exactly print quality, however this hardly diminished their jaw-dropping effect considering that they had originated 2,000 feet beneath the surface of Antarctica.

Claire examined the last image and looked at Eric. He put his arm around her shoulders and squeezed. "You're not going to like me for saying this," he said. "But he's right. You have to go."

She nodded. "Let's take a walk."

Night walks were part of Claire's self-prescribed therapeutic regimen to enable her to better cope with her fear of the dark. The concept was a simple one and relied on the same basic principle as that of a vaccine: expose herself to small doses of the source of her affliction and she would, at least theoretically, develop a resistance to it. Although the results had not been as immediate as she would have liked, she was making progress. It was all about establishing comfort zones. There was a time when she'd refused to drive at night, the mobile fortress of her car an inadequate shield against the ubiquitous domain of her fear. Employing the same technique she had gotten over the worst of it and was now able to get herself around by car after dark when necessary.

Walking at night, Eric liked to tease, was a "big step." Minus the protective barrier of her car, the nightly jaunts took exposure to another level. She was even beginning to feel, for lack of a better word, *relaxed* provided she didn't stray too far from Eric's side and the comforting glow of the streetlamps. But she was still a long way from achieving her ultimate goal: total darkness, complete isolation, unfamiliar setting, and peace of mind.

Case studies had been written about dysfunctional relationships like her parents'. Claire's father had been a hard-nosed alcoholic whose grip on reality and self-control diminished in direct proportion to amount of alcohol he'd consumed in any given time span. His life, as Claire's mother had become increasingly aware, was governed by this dangerous equation. Two to three drinks and he'd become verbally abusive, his anger boiling over in great baritone waves the neighbors in the placid Orange County suburb in which they lived deliberately ignored. Four to five drinks and the man who'd contributed his DNA to Claire's genetic makeup would become irrational and irate. He would storm around the house kicking the walls and furniture, muttering terrible things under his breath in a low guttural voice. After six drinks, James Shelby, husband and father, electrical systems analyst for Lockheed, would become someone—*something*—else altogether. It was a terrifying metamorphosis that Claire, who was only ten when things had come to a terrible climax, could not rationalize no less hope to understand.

Her father's worst episodes typically evolved out of some sort of accusation aimed at her mother. To the best of Claire's knowledge none of these were grounded in reality: wild declarations of infidelity, insensitivity, disrespect. Fueled by his wife's denials and claims of innocence, her father's paranoia would gather force, his long, angular frame acquiring the dark, foreboding mass of a thunderhead preparing to unleash an unspeakable wrath. Each episode was uniquely awful and frightening. Claire had often wondered if the man stalking through the house after her mother was actually her father at all. At various times in her life, she had believed that he was some kind of monster—a werewolf maybe—only it was what came out of the bottle and not the transmutative light of the full moon that changed him into the growling, uncontrollable beast they feared.

When sober, Jim Shelby was warm, loving and affectionate. Although such memories of him were dim and deferred to the greater staying power of his menacing alter ego, Claire vaguely remembered instances when she'd felt totally safe and protected beneath the umbrella of her father's watchful eyes. Often, he would play with her, gladly giving himself over to games of make-believe and childish whimsy. Hide and seek was Claire's favorite. For what seemed like hours she would hide somewhere in the house—in closets, under beds, behind doors—and her father would patiently hunt for her, calling out in a playful voice, "I'm going to find you." Tucked stealthily away in her hiding place, Claire would giggle and tremble with nervous glee, trying not to reveal herself to her father's tickling hands. But, again, this was when he was sober.

The ugly, grumbling monster that lived in her father's shadow liked to play games too. But these were ghoulish variations on familiar themes all the more terrifying for their total lack of playfulness. On one particular occasion Claire's parents had gotten into it pretty bad. Fed up with her father's abusive behavior, Claire's mother had stood up to him and told him exactly what she thought. She gave him an ultimatum: either he quit drinking and learn to control himself, or she was going to divorce him and take Claire with her.

Although Claire admired her mother's courage in standing up to her husband, waiting until he had sobered up would have undoubtedly been much wiser under the circumstances. Who knows how many drinks her father had knocked back that night? One thing was certain: he was dangerously past the point of no return when his wife had confronted him in the living room. Courage notwithstanding, the actions of Claire's mother that night had sent her to the emergency room with a broken arm and a badly bruised face, but not before the most terrifying episode in Claire's young life had unfolded with everlasting clarity.

Summoned by her mother's cries—a low, pitiful, keening lament not unlike that of a wounded animal—Claire arrived in the living room to find her father cradling his battered wife in his sinewy arms, shock having by then rendered her unconscious. Sensing Claire's presence, her father looked up, tears streaming down his cheeks from wild bloodshot eyes, and motioned her towards him. Certain that her mother was dead, Claire froze. What little remained of her father's rational mind must have recognized his daughter's fear because he began to ramble on about his wife's plan to leave him and take his little girl with her.

"You wouldn't ever leave your daddy, would you, baby?" he'd asked, his voice taut with paranoid distrust.

Paralyzed by fear, Claire was unable to speak.

"We like to play games together, isn't that right, Pumpkin?" her father continued, his mind desperately grasping for something to hold onto, reassurance.

Claire wanted to run and beg the neighbors to call the police, but she couldn't move. She was transfixed, hypnotized by the deranged grin spreading across her father's face, half expecting his drawn lips to reveal long, pointed fangs.

"Hide and seek," her father declared as if by way of revelation. "We'll play right now. I'll count to twenty and you hide."

He gently laid Claire's mother on the sofa and began to count. Claire didn't know what to think. None of it seemed real. Her father had already killed her mother and now he was going to kill her too. A sudden jolt shot through Claire's body. This wasn't a game. It was life or death. She ran and hid in one of upstairs closets where her mother kept the bath towels and bed linens. It wasn't her best hiding place, but she had been too afraid to think clearly. Her father was going to kill her and she could only postpone the inevitable. Claire closed the door, retreated as far as she could into the corner beneath the bottom shelf and buried herself under a pile of towels.

"Here I come," came her father's muffled voice from the room below. "Come out, come out, wherever you are . . ."

For a time she had listened to him plodding from room to room, calling out to her, his heavy footsteps striking a chilling counterpoint to his slurred, half-human speech. Hours of interminable, terror-filled darkness gave way to a life of sinister childhood memories and irrational adult fears, but Claire's father never found her. Too afraid to move, Claire had spent the entire night hiding in the closet with no idea that her mother was simply unconscious and not truly dead. Before dawn the following morning—her father having long since lapsed into the dark, dreamless oblivion that spelled his bouts of alcoholic dementia—Claire's mother collected her from the floor of the closet and drove the two of them to the emergency room.

What had happened that night would forever alter the course of Claire's life. Her mother and father separated for a time, the former agreeing not to press charges under two conditions: one, that Claire's father move out of the house and quit drinking for good; two, that he return home when he was sober and ready to resume his role as head of the family. After five weeks of exile in a motel, he had returned home in compliance with his wife's ultimatum. And after another five weeks, he had begun drinking again, rekindling the same cycle of delusional accusations and physical abuse.

And then finally one night—in keeping with the story line that make such tales of battered women almost cliché—Claire's father had gone off the edge and almost beaten his wife to death. Claire could hardly recognize her own mother beneath the purplish mishmash of bruises and swelling distorting her face. Years later, Claire's mother had joked that it had been her plan all along to let her father tire himself out in the early rounds and then steal the bout as fatigue caught up with him. Apparently the plan had worked like a charm. After twenty minutes or so, Claire's father had dragged himself away, fists hanging like stones at his side. Tired of living in fear, Claire's mother waited until he was passed-out face down on the cold tile floor of the bathroom, rolled him onto his back and stabbed him in the chest with a kitchen knife.

It was just as well—Claire had never been comfortable around her father in the wake of that unforgettable game of hide and seek. She did her best to avoid him in those last five weeks under the same roof, but it seemed that he was lurking around every corner, and that next time he would find her no matter where she hid. Still, Claire had always believed that her mother's actions, though perhaps justified, may have gone too far. On one hand the incident had brought the two of them closer together. On the other, it had created a gulf between them. In the wake of her father's death, Claire was equal parts gratitude and resentment. Once again, she could live without fear, but she was also living without a father.

She knew it was foolish, a vestige of ancient history and childhood emotional trauma, but somehow every horror from that period in her life—including the death of her father and mother's subsequent criminal trial—was indelibly linked to that small eternity she had spent buried in the lightless depths of the closet. Her fear of the dark was every bit as tangible to her now as had been her fear of being raised an orphan prior to her mother's acquittal on grounds of self-defense. Although her father was no longer in her life, Claire was forever haunted by the night she had spent huddled against the darkness and the demented pitch of his searching voice. When the lights went out she could hear him calling out to her just as clearly today as twenty-some years ago, a tortured howl slipping along the periphery of her imagination like a recurring nightmare.

Though Claire was guarded with information about her past and its effect on her, Eric knew better than to stray from their familiar well-lighted route. Every now and then, she discussed something from her childhood with him, but not to the extent that he had a fully-formed image of that terrible period. He knew that she slept with a nightlight, that unlit spaces aroused something foreboding in her, and that it was better not to force the issue. She appreciated his sensitivity and understanding, his light-handed approach to making her feel comfortable, and more importantly, normal. Since ovarian cancer had claimed her mother's life eighteen months ago, Eric was the only true confidante she had left. It was no wonder he was surprised when Claire suggested that they diverge from their usual route and walk down one of the unlit nonresidential streets north of the oil refinery.

"It's dark," Eric informed her plainly.

"That's the idea," she countered coyly. "I was thinking we could make out for awhile. This time where no one can see us."

Eric didn't exacerbate the situation by hesitating; he simply took her hand and followed her into the darkness. Claire's heart raced but she steeled herself against the torrent of fear charging through her veins. She needed to do this, to test herself. In another few weeks she'd be enwombed in perpetual night. If she couldn't keep it together for a few brief moments with Eric holding her hand, then what made her think she could survive for weeks without a flicker of daylight? Angered by her own frailty, she fought the urge to retreat into the light. She recognized the hot chemical rush from a thousand similar episodes in her life, moments when panic crept into her mind and sent her scrambling for the nearest patch of light or a couple of Ativan, whichever was closest.

They stopped mid-block in front of a dilapidated storefront where, during business hours, men in greasy coveralls rebuilt automotive transmissions. Eric encircled Claire in his strong comforting arms and pulled her into him.

"You're shaking," he said. His voice was warm and soothing. "Are you sure you want to do this?"

Claire virtually attacked him, her fear igniting a flurry of passionate caresses and deep, groping kisses. Eric responded in kind, until the two of them were rushing back to his house to fuck each others' brains out all over again, the darkness at their heels like the breath of something real and unmistakably evil.

Christchurch, New Zealand
GPS Coordinates: −43.531637, 172.636645
March 17, 2010

It was after midnight when Claire, Ethan, and the other members of the team touched down at Christchurch International Airport, the black sky scuffed with ragged moon-illumined clouds. The further they dipped into the southern hemisphere, the scarcer daylight would become. Claire likened the gradual onset of perpetual night to standing in the bottom of a hole she, herself, was digging. Down and down and down while high above the opening pinched slowly closed, stranding her in the thickening darkness with nothing to keep her company but all the skeletons she had unburied along the way.

She would've enjoyed the opportunity to explore Christchurch but they were only going to be on the ground long enough to transfer their gear to a Hercules C–130 before continuing on to McMurdo Station. With budget oversight committees constantly breathing down their necks, government agencies were more than willing to avail themselves of commercial airlines if it meant saving a buck or two. However, jets like the Boeing 737 they had flown from Los Angeles were ill-equipped for travel to the remote destinations linking earth's rugged white underbelly to the rest of civilization.

"We have a couple hours on the ground before we're back in the air." The deep voice belonged to Sergeant First Class Amir Price. At twenty-seven, he was the only African-American among them. He embodied the rare combination of energetic intelligence and athletic musculature prized by the ancient Greeks. As assistant JPAC team leader he was responsible for handling the logistical end of the operation: travel, equipment, supplies. In his own words, 'the nuts and bolts.' A devout Muslim, he'd spent the majority of the flight with his nose buried in the pages of the Koran. "The flight should take about eight hours," Price continued. "No meal service this time around, so grab a bite and stretch your legs. I'll make sure our gear ends up where it's supposed to."

"Who's hungry?" Team leader Major Frank DeLuca, an expert in mortuary affairs with more than a decade of field experience, was running the show. Although he exercised his authority with a light hand, it was obvious that his team admired and respected him. Lean and visibly health conscious, it was probably the grim nature of his work that was indirectly to blame for the filigree of broken blood vessels imparting a roseate hue to his nose and cheeks. A drinker, thought Claire.

"You buying, Major?" asked First Lieutenant Dale Bishop. A forensic odontologist, his pre-packaged introduction had included something about being a Salt Lake City Mormon who had traded the Tabernacle Choir and clean air for a career in grave-robbing. He had blue close-set eyes, neatly-trimmed blonde hair that was receding above the temples, and perfect teeth. Bishop wasn't fat, but was saddled with the relaxed midsection often worn by men in their late thirties.

"On a government salary?" DeLuca scoffed. "You've got me confused with McKenzie. He's the one pulling down the fat paycheck."

"Why not?" said Dr. Larry McKenzie, a forensic anthropologist, and only civilian member of the JPAC team. "Can't take it with me."

As a fifty-five year-old JPAC rookie, McKenzie endured his fair share of good-natured hazing from the others. For more than two decades he had consulted for various law enforcement agencies throughout North America, applying his expertise both at the crime scene and in the courtroom. When JPAC had offered him a position with the Central Identification Lab in Oahu, he'd accepted without hesitation. Leaving behind the clamor and filth of Chicago was a dream come true. His easygoing manner, attentive smile, and evenly tanned skin suggested that he had been making the most of his new home in the tropics. A Johns Hopkins School of Medicine alum, he would also be acting as their medic.

"I take back every nasty thing I ever said about you, Doc." Second Lieutenant Trevor "Witz" Witzerman hardly fit the GI Joe stereotype. Somehow he had managed to retain the narrow shoulders, sloping posture, and generally awkward physique that basic training eliminated in all but the most obstinately unfit. In spite of a meticulous comb-over camouflaging the widening gyre of bare skin consuming the crown of his skull, Witz was losing a war of attrition with pattern-baldness. A communications technician, he would serve as the team's eyes and ears.

"What about you, Hatcher?" DeLuca asked.

Hatcher checked his watch. "I'm not that hungry," he said. "I think I'll hang back and give Sergeant Price a hand with the gear."

DeLuca turned to Claire without missing a beat. "Dr. Matthews—what do you say? Join us?"

"Just don't get your hands too close to my mouth," Claire warned. "I plan on pigging out if this is going to be my last real meal. I hate to imagine what we'll be eating once we get there."

While DeLuca ran some last minute instructions by Price, Hatcher approached Claire.

"Do me a favor," he said, lowering his voice. "See if you can round up a decent bottle of champagne. You might want to check the duty-free shop. It doesn't have to be French or anything—as long as it's got bubbles." He pressed a $20 into her hand. "This ought to cover it."

"Would you prefer Cristal or Dom Perignon?"

"I don't know," he replied distractedly. He was listening in on Price and DeLuca. "You choose."

So Hatcher thinks he's going to get his cork popped. You didn't really think he'd invited you along for your scientific expertise, did you? The only female experts he takes seriously show up for work in hot pants and stiletto heels. What the hell . . . If humoring his seedy little fantasies helps get me in the door, then so be it. It's not as if the two of us will be spending much time alone together.

Though neither DeLuca nor any of the JPAC team were the least bit gung-ho, Claire was glad that they had opted for civilian attire or "civvies" for the expedition. It was more comfortable this way, less uptight. She could mingle openly without feeling as though she was part of some misguided "peacekeeping" operation that invariably proved to be another black eye for the United States. She had to give Hatcher credit—a few minutes alone with these guys and it was easy to forget that olive drab was their color of choice.

And what about her? A lone pair of ovaries adrift in a sea of testosterone. She was the team's resident authority, as close as they had to a definitive source on what may or may not have influenced the disaster at the first station. Claire's presence hinged largely on a hunch, a theory, the fantastic account of a science-minded Catholic missionary who was ultimately excommunicated for heresy. No one even knew if Alan and his team had found what they had been looking for. Stromatolites at the bottom of a lake in Antarctica were one thing. But *S. iroquoisii*, what Father Terrero called the Devil's Hunger, was entirely another. Then again, no one knew exactly where prions originated. Their existence was every bit as mysterious as the organisms themselves.

Despite her predictions of wholesale gluttony, Claire had scarcely managed to choke down a single hotdog and a handful of salt and vinegar potato chips before she was suddenly abandoned by her appetite. At first, DeLuca and the others were like a typical family enjoying a meal together—small talk mostly. World events, the lousy movies they had watched on the flight over, progress reports on the wife and kids. It wasn't long, however, before they were discussing the job that lay ahead of them and the obstacles they would most certainly encounter. Soon they were trading horror stories about "analogous accounting operations"—Baghdad, Oklahoma City, a handful of US embassies—and the gruesome spoils of their trade. "Accounting" because this is what the military called the macabre business of pinpointing the who, how, when and where of death. "Analogous" because all of the operations in question involved maximum damage and minimum remains. Scraps of flesh, bone fragments, charred teeth, *dust bunnies* . . . They were expert at piecing together the gruesome handiwork of explosions. Whether deliberate or accidental, the difference promised to be negligible. Claire realized that their clinical objectification of death wasn't malicious or insensitive; it was simply professionalism at work. For DeLuca and his team, this was shop-talk, the work-related chatter of a 9 to 5 like any other. They didn't know Alan was her friend. That it would be his flesh and bone they would be picking out of the ruins less than forty-eight hours from now. So rather than going off on a self-righteous tirade about their callousness, Claire politely excused herself from the table.

"Don't tell me you're stuffed already?" DeLuca asked. "This will be the last real food we'll eat for the foreseeable future. No Mickey D's where we're going."

"There's something I forgot to bring—girl stuff," Claire stammered. She fought back a wave of nausea.

"We did it again," Bishop interjected decisively. A disciple of the low-carb movement, he was working on his third hotdog minus the bun. "Look at her—she's about to barf."

"No problem," said McKenzie. "Let's change the subject. We can talk about—I don't know—what it's going to be like without daylight. Being a night owl, myself, I'm actually looking forward to it."

The last ounce of blood drained from Claire's face. Her chest was tight. "Seriously," she said. "I'm fine."

She escaped to the ladies' room and popped two Ativan. *Girl stuff*—if only it was that simple. She was already two weeks late. It didn't help any that her stress level was through the roof. She looked at herself in the mirror: tired, scary, and jet-lagged but not pregnant. It was probably all the extra exercise she'd been doing lately to help cope with her mother's death. The dredged up memories of her father and finding out about Alan had delivered the knockout punch. So there it was. Stress coupled with too much exercise was to blame. After all, it wasn't unusual for athletic women to miss a cycle every now and then. She couldn't have her life turned upside-down and expect everything to continue like clockwork.

Claire splashed cold water on her face, dried off and sought out the airport convenience store. Luckily, it was open twenty-four hours; otherwise, she may have actually had to address the litany of worries plaguing her mind. Thumbing through the *London Times* she came across a list of expeditionaries who'd perished in Antarctica since its discovery in the early 1820s. Last in a relatively modest timeline obituary were the names of Alan and the five other team members who now occupied an insignificant slot in polar lore. It was going to be difficult working in the shadow of so much tragedy and loss.

"The *Times of London*—good paper. I guess I should've known I wouldn't catch a woman like you reading *People*." It was McKenzie. He rested his hand on her shoulder.

"And what's wrong with *People*?" asked Claire.

"Nothing I guess, other than the fact that it's dull and superficial and trite."

Claire folded the newspaper and returned it to the newsstand. "I made a fool of myself, didn't I?"

"Not at all," said McKenzie. "It was our fault. In this line of work you can become so damn desensitized that you sometimes forget death isn't a way of life for everyone."

"Usually, I'm not so squeamish," Claire explained. "It's just that a close friend of mine was there when the station . . . I guess I'm having a hard time with the thought of what we might find."

McKenzie frowned. "Aren't we a merry crew of assholes? Doctor Hatcher didn't tell us."

"That's Ethan for you."

"You two aren't? . . ."

"Aren't and never will be," Claire finished emphatically. "What about you? What's a nice guy like you doing in a place like this?"

"Bad ticker." McKenzie rapped on his sternum and smiled. "My cardiologist told me I needed to slow down. Chicago's a big, noisy city that's home to some really bad people—the excitement was killing me. Believe it or not, the South Pole will be like taking a vacation."

Claire awoke to find Hatcher's hand planted squarely on her thigh. His voice was barely audible above the deafening noise of the C–130's four massive turboprops. She checked her watch. They had been in the air for nearly eight hours more. McMurdo couldn't be far.

"Sorry to wake you," he said, "but you'll want to see this."

Claire was considering what to do about Hatcher's hand—break it or simply pretend it didn't exist—when the world beneath them caught her eye. Though hanging low on the horizon, the morning sun gave off a fiery incandescence, igniting a conflagration of whiteness that burned from horizon to horizon. The outer edge of the continent comprised a vast mosaic of colossal ice sheets. Pressure ridges erupted where the sheets converged, jigsawing this way and that into diminutive mountain ranges. There were more shades of white than she had ever thought possible, a million random surfaces reflecting the silvery dusk with a chaotic brilliance that dazzled her eyes. Further inland, the mosaic gave rise to a vertical escarpment towering hundreds of feet above the sea. The fractured cross-section exposed a tortured landscape marbled with blue-green bolts of ice as hard as diamond and older than recorded history.

McMurdo Station, Antarctica
GPS Coordinates: −75.250973, −0.071389

March 18, 2010

Located sixteen kilometers from Williams Field—a seasonal airstrip carved into the frozen backbone of the Ross Ice Shelf—McMurdo Station was an outpost in the strictest sense of the word. Isolated well beyond the fringe of civilization in a region whose rumored existence was the stuff of globetrotting heretics until only recently, the modest community, a collection of rusting Quonsets and prefabricated warehouse-style buildings had the rugged look of a boomtown. There were no roads in or out, only a few sloppy brown tracks that allowed for travel within Antarctica's only permanent fixture besides ice—mile upon mile upon mile of ice. Not that it would have made a difference. Cut off from everything but itself, McMurdo was truly the end of the earth. The farthest point south accessible by ship, the gritty outcropping resembled an enormous scab on an otherwise pristine slab of white.

A large storage yard stacked with dozens of shipping containers stood at one end of the itinerant community. Without year-round assistance from the outside world, it would've been nearly impossible for a small family to eke out an existence no less a population that in the summer months could swell to more than a thousand. Every ounce of supplies had to be imported. Similarly, every ounce of waste, either human or manufactured, had to be disposed of elsewhere. The nearest sewage treatment plants, landfills and recycling centers were thousands of miles away. Claire shuddered at the thought of the awful tonnage periodically bellied away in sewage tankers. Although she was an Einstein when it came to the mathematics of consumption and waste, the environmental implications of such equations always had the unpleasant effect of awakening her to her own contribution to the ongoing global disaster of overpopulation. The fact that she was now in a place where natural selection had successfully excluded *Homo sapiens* only augmented her reservations about being here. Or maybe it was the realization that in a matter of days the sun would go into hiding for the next six months and leave her alone to be gnawed at by every soul-sickening anxiety she'd ever had—thousands of miles away from humanity in whose presence she realized both comfort and catastrophe. *Poof!* Gone. . . . Fade to black.

Currently, McMurdo was a hive of activity. The majority of its residents were packing up in anticipation of the long, dark winter months ahead. In less than a week, the population would shrink to a skeleton crew of less than two-hundred, and the sloppy black roads would be virtually empty. It was on one such road that Claire and the others rumbled through town in the mud-splattered four-wheel drive van that had collected them at Williams Field.

After ten minutes of jostling they skidded to a stop in front of a row of brown, two-story dormitories. The identical steel-paneled buildings, four in all, served as temporary shelters for anyone crazy enough to travel this far off the beaten path. It wasn't exactly dark out—the sky was stained with rich sepia hues, but snow landings were tricky enough in the best conditions. They would stay here until the sun reappeared before covering the remaining distance to their final destination nearly six-hundred miles farther south.

Almost nostalgically, Claire remembered the trip she had taken with the high-school ski club so many years ago . . . Remembered the budget accommodations in which she and a half-dozen of her classmates had cranked up the heater after skiing all day, and gotten tipsy on peppermint schnapps. Everything had been great until one of the girls had gotten drunk enough to ask Claire about what had gone on between her mom and dad. Was it true that she had watched her mom stab her own husband, Claire's father, to death? What was it like knowing that your own mom was ". . . so hardcore?" Did Claire have trouble finding guys who weren't afraid to date her? And of course there'd been other questions, mostly harmless, but Claire had chosen not to remember them. She had dismissed the girl's queries with a tolerant smile, intimating that she never dared break the rules set by her mother for fear of the consequences.

The reality, however, was less imminent than she had let on. The beatings, the verbal abuse, the aloneness—had broken her mother. Rules in Claire's house, for that matter any guidelines whatsoever, were virtually nonexistent in the wake of her father's death. It was true that she and her mother had coexisted under the same roof until Claire was old enough to get out and live on her own, but they were essentially strangers to one another. In life, James Shelby's abusive behavior had brought them together, engendering a need for solidarity and support. In death, he became an impassable void between them.

A cutting wind was blowing off the water, salting them with ice crystals as they hurried between the idling transport and the inn's entrance. It was good to get out of the cold, away from the wind that slashed through the lightweight pullover Claire had been wearing tied about her waist in Los Angeles earlier that day. Although the accommodations weren't exactly brimming with the old world charm of a Swiss chalet, it was warm inside and right now Claire would have gladly traded charm for warmth. The furnishings were strictly functional—phony wood grain, chromed steel, vinyl upholstery—stuff you'd expect to find in a suburban Elk's Club hall. Her room was more of the same—neutral indoor/outdoor carpeting, a swaybacked twin bed, abrasive war surplus blankets—and sadly, no bathtub. The walls were modestly decorated with framed photographs and Xeroxed newspaper clippings of Antarctic explorers from the late nineteenth century to the present day. Not much had changed over the past century. Aside from technological advances in polar gear, the modern day adventurers seemed to be cut from the same cloth as their forebears. They all squinted into the camera as if afflicted with the same visual impairment. Some things were timeless. The view from her window—a green neon sign advertising CHICO'S MEXICAN FOOD OF THE SOUTH POLE—wasn't one of them. She drew the shade and went back to sleep, jet-lagged. She stayed in her room the remainder of the day—going over her research and drifting in and out of fitful sleep—before freshening up and joining the others for dinner.

Chico's was the worst kind of dump imaginable. Although Ethan had found *Zagat* and the *Michelin Guide* to be consistently reliable in the United States and Europe, their restaurant listings in Antarctica were decidedly scant. He'd eaten here with Alan and the others a couple of months ago and had only recently been able to put the experience behind him. Nothing had changed since then other than the fact that the place was less crowded now that three-fourths of McMurdo had flown anywhere but south for the winter. Not the strands of chili pepper Christmas tree lights hanging from the ceiling. Not the gargantuan velvet sombreros and musty wool serapes tacked to the dingy walls. Not the greasy odor of a half-dozen equally grim menu selections, all of which suffered the same glistening skin of melted cheese. It wasn't that Chico's was simply the worst place in town—it was the *only* place. Fuck it—he was here to blow off some steam, and to take a few measurements. It was time to find out just how deeply he was buried in shit.

"Dinner and drinks are on me," he announced generously. "I want us to have a good time. What d'ya say—tequila shots all the way around? Christen the voyage."

"Last one standing calls a cab," boomed McKenzie.

Before long everyone was feeling good. Everyone, that is, but Sergeant Price. He was one sober Muslim. Even Claire was letting loose, pacing the guys shot for shot. Funny what a little sex appeal could bring to the table. The wet little jewel between her legs was the real catalyst behind the raucous frat-house atmosphere, not the booze. Four shots in and Witzerman's eyes were swimming in his skull but there was no way in hell he was going to bow out gracefully. As long as tits were present, the guy'd drop dead before he'd say no to another round.

DeLuca was a different story. He was like an oil tanker—the more booze he poured into himself, the smoother he rode.

Ethan stole a look at Claire out of the corner of his eye, the slow burn of alcohol exposing a moment steeped in slippery subtexts. She was chatting it up with Bishop and Price. Vanilla and chocolate. The three of them were really having a good laugh about something. Pure fucking hilarity.

Remember Alan, you dumb bitch? I said I wanted us to have some fun, not forget why the fuck we're here. And what's going on in that thoughtful gray head of yours, Dr. McKenzie? 'Doc.' Maybe you'd like to watch Shaka Zulu and Pee Wee Herman lay the pipe to our girl? I bet that's it. Mrs. McKenzie isn't the horny young wet-mop she used to be. Or maybe you'd like to pop a couple of Viagra and take a stab at Claire yourself? Why the hell not? She's not going to see LA ever again, is she?

Witzerman—fucking bald fuck! You're too fucking ugly to scare me. I'd kill myself if I looked half as bad as you. I really fucking would. You would've been a crib death in my house, you Rogaine-soaked Q-tip. Try anything with me and I'll carve my freakin' initials into your scalp and send your bald head home in a Rice Krispies box!

Price—you could be a handful. You one hard mo' fo, ain't you, Homeboy? Okum's muscle, am I right? You goddamned uptight holier-than-thou Koran-readin' A-hole. But you can bet, first chance I get, I'm going to clip those muscle-bound wings of yours.

"Ethan. . . . Hell-O! Earth calling Dr. Ethan Hatcher . . . Come in Dr. Hatcher . . ."

Claire: she was passing her hand back and forth in front of his eyes as if he was some sort of catatonic.

"You okay?" she asked.

"I was thinking about Alan."

"I've been thinking a lot about him too," she said. "It's hard to believe he's gone."

Ethan stared at her. "Don't do that."

"What?" asked Claire.

"That 'he's gone' bullshit. Alan's not gone, he's dead." Ethan looked around the table to see if the others were getting it. Whatever Okum had told them, he wanted to set the record straight. Alan was no traitor. He was a good scientist and a better friend. "Dead," he repeated defiantly. "End of story."

"Relax," said Price. "She didn't mean anything by it."

"What the fuck do you know, Price?" Ethan was seething. Alan's death hadn't really struck him, not really, but now that he had returned to the scene of the crime the truth was inescapable. Plain and simple, he was a murderer. "He wasn't your friend."

Price bristled but restrained himself. "I know that the captain is supposed to go down with the ship, and that you're probably beating yourself up because you weren't here." He turned to DeLuca. "Isn't that right, Major? The shrinks call it survivor's guilt."

That word . . . *Guilt.* It must have set him off. Before he knew what he was happening he lunged across the table and swung on Price.

So much for being a badass. A split-second later Ethan was face down on the table, a stabbing pain shooting through his left arm. In a single fluid motion, Price had grabbed him by the wrist and spun him flat onto his chest, scattering the table's contents. Ethan's shirt was covered with refried beans and salsa.

Claire jumped on Price and tried to pull him off of Ethan. "You're hurting him!"

"Sergeant, let him go." DeLuca's tone was calm but decisive. He positioned himself between the two men. "What the hell's gotten into you two? For god's sake, this isn't high school. You're professionals. We're a team—act like it."

Ethan straightened up and massaged the kinks out of his shoulder. The table was a mess. Witzerman looked as if he'd pissed his pants. McKenzie was mopping up a spill with a wad of napkins before it could work its way onto the floor. Price had backed off a few paces, but was still tightly wound, his eyes focused and hard. Bishop righted an overturned glass and checked to see if anything had gotten on him. And Claire—she was beautiful in her anguish. A guardian angel. His protector. She was probably the only one there who didn't have it out for him.

"Your friend is the reason we're here," DeLuca continued, gazing into Ethan's eyes. "Please, keep that in mind. We're here to help."

But Ethan wasn't hearing any of it. He was imagining Alan—his friend's charred corpse lying on the ice somewhere—broiled to the bone and lightly dusted with snow. And all because Ethan had done what every American did come tax time: cheat a little. Price had nailed it—survivor's guilt.

The air temperature outside Chico's hovered near fifty below. Ethan's first breath was like inhaling liquid nitrogen into his lungs. But he needed it this way. The more it hurt, the better. *Tequila shots—stupid, stupid, stupid! You know better than to go splashing alcohol on an open flame. Chem 101—basic shit. You've burned yourself badly enough already. Remember, this is about saving your ass. Alan's gone. Get it through your fucking head. Alan's dead because of you! Don't turn this into a murder-suicide.*

Williams Field, Antarctica
GPS Coordinates: –77.8675, 167.056667
March 19, 2010

During the long, lopsided night all of their gear had been transferred from the C–130 to a smaller aircraft better suited for landings on the brittle snow pack they would encounter further south. Part helicopter, part airplane, the peculiar vehicle looked like something conjured from the pages of Leonardo DaVinci's famous sketchbooks. Hatcher and Price had made their way to the airfield well before dawn to ensure that everything they needed for the expedition was in place. When Claire and the others finally arrived, he and Price were standing just beyond the shade of a weather-scarred hangar with their backs angled to the sun. Today it would struggle to rise just above eye level. Tomorrow the pale yellow wafer might not make it to Claire's shoulders. In less than a week, darkness would rule the world.

"Glad to see that you two have kissed and made up," DeLuca called as they piled out of the van and crunched through the snow toward the hangar. "The last thing we need where we're going is a lover's quarrel. It's plenty cold already."

"I was out of line," Hatcher admitted. "Let's just get the answers we're looking for and go home."

Claire was impressed. The Hatcher she knew never admitted fault. Maybe he *had* changed.

"I've got some B-complex in my bag if you're interested," McKenzie offered. "It'll help take some of the edge off the hangover."

"A little suffering might do me some good," said Hatcher. "Penance."

"Is this some kind of joke?" Bishop wondered aloud. He scowled at the strange aircraft awaiting them on the helipad and rolled his eyes. "Don't tell me you expect us to fly in that ridiculous contraption?"

"That ridiculous contraption is a Bell Helicopter V22 Osprey." The voice came from inside the hangar. "The future of military aviation."

A man wearing nothing but snow boots, Levi's and a white thermal top stretched tight as a drum skin across his broad chest emerged from behind Price and Hatcher. He smiled at the rest of them, his eyes concealed beneath a pair of black wraparound sunglasses with orange reflective lenses. Although his legs were short and stocky, his upper body evoked the powerful forequarters of a pit bull. His torso was girded with solid muscle. Crisscrossed by a network of fine interlocking scars, his face was hard and angular and lean. His chin was stippled with wiry cinnamon scruff, the pale rusty hue of which was echoed elsewhere in his eyebrows and the hair on his forearms.

"She takes off and lands like a helicopter, and flies like an airplane," he said, his voice flat and inevitable. "Has a range of 2,100 nautical miles. Ideal for the conditions we're dealing with."

"This is our pilot, Lieutenant Kent," said Price. "The LT's our only way in or out, so be nice to him."

As they lifted off Claire noticed what resembled a flock of big black birds winging in from the west. There were four of them grouped loosely together, heads slung low and forward like vultures scanning the earth below for unsuspecting prey. It didn't take long for her to realize that they were not birds at all but massive helicopters. These too were like nothing she had ever seen before—all cockpit and no passenger compartment. The front half of aircraft was connected to the tail rotor by a long, slender thorax. Up close they no longer reminded her of birds but of giant mechanical hornets.

"I guess I don't need to ask why we aren't taking one of those instead," Claire remarked to Price. "Nowhere to sit."

Price looked past her head at the incoming helicopters. "Those are Sikorsky Skycranes," he explained. "They're used for hauling cargo mostly. Each one can carry close to 30,000 pounds. They drop down on whatever it is they're after—usually some sort of shipping container—latch on and up, up and away." He demonstrated with his hand.

"What are those big canisters next to the wheels?" Claire asked. The pessimist in her thought they might be bombs or something.

"Extra fuel," said Price. "They're probably unloading a supply ship that's anchored offshore. Folks here are getting ready for the long, lonely winter."

"But they're not carrying anything," Claire observed.

By then however the Osprey's tiltrotors had rotated into the horizontal flight position and they were underway.

Antarctica: Approximately 150 Miles from the South Pole
GPS Coordinates: −89.23321, −19.6875
March 19, 2010

From Williams Field it took nearly four hours to reach their final destination, a vast basin flanked on one side by a range of white saw-toothed mountains, and on the other by a blinding desert of snow stretching to the horizon. The basin was a sort of natural reservoir—a mile long and half again as wide—the upper nine-tenths of which was crusted over with layer upon layer of icy strata. It was here, beneath thousands of feet of ice and snow that life had somehow managed to hold on for millennia. Although Claire had theorized the existence of such an ecosystem, she was having difficulty believing it herself now that she was actually here. No wonder the skeptics had called her crazy. Life in this place? Under all of that? Not a snowball's chance in hell. But it was true, and she was encouraged. If simple vent organisms could survive without light in a hostile environment for thousands of years, then surely she could manage for a few measly weeks.

Although it couldn't compete with the boundless urban sprawl of Los Angeles, one end of the ice field was home to a ramshackle encampment. She hoped the cluster of battered Quonsets and peripheral debris wasn't Hatcher's idea of home sweet home. Rusted-out machine parts lay strewn about the haggard perimeter, leaking waste oil and bright red hydraulic fluid that streaked the snowy landscape like blood. It was a veritable bone yard, an auto dismantler's paradise, a burial ground where all things mechanical went to die. Had it not been for the dirty footpaths snaking in and out of the depressing field of debris, Claire would have guessed that the area had been deserted for decades. As they passed over the grim settlement a half-dozen fugitive figures in heavy olive drab parkas trudged out of one of the drafty sheet metal huts, raised their arms and began . . .

"Jesus!" shouted Claire, snapping her head back from the window. "They're shooting at us!"

"That's just the Russians saying hello," Hatcher offered routinely. He smiled. "Don't worry about them. They're just a little stir-crazy. They staff the weather station year round. Things get pretty lonely down here."

"I'd hate to see how they say goodbye," said McKenzie, peering cautiously back at the volley of muzzle flashes now well behind them.

"Why do they need guns?" asked Claire.

Hatcher shrugged. "You can ask them yourself. I thought we'd pay them a visit—see if they know anything we can use."

The research station once staffed by Alan and the previous team occupied a place at the opposite end of the ice field. Much as Claire expected, it looked as if a bomb had gone off. Nearly half the station had been obliterated by the blast. What was still standing was scorched and broken. Beneath the scattered wreckage was the ashy imprint of the fireball that had killed six men in a fraction of a second. Against the blazing white palette of snow, the blast area resembled an ugly black flower. The half-mile-deep hole in the ice at its epicenter had been sealed off with a heavy steel door that looked like something you'd find guarding the federal gold repository at Fort Knox. Apparently, the CDC wasn't taking any chances until Claire and the others determined who or what was to blame for the explosion.

Further ahead, fifty yards or less, was the site of the new research station. The state-of-the-art facility, a radially symmetrical complex consisting of small outbuildings spoked into and about a larger hub, had the basic configuration of a wagon wheel. It was sleek and black and geometrically precise. The hub building, about the size of Eric's house in El Segundo, would serve as both their laboratory and lounge. Twelve smaller modules were spaced equidistant from one another around the perimeter of an octagonal ring. Of the twelve, eight were numbered—eight in broad Day-Glo yellow characters easily visible from the air. Each of these was crowned with a single police-style flasher, though at present all eight of the blue strobes were dormant. These were their sleeping quarters. Each comprised a generous eighty square feet of personal living space. The other four modules included the bathroom and storage. The entire affair, nearly three-hundred feet in circumference, was connected by a series of enclosed walkways. A vehicle, the likes of which Claire had never seen in person though was to polar exploration what the Land Rover was to African safaris, was parked near the station. The tundra buggy was a marvel of adaptive engineering—the soul of a snowmobile in the body of a tank. Otherwise, the surrounding land was blissfully well-intact, neither heaped with exanimate junk nor mucked up with non-biodegradable waste like the Russian weather station.

"Here it is," said Hatcher as Kent brought the Osprey down vertically near the station. "Home sweet home. It's not the W, but it beats camping."

"It looks like a spider web," said Claire.

"Fitting, considering we'll be trapped here for awhile." Hatcher's mind seemed to drift.

"It's huge," said Claire. Anything to not talk about the other station—the destruction, what they would soon be looking for. "So this is how our tax dollars are being spent?"

"It's worse than I thought," said Hatcher. He was fixated on the blast site. "I didn't think we'd be able to see it. Not all of it anyway. I thought that it'd be buried under a few feet of snow by now."

"A common misconception," Witz explained. "Most of the time it's too cold to snow in either of the polar regions. Air's too dry. But when it does—*Look out!* Every so often, a blizzard will kick up that can cut you in two. The ground is covered with these tiny ice crystals that are hundreds of times sharper than broken glass. With wind speeds in excess of sixty meters per second, any exposed skin can end up looking as if it's been raked over a cheese grater."

The sun loitered just above the horizon, the gray-yellow tint of a hard-boiled egg yolk. The sky was a peculiar shade of lavender-blue as if charged with ultraviolet wavelengths of light normally beyond the visible spectrum. In another hour the sun would dip from sight, plunging them into twenty hours of total darkness. In a matter of days the sickly orb supplying Claire with an aggrieved sense of calm would vanish altogether for the next four months, enabling the old ghosts as only perpetual night could. *It'll be good for you. Give you a chance to confront your fears. Think of it as therapy that won't cost you $150 an hour.*

But she was not convinced. The same rotations that urged the earth toward a rendezvous with blackness seemed to be exerting a correlative force on her mind. Each turn wound her a little more tightly, twisted her nerves a little closer to the bone.

The moment Claire stepped out of the Osprey she was struck by the unreasonable coldness of the place. The chill that assaulted her body was aggressive, hostile. She had spent time in extreme climates before—equatorial jungles where the unrelenting heat conspired to wring the body of every ounce of moisture—but nothing that compared with this. It was as if the air had row upon row of razor sharp teeth. In a matter of seconds her face was numb and she had difficulty pulling on her mittens. But she wasn't the only one suffering. The others scowled miserably, pantomiming their discomfort with an authenticity that was impossible to hide.

"Chop-chop!" Hatcher exhorted them. He was barely audible over the din of the V22's churning engines. "You think this is cold? Wait until the sun goes down. Let's get the gear unloaded and get inside where it's warm."

"You heard the man," Price shouted. "Move out!"

For fifteen minutes they labored in the icy shadow of the explosion. Claire's nerve endings were experiencing a crisis of indecision. She knew that she was cold but what little of her skin was exposed now registered blistering heat. It was as if the air still clung to the memory of the explosion that had, if only briefly, lent warmth to a place held fast in the grip of eternal winter. While the rest of them shuffled quickly back and forth to keep their body temperatures up, Lieutenant Kent, their pilot, seemed neither anxious nor cold. There was no sense of urgency in his stride—for that matter he didn't seem at all concerned that prolonged exposure, regardless of one's attire, meant certain frostbite and possible amputation. For him, unloading the plane was simply something that needed to be done on a day like any other. They were all hopping around inside the station with their teeth chattering when he finally joined them.

"You said it was warm inside," Witz complained. "I bet I could see my breath if the lights worked."

"Just don't anyone strike a match," Bishop warned. "Jose Cuervo here'll blow us all to . . ." He caught himself mid-sentence. "Forget I said anything."

Before they left the inn that morning Claire had installed a fresh set of batteries in the mini Maglite she now retrieved from one of the deep outer pockets of her parka. She twisted the anodized aluminum barrel, summoning a reassuring cone of light. Playfully, she shined it in each of their faces, shadow filling the cadaverous hollows about their eyes. Not exactly what you'd call flattering lighting, but there were no monsters here.

"I guess now's as good a time as any," said DeLuca. He unzipped a duffel bag he'd been carrying and produced seven identical cardboard boxes, each approximately four inches square. He handed one to each member of the team.

Claire opened the box and discovered what looked like a hospital identification bracelet printed with her name.

MATTHEWS, CLAIRE DR. MODULE 3

"Major," she joked, studying the ugly little plastic wristband with mock admiration. "You shouldn't have."

"Try it on," said DeLuca. "The snap is a high-frequency GPS beacon. We don't want anyone getting lost out there."

Claire fastened the bracelet around her wrist. "What's module 3?"

"Your suite . . . In case you forget."

"Thanks," said Price. "But I'm not big on jewelry."

DeLuca smiled impassively. "It's not a request, Sergeant."

"Sure, I'll put it on once I get the generator up and running."

"Now, Sergeant. Before you go out that door."

About an hour later the eight of them convened in the station's hub, a well-lighted octagonal module that doubled as their laboratory and common room. Once the generator was running it had taken the heater less than fifteen minutes to warm up the place. This was no fly-by-night operation run on a shoestring budget. As far as research expeditions went, it was first-cabin all the way. Considering they were thousands of miles from the nearest IKEA the furnishings weren't half bad. At each workstation was a padded folding chair that could easily be moved about the room, whether for work, meals, or R&R. In the center of the hub was a small sofa, a coffee table, a color television, a decent selection of DVD's, and the most welcome diversion of all—a treadmill. The kitchen was basic but functional: propane camp stove, a small microwave oven, pots and pans, dishes, utensils. Location notwithstanding, the station made Claire's apartment look like a dump.

"Everybody happy with the accommodations?" DeLuca asked.

"So this is how the other half lives," said Claire, taking it all in. "Dibs on the treadmill."

"You can thank Sergeant Price for that," said DeLuca.

"Friends in all the right places," Price acknowledged with a wink. "Besides, I'd go crazy without my hamster wheel."

"Me, too," echoed Claire. Until now she hadn't really thought about what she was going to do for exercise. Her idea of therapy involved working up a good sweat. Without exercise she may as well have herself committed.

"The Taj Mahal of mobile homes," DeLuca boasted. "Every inch is prefab from floor to ceiling. Totally modular. A few nuts and bolts here and there are all that's holding the place together." He rapped on the wall for effect. "Airlifted in piece by piece and assembled on the spot. None of this was here two weeks ago."

"God bless the Army Corps of Engineers," Bishop added wholeheartedly. "If it wasn't for them we'd be sleeping in igloos."

"Instant laboratory," said McKenzie. "Just add warm bodies."

So this was the happy homecoming. The return to Never-no-fucking-way-again-land. Ethan had known the day would come but this didn't make it any easier. They looked like overgrown children tromping single-file through the snowy twilight in their oversized powder blue hazmat suits. Lost children. Minus the hood section—really nothing more than an overturned bucket with a transparent plastic face shield—the suits resembled pajamas with built-in mittens and booties. He was too sick with anticipation and too goddamned cold to feel ridiculous, but this didn't mean that the image was any less ironic to him.

Claire trudged along in front of him, the powdery dusting of snow groaning like cornstarch beneath each step. Was she afraid? How would she hold up under these conditions? So much death and darkness—past and present intertwined. She was tough, he'd give her that. Never met a challenge she wouldn't accept. He'd banked on it. Hubris—wasn't that what the ancient Greeks had called it? Excessive pride. Some people saw it as a bad thing, but he'd always loved this quality about her. The girl was a fortress. Not an ounce of give. She was here because she wouldn't cave to her own fear.

"How you holding up?" Ethan asked, his voice muffled by the thin rubberized membrane that crinkled noisily with each movement.

The illumination from their flashlights flooded the space between them. Claire's face was beautiful inside her suit, serene. Snow White in the glass casket awaiting her prince.

"I'm good," she replied simply, giving him this quizzical look before plodding along after the others.

They reached the intact portion of the station first. This is where Ethan and Alan and the others had slept. From here it was nearly impossible to tell that anything bad had happened. Although the concussion from the blast had knocked the walls out of plumb and had exerted innumerable stresses on the structure overall, only someone with a trained eye—a carpenter or an engineer—would have noticed. Here, the damage was profound yet subtle. Superficially sound, structurally defunct. It was the same with people, Ethan mused. A word, a look, sometimes even a gesture, could reveal a lot about a person's state of mind if only one had the foresight to take notice. If he had listened to Alan a little more closely during their last phone conversation there was a chance that none of this would be necessary. That he wouldn't be here now.

DeLuca and the others waited near the supply entrance for Ethan and Claire to catch up. The last time Ethan was here Alan and the rest of his team had huddled together beneath the pallid midday sun brandishing their middle fingers in a group farewell. Funny, but it was this image—a collective fuck-you as he boarded the Air National Guard helicopter—that replayed in his mind more than any other since he had first learned of the explosion.

"Go ahead," said Ethan not wanting to be the first inside. "Key's under the mat."

The door was jammed but Price forced it open with a powerful thrust of his shoulder. He entered first, followed by DeLuca, McKenzie, Bishop, Claire and then finally Ethan himself. Flashlight beams knifed through the unlit supply room, providing them with glimpses of a disaster they could have scarcely imagined standing on the other side of the door. A doctor friend at the UCLA Medical Center had once told Ethan that the true measure of a person's health could only be determined by looking inside the body, no matter how physically fit they appeared to be on the surface. Often, the terminally ill showed no outward signs of infirmity. The station was a sobering case in point.

As far as Ethan could tell not an ounce of edible provisions remained. Although there should have been enough food to last the entire team another two months, the floor was a mess of ravaged boxes, shredded wrappers, gutted cans, and gooey pink foam that in some places was ankle deep. It looked as if a wild animal had broken in and devoured every last morsel of food en route to terrorizing the rest of the station. The bottom half of the walls were also fouled pink, the high tide mark of a deluge come and gone.

"What is this stuff?" asked Bishop, bending over to examine the festive sludge. "It looks like pink cottage cheese."

"Chemical foam," Ethan explained. "For extinguishing fires. Non-toxic and it won't freeze—I guess that's why they used it here . . . The storage tanks are outside on the roof. When the internal temperature hits a certain point the system is activated and the room is instantly flooded."

"We have the same stuff at the new place," confirmed Price. "Gas, electrical, chemical—works on just about any kind of fire you can think of. Messy as hell though."

"The explosion explains the foam," said DeLuca, squatting on his haunches. "But it doesn't explain these."

A smattering of footprints covered the floor—enough so that a significant portion of the foam had been trampled into a viscous residue exposing what lay beneath. Ethan's right foot was planted in the center of a flattened Raisin Bran box. His left foot had targeted a Styrofoam Cup O' Noodles container: pork.

"If everyone died in the blast," posed DeLuca, "how can there be footprints?"

"Or this," said Claire, her flashlight trained on the wall next to the door through which they had entered.

"What ya got?" Bishop asked.

"Looks like a handprint," said Price, pancaking the beam of Claire's flashlight under his own.

"It's definitely a handprint," said Claire. "Four fingers and a thumb."

DeLuca turned his attention from one mystery and focused it on another. "Nice," he said, straightening up. "We might be able to get a good set of prints from it. Could help us figure out who was doing what during the approximate time of the blast. Maybe someone survived the fireworks and holed up in here thinking help was on the way. That would explain some of the mess."

"If one of my team survived," asked Ethan, "where is he now? Wouldn't someone have noticed him when they set up the new place? Your guys *did* check for survivors? . . ."

"There's a possibility someone may have survived the blast only to die a short time later from his injuries. Burns, for example," McKenzie offered. "Or he simply could have frozen to death. Even with shelter, he'd be lucky to make it twelve hours without a working heater in cold like this. Hypothermia would be nearly instantaneous."

"Let me put it to you this way," said Ethan, his voice betraying his growing impatience. "Where's the body?"

"Time out," said DeLuca, "we're getting ahead of ourselves." He turned to Ethan, his eyes apologetic. "I know this is difficult for you . . . It's difficult for us—usually the friends and family of victims are thousands of miles away when we're doing our job. They're definitely not here assisting with recovery." He paused and addressed them all, his tone conveying the unique awkwardness of the situation. "At this point we're still totally in the dark about what happened here, so let's not to jump to any conclusions. Okay?"

"He's right, Ethan," said Claire, studying the handprint alongside Price. "I get the feeling that we're going to find out more than we ever wanted to know. Let's just take it slow, all right? Can we do that?"

Price's face was now inches from the wall, the handprint looming large and impossibly real. "Major," he said, "I think Dr. Matthews is right. We should take this whole thing at a snail's pace. There's more here than prints—this looks like feces."

"*Feces?* You sure?" DeLuca asked.

"I can't smell anything inside this suit," Price responded soberly. "But I know shit when I see it."

"I don't mean to keep interrupting," McKenzie apologized, "but you guys had better take a look at this." He was down on one knee in a corner of the supply room, his flashlight resting on top of an overturned produce box: HEAVENLY SPUDS.

Ethan's mind was reeling. *What now?* This was the kind of thing he had hoped not to find. *Why couldn't the whole goddamned place have been leveled? I'm not ready for this shit.* "I know what's going on here," he said, his voice drawn tight. "The Russians came poking around after the explosion to see what they could scrounge up. These tracks on the floor . . . *That*—" he scowled, indicating the handprint. ". . . belong to them. I'd bet my life on it."

"What in the name of Saint Peter?" Bishop exclaimed.

"A bed?" ventured McKenzie.

"Looks more like a nest to me," said Bishop.

"We know one thing for sure," said Price, joining the others. "The handprint by the door over there doesn't mean they were running low on toilet paper."

A nest. Bishop was right. A fucking nest. No less than forty rolls of toilet paper—an entire case—had been unwound from their little cardboard cylinders and converted to primitive bedding. The corner was clogged with wadded up two-ply and soiled bed linens. The nest had apparently been doused at one time with chemical foam, but subsequent layers of the makeshift bedding had been added to make it once again fit for occupancy. *Sven! Hamsun had obviously been letting the little bastard wander around the station unsupervised.*

"Cozy," Bishop remarked.

Claire was staring at Ethan. She wanted answers. But what was he supposed to say? He couldn't tell her the truth. Explaining the what-for of a chimp on an Antarctic research expedition was like explaining the lipstick on your collar to your girlfriend.

"Maybe McKenzie's right," suggested Ethan. "Maybe one of the team survived the blast and thought about starting a fire in the corner here to keep from freezing to death. Maybe that's what triggered the foam."

"Possible," said DeLuca, mulling it over. "But only if the system was still operational . . . Anyway, like I said, there's no point throwing around half-baked ideas until we know more."

"What do you make of this?" asked Claire. "It looks like blood." She squatted over the nest and pointed out traces of red fluid splattered in with the pink foam. It started about three feet up the wall and had dripped downward toward the floor until the cold had stopped it in its tracks. She looked to DeLuca for answers.

"One thing at a time," DeLuca reminded her gently. "Please."

The small quarters Alan had shared with Lim echoed the same state of disarray. Pink foam everywhere. Here, too, footprints spotted the floor. But it was also on the walls, and this time gravity had not been the sole force at work. Finger-painted Chinese characters rendered in clumpy pink ooze adorned the walls. In some places the vertical columns were orderly, the work of a methodical hand. In others—on the wall next to Alan's bed and continuing upward onto the ceiling—the careful artistry had degenerated into sloppy smears and squiggles.

"Anyone speak Chinese?" asked Bishop.

"Tomorrow we'll snap some pictures and see if we can get this translated." DeLuca turned to Ethan. "Whose room was this?"

"Alan's," said Claire. She had picked up his wallet somewhere and was examining his driver's license in the beam of her flashlight. "Bad picture, but his mom and dad will probably want it."

Ethan was torn. On one hand he was relieved that they hadn't stumbled across his friend's corpse. He didn't know if he would have been able to handle it. On the other hand, they needed something—if not a body then partial remains—to get Okum off his back, close up shop, and go home. In his entire life, he had never wanted to be free of anything so badly. A few more days like this and he'd beg the feds to lock him up.

"Copy that . . ." said Price, responding to the little voice coming over the speaker inside his suit. "We're on our way." He addressed Ethan and the others. "Ladies, gentlemen—Witz wants us back pronto. The wind's picking up. Says there's a nasty blow on the way. We've got fifteen minutes to get our butts back to base."

Back at the station, it was only a matter of minutes before Claire had changed into a pair sweats and cross-trainers and hopped on the treadmill. She had been thinking about it every second they had been out there in the dark, picking through what amounted to the worst kind of nightmare. Although she was fairly convincing in projecting a level of comfort that was nowhere near panic, the reality was much closer to the bone. The suit—that stupid crinkly rubber body condom—was like her personal amphitheater. It exaggerated everything: Every breath, every movement, every heartbeat resounded with awful clarity. Belly of the beast. Even her thoughts seemed to boom out loud, threatening to expose her to the others as the scared little girl she was. However, as weak and vulnerable as the possibility of exposure had made her feel, it was nothing when compared to the smell that filled the suit and forced her to breathe in her own sickening frailty. With nowhere to go, every chemical odor her body released was allowed to linger. For close to an hour she'd subsisted on a banquet of primal exhaust ordinarily undetectable to humans. It was exactly this sort of animal response to her fear of the dark—and to what they had seen in the other station—that now compelled her to run.

"Looks like you've got some competition, Price," DeLuca observed wryly. "Dr. Matthews might just be able to give you a run for your money."

Claire looked at the monitor and realized that she had been hogging the tread-mill for close to an hour. Until then, no one had said a word to her. At least not that she knew of, and she had drifted into a hypnotic state. Price was waiting patiently for a spin—stretching, loosening up, jawing with the others.

"You think so, huh?" he said. "She's got a good stride—I'll give her that."

Claire punched the STOP button and got off. "Sorry about that, Price. I guess I lost track of the time."

"You better watch out, Price," Bishop egged him on. "She's not even breathing hard." He was sprawled on the sofa munching on a protein bar.

Price handed her a towel and turned to Bishop. "The woman obviously takes care of herself which is more than I can say for you. Look at the junk you're eating . . . An overpriced candy bar, that's all it is. Some doctor is getting rich off of you and you're too blind to see it. It's all a scam. Exercise is all you need."

Bishop took a big bite. "Exercise is for suckers. A low-carb lifestyle is the thinking man's road to"—he paused and read straight from the wrapper. "'. . . a leaner, meaner you.' Twenty million Americans can't be wrong. In another six months, I'll look like you. All without doing a single pushup."

"Keep putting that junk into your body and in another six months you'll be dead."

Bishop took another bite and chewed it defiantly. "Twenty bucks says she kicks your ass." He turned to Claire. "What d'ya say? Beat him, and all the money's yours. I just want the satisfaction of watching him lose."

Right now, all Claire wanted was a hot shower and a good night's sleep. The run was a start, but in no way had she purged herself of . . . Fear, grief, confusion, shame—maybe even anger? Her mind was cluttered with raw emotions that were impossible to quantify. Finding Alan's driver's license wasn't easy for her. But it went deeper than this. As a scientist she was trained to look for causality, reason. Though at a glance none of it made sense. The handprint, pink foam everywhere, Chinese char-acters dripping down the walls, blood—*a nest*? What they needed was a behavioral psychologist, not her. What answers could she possibly hope to provide? But as her mind went round and round and beads of cold sweat skittered down her spine like parasites, an image of the culprit had begun to divide and replicate in the forefront of her subconscious. Mad Cow disease, Kuru—the laughing death—Father Ter-rero's aptly named devil's hunger: If there was a common denominator in cases of spongiform encephalitis it was an acute degeneration of the rational mind. Insanity. Fortunately Claire had yet to go through the motions of scientific process. It was the only thing keeping her from connecting what had happened to Alan and the others with the unprecedented carnage at *Mission Nuestra Señora de la Candelaria* in late August of 1871.

"Maybe later," she said. "I'm going to get cleaned up and hit the sack."

"Come on," Bishop urged. "I'll double the money."

"Drop it," said Price. "She's not interested."

Price pulled off his sweatshirt and climbed onto the treadmill. The guy was ripped from head to toe. Track and field all the way. He was showing off, but good-naturedly. Still, the message was clear. He was no couch potato.

"I didn't say that," Claire corrected, her competitive spirit intervening where reason should have prevailed. "I'm just a little tired right now. It's been a long day. Give me until tomorrow. Then, if you're still up to it—"

"You're on," said Price. "Bishop, you'd better start counting your pennies."

"I don't want this to be about money," said Claire, feigning nervousness. "This is about me kicking your butt."

Witz clapped Bishop on the back and laughed out loud. "Oooooh!" he chided in a sing-songy voice. *"Price is gonna get beat-en by a gir-irl!"*

"Who wants another beer?" asked Kent. He stood by the refrigerator in his orange iridescent sunglasses, a crude smirk carved into the lower half of his face so that the overall effect was like that of a talking jack o' lantern. "Doc? You look like you could use a cold one after working up a sweat like that."

"How 'bout a rain check?" said Claire. She wasn't comfortable around Kent. There was a smugness implicit in his tone—the bloated self-assuredness of a body-builder. His cause wasn't helped by the fact that he hid his eyes from them. Eyes, in any creature, were evolutionary signposts providing valuable insight with regard to their environment, feeding habits, and natural disposition. "Maybe when I'm done showering."

The water pressure was hardly invigorating—an old man with an ailing prostate could've generated a more powerful stream—however the water was hot and the steam helped clear her mind. Most of her hypotheses regarding *S. iroquoisii* involved its potential influence on the behavioral patterns of early groups of hominids. By most estimations, these primitive, relatively unintelligent creatures were more aptly characterized as pre-ape than pre-human. Claire had only given limited consideration to the role *S. iroquoisii*, or any encephalopathy for that matter, might have played in the physical and social development of an organism already sitting atop the evolutionary ladder. *Homo sapiens*. Humankind.

If what she had seen in the ruins of the other station was any indication . . . But she was getting ahead of herself. They were a long way from definitive answers. Samples had to be collected, analyses performed, live subject trials. *Where in the world would they find guinea pigs out here?* A ton of questions and only one thing was certain. The impact of *S. iroquoisii* on a brainy host organism that was patently unstable, prone to conflict, ruthlessly determined, and guided by an unwavering ideological agenda could not be understated. Considering the basic biological needs of virtually every life form on the planet—sustenance, reproduction, territory—the bygone heyday of a few rowdy monkeys took on a very different complexion when applied to the world of men. Given humankind's inglorious track record with world hunger, overpopulation and war, widespread infection would almost guarantee the greatest mass extinction since the dinosaurs.

Claire was doing a pretty good job of freaking herself out when her thoughts were interrupted by a knock at the door. "I'll be out in a minute."

"Take your time," Hatcher joked. "I just wanted to make sure you hadn't drowned in there."

Not thirty seconds later, she was rinsing her hair when the bathroom door opened and closed. She couldn't hear anything above the hiss of the water but had a creepy feeling that she wasn't alone. "Wow, Hatcher, I didn't realize that you'd gotten so desperate in your old age." No response. She heard someone rustling around. She cranked closed the valve and threw open the plastic shower curtain.

It had only taken a few minutes for the tiny bathroom to become entirely choked with steam. The shower, sink and toilet were all crowded into a space not much bigger than a gym locker. If the bathroom was any smaller Kent would have been sitting in her lap, a grim prospect considering that he was totally naked. But it wasn't his nakedness that bothered her. Actually, had it not been for his eyes, he would have looked totally ridiculous, pitiful even, standing there all muscle-bound in the swirling mist with a beer in his hand. But his eyes—they were like stab wounds. It was as if evolution was slowly erasing them from his skull in favor of other less conventional senses. He was smiling.

"What do you want, Kent?" she asked brusquely, yanking her towel off the curtain rod and covering herself with it.

"I brought you that beer," he said.

"DeLuca told me to be nice to you, or I'd kick your ass for this little stunt."

Kent's expression was changeless as she gathered her clothes in a bundle and squeezed past him into the corridor. *Relax—nothing happened. He's just a creep.*

She turned the corner in a hurry—the outermost corridor was all corners—and bumped into Hatcher. She jumped.

"I didn't mean to scare you," he said, looking pleased with himself. He had a towel slung around his neck and a shaving kit tucked under one arm.

"You startled me, Ethan," she corrected. "You didn't scare me."

"How's the shower?"

"Good. But you might want to wait a few minutes. Kent's in there."

"I thought you were alone."

"Apparently I wasn't."

Hatcher looked as if he had bitten into something rotten. "With Kent—that puffed up little gorilla? You're kidding?"

"Fuck you, Ethan. You're not my daddy."

She pushed past him and didn't look back. Tears clouded her eyes.

"I missed you at breakfast this morning," said McKenzie. "Sergeant Price whipped us up some mean powdered eggs and bacon."

He crunched through the snow alongside Claire, the wrecked station lying just ahead. A slim metallic case dangled from one of his gloved hands. DeLuca, Bishop and Price all carried similar cases. It was an odd sight—four men wearing blue rubber suits tromping to work in the dusky light. Astronauts with briefcases. Fifty yards of wide open polar freeway, but to Claire it was the worst commute in the world.

"It's 4:00 AM," she replied. "Eat any earlier and we might as well call it dessert."

"Forget about keeping track of the time down here," said Price. "It's best to just go with the flow."

"He's right," Ethan called back to her. Today, he had taken the lead. "After a week in Antarctica you won't know which end is up."

"So that explains why you were talking out of your ass last night," Claire remarked dryly.

"You're not still upset about that?"

"Concerned is more like it," she explained. "You're a scientist—stick to the facts."

The wind had died out completely while they slept. The sky was now a dingy gray panel scoured of color. What lay before them was a landscape etched to the bare bone—a numbing emptiness as painless and pure as crib death. Here, an able-bodied person could slip into nothingness without a whimper. What the sun offered in the way of light and comfort was not expressed in warmth. It stalked the horizon like a rheumy eye, cold and ashen, a dispassionate observer to the puny lives of men.

Surprisingly, the station was even more ominous than when it had been cloaked in darkness. Using flashlights they had only been able to explore it in bits and pieces. Now with the benefit of daylight, it stood before them replete in its own devastation, a sprawling structural cadaver awaiting post-mortem. Hatcher, Bishop and Price resumed where they had left off the night before—in the rear of the station, the living quarters. Claire, McKenzie and DeLuca continued around to the front of the station—the site of the explosion and possible cause of all this.

"It's hard to imagine that there's a lake down there," said Claire. She stood next to the circular steel lid sealing off the hole from the outside world.

McKenzie nodded in agreement. "If we could get it open we could set up a little hut, stock it with brandy and do some ice fishing."

"They really don't want anything getting out," Claire observed.

The cover was a stupid precaution. Typical bureaucratic overkill. It was one thing to Shanghai an organism to the surface, but to think that it would willfully abandon a comfortable habitat miles down for this was ludicrous. About the only purpose she could imagine the steel barrier serving was to keep people from falling in. Like McKenzie said—a giant manhole cover.

"Come on," said DeLuca abruptly. "We've got work to do. I don't want us to be out in the cold for more than two hours at a time."

It was −61°. Cold by any standard. But it could, and would, get much colder.

There was absolutely nothing left of the drilling room, nor of the corridor that connected it to the rest of the station. Scattered debris—but nothing intact. The explosion had reduced this section of the station to its constituent parts: splinters of wood, metal scraps, wisps of yellow fiberglass insulation, and a ubiquitous dusting of mystery detritus—the stuff Claire didn't want to know about. Most of it could have easily been swept into a dustpan. The ironic thing about it was that she didn't have to be here, not outside. Not freezing her ass off while Witz and their trusty pilot, Kent—okay, so the asshole was added incentive for her being here—stayed cozy and played cards. Her turn would come in the lab back at the station.

Before setting out, she had told them that it was premature to make any guesses. DeLuca was adamant that she not feel obligated to accompany them, but she had insisted. *Insisted! Stubborn girl. Are you crazy?* She might've even changed her mind had DeLuca not worked so hard to make her feel as though she'd come unglued at the first sign of anything unpleasant. *Sit this one out and no one will think any less of you. Stay warm, work on your needlepoint. Leave the dirty work to us men.* Although he hadn't put it this bluntly, the message was implicit in his demeanor. Hatcher knew as little as she did about forensic science, but DeLuca hadn't discouraged *him* from tagging along.

"You sure you're okay with this?" DeLuca asked.

"Couldn't be better," she replied cheerfully.

He smiled compassionately and clapped her on the shoulder. "Well, then, Dr. McKenzie and I are going to get started. If you see anything that catches your eye let one of us know and we'll bag it for you. And be careful where you walk."

DeLuca picked a clear spot in the snow and laid his futuristic attaché case on one side. Nothing was easy given the limited mobility offered by the hazmat suit, but with a little bit of fumbling he managed to pop open the lid and expose the contents. In addition to a variety of specimen containers, the case contained a fairly general array of tools: a roll of transparent packing tape, tweezers, X-acto knife, needle-nose pliers, soft bristle paintbrush, tape measure. The sort of stuff most people kept at home in the tool drawer. One item, however, caught Claire's eye. Not because it was all that remarkable, but because a hand-held vacuum cleaner wasn't the sort of thing she imagined to be a professional scientist's instrument of choice. Of course she understood the attraction when she saw how efficiently DeLuca sucked up specimens from the surrounding ice for subsequent analysis back at the lab. *Dust bunnies—* finally an answer to the question that had been nagging her since Christchurch.

Her own treasure hunt wasn't nearly as methodical, and for the first half hour or so she did as DeLuca had suggested and watched where she walked. She was so intent on the placement of her feet that she hardly noticed the fallout of debris all around her. No use lying to herself—she was afraid of what she might find if she really opened her eyes.

Claire began with a cursory examination of everything that DeLuca couldn't get up with his vacuum. It was just a hunch, but she got the feeling that he wouldn't have bothered with the small stuff first if he had not believed that therein lay the best possible chance of discovering human remains. The time would come when she'd have all of that she could stomach. For now, she was going to play it safe.

Frying pan—good start. Nothing here. A square stainless-steel grate—burned and disfigured. Maybe they'd been barbecuing? Bad pun. A salad fork, a coffee pot . . . A burned piece of wood—watch out, nails. A? . . . A? . . . What the heck is that? . . . With her toe, she nudged the object onto its side. *A chainsaw? Ask Ethan, he'll know. A shoe . . . A shoe? . . . Oh, god, it is a shoe . . . Relax, there's nothing in it! Accent seasoning salt—MSG city! Maybe this is what killed them.* So far the search was going exactly as she'd hoped—nothing that would give her nightmares.

"Frank, give me a hand over here. I think I got something." It was McKenzie. He was standing in the open end of the intact portion of the station—what remained of the common room.

Cross-sectioned by the blast, Claire could see inside the walls, ceiling and floor. Badly charred insulation a foot thick was exposed to the elements where no less than a third of the entire structure had been ripped off its foundation and blown to bits. While the damage was nowhere near as extensive as where she was standing, it was worse in that enough remained to easily connect the devastation with those who had died. This was where Alan and the others had enjoyed a little R&R between shifts.

DeLuca was occupied transferring the contents of the Dustbuster canister into a plastic baggie. "Give me a minute," he said. "On second thought . . ." he continued, calling across the field of debris. "Dr. Matthews, how 'bout giving Dr. McKenzie a hand? That okay with you, Larry?"

McKenzie stopped what he was doing. "I'm not really sure what I have here," he replied, his voice tinged with reservation. "I think it might be best if you assisted. I can wait."

"We don't have a lot of time," DeLuca answered impatiently.

Claire had known from the beginning that things were going to get harder before they got any easier. "On my way," she called. She didn't want this damsel in distress thing dragged out any further. Chivalry was dead—she'd see to it.

The floor of the station rested on a foundation elevated two feet above the surface of the ice. Because of the suit's inherent awkwardness Claire was forced to sit on the shorn edge of the floor and swing her legs up. Although she thought the suit was overkill, she was mindful of snags as she rose to her feet. Exposure at this stage of the game meant quarantine. DeLuca was very clear about the protocol established by the CDC. No exceptions.

McKenzie was examining a badly damaged section of wall—the only portion of the common room left standing. "How can I help?" Claire asked, peering over his shoulder.

"You see this little hole here?" he said, directing her attention to a small perforation in the charred paneling. "There's something lodged in there, but my mask is fogging up and I can't see well enough to get it out. I guess my eyes aren't what they used to be. Here, try these." He handed her a very slender pair of needle-nose pliers.

Claire saw what he was talking about—a small irregularly shaped projectile of some sort—but she couldn't get a good enough grip to dislodge it. "I'm afraid that if I'm not careful I'll damage it somehow," she said. "Maybe if we cut away some of the wall here it'll be easier to get at."

"Good idea," agreed McKenzie. "This ought to do the trick." He handed her a pen knife.

Fabricated from an energy efficient composite of wood cellulose and polyurethane resin, the wall was relatively soft. Its chief purpose was to serve as a barrier and sound-proofing, not as structural support. In a few minutes Claire had managed to excise a significant portion of the space age material from around the perforation. The mystery projectile now sat at the bottom of a small crater—a tiny meteorite. The glint of silver amalgam caught Claire's eye.

"Is that what I think it is?" she asked.

"I'm afraid so . . ." said McKenzie. "But, hey, that's good news. Easy to ID. Bishop will be thrilled."

"But how did it get stuck in the wall?"

DeLuca had joined them. "Shrapnel," he explained concisely. "In explosions as big as this, parts of the victims not instantly incinerated are propelled through the air at thousands of feet per second. Because teeth are so hard they often survive the blast undamaged. They become bullets, in effect. Sometimes we actually find corpses with pieces of other corpses lodged inside of them. In rare instances, skeletal shrapnel can actually be linked to the cause of death. In the Oklahoma City bombing, a police officer was killed by a woman's—"

Claire broke him off in mid-sentence. "I get the idea," she said. "Remind me not to ask any more questions."

Their shadows had grown considerably longer by the time the two hours were up, the sun sinking like a stone on the horizon. Daylight happened in the blink of an eye this far along in the ecliptic. Night, on the other hand, was in no great hurry. When the other half of the team met up with them not far from where McKenzie had plucked someone's molar from the wall, it was shortly after 6:00 AM. Just about every cliché she could think of was apropos of the stricken expression worn by Hatcher, so she settled on one.

"You look like you've seen a ghost," said Claire.

His face was drawn and waxen beneath the face shield." I don't know what could've happened. I was only gone a week. It's like they all went nuts."

"Maybe they were high on something." She, too, was reaching, groping for answers. "Are you sure no one brought any drugs along—maybe one of the guys you didn't know so well?"

"Drugs?" he echoed feebly. "No way . . . Maybe . . . I don't know. It's possible, I guess. I'm not sure of anything anymore."

The way Bishop and Price were behaving—two guys who'd supposedly seen it all—confirmed the horrified look of perplexity on Hatcher's face. They quietly conferred with DeLuca and McKenzie, mumbling not of discovery, but revelation. McKenzie dangled a small plastic baggie in front of Bishop. They reminded her of Smurfs in their blue hazmat suits.

"We found a tooth stuck in the wall," said Claire, speaking as much for her own benefit as she was Hatcher's. She didn't want to be alone with her thoughts right now. "A tooth. I'm not sure I want to understand something like that. I'm not sure I can."

Hatcher wasn't listening. He had shrunk into a ball and was sitting on the floor of the derelict station hugging his knees. Mute sobs wracked his body.

So much for remaining clinically detached and keeping his head on straight. Ethan was losing his edge and it was pretty fucking obvious to the others. *Crying like a goddamned child. Pull it together.* What he'd seen back there—this whole miserable business—defied explanation. Not that he especially wanted an explanation, or even cared if Okum's little witch hunt produced real answers. This shit they were dredging up was giving him ulcers. Much more and he'd be chugging Pepto Bismol martinis just so he could sleep at night.

"What was in the other rooms?" Claire asked him, sagging back behind the others as they ambled home through the permanent dusk. "What did you see?"

"I don't know," Ethan replied flatly. His voice was off key and lifeless, a peculiar counterpoint to the monotonous crunching of their feet.

"What do—"

He stopped and looked Claire squarely in the eye. "I don't know," he growled. "Aren't you listening to me? I said, *I—don't—know.*"

Claire, too, was shaken by all of this, and Ethan instantly regretted his demeanor. Right now she was the only one he could trust, the only one who remotely understood what he was going through. "I'm sorry," he said. "This just . . ."

She reached out and touched him on the arm with her gloved hand. A thin, joyless smile crossed her lips. "Me, too."

DeLuca and his team were like kids counting up their loot the morning after Halloween. They couldn't wait to compare the specimens each had collected from the derelict station. Although McKenzie's tooth garnered top honors, they had all made out like bandits. Price had his feces—collected from the handprint on the wall of the supply room as both a fingerprint on a strip of transparent adhesive tape, and as a scraping suspended in a liquid medium. Bishop: a fistful of cotton swabs anointed with residual traces. From the rim of the toilet, the drain in the bathroom sink, the shower pan . . . From everywhere a healthy dose of disinfectant was warranted. He had spent nearly the entire two hours poking around the bathroom. Ethan attributed Bishop's seeming thoroughness to the luxurious warmth generated by the propane space heater he had used to make the iced-over fixtures more amenable to specimen-gathering. He had also snapped several megabytes of digital stills, a macabre photographic record of what Ethan's team had left behind. Together, the swabs and the voyeuristic imagery evoked a kind of sexless pornography. And let's not forget DeLuca's bid for *Good Housekeeping's* Man of the Year honors—a clutch of zip-sealed dust bunnies that would have given the CEO of Hoover vacuum cleaners a hard-on.

While the others settled in at their workstations, Price produced a comparison chart from a poster tube and tacked it to the wall. The names of the previous team were listed alphabetically from top to bottom, including Ethan observed distrustfully, his own. Each name was followed by a shadowy image of a familiar zebra-striped chain. At a glance the chains were more or less alike; however, closer examination revealed that each was profoundly different from the next. DNA. JPAC's objective was twofold. First—find a match for everyone on the list, except of course Ethan. Second—prove that everyone had died in the blast. DeLuca admitted that it was going to be difficult differentiating between those specimens that were direct byproducts of the blast, and what he called "breadcrumbs."

This was probably going to turn out to be one of those things Ethan would've rather not known, but he asked anyway. "Breadcrumbs?"

Price explained. "Every human being—every living creature for that matter—is constantly rebuilding itself. When a new cell is born an old one dies off and is left behind. A fair amount of the dust in your home is composed of cellular debris—hair, skin. Breadcrumbs—" he concluded logically. "We leave a trail wherever we go."

"Follow the trail and you'll find your man," McKenzie added.

"Now that you know about breadcrumbs," said DeLuca, "why don't you fill us in on this whatever-it-is we're keeping an eye out for."

"Don't look at me," said Ethan. "Claire's the real expert here. *S. iroquoisii* is her baby."

Claire fixed him with a thankless smirk. "I'm not sure I like the analogy, but I guess it beats dying an old maid. In nearly every case of spongiform encephalitis the infected brain tissue exhibits traces of tiny rod-shaped particles. Although the relationship of these particles to the infection itself isn't clearly understood they are as good an indication as any that prions were present. In *S. iroquoisii's* case these particles should be relatively big—visible under a standard light microscope. Otherwise Father Terrero wouldn't have been able to see them."

"Father Terrero?" DeLuca asked.

"A nineteenth century Spanish missionary," Claire explained. "He documented a case of spongiform encephalitis affecting a group of Iroquois Indian braves who took part in a rather infamous killing spree in the 1870's."

"You're shitting me?" said Bishop.

"I know it sounds farfetched," said Claire, "but Father Terrero was also a scientist. Even by today's standards his methodology was sound."

"So where do we look?" DeLuca asked.

"Any intact tissue would be a good place to start," said Claire.

"Why here?" asked DeLuca. "Why Antarctica?"

"The ecosystem that spawned *S. iroquoisii* is very, very old. A billion years, maybe more. I'm not sure how much you know about paleogeography, but the earth was like one big Petri dish back then, a great big lukewarm ocean teeming with early microbial life. *Iroquoisii's* ecological niche was extremely specialized. He would've died out as an independent species the moment the seas began to cool."

"So *S. iroquoisii's* a *he*?" Ethan remarked sarcastically. "Isn't that a tad bit sexist? Why not an *it*? Or a *she*?"

"Classic Napoleon complex," Claire elaborated. "Doesn't fit the profile of a she. *He*," she continued, "is a total control freak."

"Easy, girl," said Ethan. "I'm just busting your balls."

"As I was saying . . . there's a chance that *he* managed to hang on in a few isolated pockets. But only in especially temperate zones on or very near the equator."

"Antarctica's nowhere near the equator," said Witz, echoing what all of them were thinking. The balding little putz was hardly paying attention. He was fiddling with a handheld electronic device that was like one of those portable video games you see lulling kids into a state of slack-jawed rapture.

"Not in this day and age," said Ethan. "But two-hundred million years ago the land we're standing on was part of a supercontinent called Gondwanaland. As the giant landmass was forced apart by the processes of plate tectonics and seafloor spreading much of what once rested near the equator drifted into the southern hemisphere—South America, Australia, Antarctica. And everything else came with it. Like one big Noah's Ark."

"Very good, Ethan," said Claire. There was a note of condescension in her voice that Ethan found sexy in a kinky, B&D sort of way. "So you actually read my article. You're not just looking at the pictures anymore."

Ethan took a bow and flashed her an ingratiating smile. "That month's *Playboy* got lost in the mail."

"So you see," Claire ignored him, "I didn't actually pull Antarctica out of a hat. Like a hunter, I tracked her from where she used to call home. What better place to look for the origins of life on earth than going right to the source?"

"And Antarctica's a *she?*" Ethan remarked wryly. He loved toying with Claire. Back when they were together verbal repartee had constituted a significant portion of their foreplay. He'd say something nasty, she'd say something nasty back, and before long they'd be ripping each others' clothes off.

"Strong, beautiful, mysterious—absolutely."

"What about inhospitable and frigid?"

"She wasn't always that way," Claire replied matter-of-factly. "She, like Africa, was once a cradle of life. But that, as they say, is ancient history."

"Maybe we're better off," Bishop observed innocently.

"You're probably right," Claire agreed, combing a loose strand of hair from her face. "*But S. iroquoisii* isn't a pathogen in the modern sense of the word. In fact, he's not all bad. Our susceptibility to him—correct that, our *ability* to utilize him genetically—is probably what gave us a leg up over every other creature on the planet. We are where we are today—as a species, as a civilization—because of him. Just as ancient retroviruses make up a part of the human genome and better enable us to cope with disease, *S. iroquoisii* has better enabled us to meet the challenges of our physical environment. Without him we might still be swinging from the trees."

"I'm lost," said Bishop, a perplexed look spreading across his face. "What exactly does *he* do?"

"I've been asking myself the same question going on five years now," Claire admitted candidly. Her dark eyes gleamed with the allure of possibility. "My best guess is that he targets receptor sites within the affected host. The response then varies with regard to the location of these sites. In primitive sea life such as jellyfish, *S. iroquoisii* may have influenced the feeding behavior, and thus the patterns of vertical migration that ultimately brought life out from the deep and into the light of day. At this point it's all mostly theoretical."

"Where does man come in?" asked Price. "We're a long way from jellyfish." He looked at Bishop who was snacking on another protein bar. "Most of us."

"That's where it gets tricky," said Claire. She raised her eyebrows in an expression Ethan remembered from grad school. "Personally, I think *S. iroquoisii* influenced genetic drift. Between two and three million years ago several different species of pre-humans existed on the planet simultaneously. Of these, only a select few ever evolved into modern *Homo sapiens*. The rest, Neanderthals and Cro-Magnon for example, died out rather quickly and unceremoniously."

"Don't let Kent hear you say that," Bishop remarked snidely. "He's likely to hang himself when he realizes he's the last of his kind."

"No one knows why for sure," she said. "The fossil record is pretty patchy, but recent finds suggest that in certain isolated pockets the transformation may have been extremely abrupt. At least in evolutionary terms—a spike so to speak. A few hundred years, maybe less."

Price snapped his fingers. "Just like that?" he stated skeptically. "Boom! From traveling by swinging vine to hybrid cars?"

Claire took the joke in stride. "Pretty close. But that's not what interests me . . ."

"You want to know how a bunch of scrawny, physically overmatched ape-men managed to survive when the great big hairy badasses living next door couldn't hack it." Price glowered imitatively and beat his chest for effect.

"Brains," Ethan answered. "Superior intelligence."

"He's right," said Claire. "But that's still not what we're after. It's how we got these big brains of ours in such a relatively short time that has science scratching its head."

"Well, then," said McKenzie, "what's the verdict?"

"Chemicals," Claire responded simply. "We all know that every creature on the planet is the sum of its chemical impulses. But how these chemicals derived has proven to be one of science's great enigmas. It's one thing to chart the patterns of physical evolution through the examination and analysis of transitional species. Charting the evolution of the chemistry of the brain is another ball of wax altogether. Because ancient earth comprised a smorgasbord of chemicals in their elemental state, it only makes sense that the earliest forms of life borrowed from this incredibly rich primordial soup along the way. Trial and error proved which combinations worked best in any given environment. Man—rather, the *brain* of man—is the most successful chemical combination to come along in the past two million years."

"Then what you're saying is that *S. iroquoisii* is one of the chemical sources we borrowed from?"

Claire nodded. "One thing science has shown us in the past couple of decades is that there's a molecular basis for virtually every form of behavior."

"So *S. iroquoisii* is still part of us?" DeLuca asked.

"He's there all right," Claire confirmed. "Lurking inside your brain—probably in the structures of the amygdalae and the archipallium—in the form of specialized receptor sites."

"These receptor sites . . ." asked McKenzie. "What do they do exactly?"

"Hunger, self-preservation . . ." said Claire. "Aggression. They oversee all the functions of the primitive brain."

"Your boy sounds like a real sweetheart," said Bishop.

"You wouldn't want to meet him in a dark alley," Claire agreed.

"If he's inside of us right now," Bishop asked, "why aren't we killing each other?"

"Aren't we?" she replied matter-of-factly. "Iraq, Afghanistan—take a look around. Killing is what we do best."

"She's got a point," said McKenzie.

"Ordinarily our receptor sites receive these chemical impulses in small doses influenced by environmental stimuli. If we're hungry, we eat. Threatened—we either run or fight. However, if we received *S. iroquoisii* from an exogenous source—if we caught it from someone or something else—those same receptor sites could easily become overloaded."

McKenzie added another shot of whiskey to his coffee. "The same thing happens with drug use. The chemicals react with naturally occurring receptors but elicit responses far exceeding those brought about by endogenous sources."

"Feeding behavior, for example," Claire elaborated. "Evolutionary biologists, myself included, now believe that certain dietary modifications were responsible for the dramatic increase in brain size in pre-humans. This marked shift in eating habits may have been triggered by exposure to *S. iroquoisii*."

"By 'dietary modifications' you mean what exactly?" asked Price.

"You're not going to like this," said Claire. "But the original Atkins Diet. Protein. Meat. And lots of it. Lieutenant Bishop would've fit right in. The fossil record suggests that early primates were largely vegetarian. Then suddenly—no one knows exactly when—meat became a dietary staple. Insects, birds, rodents—each other when alternate sources became scarce or unavailable. This abrupt transition is marked by the addition of two prominent features: modified dentition—specifically the addition of incisors, our meat-cutting teeth. And a correlative increase in brain size due to greater protein intake. Everything else followed."

"There's more?" said Price.

"The increased demand for animal protein necessitated an entirely new lifestyle. There's not much in the way of prey high up in the treetops. We climbed down out of the jungle canopy, learned to walk upright, taught ourselves to hunt, elected Charleton Heston President of the NRA . . ." Claire rolled her eyes and shrugged. "And the rest, as they say, is history."

"Sizzler, Black Angus, Big Macs . . ." Price added.

"So what you're saying is that *S. iroquoisii* is responsible for blocked arteries and colon cancer." Bishop slapped Witz on the back and chuckled.

"You're not seeing the bigger picture," said Ethan. "More meat means bigger prey. Bigger prey means greater danger. Greater danger means we needed bigger balls . . ."

"What Hatcher is trying to say is that an increase in aggressive behavior was the natural by-product of all this. Early man needed violence more than ever to sustain himself, to solidify and maintain his position atop the food chain. Natural selection is powered by competition; therefore, violence became a staple of existence."

"Only the strong survive," Price observed soberly.

Claire nodded. "Strong, violent—it's all a matter of perspective. New Guinea islanders, for example, were notoriously cruel toward members of rival tribes. They regularly conducted hunting parties to exact vengeance for family members slain in battle. It was customary to dine on the flesh of their captives as a form of restitution. Although their logic was misguided—having more to do with spiritual beliefs than basic nutrition—the tribesmen correctly believed that eating their enemies made them stronger. This ritualized behavior also brought about the appearance of Kuru, another form spongiform encephalitis that nearly drove many of these tribes to extinction. Finally, the government intervened, the tribes stopped eating each other, and the Kuru prion effectively fell off the map."

"And to think I've been wasting my money on vitamins all these years," remarked Price.

"Meat, aggression—it's like the snake that feeds on its own tail," said Claire. "One perpetuates the other."

"Anything else?" DeLuca asked.

"Oh, yeah," Claire added casually. "I almost forgot . . . There's a good chance that *iroquoisii* may also greatly increase sex drive."

"Now you're talkin'," said Witz.

"The archipallium—the section of the brain responsible for aggression—is also the source of self-preservation. Although we don't often think of it in these terms, reproduction is a proactive defense against extinction. In fact, humans and dolphins, both big-brained creatures, are the only species we know of that are sexually active year-round."

Witz set aside his electronic weather gadget and appraised Claire hopefully. "Tell me more."

But Claire wasn't listening. Ethan could see the consternation in the down turned corners of her eyes, in the furrows of her brow.

"The archipallium," McKenzie mused. "The old reptilian brain. The piece of work you're describing sounds like a handful."

"Fuck you to death and then eat you for dessert," said Bishop.

Claire spent the next several hours watching DeLuca and his team study and catalogue their specimens. She felt like a pest questioning them about this, confessing her ignorance about that. But they were all very informative and before long she was so immersed in the work that she was nearly able to forget the reason behind it and concentrate solely on the science. Their efficiency and expertise was remarkable, navigating data and intricate procedures with a fluency born of intensive training and experience. Employing the latest in forensic technology, keen eyes, and old fashioned deductive reasoning, JPAC made finding a needle in a haystack look like child's play. There was a strange kind of beauty in their methodology, a careful choreography of scientific ritual and practice that had always appealed to Claire. Science was pure and elemental, as much a component of the human experience as was love. She was quickly reminded, however, that death shared equal billing.

Bishop was the first to record his findings on the large grid Price had affixed to the wall above the workstation. Using dental records, a fairly recent x-ray, and digital odontography, he was able to identify with 90 percent certainty the true owner of the tooth McKenzie had found. In another five or six hours, comparison analysis of mitochondrial DNA extracted from the root of the tooth would remove it from the realm of reasonable doubt. Claire, however, was already convinced. It wasn't the least bit scientific, but she trusted enough in percentages to pity Alan the unique projectile jettisoned from his skull by the force of the blast. Having it up on the wall spelled out in red grease pencil for everyone to see somehow made it real, unequivocal.

WHITEHURST, ALAN DR.: RT. 2ND MOLAR/UPPER; EAST WALL, COMMON ROOM

"I'm sorry he had to be the first," said Bishop.

Claire could tell from the awkward tilt of Bishop's expression that this was one aspect of the job with which he didn't have any experience. He was uncomfortable and it showed.

"You're just doing your job," she assured him.

Although this wasn't easy for Claire, she had built up a sort of immunity to bad news during her mother's drawn-out battle with cancer. Diagnosis, surgery, chemotherapy, radiation. It was one blow after another until her mother finally lay dead. Conversely, Hatcher was a newcomer to all of this. Grief was still foreign to him, an invisible enemy against whom there was no defense. The breakdowns he'd suffered at Chico's the other night and now today at the derelict station . . . This was only the tip of the iceberg. Claire knew from her own experience that the outer manifestations of grief were nowhere nearly as violent as the savage assault it waged on the heart. From the moment they had arrived she wondered how Hatcher would react when confronted with the physical evidence of Alan's death. Perhaps they all had, for he was suddenly caught in a crossfire of curious glances.

He exhaled and looked at Bishop dazedly. "Are you sure it's his? You said 90 percent . . ."

"We have to wait for McKenzie to run the DNA—" Bishop explained. "But . . ." He stood there wringing his hands, unsure how to proceed. "Okay, it's like this. When I say 90 percent that means if the specimen was collected in Vietnam or Iraq or New York—basically anywhere in the world but here. What I mean is—"

Sensing that his man was in trouble DeLuca intervened. "What Lieutenant Bishop is trying to say is that the tooth definitely belonged to your friend. There's just no one else down here . . . The population is too small. We're still going to check the DNA against the maternal bloodline, but at this point it's merely a formality."

Laughter blared from the television. Claire could see Kent out of the corner of her eye. He was kicked back on the sofa twitching his pectorals so that his entire chest jumped at irregular intervals. Witz sat next to him, half-asleep.

Hatcher was expressionless. "So you're absolutely sure?"

"*Absolutely* is a loaded word in this business . . ." said DeLuca. "But, yeah, we're absolutely sure."

"McKenzie, Price—you guys agree with them?"

McKenzie and Price both nodded.

Hatcher was almost too calm, and this made Claire nervous. His earlier breakdowns had seemed to foretell an impending crisis of a much greater magnitude. But here he was taking in the confirmation of Alan's death in relative stride. Shock maybe. Or denial.

"If it makes you feel any better," offered Bishop, "he died instantaneously. The annealing on the surface of the tooth indicates extreme heat. For all intents and purposes, he was standing inside a crematorium."

Hatcher was slow to respond. "Everybody happy?" he asked, collecting Alan's tooth from a specimen dish next to where Bishop had been sitting. "Bishop, Price—you guys happy? McKenzie? . . . What about you, Major? One down, five to go . . . Because I sure feel better." Hatcher pinched the tooth between his thumb and forefinger and calmly studied it.

This was not at all what Claire had expected.

Hatcher looked at Bishop. "This burnt part?" he asked. "This is what you meant by annealing?"

Bishop nodded.

Hatcher made a fist around the tooth and started out of the room. The TV intensified its obnoxious assault on the awkward silence that ensued. A woman was singing an off key love song about someone named Harold.

"Hey, Doc—" DeLuca called after him. "Sorry, buddy, but we need that tooth. Standard operating procedure."

Hatcher stopped and wheeled on him. "Fuck standard operating procedure!" he growled, brandishing the fist with the tooth in it. "This comes back with me. A minute ago you said this was Alan's tooth. Absolutely certain—remember? Well, now it's mine. Tell Okum if he wants a souvenir that I'll stick it up his ass myself next time I see him. Otherwise, back the fuck off."

Hatcher turned and stormed from the room.

"I better go talk to him," said Claire.

"No, this is on me," said DeLuca.

Ethan had no sooner closed the door to his quarters when he found himself once again face to face with DeLuca. His blood was still pumping from their exchange in the common room only moments ago. DeLuca could spout procedure until his salivary glands ran dry and started spewing up dust but there was no way in hell Ethan was giving up Alan's tooth. He wasn't even sure of his motives, only that he'd rather die than let it go without a fight.

"Listen to that wind," said DeLuca. "It's really moving." He cocked his head to one side and listened.

Ethan could hear it too—a raw, palpable force buffeting the walls of the station, but he had grown used to it during his previous sojourn. It was now like freeway noise to him—a low, whisper-roar that made him long for the creeping predictability of rush hour on the 405.

"I'm not giving back the tooth," said Ethan.

DeLuca closed the door behind him. Gone was the paternal front he put on for the others. His affable, domesticated smile gave way to an effortless snarl. "Keep it," he said. "Only watch what you say. You and I are the only ones here with perspective. The others have no idea what we're dealing with. As far as they know it was all a freak accident—the discovery, the explosion. We're the cleanup crew, nothing more."

Ethan had been waiting for this. "How stupid do you think I am? I've seen how you look after your men. You wouldn't turn them loose down here blindfolded. You couldn't. Not like I did." But he was beginning to wonder. There was more to DeLuca than he'd first believed. A simmering menace.

"Sometimes blindfolded is best. My men know enough to get the job done. We're military—we don't ask questions, we follow orders. You, on the other hand, know enough to fuck up everything."

"Well, pardon fucking me, I didn't ask for this shit."

"All I'm saying is that we'll get out of here a lot quicker if you stop blurting out whatever pops into your head and let me take care of things."

"Forgive me if I don't have total faith in your judgment, but aren't you the one who let Claire tag along this morning? Don't let the perky tits and ass fool you—the girl doesn't miss a thing."

"Dr. Matthews lacks context. She was lost out there. I could see it in her eyes."

"If she knew about any of this she'd crucify me."

"Once she gives us what we're after we'll put her on the first bus home."

"What about me? Okum didn't give you any *special* instructions? You said it yourself—I know enough to fuck up everything."

DeLuca blinked and just like that he was his old congenial self again. "Listen to that wind blow. Sounds like it's gonna rip the roof right off of this place."

10:31 AM and Ethan had already been awake for more than six hours. And it would probably be another ten before the DNA and other test results were analyzed and everyone turned in for the night. If this continued he'd never be able to get his sleep cycle back on track. He was wiped out, but at least he wasn't freezing his ass off, not like with Alan and the others. The new station was virtually airtight in case of quarantine. Each room was a self-contained unit. If a member of the team became infected, any or all of the rooms could double as isolation wards.

Ethan had just begun to drift off when he was snatched from the brink of oblivion by an ear-splitting roar. For a moment the real-world cacophony connected with his dream and he was inside the station with Alan and the others when four-hundred gallons of gasoline ignited and ripped their world to pieces. And then he was on his feet, Alan's tooth still clenched in his fist, staggering through the low-ceilinged corridor in a groggy haze.

"You're just in time for the big race," Bishop announced as Ethan burst into the room.

"Grab a seat and place your bets," said Witz.

Calm down, they're all here. They didn't ditch you. Calm down.

DeLuca looked at Ethan with pitying eyes. He and his team had set up folding chairs around the treadmill and were watching Claire hammer out a blistering pace. Her hair was back in a ponytail and Ethan was momentarily mesmerized by its rhythmic bounce. "What's that noise?" he asked.

"Just Kent keeping the engines warm," Price explained. "The pistons will crack if they get too cold." He was standing alongside the treadmill, stretching and limbering up. "You ought to know that by now. He's been doing it every four hours since we got here."

"You didn't think we were going to leave you here?" Witz joked.

Ethan simply glared at him.

Claire jabbed at the control console and kicked up the pace. Beads of sweat bristled on her forehead. Her face was flushed, but she was breathing evenly and had a good relaxed stride going.

Price checked his watch. "Two more minutes."

"If you want to get in on the action, Doc," said Bishop, "now's the time."

Ethan shook his head. "I'll hang onto my money until the rematch when Claire runs second. She's better with a challenge in front of her. This way all Sergeant Price has to do is outpace her by a tenth of a mile and he wins."

"Think you can take her?" Price challenged.

"No way," Ethan admitted. "I've been down that road before. It just goes and goes and goes."

Claire hadn't pushed herself hard enough. Hatcher was right. Price had keyed in a pace that would edge her by a tenth of a mile and was now simply going through the motions. With less than a minute to go he hadn't even broken a sweat.

"Pay up, gentlemen," said Price. He smiled broadly as he hopped off the treadmill. "And no personal checks."

Claire walked over to him and shook his hand. "Congratulations, now I think I'll go bury my head in the snow."

"It wasn't that bad," Price assured her. "Besides, Hatcher was right. I had the advantage. Next time I'll run first."

"Rematch *mañana*?" Witz pressed. "Double or nothing? We'll put up the money."

"I don't know," said Claire. "He beat me pretty bad."

"Come on," said Bishop. "It'll be fun."

"Give her a break," said Price. "The woman has a conscience. She doesn't want to lose any more of your money."

Claire studied the faces gathered around her. *Men.* When women were involved they were like jackals on the blood trail of a wounded gazelle. *Wrong girl.* "Tomorrow it is," she responded decisively.

"You've got balls," said Price.

"Remind me to give you a lesson in anatomy after I kick your butt."

Ethan held out his hand to Price. "Twenty bucks."

Price reluctantly turned over a share of his winnings.

"What's this?" Claire asked suspiciously.

"Information," Hatcher explained. "I told Price how he could get you to race him as many times as he wants."

"Really?" Claire inquired. "How's that?"

"Act like you don't stand a chance," said Hatcher. "It's how I got you to sleep with me in grad school."

"By that point, I would've done just about anything to get you to stop begging."

It wasn't an easy pill to swallow, but he was right. Claire's pride was her only true vulnerability. Old Nosworthy, for example—all he'd wanted from her was a formal apology. After all, he'd taken his fair share of heat for the Ha Tinh debacle. But Claire wasn't sorry for what she'd done—it was the right thing to do—and nothing in the world was going to make her claim otherwise. The same was true of her fear of the dark—she expended as much energy justifying its paralyzing influence on her life as she did rebuking herself for behaving so childishly. Maybe her mother was right. Maybe Claire was making excuses. Blaming her abusive father and Nosworthy was easier than admitting that she was the sole architect of her own miserable existence. Pride may not have been the source of her weakness, but it certainly exacerbated what was already there.

Claire joined Price in the storage room for a grueling hour of pushups, sit-ups, and other less orthodox strength-training exercises. Boot Camp Hell, he called it. She was grateful for the distraction. When she wasn't keeping herself busy her father's voice crept into her mind and poisoned her thoughts. She could feel the blackness pressing in around them, his voice threaded in with the wind.

"Is that all you got?" Price barked. "Thirty lousy pushups."

Claire collapsed to the floor, her arms like rubber bands. "You're a man," she panted. "Your upper body is naturally stronger than mine."

"You're not going to catch up lying on the ground panting like a sick dog."

Claire hoisted herself up off the floor and continued until her arms gave out. She rolled onto her back and looked at Price who was sitting on a shipping crate. "So what do you think of all this so far?"

"Right now it doesn't make any sense."

"Will it ever?"

"I thought *you* were going to tell us whether it did or not."

"I'm not sure I can."

"No one expects you to pull a rabbit out of a hat."

"That's not the problem," said Claire. "I'm afraid of what I'll find if I look hard enough."

Understanding illuminated Price's eyes. "So that's why you backed off earlier. That didn't seem like you—letting the men have all the fun."

Claire had a workstation of her own, but she had yet to take the driver's seat, choosing instead to await JPAC's initial findings. That Alan's name had come up first only proved that she wasn't cut out for this.

"Yeah, well—I didn't want to step on any toes," Claire lied. "You men are sensitive like that."

Price gazed evenly at her. "Bullshit."

"You don't understand," said Claire. Terrifying images filled her mind.

"Try me."

"If *S. iroquoisii* gets loose we could find ourselves in the middle of another Stone Age. Tribal warfare on a global scale. Only nowadays the clubs we carry into battle can smash entire cities."

Price had done the work on the fingerprints he had collected from the fecal hand-print and had then turned the remainder of the sample over to DeLuca for detailed analysis. Seeing that they had yet to identify a decent tissue sample, Claire decided it was as good a place as any to begin her search for what she was beginning to hope she wouldn't find.

"You have a chance to analyze the specimen I collected?" Price asked.

"Briefly," replied DeLuca. He was crunched over a folding table dissecting one of his dust bunnies. With tweezers and a jeweler's loupe pinched in one eye, he gathered bits of trace evidence no bigger than grains of rice.

"Well?" said Price. "The suspense is killing me."

DeLuca set the tweezers on the table and looked up from what he was doing. His right eye was enormous beneath the loupe's magnifying lens. "See for yourself."

He selected a numbered slide from a plastic box and loaded it into a digital microscope that was wired into his laptop computer. He gently touched the mouse pad and the screensaver—a postcard-style picture of a palm-studded atoll somewhere in the South Pacific—gave way to an unfocused image. A few jabs at the keyboard and *voila*—high-res video of the world of the infinitely small.

"Is that *iroquoisii*?" Price asked.

Among other less significant items—remains of bacteria indigenous to the human intestinal tract—something far more revealing occupied center stage. Claire immediately recognized the hearty little swimmers even though now defunct and stripped of their frantic motility. "Not exactly," she answered.

Once oriented, it hadn't taken Price's discerning mind but a few instants to make the connection. "Don't tell me," he said. "That's the Pony Express, isn't it?"

"It looks like a couple of Hatcher's guys were mixing business with pleasure," DeLuca remarked blandly.

"Do you have any idea who?" asked Claire.

"The sample was pretty small," said DeLuca, "but Bishop is running it through PCR as we speak. We should have enough DNA in another hour or so to give us some answers."

Hatcher was eating a bowl of cereal in the kitchen area when Claire and Price had first entered the common room. Somewhere along the way he had quietly joined them, and now stood watching over their shoulders in mute horror.

"If it's Alan's I don't want to know." With that said, he stole away just as quietly as he had arrived.

"And the feces?" Claire asked.

"Piece of cake," Bishop called over from his workstation. "Arthur Leonelli . . ." He checked a fact sheet lying on the table in front of him. "Professor of hydrology at the University of Washington."

"Hey, McKenzie," said Price. "You get a chance to run those prints?"

McKenzie closed the lid on a DNA centrifuge and flicked the ON switch. The machine thrummed to life. "Prints also belonged to Leonelli."

"I'm beginning to think we'd be better off not knowing what went on here," said Price.

DeLuca was stressed. He massaged the back of his neck and grimaced. "Let's try to stay objective until we have all the facts.

Ethan wondered if he would ever be able to get any sleep around this place. His head throbbed, his stomach was all knotted up, and his mattress felt as if it was stuffed with old shoes. And these were the bright spots. If it wasn't Kent revving his engines every couple of hours like a frustrated Hell's Angel, it was the wind. Wind, wind— always the wind. Between the way the walls trembled and the low, plaintive whis- tle cutting through the night, he may as well have been stretched out on a wooden bench in a train station. Add to this the possibility that Alan had been . . . *had been . . . Had been what!? Don't be such an asshole. He was your best friend—you knew him better than that.* Then again what he once knew, or what he thought he had known was a thing of the past. Ancient history. Turned upside-down by a goddamned tooth. A few short months ago Ethan had been living his life. A good life. No complications. No hassles. *Now look at yourself—standing in the middle of a shitstorm without an umbrella.* He could barely keep his head above the rising tide. When the knock at his door came, he almost welcomed it. Not above sleep, but almost.

"Ethan?" It was Claire. "You in there?"

"Later," he moaned. "I'm sleeping."

"Make yourself decent, I'm coming in." She opened the door and stepped into the room, clutching a squirt-bottle of water in one hand. She squeezed some into her mouth and commented, "Love what you've done with the place."

"I said I was sleeping."

"With the light on?"

The truth: he'd been lying there contemplating Alan's tooth for the good part of an hour. He'd tucked it under his pillow the moment he'd heard Claire's voice.

"Make yourself at home," he offered ironically.

"Remember, you started it the other day when you barged into my office. At least I knocked."

Ethan rubbed his eyes. "Hand me that bottle of pills on top of my bag, will you? I've got a brutal headache."

Claire picked up the bottle and rattled it. She read the label. Skepticism creased her brow. "You're taking Xanax for a headache?"

"I'm taking aspirin for the headache," he explained. "I'm taking Xanax so I'm not so wound-up. You oughta try it sometime."

She shrugged and tossed him the pills. "Would you like a sip of my water to wash those down?"

He shook his head no and uncapped the bottle.

"Is there something you're not telling me?" she asked.

"There are a lot of things I'm not telling you." He popped two of the small white pills into his mouth and chewed them into a bitter paste. "Why?"

"Don't be obtuse. You asked me to be here, the least you can do is be straightforward with me."

He'd known this was coming. A hunch, woman's intuition, a keen eye for bullshit—call it what you will. Claire was not the sort of person you could slap a pair of blinders on and walk off a cliff.

"How you holding up so far?" he asked. "The darkness getting to you?"

"Did your team find something I should know about?"

He was momentarily stirred half-upright. "Did *you* find something?"

"Is there an echo in here?" Claire looked frustrated. She collected her thoughts and started again. "No, I didn't find anything. The feces were negative. No sign of *S. iroquoisii.*"

"And the? . . ." The thought alone made him squeamish. "*You know—*"

"Don't worry," she replied drearily. "It wasn't your body that kept Alan hanging around all these years. Though frankly I can't imagine what did."

Relief washed over Ethan and he slumped into the mattress. He didn't need any revelations—not at this juncture. The light seemed to dim. Finally, he was getting somewhere. Sleep was just around the corner—he could feel it. "If we get lucky . . ." he mumbled, remembering DeLuca's words.

"Who's Okum?" Claire asked.

Ethan's eyelids drooped, but Claire blasted him in the face with a stream of water from her squirt-bottle.

"What the fuck? . . ." he sputtered. "I was almost asleep."

"It was an accident," Claire replied brusquely. "Now who's Okum? You mentioned his name earlier when you stormed out of the lab with Alan's tooth wrapped up in your fist."

"Jesus, you sound paranoid." Ethan wiped the water from his face with the back of his sleeve. "Okum's this guy who investigates big money insurance claims. The asshole wants proof that everyone died in the explosion. Otherwise, his company won't make good on the claim filed by the expedition's financial backers. JPAC agreed to allow Okum to review their findings when we get back."

"The expedition was insured?" Claire asked, her facial expression underscored with doubt.

"For nearly ten million dollars. Igor—the probe we used to drill through the ice and record those images I emailed you—was valued at more than half of that. The remainder was intended to cover miscellaneous equipment, the station, and personal injury for every member of the team. It's one of the reasons why coming back to this hellhole was so important to me. We can't bring Alan back, but at least we can make sure that his parents end up with a nice chunk of change. It's how you're getting paid."

"Why did you wait until now to tell me all of this?" Claire was disappointed. He knew the look well.

"Because I hoped it wouldn't come up. I'm sorry. I should've been more straightforward with you. So that's the big secret. Now you see why I've been so bent about all of this. It makes me sick that my best friend has been reduced to a dollar value. But it's the best I could do under the circumstances."

As lies went, this one was truly inspired. Not only had Ethan scattered Claire's interest in Okum, he was pandering to one of her most deeply held beliefs—that money lies at the core of everything rotten. He had admitted withholding information from her, but only with the added bonus of ingratiating himself to her way of thinking.

She chewed on it for a few moments before speaking. "Are we insured?"

Ethan had anticipated this. Here was an opportunity to really sell it. "Afraid not," he said artfully and looked away.

Ethan had realized early on that appeasement for Claire meant seeing herself as a martyr. He had never known anyone who was so hard on themselves. It was too bad, but she had really grown into the role living in exile these past few years. One had merely to supply the hammer and nails and she was more than willing to undertake the dirty work of crucifying herself. In this way she was like her mother. There was no pleasure in playing her against herself—especially after all he'd put her through since Vietnam—but the less she knew about their reasons for being here, the better chance he had of getting them both home intact and alive. He didn't want another death on his hands, particularly hers. Even after all this time he still cared for her.

"Why?" she asked.

"No one would touch us this time around. Too risky. Anyway, it's in the hands of the government. If anything bad happens—so what? What's a few million tax dollars? Plenty more where that came from, right?"

"That reminds me . . ." she broke off casually, apparently satisfied. "Dinner'll be ready soon. Price wanted me to let you know."

"Tell him thanks, but I'm going to try to get some sleep."

Claire stopped at the door on her way out. "What kind of food did you guys eat the first time around? I know Alan couldn't cook, and you're no wiz in the kitchen."

"Nothing special. Everything was pretty much dehydrated. Compliments of the Just-Add-Water Gourmet."

"No barbecue?"

"Barbecue . . ." he chuckled. "Even when the sun was up it was fifty below out. We'd have been lucky to get a fire started."

"Because I found this metal grate near the site of the explosion . . ." she went on. "I don't know, it just seemed out of place, that's all. It reminded me of a grill from one of those portable hibachi barbecues—you know, the little rectangular ones you bring on picnics. Only this was bigger." She approximated the general dimensions with her hands.

Okum's monkeys! A cage door—what else could she be talking about? He'd wondered about them earlier—when a hairy limb was going to turn up in the wreckage and point Claire down a path of inquiry without end. Fortunately, she was way off base. *Time to throw her another bone.* "Now that you mention it, Leonelli—"

"And you couldn't have done any grilling indoors, or it would've set off the fire extinguishers. You would've had pink foam everywhere."

Shit! Like he'd told DeLuca, nothing got by her.

"Oh, I'm sorry," said Claire. "Did I cut you off? What about Leonelli? You were saying? . . ."

The onset of perpetual night in Antarctica entailed more than just the changing of the seasons. It was the cosmic equivalent of a psychotic break. Summer on the white continent was governed by what climatologists called "fads," capricious weather systems that came and went like fashion trends. Winter, however, was a source of pure malignance. A ravenous white locust swarm that devoured everything in its path. The wind could blow so hard and for such extended duration that the landscape itself could be reshaped, disfigured, carved anew as if by knife-blade. And when the veil of darkness finally lifted what was once familiar was often unrecognizable. It was both good news and bad news that they found themselves straddling this seasonal cusp. Bad news because inclement weather conditions had kept them off the site of the derelict station for nearly four days. Good news because it could have just as easily been forty.

It was this loss of precious time that had prompted DeLuca to step things up and conduct the evidence-gathering end of the operation in three-person shifts beginning each day at sun up. Now that they'd had a chance to survey the site and complete their preliminary analyses, he had concluded that expediency was the best and only way to prevent further loss of evidence to the elements. If they futzed around too long there'd be nothing left for them to find. Though Witz had been tracking the weather via satellite uplink and was guardedly optimistic about the long-range forecast, there was no guarantee that it would hold.

Although Claire had been anxious to return to the site armed with a new awareness of the previous expedition's objectives and a growing burden of suspicions, this was not why or how she had hoped to secure a slot with the first shift to return to the derelict station.

The day before yesterday she was showering after one of her grueling workout sessions with Price when the power suddenly cut out. One moment she was enveloped in a warm cascade of water and steam, the next, she was trapped inside a vertical tomb—alone, cold, smothering in balmy darkness. She'd managed to hold on for what seemed like an eternity—comforting herself with logic and a useless array of empowering phrases—but the tricks the shrinks had taught her were no more effective now than at any other time of crisis in her life. Avoidance was, and always would be, her primary coping mechanism when it came to her fear of the dark. It wasn't a cure but worked well enough in Los Angeles where day and night divided the cosmos equitably. But here, this time of year . . . *What did you expect?* Denial and a stiff upper lip could only go so far. She had cheated her way through this much of it, back-burnering her fear as much for Hatcher's sake as her own. A small part of her had even begun to believe that she was doing okay, reaping the benefits of immersion therapy. But then she hadn't really immersed herself, had she? As long as she remained inside the station she was insulated against the darkness. Pathetic, but this was her security blanket: warm, windowless, well-lighted.

Then the power had cut out and it was as if someone had broken open an anthill and a billion particles of darkness had crashed over her in a single voracious wave. She screamed, crumpling into an insignificant ball of childish fright and torment. And when the lights had come back on—all of this because someone had forgotten to put fuel in the goddamn generator—they were standing over her, Hatcher and the others. A portrait of shame and concern.

"She's afraid of the dark," Hatcher explained simply. He then covered her with a towel in an uncharacteristic show of compassion and ushered the others from the bathroom so Claire could be alone in her humility.

No one had spoken of it since. Not Hatcher. Not DeLuca. And certainly not her. But it was on all of their minds—she was sure of it. How ridiculous she must have looked to them—as vulnerable and afflicted as a victim of real tragedy. Now whenever she was around them she was uncomfortably self-aware. Her nakedness in the shower now manifested itself in a more profound and personal way. She had been rendered emotionally naked and this added degree of exposure was that much more awful to bear. The group dynamic, though, did not change, and for this she was grateful. Everyone went on as if nothing had happened, and Claire was more than willing to entertain their polite delusions.

She was sure the incident in the shower was why she had been selected as a member of the first shift. DeLuca hadn't come out and said as much—he wouldn't out of respect for her—but Claire knew that it wasn't accidental. Out of pity, he had given her the remaining daylight. A scant two hours of comfort in a world that had grown irrevocably black in the past forty-eight hours.

Although she, Price and Bishop were saddled with the burden of setting up a perimeter of floodlights, lugging the heavy equipment across the ice was infinitely preferable to the darkness that would await the next team. Standing in the field of debris near the blast's epicenter, the urgency upon which DeLuca had based his decision to step things up became abundantly clear to her. According to Witz, the gusts that had driven them off the site four days ago were mild when compared to those that ravaged the dark winter months ahead. The field of debris was much less localized than it had been. Scattered and rearranged as if by an oceanic current, it was now spread out over a much greater circumference.

If nothing else, their preliminary findings had convinced DeLuca that the cumbersome hazmat suits were an unnecessary precaution. So far *S. iroquoisii* was nowhere to be found. Claire wasn't as warm like this, but a thick neoprene mask and polarized goggles kept her face from freezing.

"Plug us in," said Price, "and make sure we have power."

For electricity they had run a power cord all the way from the new station. This had been Claire's responsibility. Fortunately her load had grown lighter with each step. Otherwise she would never have made it. She did as Price had asked and connected the floodlights. White halogen illumination displaced the murky dawn.

"We're in business," announced Price. "What about you, Bishop? Got juice?"

Bishop didn't respond. Something had caught his eye near where he was setting up the floodlights. He'd dropped to his knees to get a closer look. He was now using his gloved hand to gently dust away a partial covering of snow from the object in question.

"What is it?" Price called over to him.

"Nothing . . ." Bishop replied wonderingly. Even at thirty-plus feet Claire could see the look of astonishment trapped beneath his goggles. "You guys finish what you're doing."

But Claire was already on the move. In all probability, Hatcher had lied to her about the metal grate. If not overtly, then by omission. Of course he would try to dismiss his confusion as a side effect of the Xanax, but she knew better. Though why and about what he had lied was still unclear. If Bishop had discovered something significant Claire wanted in on the ground floor. From now on it was eyes wide open.

"Is that a—?"

Bishop sat on his heels and nodded. "I know it's not easy but we see this sort of thing all the time." He looked over his shoulder. "Price, bring one of those kits over here, will ya?"

It had been one thing for Claire to tell herself that she was ready for anything, but finding someone's index finger beneath a thin dusting snow wasn't the *anything* she had prepared herself for. But here it was, cocked at the second knuckle like a comma in a half-uttered phrase. It was odd—a finger alone and disconnected. No context, no frame of reference. A glass slipper without an owner. No brain to articulate it, to tell it what to do. Smaller than she would've thought, yet larger for the same reason. This was a piece of someone—insignificant by itself, but essential as part of the whole. Only something terrible could divest one of interest in such a coveted asset. From the cradle to the grave. Bishop collected the finger with a forceps Price handed him, and deposited it into a small Ziploc bag.

While waiting out the storm DeLuca's team had positively identified two more victims of the blast from partial remains: Gary Northcutt and Kjell Hamsun. Combined, there wasn't enough left of the two men to fill a coffee cup: a diamond-shaped fragment of occipital bone, a partial vertebra that looked as if it had been ejected out of a supernova, and bits and pieces of uncertain origin. No soft tissue, though. Nothing that might harbor traces of *S. iroquoisii*. The finger was a real opportunity.

"May I?" Claire asked.

Bishop handed her the Ziploc.

The flesh along the top and bottom of the finger had a sort of raw, freezer-burned look—a mottled mingling of gray and bluish-white. The fingernail was chalk white but for a thin ochre crescent underscoring the lead edge after the fashion of a French manicure. The flesh on the sides of the finger had a sort of patina to it, a warm bronzing that was deepest and darkest at the high points and diminished to virtually nothing in the articulation valleys marking the knuckles. Tiny black particles—Claire assumed they were bits of ash—speckled the singed flesh.

"This discoloration along the edges . . ." said Claire, holding the bag up so Bishop could see it. "What do you think caused it?"

Bishop peered at the finger. "Heat from the explosion most likely."

"You said the heat generated by the explosion was thousands of degrees. Wouldn't the entire finger have been incinerated? Or charred beyond recognition? I'm no expert, but this looks more like the result of something you'd see on the *Food Network*." Claire studied Bishop's eyes.

Price laughed. "What are you trying to say?"

"Nothing," said Claire. "The way it looks—the browning here—just reminds me of when my mother used to braise chicken drumsticks for *coq au vin*."

"You've been hanging around us too long," said Bishop. He patted her on the back. "But you're right—it looks like link sausage that needs a couple more turns in the frying pan."

"It's actually the way the bone looks that put the thought in my head." Claire shook the finger into a corner of the bag so that the severed end was clearly visible. "See how clean the cut is . . . Right here. The end of the bone is uniform. I don't know . . . I'm probably crazy, but it looks deliberate. An explosion couldn't do that, could it?"

"Absolutely," Price explained. "Razor sharp debris, broken glass, pieces of metal traveling at hundreds of feet per second . . . The thing about explosions is you never know what to expect."

Bishop gave a gentle tug on the bag and it slipped from between Claire's fingers. He studied his find one last time before placing it in the specimen kit. "You said you wanted a tissue sample. That's about as big a chunk of tissue as I expect we'll find." His blue eyes twinkled strangely.

"Shouldn't there be more of that?" asked Claire. "Parts?"

"Parts?" Price echoed.

"Fingers, toes? . . ."

"I don't know about you two," Bishop interrupted, "but I can't feel my fingers *or* toes. I need to get my blood pumping or I'll be frozen in place."

They combed the blast perimeter for remains, expanding their search to keep up with the thoughtless hand of the wind. Claire was optimistic that the finger could provide them with information. There was a good chance that *S. iroquoisii* would reveal itself in trace amounts provided the sample was large enough. She was considering how to best exploit the sudden abundance of tissue at her disposal when she happened upon something familiar. It was the metal grate, Hatcher's alleged barbecue grill.

She knelt and examined the grate—this time more closely than before. If she could only find some sort of identifying mark—a serial number, or . . . *Jackpot!* A small steel nameplate was welded to the bars near one of the corners. The surface was badly charred and smudged with ash, but using her glove and a sprinkling of ice crystals as a mild abrasive she managed to buff away enough so that a single word became visible. She immediately recognized the logo from a handful of specialized biology labs she'd reluctantly attended as a grad student.

LAB-I-TAT

Claire held the grate in front of her face and looked through the slats. *A cage! How could I be so blind? Lab animals. The first team was working with lab animals!* So Hatcher and the others had planned on more than simply proving *S. iroquoisii's* existence. They wanted to test it out for themselves. Claire had no idea why—evolutionary biology wasn't exactly Hatcher's forte. But then it was obvious, wasn't it? *S. iroquoisii* was the only thing he hadn't taken from her. Not yet. And now the CDC was trying to take it from him.

She admired the poetical symmetry of events, but why include her at all? Why expose himself like this? Simple, Hatcher was an armchair scientist; he needed a technician to quantify the data. Now that Alan was gone, Claire was his best shot at nailing down the facts. He knew she'd fight for her baby, that she'd go to just about any length to remove it from the realm of menace. She would make the CDC understand, convince them not to poison the lake. Hatcher could then publish the findings and collect the accolades.

"What you got there?" Price asked.

"Junk," said Claire, chucking aside the grate.

She doubted that JPAC had the faintest idea of the extent to which it was being used. Or was even interested for that matter. Hatcher had it all figured out. The CDC would get their proof that everything was hunky-dory, Okum could confirm that the insurance claim was legit, and Hatcher, the scheming bum, would come out smelling like a gardenia. Scientist, concerned citizen, dedicated friend. *God, it was sickening.* If Claire was just a little more vindictive she could've blindsided him right then and there with a minimum of collateral damage. Alan's parents would still get the insurance money, but as for the rest of it . . . By overstating the threat, she could've easily convinced the CDC to proceed with its plan to poison the lake. It was the last thing in the world Hatcher would've expected of her. Infanticide on a grand scale. Especially not after . . . The look on his face would have almost been worth it. But she was lugging around too many skeletons already. She couldn't. She wouldn't. This was a one-of-a-kind ecosystem. Claire was too close to realizing one of her life's greatest ambitions to turn back now. At the very least she could hang with it a few more days, take a closer look at the finger, stick with the program. In other words, she would play along like a good little dupe while figuring out a way to beat Hatcher at his own game. *S. iroquoisii* could either take its place among evolution's exalted success stories, or Claire could do nothing at all and allow the most meaningful discovery since DNA to languish in base ignominy like the hapless dodo.

If there was a silver lining to all of this, it existed in inverse proportion to the growing awareness of her naiveté. More and more it was looking as if Hatcher was confident, perhaps even certain, that *S. iroquoisii* was a reality. But he wasn't just going to come out and say it. This saddled Claire with the burden of proof.

As she explored the intact portion of the station she found herself walking a fine line between morbid fascination and professional curiosity. She had done a lot of thinking since McKenzie had first asked her about the potential effects of *S. iroquoisii* on human hosts—its calling card. And the more she had thought about his question, the more she disliked the answers she was coming up with. Primitive organisms were one thing—their biological needs existed in a pure and fluid state, unimpeded by the irrational and lofty demands of the human ego. Simple creatures, simple needs. Territory, sustenance, reproduction. For millions of years nearly every species on earth had pursued these ends with indefatigable vigor. And but for one notable exception, none had ever succeeded to the extent that its survival ethic had gone and upset the natural equilibrium.

Of course the one notable exception was man. *Homo sapiens* had thrown everything off kilter the day the rough beast had slouched out of the jungle three million years ago, give or take. For man, it wasn't enough to merely survive. Gratification, both physical and psychological, was his hallmark. While other life forms adapted to accommodate the equilibrium, mankind had a nasty habit of going for broke with anything he laid his hands on. Give an amoeba a few extra drops of pond water and it was happy to while away the afternoon doing the backstroke. But give a man a few of those same drops and he was apt to develop a thirst for empire: Genghis Khan, Henry VIII, Hitler. Extrapolation was the magic word. Reproduction begets destructive lust: Don Juan, the Marquis de Sade, Caligula. *The traces of semen in Leonelli's feces?* Sustenance: obesity, bulimia, Father Tererro's Iroquois braves cannibalizing their victims. Goodbye, equilibrium. Hello, winner-take-all.

Even apes, our evolutionary cousins, didn't behave this way. Blame it on an undeveloped sense of manifest destiny, but no one could tell her that the nest in the corner of the storage room was the work of a human. Claire had wondered at the identity of the occupant of the LAB-I-TAT, the mournful eyes she might've seen staring back at her from behind the cold steel grate. Now she had her answer—forty rolls of toilet paper clotted with pink fire-extinguishing foam. She remembered her Jane Goodall. *Too well . . .* she'd been showing the Gombe documentary to her general biology class every fourth week of the semester for the better part of five years. Chimpanzees. The Cadillac of lab animals and closest thing to an analog of man.

Claire collected several dozen coarse black hairs from the makeshift bedding and sealed them in a specimen bag. Her newfound awareness begged another question— this one, potentially more revealing than any she had asked as of yet. How far had the previous team progressed in their work? Had they actually introduced *S. iroquoisii* to a living host—the chimp? If so, what had been the effect? Fireworks or a dud? How long did it take the chimp abandon its "home" in the LAB-I-TAT and set up camp in here, in the storage room? Before the explosion or after? Who had decided that the cage was no longer appropriate—the chimp or the scientists? When, and under what circumstances? Even chimps born and bred in captivity could be a handful.

Claire was squatting over the nest, fast-forwarding through one scenario after another when she was overcome by a very old and sickening sensation. The cool insect skitter of watching eyes electrified her spine. She peeked over her shoulder: alone. It was getting to her—the cold, the darkness, the ugly little pieces falling into place one by one. The derelict station may have no longer been capable of serving the interests of science, but it made one hell of a haunted house. The chill that plagued her was real though. She had better get moving before hypothermia got a foothold on her circulatory system.

It was true what they said—the clothes make the man. It was also true that a good dresser knew how to accessorize. For southern belles it was the corsage. For homicidal nut jobs . . . Well, Ethan had just what the costume designer ordered. In fact, he had only minutes ago laid his hands on it. And purely by luck. Ninety-nine percent perspiration, one percent inspiration—his ensemble was now complete.

If there was any doubt as to just how whacked-out he looked—black hooded parka, heavy black insulated pants, black goggles with reflective lenses, black mask—it was swiftly laid to rest by Claire's reaction as she emerged from the storage room and saw him looming there in the half-lit corridor clutching Ellis's ice axe. He was an ominous sight—world-class mountaineer, Reinhold Messner meets Darth Vader. Poor, unsuspecting Claire was too busy making lemon popsicles in her pants to offer an intelligible critique but he could weigh-in with her later. A shrill note—half hiccup, half shriek—escaped her lips before she could rein it in. Ethan forced himself not to laugh. It was cruel, particularly after her little breakdown in the shower, but she had asked him not to treat her any differently than before. Hell, she'd practically begged.

"Asshole!" Claire blurted as she attempted to storm past him.

The corridor was narrow and he easily blocked her path. "I'm sorry," he said, unable to stifle a chuckle. "I couldn't resist when I saw you in there all alone."

"Okay, Ethan, you got me," she choked. "Now let me go, I've got work to do."

Claire almost never lost her head, but he could make out enough of her face beneath her goggles to see that she was genuinely scared. He'd gotten the answer he was looking for: the armor was still off.

"I was only having a little fun," he said.

Claire was rigid, unresponsive. She looked him squarely in the eye although he knew it was merely coincidental. His eyes, after all, were hidden behind a convex plastic mirror.

"Go ahead," Ethan invited her, raising his arms over his head. "Take your best shot. I have it coming."

Claire's response was so sudden and decisive that he didn't have time to brace himself. She caught him just beneath the ribs with this sort of lightning quick judo punch that expelled the air from his lungs in a hoarse whoosh. Gasping, he doubled over and she breezed past him.

"Don't worry about me," he moaned. "Just a punctured lung. Nothing a few hours of emergency surgery won't fix."

Ethan dragged himself into his old quarters, threw back the blankets now covered in pink foam, and collapsed on the bed. He lay on his back and stared at the ceiling. After a minute or two, the nausea dissipated. No bones about it, Claire brought out the masochist in him. He'd probably never be able to hold down solid food again, yet all he could think about was how good she looked on the treadmill losing to Price each day. Not an ounce of jiggle anywhere on her from head to toe. Daddy Jim may have been a raging drunk and wife-beater, but this hadn't prevented him from siring some pedigree hoof.

Based on the initial damage reports, Ethan had assumed that what little he'd brought in the way of personal property had been destroyed. He hadn't even given the situation much thought until now. Most of it was easily replaceable and not particularly valuable. There were two items, however, that he hoped dearly would turn up. The first was an authentic game-worn Kirk Gibson Dodgers jersey that Ethan wore when he needed good luck. Given to him by his father in acknowledgement of the completion of Ethan's doctoral dissertation—a Hatcher family first—the jersey had never let him down. It was as close to a sacred object as there was in his life. That he had forgotten it for a time proved just how preoccupied he had been with all of what had been going on.

The second item, the one his ass depended on, was a handheld digital camcorder that Okum had provided so that the team could chronicle the expedition. Compact and highly sophisticated, the slick little camcorder embodied the latest in HD technology. Small enough to be easily concealed and good in just about any light, it was ideally suited for the amateur boudoir videographer. Ethan had even thought about keeping it for himself when their work here was done. One could argue that this would've been pushing his luck, but of course he had devised a little something to cover his skinny white ass. By sending him to Antarctica, Okum had actually done him a favor. Albeit in a roundabout, punitive sort of way.

Ethan understood that Okum's insistence he record every phase of their work was just one more way of keeping tabs on him. Ethan planned on fulfilling his end of the deal by providing Okum with the best damn collection of home movies the bastard had ever seen, but he also planned on keeping a copy for himself. He would present it with the rest of the team's findings after lying low for a bit upon his return to Los Angeles. Considering the magnitude of the discovery, he would become a household name overnight. Uncle Sam wouldn't have the balls to touch him then. Out of fairness he wouldn't mention their interest in Ivan as a bio-weapon. And they wouldn't dare kill him. They couldn't. *Listen up, Wayne, I've taken measures to ensure that our secret remain a secret as long as I find myself in good health. Capiche? But if I so much as catch a sniffle . . .* Even if Okum popped off and went public with Ethan's financial transgressions, there wasn't a university on God's green earth that wouldn't be willing to look the other way and roll out the red carpet. Anything shy of cold-blooded murder would be peanuts when stacked against the kind of cachet a Nobel Prize would earn the name Dr. Ethan Hatcher, not to mention any institution with which he was associated.

Before Ethan had believed that everything had been destroyed, he'd envisioned select episodes from the historic record becoming part of a *Discovery Channel* prime time special. But of course that dream had died when he'd learned of the utter devastation left by the explosion. So complete had been his own devastation that it wasn't until just now that it occurred to him that the camcorder may have actually survived. *If so* . . . And like that he was back on his feet tearing the place apart.

Nothing was where it should have been. By all appearances the room had already been ransacked. He rummaged through a mishmash of wadded-up clothes, assorted personal effects and noxious pink goo, but his Kirk Gibson jersey was gone. *Fuck!* It was all Ethan had left of his old man. That and regrets. Talk about a punch in the gut! He continued his search for the camcorder, however after several minutes had turned up nothing but the lens cap and a trampled-on product registration card. What he was really after were the extra memory cards they had brought—four total, one of which he'd filled and swapped out for a blank before he'd left for LA. Where the others had gone was anybody's guess. Just as it was anybody's guess what, if anything, the cards contained. 100+ gigabytes of irrefutable evidence . . . *maybe*. Those cards might hold his Get Out of Jail Free card. If they existed in any way, shape, or form he had to find them.

Ethan was sucking wind by the time he had finished searching the room Northcutt had shared with Leonelli. It was more of the same. Junk everywhere, but no memory cards. He was emptying the contents of someone's brown vinyl shaving kit onto the floor when DeLuca poked his head in the door.

"What are you looking for?" he asked, regarding Ethan with circumspect eyes.

"I want to know what happened to my team."

DeLuca entered the room and looked around. "About that," he said casually. "I think it would be best if Dr. Matthews and yourself left this end of it to us from here on out."

Ethan removed a bottle of Old Spice from the shaving kit, unscrewed the cap and wafted it under his nose. The high concentration of alcohol in the cologne had prevented it from freezing. "What'd she find?"

DeLuca dug a baggie out of his pocket and dangled it in front of Ethan's face. "Actually, it was Bishop's find. However, Dr. Matthews made some interesting points."

"A finger, so what?" Ethan was too concerned about the disks to give it much thought. "Isn't that what explosions do?" He capped the bottle of Old Spice and returned it to the shaving kit.

"Whoever the finger belonged to didn't lose it in the explosion. At least it doesn't appear that way. The cut is too neat. It looks deliberate. There, at the juncture of the metacarpal and phalange . . . See how the edge of the bone is smooth—"

Ethan lost track of what he'd been doing. This was more than even the Xanax could handle. "Yes, I see," he replied calmly. "You can get it out of my face now."

"And take a look at these burns. They're not what we usually see in cases like this. The charring is only superficial, much too even for the suddenness and intensity of the heat we're talking about."

The shaving kit slipped from Ethan's hand and fell to the floor. "What's this got to do with Claire? . . ." he stammered. ". . . Dr. Matthews?"

Unflinching, DeLuca returned the baggie to his pocket. "She said the browning reminded her of when her mother used to prepare *coq au vin*. I might not have thought of it myself if she hadn't pointed it out."

"What's that supposed to mean?" Ethan didn't like where this was going.

"Maybe your guys ran out of food."

Ethan cut him off. "Just stop. There was enough food here to last them a month. Even if they had run out, all they had to do was dial up McMurdo for a little room service."

"You've seen the storage room . . . Look at this place. You remember what Dr. Matthews said about Ivan kicking up the biological imperatives—territory, reproduction . . ." DeLuca paused and concluded his point with greater emphasis. ". . . *sustenance*. If there's one thing history has taught us it's that the way to a man's dark side is through his stomach. Under the right circumstances hunger can be a powerful enemy. Just ask Jeff Dahmer."

"What do you plan to do with Claire? She's not going to just sit tight and look at Facebook all day."

"We'll keep her busy in the lab until we wrap things up. Let her do what she was brought here to do—give Ivan a face. If that doesn't do the trick, I've got a little surprise for her."

Ethan didn't want to know but he asked anyway. It was becoming a bad habit of his. "Surprise?"

"You just do your job and let me worry about that."

"You know what, DeLuca, get fucked."

DeLuca continued with the imperturbable calm of a funeral director. "You'll be glad to hear that we might be out of here sooner than we thought. Heck, if it wasn't for the chimp DNA that keeps popping up we might already be home."

"It's still too early to be jumping to any conclusions," said Ethan. He needed time. He needed to find those memory cards. Without proof that Ivan existed he was screwed. "You said so yourself."

"That was before certain facts came to light."

"Piss off."

"Price heard back from our translator. Those Chinese characters scribbled on the wall in Whitehurst's room . . . among other less intelligible things, it was a last will and testament."

Whether it was Hatcher's little scare back in the derelict station or the trek home through the diminishing light, something had put Claire on edge. Even with some of the pieces falling into place she couldn't pretend to understand what had transpired in the last days of Alan's life. And this—not knowing—is what grated on her the most. Ignorance was vulnerability. She had even begun to second-guess herself. The hairs, for example—why had she even bothered to collect them? She knew they belonged to a chimp, just as she knew that the LAB-I-TAT had not housed a man. No matter how deep she dug she wasn't going to get the answers she was looking for. Wasn't it enough to see that Alan and the others were acknowledged for their discovery? She was doing it again—planting the flag before she had reached the summit. Despite how things looked, nothing had actually been confirmed. *S. iroquoisii* was still only a theory. Maybe Hatcher was right. Maybe she was being paranoid. She was upset because the expedition's objectives didn't fall in line with her own idealized sense of right and wrong. She had to let go of this chip on her shoulder—this me against the world mind-set. She didn't need another pygmy rhinoceros on her back.

It was a thing of beauty to see Price run. After losing to him on the treadmill five days in a row, Claire was convinced that it didn't matter if she ran first, second or downhill. She was beginning to think that he was unbeatable. He could sustain a pace that would have qualified him for any number of Olympic events, or so it seemed. The guy was just so fit and so determined that it was like racing Secretariat. If there was one thing Claire had learned getting her ass kicked day in and day out, it was that she was an even bigger glutton for punishment than she had realized. The worse she lost, the more she pressed for a rematch. Even their post-run workouts were now presided over by a competitive atmosphere although Price was clearly her superior in every physical challenge they had so far attempted. It was fun but it was also pitiful. Claire knew that she was trying to get back what she had lost when the lights cut out. She wasn't only competing against Price, she was competing against herself. One way or another, the outcome was the same. She was losing, and she was losing badly.

Price was coaching her through a relentless circuit of pushups, crunches and leg raises when Hatcher poked his head in the storage room door.

"DeLuca's done with the finger," he announced simply. "He says it's your turn now."

Before Claire was allowed to undertake her hunt for *S. iroquoisii*, DeLuca had first wanted to run some tests of his own, the most relevant of which involved establishing the victim's identity by way of fingerprint analysis.

"It was an easy match," he said. "But it doesn't really help our cause all that much. The finger belonged to Northcutt. We still need to account for the whereabouts of Ellis, Schmidt, and Lim."

"What about Leonelli?" asked Claire. "Anything else turn up yet?"

"Leonelli's right here," said McKenzie. "We found him during the second shift about twenty yards beyond the blast perimeter. The wind must've uncovered him. That's probably why we missed him before."

Claire was confused. McKenzie hovered over a large, rectangular Tupperware casserole that was loosely covered with one of those cheap decorative dishtowels bundled three to a pack featuring various kitchen motifs—in this case mushrooms and onions. Like a magician unveiling his latest illusion, he whipped off the dishtowel and revealed what lay beneath. Even though the gruesome artifact had been exposed to the elements for several weeks, the stench of charred flesh still hung over it. Nothing Claire imagined could have driven off the stubborn odor that flooded her nostrils and sluiced down the back of her throat like wet cremains. She clamped her hand over her mouth and nose to keep the contents of her stomach from coming up. It was the smell more than anything—the extreme caramelization of fats and proteins and chemical residues she innately recognized as those carrying on the mechanical processes of life in her own body. She could see herself in the burned-out eye sockets staring back at her from the blackened husk, a partial bust—really that's all it was—wedged diagonally in the burp-seal container, but still worse, worse by any thinkable standard, was the fact that she could smell herself on death's ashen breath.

"Notice how his teeth are clenched . . ." McKenzie directed her, indicating the blackened dentition with a pencil eraser. "We see this in burn victims quite often—the body closes off the airways to protect the lungs."

Bishop nodded in agreement. "The dead never give up their secrets without a fight."

Before Claire could recover, Hatcher jumped in and threw the dishtowel back over the remains. "What the hell's wrong with you?" he demanded, swelling angrily before McKenzie.

"I thought—" McKenzie began.

"Like fuck you did!" Hatcher shouted, wheeling on DeLuca. "This was your idea." He grabbed DeLuca by the shirt and got in his face. "Leave her the hell alone!"

DeLuca started to say something but Claire interrupted before things got any uglier. "Ethan, I'm fine. The smell got to me, that's all. Seriously," she said, taking him gently by the arm. "I'm good."

"She's good," DeLuca echoed. "She's a big girl, she can handle herself." He was calm and made no attempt to extricate himself from Hatcher's grasp.

Although Claire acknowledged what DeLuca was saying she got the sense that his motives weren't exactly in keeping with his words. She knew when someone was feeling her out, looking for a soft spot. Rubbing her face in it like that was a cheap shot, but it wasn't anything new to her. Most men simply couldn't resist an opportunity to flex their lack of compassion. That's what made Eric different from the rest. To him, compassion was a sign of strength not weakness.

Hatcher glared at both of them, released DeLuca and stormed from the room. Claire stuck to her story, even going so far as to express a desire to examine Leonelli's remains when McKenzie had concluded his analysis. "The skull seems to be more or less intact," she remarked with the effortless detachment of her male colleagues. "I'd like to take a look at some of the brain tissue if any survived."

Northcutt's severed index finger awaited Claire's inspection like a cheap Halloween prank. In thawing, the flesh had lost some of its earlier bluishness. What was not ghostly pale was tinted a rich golden bronze. She couldn't help thinking it again—*coq au vin*. Although the process of decay had been held in check by the extreme cold, the finger now emitted a pungent odor that was partly familiar. A stranger to decomposition, she wrote it off as one of many chemical signatures all humans have an indigenous understanding of, much like the smoky breath of Leonelli's scorched remains.

Using a scalpel, she shaved away several paper-thin pieces of the dermis. These, she examined under a microscope though she didn't expect to find anything in samples of superficial tissue. *S. iroquoisii* would almost certainly be a deep diver, a traveler of the arterial conduits that supplied the brain with life. But that would come later. As she cut more deeply into the flesh she was disappointed at the scarcity of blood. What little remained was totally congealed and more closely resembled grape jelly than blood at all. It didn't take Claire long to realize that Northcutt's finger wasn't, as Bishop had intimated, ready to give up any secrets.

An evening out—it was exactly what Claire needed. She and the other members of the team—all except Kent who had remained behind to keep an eye on his precious Osprey—piled into the tundra buggy and slowly picked their way across the ice field with Hatcher at the helm. Although this was the guy Claire had once tried unsuccessfully to teach to parallel park, he was fairly competent with the tandem joysticks used to guide the growling machine as it crunched noisily over what sounded like a mixture of broken light bulbs and eggshells. Tiny cyclones of ice crystals zigzagged in and out of the blinding swath of the buggy's oversized halogen headlamps. The passenger compartment was laid out like that of a school bus. Six parallel rows of molded plastic bench seats, two on each side of a central aisle, provided adequate seating for twelve. Unlike most of the hand-me-down junk that wound up on research expeditions everything seemed to be in good working order. This wasn't some aging beast of burden put out to pasture by an erstwhile philanthropist hoping to cash in on a good tax write-off. It was even clean. The residual scent of a strong commercial antiseptic occupied the cozy bubble of warmth shuttling them across the ice.

"So tell me again," said Bishop. "Why are we doing this?"

"*Glasnost*," said Hatcher. "Besides, it'll be nice to have a home-cooked meal after all that packaged junk we've been eating."

Just inside the entrance of the Russian station stood a fifty-five gallon fuel drum filled nearly to capacity with homemade vodka. A length of black rubber hose used to siphon the contents within lay coiled atop the drum like an asp prepared to strike at anyone unwary or unwise enough to pass within reach of its fangs. Into which category Claire fell, she didn't know exactly. Soon enough though she would discover just how apropos was her first impression of the drum and its menacing keeper. Her first sip convinced her that the dubious libation certainly had bite and was not as smooth as the silk lining Lenin's casket as Zhenya, a small scruffy man wearing several layers of clothes, had suggested while topping off battered tin cups prior to dinner. But she was getting ahead herself.

Although the drum of vodka was, with regard to scientific expeditions, odd by conventional standards, it was totally in keeping with the rest of her immediate surroundings. The interior of the station was every bit as disheveled and defunct as the snow-blown junkyard through which they had passed in attempting to locate the entrance. Inside and out, the place looked as if it had been decorated by the indiscriminate hand of a suicide bomber. There was no way of knowing with any degree of certainty what was debris and what was still being used. *Russian moonshiners*, thought Claire, as she sidestepped a computer lying in several pieces opposite the drum of vodka—a tangle of wires and disembodied circuit boards.

Whether out of whimsy or boredom—she was inclined to think of it as the latter—someone had placed a crude likeness of a bird fashioned from a soda can in the center of the tangle of wires as if nesting. It was a theme echoed elsewhere in virtually every corner of what was to Claire looking more and more like a backwater shanty and not a hub of scientific observation. The place was inundated with the ungainly creatures, dozens of them, hundreds, hatched from virtually every flavor of soda known to man. They dangled from the ceiling on lengths of dental floss though it was easy to imagine that jagged razor-sharp wings held them aloft. Coke, 7-Up, orange, ginger ale, root beer—premium and discount brands alike, diet and caffeine-free—an avian taxonomy rendered entirely in aluminum. The curious little birds occupied the nooks and crevices between pots and pans, stacks of unlaundered clothing, dog-eared books and government manuals, spent propane canisters—all of which were scattered about the perimeter of the room. They were either on, next to, or inside virtually everything. Like an ecosystem stripped of its natural predators, the station was being overrun.

Claire nearly stepped on one as she squeezed in the door to make room for the others behind her. It was eerie—all these birds. The idea that someone would lend so much of themselves to such a frivolous pursuit was creepy. The tedium, the pure stir-craziness of it . . . It was disarming to say the least. But if she had been disarmed by the multitudes of soda can birds all around her, then it was safe to say that she was blown away by her first impression of their hosts.

There were four of them, all relatively young, and none of whom acted the part of dedicated climatologist. Zhenya, the one who had greeted them at the door, was perhaps twenty-five though would have had no trouble convincing Claire that he was closer to forty-five. He had striking blue eyes, though the whites were dull and ashy, full, almost feminine lips, and a head of unkempt ginger hair that hadn't known brush or comb in ages. He wasn't gaunt exactly, but his cheekbones and jaw line had acquired the lean angularity that comes with poor nutrition.

Maksim (to them he was simply Max), wore the gloomy smile of a paint-by-numbers portrait of a hobo. Like Zhenya, he was grubby and unshaven. His clothes looked slept-in and had the soiled sheen of homeless shelter hand-me-downs. Although friendly enough, it was difficult to get a handle on what made him tick. No sooner would he embark on one course of dialogue then something totally unrelated would snag his attention and he would go rambling off in another direction. Claire wondered how a poster boy for ADD had been able to make it all the way through school and land such an important post with the Russian Weather Service.

Shurik was a big man with ponderous features and flesh that was the pinkish-brown hue of bologna. Apparently, he was the one in charge of the weather station, though Claire wondered at his qualifications. Although his English was considerably better than the rest of the team, Claire didn't see a connection between bilingualism and rank in a region whose official language was spoken by some seventeen species of penguin, but not by any humans. Nonetheless, the others deferred to him—never directly, though with a tacit awareness of his place atop the chain of command. Shurik had blunt powerful limbs, a low barren voice, and regretted his small badly weathered ears, above and about which his hair was cropped almost to the root. This was in discrepant contrast with the roiling jet-black beard thicketing the lower half of his face. When he spoke—usually in an aggressive surge dominated by gruff imperatives—his coffee-stained teeth flashed wolfishly. Claire's first impression of him was that of a character from, of all things, a Russian fairytale. A solitary woodsman or a fugitive baker who counted unsuspecting children among the many secret ingredients in his delicious potpies. His eyes were too small for his face and were opaque with the inbred resignation of a beast of burden. He carried himself as if evolution had equipped him to bear the weight of the world on his broad shoulders, and it was perhaps because of this that Claire felt sorry for him.

Finally, there was Alyona, the only woman among them. And only she seemed to have eluded the ravages of confinement and isolation. Then again, she *was* wearing makeup. So it was only a little eyeliner and a pat or two of powder to buffer the body's natural oils and give her complexion a matte finish . . . Beneath it all she was perhaps just as dissipated as the others. *Who are you kidding? Admit it—the girl's a knockout. Look how the men are drooling over her.* Slap a designer evening gown on the exotic beauty and she could have been the next Bond girl. Dark straight hair, perfect bone structure, large cola-colored eyes. She was probably from one of those out-of-the-way villages that no one knows about—unspoiled by hybridization and genetic drift—where virtually every girl for generations is blessed with the undiluted beauty of her ancestors.

Claire's first impression of the motley group opened her eyes to an unimagined level of hardship. Of the four of them, only Alyona seemed to be keeping it together. *Seemed* because she and Hatcher had somehow managed to become lovers. Although Claire's ex would stick his dick in anything not marked high voltage, this failed to explain the other end of the equation. *So this is why Hatcher had been so gung-ho to make the trip across the ice . . .* Claire should have known. Only two things in this world—money and sex—ever truly motivated him. Everything else he did was simply window dressing, angles intersecting his seedy wants.

Almost immediately Claire was struck by the temperature of the room. At first the heat was comforting, a welcome reprieve from the stinging cold of outdoors, but soon she was overwhelmed. Gradually, she stripped away her outer layers of clothing until she wore nothing but a pair of insulated pants and the thermal underwear top that had become a second skin to her. Witz was next—after him it was McKenzie, then Price—and before long only the Russians remained in their heavy military issue parkas and polar pants, immune to the obscene heat that gushed out of an old propane heater Claire hoped would break down.

They were too far from civilization, too grateful for companionship to feel awkward as the introductions were made. Alyona launched herself into Hatcher's arms while the rest of them rolled their eyes. Claire received a similar welcome from the Russian men as they climbed over one another to be the first to give her the grand tour of what they had befittingly dubbed the Gulag. And for a time everything was right in the world as they talked and laughed and got to know one another over the vodka that was as well-mannered and subtle as napalm.

"To cold weather and warm bodies," Hatcher toasted, his arm slung low over Alyona's hips.

"Na staróvya!" the Russians chorused.

With the exception of Price they hoisted their tin cups and choked down the high-octane ice-breaker.

"To Kesha and Georgiy!" Zhenya declared in flamboyant, thick-accented English. "Vwe eat better tonight be-coss of you." He hollered something in Russian in the direction of the kitchen, the distant clatter of pots and pans the only response he got.

"Here-here!" McKenzie agreed and knocked back the rest of the awful spirit with a satisfied grimace.

Before long they had broken into smaller more intimate pairings. McKenzie and Price occupied a space near the entrance, hoping to catch a bit of the cool air that seeped in around the drafty edges of the ill-fitting door. Alyona and Hatcher groped one another on a swaybacked sofa that looked like something you'd see curbside on trash day in one of the many inner-city neighborhoods outlying Los Caminos. DeLuca and Max chuckled loudly, though about what exactly wasn't apparent, celebrating each other with drunken overtures. Bishop and Shurik disappeared into another portion of the windowless complex and were not heard from again until shortly before they all sat down to eat. And throughout it all Claire and Zhenya and Witz made small talk that always worked its way back to the topic of sex.

Before long, the aroma of spices and sizzling animal fats filled the room and they all sat down to dinner around a large makeshift table that Shurik explained had been fashioned from the Plexiglas windshield of a supply helicopter. Claire had thought it a little strange that Georgiy and Kesha, neither of whom spoke a word of English, were not introduced sooner, but her doubts were quickly laid to rest as the two men emerged from the kitchen bearing a modest feast of Russian favorites. Although the hygiene level may not have been up to Health Department standards, it was apparent that their hosts had pulled out all the stops. Claire promised herself that she would steer clear of the kitchen and eat with a gusto befitting the Russians' hospitality.

From the moment the first plate of food was placed on the makeshift table the meal progressed with all the restraint of a hundred-yard dash. Even Alyona kept pace with the men, attacking her food as if she had been raised by wolves. It was comical—the chewing and slurping and obligatory snippets of conversation squeezed in between mouthfuls.

"Tell me, Alyona," said Claire. "What's a nice girl like you doing in a place like this?"

"You mean vaht she is doing vwiss bunch of Cossacks?" growled Max, slipping the question past the partially-masticated contents of his mouth. Between his gruff mannerisms, untamed black whiskers and wild bloodshot eyes he was every bit the uncultured ruffian to whom he alluded.

Alyona pinched Max's scruffy cheek. "I can—how you say?—handle myself. If he is bad boy . . . Yes—this is how you say . . . *Bad boy*? I cut off *muda*." She scissored the air with her fingers.

When the laughter subsided it was Zhenya's turn. "Yes, Aly, tell how you end up vwiss so many vwild animals in coldest place on earth." He smiled across the table at her, his crooked yellow teeth gilded with plaque and gray strings of stew meat.

Alyona snapped something at Zhenya in her native tongue—*a threat?*—and the other Russians laughed. Zhenya must've gotten the message because he fell dead quiet.

Claire and the other members of the team looked to Hatcher for answers.

"Don't ask me," he said. "But I'd like to know." He looked at Alyona. "C'mon, Aly, give it up. We're all adults here."

Alyona scanned the faces around her and with a bored look said, "I vwoodn't—how you say?—fuck doorty old pig." She curled her upper lip in disgust. "So they send me here to vwatch vweether and make snowman."

"Whatever happened to Siberia?" McKenzie asked. "I thought that's where they sent all the bad Russian girls and boys."

"In Siberia, vweenter is only ten months," Shurik said wearily. "In South Pole, vweenter is 20,000 years."

"I don't know about the rest of you lightweights," said DeLuca, "but I'd like some more of that stew." He handed his plate to Georgiy who presided over the steaming pot wearing dirty orange oven mitts. "A big piece of meat, if you've got it."

"So, who else will have more?" Shurik demanded robustly. He stopped to survey the bedraggled contents of Price's plate. "The meal, Sergeant, you not like?"

"The meal is excellent," Price replied sincerely. "It's just that I can't eat pork. I'm Muslim—it's against the rules. I shouldn't even be eating this because I'm still getting some of the juices, but it's just so good I can't resist." He smiled and awaited Shurik's response. "The meat—it is pork, isn't it?"

Shurik looked surprised. "*Da* . . ." he affirmed uncertainly. "Oink oink!"

"You don't know what you're missing, Price," said Bishop. He was working over a piece of meat when he suddenly stopped chewing. His jaw froze and a strange look took hold of his face. He worked his lips around and pushed something out of his mouth with the tip of his tongue, grabbing it between his thumb and forefinger so that he could examine it in the light.

"Vwhat ees it?" Shurik demanded.

"Nothing," said Bishop, shrugging it off. "Just a hair. No harm done."

Shurik plucked the hair from between DeLuca's fingers and held it in front of Kesha's face. The sickly-looking cook was about to say something when Shurik flicked the hair at him and slapped him across the face. The table fell silent.

"Look," said Bishop, digging in. "It hasn't slowed me down any."

Shurik was not appeased though. He stared coldly at Kesha who sat at his place fidgeting nervously.

"Beats the hell out of SOS," Bishop continued, smacking his lips heartily between bites.

"More vodka!" McKenzie demanded merrily.

This got Shurik's attention and he snapped out of it. "Vwhat ees S-O-S?" he asked, a beat behind the conversation.

"Shit on a shingle," DeLuca explained. "Army chow."

The Russians looked puzzled.

"It means God help us if we run out of booze and have to endure this place sober," added McKenzie, raising his cup. "Now where's that rotgut?"

They joined him in a toast and returned to eating. After dinner they again broke into small groups and set about the business of digesting the heavy meal. Hot and bloated, Claire was ready to call it a night. However it was clear that Hatcher had other plans. He had his arms locked around Alyona's waist and was maneuvering her toward the gloomy passage that served as a conduit to the rest of the Gulag. The girl was in for the wildest thirty seconds of her life.

"I vwill show you '*rrr*ound," said Zhenya.

A bit on the tipsy side, Claire didn't feel like doing much of anything, but Zhenya gave her a friendly nudge and she reluctantly followed him into the kitchen. The walls were textured with grease and spatters of food grime. Kesha and Georgiy ignored them, staring blankly at one another as they scraped clean the dishes—all the lumpy brown stew muck and clotted sour cream—that had just been cleared from the table. It was a peculiar look they wore, a look Claire was sure spoke volumes, but on what subject she couldn't even begin to fathom. She'd seen it before—during dinner all of the Russians had lapsed into it at one time or another. Claire had assumed the language barrier was to blame. Or maybe it was because they'd been cut off from the outside world for so long—a mild strain of cabin fever taking hold. But who was she to judge? She was hardly at her own best—physically or mentally. Between Alan visiting her every night in her dreams, and the fact that her body was so out of whack that it looked as if she was going to miss her period for the first time since Hatcher had . . .

Yuck! What the hell? . . . As Claire looked away her eyes latched onto a fairly large and ambiguous slab of meat resting on a butcher block in a pool of its own thick blood. The top half was still matted with coarse black hair. Before she could ask, Zhenya spun her about and whisked her away.

Most of the Gulag looked as if it had been inhabited for decades by a cult of packrats. Junk lined the walls of the main corridor, a claustrophobic passage scarcely seven feet high. Every now and then she would catch a glimpse of something vaguely familiar—an old manual typewriter, a defunct toaster oven, a dress maker's mannequin—swamped in Russian newspapers, paperback novels, burned-out light bulbs and always more soda can birds. One wall of the corridor, from top to bottom, was covered with the torn-out pages of a book, hundreds in all. Here and there, lines, entire passages, sometimes even nearly a page had been blanked out with black marker. Zhenya explained that it was all part of a game in which they pared away bits and pieces to ferret new shorter stories from the larger whole. Kesha, the bookworm of the group, had started the game as a diversion from the drudgery of their daily lives. Claire guessed that nearly 80 percent of the entire work had been obliterated in favor of the remaining text.

"What's it about?" asked Claire.

"Ee deez about oos an'deez plaze," he explained in thick-accented English.

"Drama, comedy, romance?"

Zhenya thought it over. Claire wasn't sure that he'd understood the question but before long he replied, "Ee deez like bad dream."

"You mean a nightmare."

"Nightmare—ee deez good vword for deez plaze?"

"That depends."

Zhenya's eyes gleamed darkly. "Here, dey send me to die."

The place was unthinkably depressing, a labyrinth of dim narrow corridors and drafty little rooms presided over by a state of morbid disrepair. There were actually holes in the walls, many of which had been patched with scraps of wood while others were merely plugged with wadded-up rags or bandaged with peeling strips of duct tape. Cold air bled through in the places where these and other quick-fixes had been applied in a sort of structural first-aid.

Zhenya led her to a storage area that had actually begun to fill with snow. For a moment her guide brightened, confessing that he had accidentally backed into the station with the tractor they used to haul in supplies from their sister base fifty miles to the east. Claire was grateful for the rush of cold air. In the last few minutes the vodka had begun to assert itself, causing the floor to roll gently underfoot. She reached for the wall but missed; only Zhenya's quick hands prevented her from going down.

"Whoa!" he exclaimed, wrapping his arms around her waist and drawing her into him.

Claire chuckled awkwardly and tried to squirm free of Zhenya's opportunistic grasp, but he cuffed her savagely on the side of the head.

Claire came to in a cramped unkempt room that smelled like a cage. Her head was swimming but she could focus well enough to realize that she was stretched out on a dingy bed, the ceiling over her head cluttered with old photographs of people and places she didn't know. For a moment she thought that she'd imagined Zhenya hitting her—that she had simply blacked out—but then the pain in her head arose from the depths of unconsciousness and she felt his breath, shot through with phlegm, gum disease and boozy ferment, invade her ear.

"Look," said Zhenya. He was cuddled against her, one arm wedged under her neck, the other pointed toward the ceiling at a photograph of a young man wearing a military uniform. He was standing in front of a little yellow house with a rose garden.

"I'deez me—Zhenya! I am hanzum yoong man, *da?*"

"*Da!*" Claire chuckled. Fog pressed in around the edges of her vision. She was fading out again.

Zhenya sat up abruptly and slapped her across the face. The fog broke and Claire heard Hatcher's voice somewhere close by. A moment later Alyona laughed and Claire was able to make the connection. The two lovers were mixing it up in the adjacent room, a thin plywood wall all that stood between her and possible rescue. Before she could scream for help, though, Zhenya jammed the bound edge of a paperback novel into her mouth, forcing her jaw apart and pinning her tongue to the back of her throat so that it blocked her airway. Scarcely able to breathe, Claire gagged on the musty archival scent of rotting paper.

He was going to rape her. Claire had never considered the possibility of becoming a crime statistic. This didn't happen to strong women. But it *was* happening and she was weak, weaker now than she had ever been in her life, and she would be lucky if Zhenya didn't suffocate her in the process. He released the book and hit her again, this time just under the left eye. The happy-go-lucky demeanor he'd worn during dinner had given way to a determined stare that inhabited her entire field of vision. And then he was tugging at her pants, breath rattling through clenched teeth, sweating, and she tasted the greasy beads trembling on his upper lip as he smothered her with violent kisses.

For a split-second she thought she saw Shurik standing over them—a bearded silhouette really, obscured by the concussive haze enveloping her brain. But the room was carouseling, her ears were ringing, and she didn't know what to think. But then she saw him again, this time more clearly than before and he was clutching a—*tennis racket?*—over his head. So she was hallucinating after all. However, she was not so convinced that its sudden downward trajectory failed to make her look away. Zhenya reared back and stiffened. A trickle of blood snaked down his forehead, across the bridge of his nose and hooked under his left eye, only the white of which now showed. Shurik then grabbed Zhenya by the collar of his parka, heaping him onto the floor.

Claire was still too weak to move. "Thanks," she said, acknowledging Shurik with a feeble smile. "Can you help me up?"

Shurik lingered over her, his massive torso eclipsing the only light in the room, a single naked bulb burning overhead. Claire asked again. This time, he pressed in closer. There was a low, predatory pitch to his breathing and Claire realized that he was sniffing her, circumnavigating the line of her collar with his nose.

"Back the fuck off!" It was Price. He forced himself between Claire and Shurik and slung her arm over his shoulder. Shurik began to say something but by then Price was dragging Claire from the room and calling out in a loud, stern voice: "Zip it up, Hatcher, party's over!"

Where had the time gone? Claire had been in a funk since their cozy little get-to-gether with the Russians four days ago—and there were reasons for this, damn good reasons—but her mood hardly explained the sense of total detachment she was feeling. *Snap out of it. You're probably catching a cold.* It was a known fact that depression could weaken the immune system. But then again her altercation with Zhenya—*so that's what you're calling it, an altercation?*—may well have been the reason behind the soreness in her limbs. If the bruises were any indication . . . *Altercation—listen to yourself. Call it what it was. The creep tried to rape you. And he would have succeeded if Price hadn't come to your rescue. Your wounded pride's the reason you feel like shit. It's why you're out here playing peek-a-boo with the sun when you could be keeping warm back at the station.*

Claire's pride explained a lot of things, but it didn't explain the chimp carcass she had seen lain out on the butcher block the other night. Or had she? . . . *You don't know what you saw that night. Not really. Your mind was all mucked up from the drugs Zhenya slipped you. And you were stressed. There you go again . . . Get over yourself! Stressed . . . You were scared shitless! The chimp was a hallucination, a projection of your fucked-up subconscious. You found the cage and then the nest, and your mind wouldn't let go. Nothing is what it seems anymore.*

In less than an hour it would be pitch black and she'd be out here alone with only Witz to protect her from the monsters. And yet she wasn't afraid. Not really. Or was she? Deep down she could feel the carbonated sizzle in her bloodstream—a slow percolating buzz that ordinarily honed her senses to knife points—but it was different than before. Remote. So she wasn't about to trade in her sunglasses and tanning oil for a pair of night-vision goggles, a quiver of wooden stakes and a graveyard shift as a vampire hunter. No matter how good the pay was. But she may have been growing accustomed to the darkness. In the past twenty-four hours she had given very little thought to the sun's absence in the sky each day. True, there were other things on her mind, but there was more to it than this. It wasn't that the darkness had sneaked up on her. She could spend the day in a lighted room without windows or clocks and still detect the onset of night with the sixth sense of a bat. Its presence was as unequivocal as cancer—voracious, terminal, black—amassing strength in her central nervous system and branching outward into her extremities, consuming all that was vital and alive.

Since her breakdown in the shower she had done her best to force the ugly truth of it into a far corner of her mind—conceal her fears from the men and spare her the macho chiding and broad shoulders to lean on. Though she hadn't expected to overcome it so completely, so abruptly. If she was still afraid of the dark she had somehow managed to camouflage it from herself. Again, maybe it was the drugs Zhenya had slipped her. The mystery compound had boiled away Claire's fear, leaving behind a gloomy vapor that was merely evocative of the terror she had once felt. Ultimately, though, it wasn't triumph but indifference. Just as her volunteering to accompany Witz on this little mission of theirs was not a display of courage but a show of apathy. She just didn't give a shit. After what had happened to her—*almost happened*—at the Russian station she had clicked off. She was now sleepwalking, her autonomic systems running the show. Shock had done this. Rather than allowing the emotional trauma to fry her circuits her mind had placed her body on life-support and had then disconnected itself. Cruise control. There was nothing magical about it. This was self-preservation at work. When the time was right her mind would reconnect itself and she would then have to deal with the consequences. For now, however, she was free.

Two days ago she would have been paralyzed by fear to be out here like this, the black tide pressing in around her. She had covered the same stretch of trodden snow before, however the path had been illuminated by a blinding crossfire of floodlights between the derelict station and the improvised morgue she had called home for nearly two weeks. A conflagration of mean white light had bridged the bottomless gulf of perpetual night. *Had*—past tense. High winds had knocked out the floodlights and no one had been out to repair them since. Although it lay only a hundred or so feet ahead, she could barely discern the derelict station in the dusky light. Not since Claire had sought refuge in the linen closet—an unwilling pawn in her father's nightmarish game of hide and seek—had she given so little thought to the impending night.

The same winds that had knocked out the floodlights had disabled the relay antenna they relied on to stay connected to the outside world. Located atop an icy ridgeline several hundred feet above the station, the dish relayed satellite signals that may otherwise have been lost to magnetic interference that was typical of the poles. For a day and a half they had been unable to communicate with anyone beyond shouting distance. She had been talking to Eric—tiptoeing around what had happened at the Russian station—when a powerful gust came along and took him away from her. They had also been forced to go without the weather forecast, dangerous business considering that Kent refused to fly without it. These concerns, among other more pressing matters, had made reestablishing this vital link a top priority. When the winds had finally quieted down, DeLuca had instructed Witz to ascend the ridge and repair the relay. Claire surprised herself and had volunteered to accompany him. She was sick of being everyone's charity case.

Silvery gusts of breath coalesced in front of them like ghosts spawned from their lungs. The slope was not particularly steep although an icy crust made the footing unsure, the going treacherous. Although crampons had been brought for every member of the team, neither she nor Witz had thought to use them. They hoofed carefully upward toward the relay dish, though neither was overly concerned with the potential consequences a single misstep could entail. They were alone with the crunching noise of their footsteps, the doleful howl of a steady wind, and the singular desolation of the last continent on earth to be settled by humans. Not that an itinerant population of scientists and support personnel constituted a bustling metropolis. Quite the opposite, in fact. Claire would forever remember McMurdo as having all the hominess and permanence of a truck stop. But out here—where culture and community were about as near as the lively streets of Caesar's Rome—the terrible grandeur of the wilderness surpassed even her most dreaded expectations.

"I hate it here," Claire commented without emotion. "I can't feel my toes."

"This is nothing," said Witz casually, pausing mid-slope to catch his breath. "Like summer in Barbados," he went on. "Let's take a look at what the mercury's doing. Hold the flashlight so I can see."

Witz pawed at the pale gray front of his hooded parka, a layered amalgam of Gore-Tex and bonded-polymer insulates one hundred times warmer than goose down. The extreme conditions experts at The North Face had equipped their top-of-the-line polar shell with an oversized zipper pull. This simple addition enabled Witz to access the inside pocket without removing his mittens, a distinct advantage in a climate that could impart a glassy brittleness to exposed flesh in a matter of minutes. It was here that he carried the handheld weather computer Claire had first noticed on the flight from Christchurch. Over the past couple of weeks she had gotten used to seeing him with the little black box affixed to his hand—punching buttons and staring raptly at the luminous display. The average teenage boy spent less time playing with his penis and was perhaps no more ignorant of its advanced functions than the taut little man standing before her cursing at the sophisticated piece of hardware. Claire tried to restrain a chuckle as Witz fumbled with the ON switch.

"Take off your gloves," Claire suggested. "It'll be easier that way." She was anxious to keep moving. This cold she had caught—*so this is how you intend to explain your lightheadedness?*—had made her that much more susceptible to the sub-zero chill.

Witz grumbled something about the weather computer's designers making the switches more user-friendly and removed his right glove. "If I get frostbite, I'll sue the manufacturers," he threatened.

"*Frostbite*—in this heat?" Claire was incredulous. "I bet there wasn't one reported case of frostbite in Barbados in the last hundred years. Sunburns you could toast marshmallows over . . . But no frostbite."

She knew that Witz was smirking at her beneath the neoprene mask that covered every inch of his face not protected by the goggles he wore to keep his eyeballs from freezing. He stabbed at the buttons on the weather computer and held it over his head for several seconds. He then checked the display.

"I'd like to get up a little higher," he said. "Out of the basin. We'll get a better reading that way."

Claire slogged after him up the vitreous slope. They stopped where it plateaued on an icy mesa overlooking the massive basin in which they had taken up residence. She could just make out the station in the brittle starlight where it lay atop the snow in stark relief like an ancient cryptogram of a black sun. Not that she particularly gave a shit, but she wondered if Hatcher was ever going to come out of his quarters again. About the only reason she even gave it a second thought was because his self-imposed exile had apparently been precipitated by something that twenty-four hours, Hatcher's unexplained reclusiveness had given them all something to wonder about, but no one seemed to care anymore, including Claire.

Witz sighed deeply and plopped down on his butt in the snow. He looked like a little kid sitting there in his puffy polar gear, legs stretched out before him. He wedged the flashlight between his thighs so that the beam illuminated the lower half of his face.

"Elevation getting to you?" Claire asked.

"Maybe that's what's it is," he replied. "I've just been really run down the past couple of days. At first I thought it was a hangover or something I ate."

"Monkey meat," Claire stated frankly.

It wasn't clear whether Witz had heard her or not. Once again he was grappling with the weather computer. He hadn't learned from his earlier difficulties and his expression contorted angrily as his efforts to key in the necessary commands were frustrated by his gloves. Without warning, an enraged growl issued from somewhere deep inside of him and he hurled the device across the mesa. It landed approximately twenty feet away and skidded over the ice, stopping just shy of the edge of the slope they had just ascended. A few inches more and it would have gone skittering down the slope and into the basin. Lost, no doubt, in one of the numerous fissures that scarred the ice field.

"That was smart," said Claire.

"Thing's a piece of shit."

"What about checking the temperature? You said you wanted an accurate reading."

As quickly as he'd lost his temper, Witz had settled back down. "It's cold . . ." he replied dully. "Too fucking cold. Attaching a number to it won't make it any warmer." "I'd still like to know."

As much as Claire wanted to fix the relay and get back inside, she was determined to satisfy her curiosity. Lately, she had been colder than usual. She could literally feel it in her bones. Even when she was inside the station, it didn't seem that the heater was capable of providing her with adequate warmth. Like the others, she had resorted to wearing her cold weather gear nearly round the clock.

Claire was finding out just how lean the air could be at 6,000 feet above sea level. The wind had transformed the snow atop the mesa into an icy matrix approximating frozen milk in both appearance and slickness. She scuffled toward the edge, half-walking half-skating, the waffled soles of her boots offering next to nothing in the way of traction. *Crampons—next time.*

The station, the field of debris, the ugly black smudge marking the epicenter of the explosion: all were located at the edge of a sweeping depression. A great, white, flat expanse marking the frozen-over surface of the subglacial lake. At one time, the low browbeaten peaks that ringed the basin towered well above the ancient reservoir that once sparkled in their lap, liquid and blue. However, 100,000 years of accumulating snowfall had more or less equalized the disparity between lakeshore and mountaintop. For a moment, Claire was able to step outside of herself as she took in the eerily beautiful landscape that shone cobalt in the muted light of the moon hiding somewhere not far below the horizon.

Before the relay went down she'd spoken with Eric every couple of days—had told him how much he would have admired the stoic beauty of the place, the foreboding majesty of the frozen kingdom of the narwhal and the emperor penguin. He'd joked that he was going to hop on a plane and come join her, that he had friends in high places. At the time, Claire wished he wasn't joking. But she was no longer afraid and now resented herself for needing him like that.

Zhenya, the little prick, had reminded her that you were never really anything but alone in the world. Alone and exposed. It wasn't so bad though. Self-reliance was the essence of survival, the cornerstone of evolution. There wasn't an organism on the planet that wasn't looking out solely for itself, that wouldn't gladly subsist on the miscues of its contemporaries to nourish its own evolutionary aspirations. She was alone and this is the way it was meant to be. Away from the ubiquitous din of civilization, electric lights, the white noise of traffic and voices and the beating of hearts not her own. She may as well have been a million light-years from the nearest 7-ELEVEN because there was nothing to suggest that humankind existed. Not now, not then, not ever. Nothing, that is, but the faint yellow light of the Russian station—a single pathetic bulb pitted against the yawing abyss of space—at the opposite end of the depression.

She returned the weather computer to Witz who was now huddled over the relay dish—a small circular unit about the size required for satellite TV. He was performing a systems check. "There's no reason this shouldn't work," he blustered, snapping closed the access door in the unit's base.

"The cold?" Claire offered.

"Maybe."

"Here's your weather gizmo," she said handing him the maligned device. "Next time, you go get it."

Claire stood with her back was to the gusting wind, shielding herself against stinging drifts of ice pellets that peppered her like birdshot. Although her ears were muffled against the cold, she could hear Witz beating the blood back into his exposed hand so that he could key in the functions necessary to complete his data-gathering.

"Hold the light," he shouted, his voice whisked from the mesa as soon as it left his mouth. "I can hardly see what I'm doing."

Since leaving the sheltered cove of the basin the wind had picked up considerably. For the most part its bark was worse than its bite, a steady assault that ruffled the storm shutters but nothing they couldn't handle. Occasionally, however, they were surprised by a ferocious gust that lit into them with a sudden fury, a resolve born of eons of meteorological angst.

It was as Claire swung about to better position the flashlight for Witz that the sound of gunfire first reached her ears. It was scarcely audible above the wind that roared across the mesa, a halting succession of metered shots followed by a rolling staccato burst. But it was there, and it was unmistakable. Any doubts she may have had were quickly dispelled as more gunshots rang out—a furious exchange muted by the distance but impossible to ignore. There could only be one possible source: the Russians. Zhenya, Shurik and the others had finally lost it. Apparently, Claire's own nightmare experience with the crazy assholes was only a preview. She and Witz stopped what they were doing and traded looks.

"Is that what I think it is?" Witz asked.

Claire was about to respond when she was struck full force by the sort of gust that all but the most unfortunate of Americans know only from the eight o'clock news. She recognized the Herculean blast from countless reels of natural disaster footage. This was the invisible brute that overturned cars for sport, ripped houses from their foundations, made a tossed salad of shingles and family albums and all manner of ir-replaceable mementos, played jump rope with power lines, propelled stalks of wheat like bullets into the flesh of panicked livestock. One second Claire was doing her best to ignore the bitter antagonistic cold, the next it was if the hand of God had knocked her off her feet.

Panic pulled at her from a thousand directions, a visceral thrashing in the pit of her stomach, as she scudded down the icy slope on her back, headfirst. She kicked her right heel down hard against the ironclad snow pack and simultaneously swung her left leg outward. Twisting at the waist, she spun herself around. Now what? She was schussing down the slope at breakneck speed. It wasn't so much the momentum that scared her, it was the fact that she was now truly alone, the illimitable darkness rushing to overwhelm the frail sense of security she had manufactured at Witz's side.

The flashlight . . . She must've dropped it in that first instant when she had attempted to break her fall. Now it lay somewhere on the mesa above her, a reassuring sweep of light playing out over the snow. She tried to slow her momentum by digging in her heels, but the ice was too hard, too slick. In a matter of seconds she had tobogganed past the station, past the ugly black cancer on the snow that occupied her thoughts like a grim prognosis. They were not in her path—a collision was out of the question—however for a split-second each had occupied the same plane as she, and she now felt them drifting helplessly away from her.

Until now she hadn't realized just how dished the basin actually was. But now she understood. Gravity needed very little help to get its point across in this frozen, frictionless world. She had slowed, yes, but the slowing too was interminable—taunting in its leisure—still waters peeling quietly into a raging falls. By the time she came to a complete stop she'd be who knows how far away from the station. Freezing to death alone in the dark. When the rescue attempt failed—or was deemed pointless—they would launch a recovery operation. Funny, she thought, the semantic gulf separating two such relatively similar terms. Rescue. Recovery.

Alive. Dead.

Again, she tried to stop herself, but it was pointless. The ice was just too slick. No matter how hard she fought it, she was moving further and further away from possible rescue. Closer and closer to recovery. From alive to dead. A couple of hours, tops—that's all it would take to freeze her solid. Her blood would thicken, her heart would slow against the congealing tide, and her joints would stiffen until she was paralyzed. But wait, it was only –38°. That is what Witz had said? This was nothing. Not the way she was dressed. Her polar shell was rated to –50°. She was better insulated than a polar bear. Virtually anywhere on earth she could survive until the sun came up . . . But really, that's what all of this was about, right?

The sun. Daylight. Her security blanket. The unpretentious disk in the sky that most take for granted wasn't coming up any time soon. Not for months. Not really. Even when the sun reached its apex—cowering deep in the shadow of the horizon like a peeping Tom—the sky overhead would be little more than a dusky shade of brown. The solar murk that she pined for each day was really just a variation on the theme of night. She was scared out of her mind, and it sickened her to feel so helpless against something that couldn't directly harm her.

Then, for the second time in as many moments, the world fell out from under her. She had been too panicked about the intangible menace that had been bullying her since childhood to consider the real danger all around. Jagged fissures, some wide and deep enough to swallow a school bus, scarred the surface of the vast depression. This was one of the primary reasons they needed Kent and his Osprey.

Vertical takeoff and landing capability was essential in a region where long runways were made impossible by the ever shifting ice.

Witz had suggested that atypical shifts in temperature and an increased level of solar radiation had transformed the ice field into a treacherous cloisonné of yawing chasms and natural trapdoors camouflaged by glassy panes of ice. The data was irrefutable. Blame it on CFC's, fossil fuels, the destruction of the rainforests, or the natural geologic cycle—it all boiled down to an irreversible global catastrophe that was already well underway. Claire still had enough of her wits about her to realize that it was one such chasm—cold and dark and deep—that had bared its fangs and made a meal of her.

One thing was certain; if she survived she was going to have one hell of a bruise on her ass. She'd landed on an icy ledge about five feet beneath the surface, the impact reverberating up the shaft of her spine. She had also whacked the back of her head going over the edge of the crevasse, but otherwise was still in one piece and lucky to be alive. She didn't dare attempt to extricate herself from the crevasse without first attempting to ascertain its dimensions. She was more than capable. She could do twenty pull-ups no problem—strong as an ox, according to Price. But upper-body strength wasn't the issue. This was about playing it smart. Without the flashlight she had no way of knowing just how far the crevasse dropped out below her. Two feet? Ten feet? A thousand?

She explored the crevasse with her hands, however her gloves effectively blinded her sense of touch. Other than an odd chunk of ice jutting between her legs, she could make out very little of her surroundings. She still had her voice though. "Witz!" she called.

"Claire!" she could hear him shouting. "Where are you?"

"I'm in a crevasse! Follow my voice."

"I'll get help and come back for you," he replied. There was a strange quality to his voice; it was at once both near and far away. A trick of the vast horizontal emptiness. The words passed over the top of the crevasse with an irrevocability that terrified her.

"I'm not too deep. You can pull me out by yourself."

There was a moment of silence followed by what she'd most dreaded to hear. "I'll be right back," he said. "I promise."

Fuck it. This was no time to be proud. The thought that she would be left alone out here with nothing but the melancholy voice of the wind and the smothering coffin-lid of night severed the delicate membrane of connective tissue binding her to reason and self-control.

"Don't leave me!" she cried out. But there was no answer. He was gone. *This can't be happening*. . . "Witz!" she shouted.

"We didn't come all this way to play in the snow. We've got work to do." It was Witz, his head silhouetted against the darkening sky above the crevasse.

"Asshole," Claire uttered sincerely.

Witz fumbled with the switch on the flashlight. *Click-click. Click-click.* "It was working fine just a second ago. It must be on the fritz since you dropped it." He cuffed the barrel of the flashlight against his palm and the beam flickered to life. A second later they were both screaming.

It had started with Witz—a rippling crescendo that tore through the night—and surged over into Claire as light illuminated the crevasse. Claire's assumption that what she now straddled was an odd-shaped chunk of ice—*Why should I have thought any differently, everything out here is ice?*—was only partially accurate. Indeed, ice was now a constituent element of the grotesque curio jutting obscenely between her legs, but no more so than flesh and blood and bone and the myriad other components that make up a human being in life. But there he was, gray-blue in the feeble shower of light, grinning maniacally like someone who has discovered too late that the secret of life is a tasteless joke.

He was Asian—this much was clear even beneath the sugary dusting of frost that coated every square inch of him. His eyes, although open, were little more than paisley slits forced upward at the outer corners by the arrow points of his demented smile. His hair was short and black and symmetrical so that it offset his face as would a picture frame. Ice crystals were threaded along each shaft like seed pearls; even his eyelashes were bejeweled with the twinkling crystalline specks. Horror gave way to morbid curiosity and scientific detachment as Claire attempted to apply what she knew of reason and probability to an equation that would add up.

"Witz, give me the flashlight."

"I'm going back," he stammered. "We need to tell somebody. Hatcher . . . Doctor Hatcher will want to know."

"Looks like you can cross another name off your wish-list. If I were to take an educated guess, I'd say we just found Hatcher's missing marine biologist."

It was clear from the position of Lim's body that he'd been trying to climb out of the crevasse when he had succumbed to the freezing cold. His bare arms, one of which was badly broken midpoint between the wrist and elbow, were fused to the ledge on which Claire sat. She knew the arm was broken—it was his left arm—because the fractured ulna had erupted through the overlying soft tissue. That a considerable amount of blood was present at and around the site of the wound—frozen though it was in a crimson-black upwelling that resembled a disfigured rose—indicated that Lim's heart was still pumping when he had fallen into the crevasse and injured himself. In a last-ditch effort to prevent himself from bleeding to death, he had secured a length of nylon cord—*a drawstring?*—just above the wound so that it acted as a tourniquet.

Although the wound itself provided a grim point of interest, Claire wanted to know why anyone would venture so far from the relative warmth and safety of the station. The fact that he wasn't wearing a jacket suggested he hadn't been thinking straight, or that circumstance hadn't afforded him the luxury of being well prepared.

Whatever the case, in sub-zero weather, sweatpants and a T-shirt equaled suicide. Of this equation, she was sure.

Claire ran the beam over the rest of his body, taking note of two things: The crevasse was only a fraction as deep as it was long, perhaps eight feet from top to bottom; and Lim was wearing a jacket after all. Just not on his upper body where it belonged. What she'd mistaken for sweatpants was actually a parka similar to her own although it clearly belonged to someone much larger than either of them. Lim's legs comfortably occupied the sleeves. And the waist, now inverted, was cinched with duct tape snugly above his hips. Claire took one last look at his face—the unchanging marbleized expression evocative of renaissance statuary, a lost Michelangelo—before Witz hoisted her to safety.

Once she got over the shock of finding herself trapped in a crevasse alongside a dead man, she began to question Lim's state-of-mind. She had plenty of time to think about things on the long walk back to the station. It was stupid of him to risk the ice field instead of waiting in what remained of the station for help to arrive, but she couldn't honestly say that she would've reacted any differently under the circumstances. Ears ringing, heart racing, head pounding from the blast—panic wasn't an easy thing to pin down. It did different things to different people. Ultimately, did it even matter? Ellis was the only member of Hatcher's original team whose remains hadn't been identified. Six down, one to go. Maybe there *was* a light at the end of the tunnel.

When she and Witz returned to the station only Price was the least bit interested in their discovery. DeLuca, McKenzie and Bishop hardly even stirred. All three sat wedged against one another on the sofa like frat boys after a night of heavy drinking. Empty food and drink containers littered the floor at their feet. All three of them were wearing their parkas.

"Close the door," groaned McKenzie. "You're letting out the heat."

"Did you fix the relay?" DeLuca inquired distantly. His eyes were dull and cavernous. He hadn't shaved in nearly a week.

"Maybe you didn't hear me," said Claire. "We found a man frozen in the ice."

"It's Lim," Witz confirmed absently. He'd moved away from the door and had anchored himself beneath the heater vent blowing downward from the ceiling. He closed his eyes, tilted back his head and let the warm current of air radiate over him.

DeLuca sprang off the sofa and spun Witz around by the shoulders. "Listen to me!" he snapped. "I asked you a question, Lieutenant, and I expect an answer. Did you fix the relay?"

Witz squirmed uneasily and stared at the ground. "Not exactly."

Claire had never seen DeLuca like this. He was seething. She forced herself between the two men before things could escalate. "It was my fault," she said. "I slipped on the ice and fell. If it wasn't for Witz I'd still be out there." Claire paused. "With all due respect, Major, you're the one who's not listening. There's a dead man out there."

Price stepped forward and took DeLuca by the arm. "Dr. Matthews is right, Frank. We can worry about repairing the relay later. Right now, we need to get out there."

But DeLuca was somewhere else, his anger from a moment earlier surrendering to a look bordering on despair. Worry lines crimped his brow. His hair was grayer than Claire had realized. "We have to make a report . . ." he uttered vacantly. "Twenty-four hours—that's what he said. . . . Twenty-four hours or . . ." DeLuca tried to go on but by then he was trembling violently and the words rattled back into his throat.

Price slapped him across the face. The room was suddenly quiet. Only the wind was audible, a low dry scraping at the walls of the station. Claire expected . . . She didn't know what to expect—a fight? Threats of a court marshal? After all, Price had struck a senior officer. But DeLuca looked relieved, grateful even, and simply nodded in acknowledgement of Price's earlier suggestion.

"Has anyone checked to see that the generator has enough fuel?" asked Price.

"I topped it off an hour ago," replied Bishop. "Nearly froze to death, but it should be good for another eight hours or so." He was eating deviled ham straight from the can. Using his fingers, he scooped up a grayish-pink glob and jammed it into his mouth. He flung aside the empty can and peeled back the pull-tab lid on another that he had stashed in the pocket of his parka.

McKenzie looked at Bishop accusingly. "You told me that was the last can."

Bishop emptied the second can of deviled ham just like the first and sucked his fingers clean. "Okay," he confessed, "*that* was the last can." His tone was cold, confrontational. Gone was the affable ex-choir boy whose honeyed voice had once thrilled the Tabernacle faithful. Despite the stifling heat inside the station, his warm, blue, close-set eyes were now frozen over. Glittering meanly, diamond hard.

McKenzie glared at him and smiled. "Remember, we're a long way from the nearest hospital, buddy boy."

Claire's patience had worn thin. "Okay," she inquired brashly, "who do I have to blow to get permission to use the car?"

That got their attention. Since Zhenya and then Shurik had tried to rape her, the sexual objectification Claire routinely experienced as a woman was more apparent than ever before. Though they had never openly discussed what had gone on in the Russian station, the mere implication of the welt on her temple and the fact that it *wasn't* being talked about had opened the floodgates to a torrent of male hormones. It wasn't as bad as all that, but she was aware of the way they now looked at her—as sustenance, food, a game animal. It wasn't quite open season, not yet, but she could feel the sexual hunger in the air. The only thing keeping the hounds at bay was each other. Lately, she'd made a point of never being alone with any of them, except of course Witz who she could handle with one arm tied behind her back. So far, Price seemed the least interested, but he was also the most dangerous. It was a combination that excited her. No point lying to herself—she liked a good stiff fuck as much as the next girl. Where was Eric when she needed him? He had a way of making her feel safe.

"What about Kent?" asked DeLuca. A pained look transfigured his face. He ran his fingers slowly through his hair, applying pressure to his scalp. "He's our only way out of here."

"Don't worry about Kent," Price assured him. "He's not going anywhere—not in these conditions. Not unless he has a death wish."

"What about Hatcher? I don't want him burning the place to the ground while we're gone."

"Good luck," said Price. "He's been all weirded out since dinner with the Russian royal family. Locked up tight. You couldn't get him out of his room if you tried."

"We'll see about that," said Claire.

Ethan had been barricaded in his quarters going on four days now. Not even the hunger gnawing at his stomach nor the thick ammoniated stink of his own waste spreading out from one corner of the room could convince him to unlock the door. What difference did it make if he smelled like he'd been living out of a shopping cart and spending his nights sleeping under a freeway overpass? There were far worse ways of dying than from poor hygiene or an empty belly. If he hadn't known it before, he sure as shit realized it now. Considering that Alyona, the crazy fucking nympho bitch, had murdered him, everything else seemed pretty goddamn unimportant. Good grooming was way the fuck down on his list of priorities. And grabbing a bite to eat was way fucking firmly dead last. One peek at the menu had straight away killed his appetite. He should've seen it sooner, before the mother of all STD's had turned his blood to sewage and left him standing graveside at his own funeral. But look on the bright side—at least he hadn't gone crying like a baby to the others and given himself away. As far as they were concerned, he was grieving for Alan, not himself.

Throughout their visit with the Russians Alyona had gone after him like a sex-starved inmate on conjugal leave from a women's prison. As much as he'd enjoyed playing the stud, his enthusiasm was offset by a growing climate of resentment brewing among Alyona's male colleagues. Ethan knew better than to go wagging his dick around another man's garden, particularly where guns were involved. It didn't make for good diplomacy.

At the first possible opportunity he had grabbed the bottle of champagne Claire had picked out for him and had steered Alyona toward her quarters where they could be alone. Actually, it was Alyona who had initiated their retreat, dragging him along by his waistband back to her den. The room—he had been here a few times before—was a gloomy little cubicle possessing all the warmth and reassurance of a free clinic. An inconceivable array of junk was piled against the walls. Ordinarily, the squalor wouldn't have bothered him. He'd take a porn star over *Good Housekeeping's* Woman of the Year any day. But right now getting laid was secondary. Ethan clung to the hope that the DVD camcorder had not been destroyed in the blast, that the Russians—*goddamn scavengers*—had made off with it along with his Kirk Gibson jersey and whatever else they came across. He still couldn't believe that Zhenya, the ballsy little prick, was actually wearing it. But then again, it was merely by chance that Ethan had noticed the jersey layered conveniently beneath Zhenya's parka as he leaned across the table during dinner and helped himself to a quivering cube of the stringy stew meat they were trying to pass off as pork.

Alyona pushed Ethan in ahead of her and closed the door. He scanned the room to see if the camcorder was anywhere in sight, but Alyona spun him around so that he was facing her and with a violent thrust of her hips sent him staggering backward toward the bed. He suggested popping the champagne—pawing at the impossible foil wrap smothering the cork—but she pressed on, an uneven tilt to her gaze. Whether it was carnivorous determination in her slow stalking pursuit or that she was now undressing with each step, something told him that she hadn't even understood the offer. If she had any awareness of her surroundings other than the nervous slab of meat he presented her, it was now being processed on an instinctive level. Army issue parka, thermal, and wifebeater—in three strides her upper half was stripped bare, her small perfectly upturned breasts basted with sweat. Army issue pants, thermals, panties—buck fucking naked! Diving into him, she half-smiled half-snarled, teeth flashing wetly, and knocked him off of his feet. She was on him before the sensation of weightlessness was gone, his freefall abruptly shattered by the bed. Before he could react, she pounced, ripping his pants down around his ankles. Ethan hardly knew what to make of it, but knew better than to open his mouth and risk killing the deal. A moment later he was inside her and from that point on it was like Secretariat thundering down the home stretch at the Kentucky Derby. She rode him with such reckless force that he was afraid to move. His pelvis took a beating but it wasn't all bad. Alyona muttered breathlessly in Russian throughout—an unintelligible stream of fuck-me talk that gave way to an urgent staccato wailing. Ethan was sure that her cries would summon the others—Shurik at least. And then she was done, her insides clenching him tightly long after she sat up and swept the loose tassels of hair from her flushed and sweat-dampened face. Ethan hadn't even come.

"Wow," Ethan remarked, summoning as much enthusiasm as he could given the fact that he'd been shortchanged. "Someone's glad to see me."

Alyona ignored him and cast an indifferent glance around the room. "I am vwanting for see-garette . . ." she said. "You have?"

"Don't smoke," Ethan replied. "But wasn't it Freud who said that penises and cigars were one in the same? Symbolically of cou—"

Alyona dismounted him abruptly and strode around the room naked, rummaging through the haphazard contents. Cursing aloud in Russian, she swept shelves bare, flinging aside anything that got in the way of her search.

"I was wondering—" Ethan probed impatiently. "Have you or any of your people been by the station since the explosion? Because there a few things of mine I'd like back if possible."

She knocked over a stack of books and fixed her eyes squarely on him. "*Nyet*," she stated flatly.

"*Nyet* what?" Ethan asked. He was getting frustrated. "*Nyet*, you haven't been to the station, or *nyet* I can't have my things back?"

"*Nyet*, vwee have not been to stayshun," she responded dully.

"That's funny because Zhenya's wearing my Kirk Gibson jersey under his jacket."

"Vwhat Zhenya vwearing?"

Ethan sat up and pulled on his pants. "Look," he said, "I don't give a fuck about the jersey. It's the camcorder." Stupidly, he pantomimed someone operating an old turn-crank movie camera.

"I know vwhat eez camera."

"It's essential that I get it back. And the memory cards—they might contain information about what happened to my team."

"I know vwhat happen to team . . ." she said, offering a little pantomime of her own. "Boom!"

Alyona abandoned her search for cigarettes and approached the bed. The feral glint had returned to her eyes. She reached out and attempted to unbutton Ethan's pants, but he stopped her. For the first time he noticed the grime under her fingernails, and thought about the ochre crescent underscoring the fingernail of the severed finger Bishop had collected from the site of the explosion. Ethan's situation reasserted itself with a singular urgency.

"The camcorder—" he asked again. "Please tell me you've seen it."

Alyona ignored him and tugged savagely at his waistband. Ethan resisted, but it wasn't easy. She was strong—stronger than he remembered.

"Look," he said, raising his voice and forcing her off of him. "I'll fuck you all night if it'll make you happy, but right now I need that camcorder! I'll tear this goddamned place to the ground if I have to."

Alyona straightened up and eyed him appreciatively. "I know vwhere is vwideo camera," she teased. "Feerst, me you fuck."

"Listen to me!" he exploded, seizing her by the wrist and spinning her around so that he was on top of her. He pinned her to the bed with all his weight. "I'm not fucking around."

Alyona winced in pain, her face contorting masochistically. "*Owwww!*" she moaned.

Ethan came back into himself and let her go. "I didn't mean to hurt you."

But Alyona pulled him back on top of her. "I like," she purred, wrapping her legs around him. "You be strong vwiss me."

"Please," he urged, "just tell me where the camcorder is."

"Joost kees, okay? Then I tell you vwhere is camcorder." She closed her eyes and parted her lips.

What the hell, he wasn't getting anywhere with reason. He hadn't noticed it earlier when lust had elevated his own body temperature, but Alyona was burning up. Her mouth, her cheeks . . . Jesus, her hands were like branding irons on his exposed flesh. When it became clear that she had no intent of letting up, Ethan attempted to pull back. She locked her arms around his neck and mashed her mouth into his, biting him on the lower lip.

Enough was enough. The horny bitch had lost her mind. Ethan could taste the blood, warm and metallic, as it gushed into his mouth. This time anger was on his side as he easily threw Alyona to the ground. He stood over her, fists poised like mallets ready to crush her skull, but she was unimpressed, taunting even. She crouched on her haunches and glared back at him. A different kind of light now burned inside of her, the bottomless wells of her pupils yawing before him so that instinctively he edged backward, awed by that terrible plunge into nothingness. And then she sprang at him, teeth bared. Ethan outweighed her by at least fifty pounds but had to fight to stay on his feet. It was like some sort of mad dance they were performing—a deranged tango—Alyona locking him up with her arms and plunging her tongue into his bloodied mouth. And then with an artfulness that caught him totally by surprise she planted her foot firmly between his legs, hooking him behind the right knee and toppled him onto his back. He impacted the floor with a resounding thump, his tailbone absorbing the worst of the impact. For only a split-second, though it was long enough to send a jolt of terror surging through him, he could not move his legs. Numbness radiated out from the point of the impact, leaving him vulnerable and open to attack. He had fucked some she-devils in his day, but other than a few fleeting reservations easily remedied by a condom, none had given him cause to fear for his safety. But that was then. As he groped for something with which to defend himself, Ethan's hand wrapped around the neck of the champagne bottle. Instinct took over and he lashed out with it, catching Alyona squarely upside the head. Stunned, she collapsed on top of him, her breath coming in slow crackling gasps that reeked of Russian rotgut.

Although there was no reason for him to expect otherwise—having never even been so much as a witness to a barroom brawl—the bottle remained in one piece. That it had not easily broken terrified Ethan. Dazedly, he let the bottle slip from his hand with a dull discouraging thud. How hard had he hit her? Obviously, hard enough to knock her out, but was it hard enough to kill her? There was the noise the bottle had made as it contacted her skull—a crisp batting practice whack—but he didn't want to think about that. Hard. He had hit her hard—not intentionally—but who was going to believe him? Especially if her brain swelled and she croaked. No blood, but already a nasty-looking welt had risen over her temple, the aggravated tissue melting into her left eye socket and pinching it closed. Regardless of his intent, it was what it was. No trial by jury down here. Guns—that's how it would be decided if Shurik or one of the others came snooping around. A man couldn't hit a woman and get away with it—no matter where he was or what the situation happened to be. The fate of Claire's father, knifed to death while in a drunken stupor, was all the convincing Ethan needed to get his ass in high gear and run for the hills.

Although numb elsewhere from shock, the feeling had returned to his legs. He rolled Alyona off of him and positioned her on the bed so that the bruised side of her head lay buried in the pillow. She was breathing so shallowly that he had to lean in close to be convinced that she wasn't already dead. If anyone popped in, they'd assume that she was sleeping. Ethan took a few deep breaths, settled himself down and prepared to face the others. *Just round 'em up and go. You can explain yourself later.*

He was halfway out the door when a commotion erupted in the hall—stressed voices, the scuffle of feet—and he hurried back to the bed. Purely instinct. He draped himself over Alyona and pretended to be making out with her. If she came around now he was fucked. A second later Price was banging on the door and demanding that they leave. Ethan didn't know and didn't care. He was moving toward the door a second time when something caught his eye. Scarcely larger than a paperback itself, the camcorder was wedged in a row of books atop a tier of homemade shelves against the wall at the foot of the bed. He could almost feel the lens watching him—reflective, inscrutable, auto-focusing—an infallible witness to his misdeeds. Dr. Ethan Hatcher: abusive boyfriend, murderer, necrophiliac. He might get his fifteen seconds on TMZ after all. The little green recording light was on. No wonder Alyona hadn't wanted to give up the camcorder just yet—Little Miss Freaky had been preparing him a filthy keepsake. Shame she was totally nuts. The memory cards were there too—several in all blessedly intact in the zippered storage case—also wedged in amongst the books.

It was bad enough that Ethan hadn't showered in way too fucking long—*ripe*, there was no other way to describe the aged stink coming off his body—but the fact that he'd resorted to pissing in the corner of his room . . . Hell, it proved just how much things had changed since their fucked-up little get-together with the Russians. He was becoming like one of those shut-ins you hear about on the nightly news who'd rather shoot it out with the authorities than take out the trash or remove the aluminum foil from every window in the house. Long toenails, greasy hair, a fervent distrust of everyone and everything including soap. What a fucked-up way to go.

Ethan had never liked reruns—in fact, he despised them—but the drama captured on the memory cards was not your standard primetime fare. HBO would've run the other way. It was impossible to say exactly how many times he'd already watched it from beginning to end, only that the answers he'd been seeking the first time through were now the same answers he wished he'd never gotten.

Ethan watched from the beginning, retracing the catastrophe all the way back to the first day of the expedition, hoping to pinpoint what had gone wrong. He, himself, figured prominently in much of the earlier footage but that was from another time, another life, and he recognized himself only distantly like a reflection of a reflection of a reflection. Most of it was pretty routine, but the last card, the final installment in an increasingly disjointed anecdotal record, was as close to a Lee Harvey Oswald as they were going to find.

It wasn't the actual footage that troubled Ethan—though there were certainly moments that raised questions . . . It was the mood, a strange atmosphere, call it what you will. Outwardly, these were the same men he had left behind only days earlier, yet they were somehow different. Gone was the spark, the easy banter, the camaraderie that had united them in their work and had enabled them to overcome the terrible solitude of Antarctica. There now existed in its place a climate of apprehension and quiet reserve. Budding paranoia, active distrust. The last card chronicled the profound shift; it was enough to convince Ethan that Ivan the Terrible had crashed the party not long after his own timely departure.

Alan had done most of the recording in Ethan's absence, capturing just enough of the team's daily activities to assemble a roughly chronological progression of events. The time/date stamp on each file provided a to-the-second account of the team's last days. Ethan already knew about the discovery of the vent community on the lake bottom. What he couldn't possibly have imagined was how stupidly his team had behaved in the wake of its discovery.

He would have believed that it was all just a put-on to get his goat had they not filmed themselves actually eating the shrimp. Even Ellis, Mr. Practicality, had agreed to Leonelli's half-baked suggestion. Ethan's first instinct was to blame himself. All of this could have been avoided if he had just leveled with Alan and the others from the beginning. Then again, they should have known better. They were scientists, not aborigines. You just don't eat whatever the hell you find crawling around under the nearest rock. Not only was it risky and unprofessional, it simply wasn't good judgment. Unfortunately, a lack of good judgment wasn't all they'd shown.

Ethan's guilt—a great big nagging crapload of it—was complicated by the fact that after going over the footage for the umpteenth time he felt as if he was right there with them. It may not have been reality—not his old reality, not the Los Angeles reality he knew and loved, fuck no, not even close—but the first time he had opened his eyes to their world he had embarked on a journey into an alternate reality that would ultimately claim him as a permanent resident. The images projected on the tiny display grew and enveloped Ethan so that he no longer had to hold the camcorder inches from his face to experience everything. From the vibrations in the air to the chemical burn of adrenaline to the static field of paranoia, he was right there with them.

But that wasn't even the worst thing about it. As much as he was becoming a fixture of their last moments on earth, the events remained untouchable, immutable, digitally encoded on a scrap of silicon. No matter how badly Ethan wanted to stop Alan and the others from repeating the same mistakes that had gotten them dead, to impose his will on that one terrible eye-blink in history, he was powerless to intervene. He could only stand by and watch as the events unfolded time and again with the same singular purpose and dread. So this was Hell.

Ethan could taste the warm waft of garlic in the air as Leonelli served each of them a portion of golden-brown shrimp. The clink of utensils and grunts of approval, the smacking of lips and hearty compliments circulating around the table. Northcutt scarcely breathed between mouthfuls, and Lim nodded enthusiastically with each bite. Hamsun ate with his big brutal hands—Ethan knew all too well—both stuffing himself and feeding select morsels to Sven who now sat in Ethan's seat, a pair of astute brown monkey eyes peering hungrily over the edge of the table, his bristling black dome bobbing enthusiastically. Ellis said something to Schmidt about ". . . how the other half lived" and they all laughed and toasted their discovery with coffee mugs of red wine. Ethan was now living through Alan's eyes.

On the next file, Igor was up and running. They had begun to collect data on the vent. Although only twelve hours had elapsed since the meal of tainted shrimp, the team was already exhibiting the effects of what Alan would later report to Ethan as a case of the flu: sore throat, fatigue, stiffness in the joints. Leonelli was hit first and hit hardest. Alan had recorded the stricken hydrologist lying in bed, mumbling incoherently in a state of semi-conscious delirium. Forty-eight hours later they were all sick with flu symptoms. The filming stopped but for a brief clip of Alan documenting the site of the infection. "Welcome to the ICU . . ." he joked feebly, looking in on each member of the team, prostrate and shivering and babbling in their beds. Before signing off, Alan had turned the camcorder on himself. Ethan was stunned at how devastated his friend looked—waxen, quivering, malarial.

Soon enough the mystery illness had seemingly run its course. The team was up and about, but they all suffered from a lingering chill. Schmidt and Ellis argued over whose turn it was in the Meat Locker, and Leonelli wondered aloud why it was so fucking cold inside the station. The thermostat had to be wrong, stabbing the wall-mounted unit with his index finger. No way was it over 80°—not even close!

Roughly four days—ninety-six hours—after the fateful meal, Hamsun emerged from the hallway and stood before the others who loitered about the common room. He was wearing his parka and grinning stupidly. Moments later, Sven emerged from the shadows carried along on his ugly flat feet by a kind of rocking monkey-swagger. He was wearing Ethan's Kirk Gibson jersey, the hem of which touched the floor and trailed behind him as would an evening gown. Laughter, applause, Alan saying: "Someone remind me to erase this before Hatcher gets back . . ." Blackness. Next segment.

The station door swung open and in scuffled Leonelli. Someone out of the frame of the picture said, "The prodigal son returns" before he entered the frame of the picture. A second later Alan quipped, "Honey, I'm home!" and activated the zoom feature. Leonelli's face surged into the foreground. The first few times Ethan had watched the video he had instinctively recoiled as Leonelli pressed towards him. The clarity was unreal, the focus tight, the fidelity digital. Leonelli was covered in blood. He was not looking at them however, but through them. A thousand-yard stare, the bright whites of his eyes contrasting starkly with the frozen mask of blood. The camcorder microphone picked up the shallow diastolic of Alan's breathing. "Close the door," he urged. "You're letting out the heat."

Twenty-seven hours after Leonelli had shown up covered in blood—*no call? no freaking S.O.S? no Ellis!*—Alan sat recording in the quarters he shared with Lim. The only source of light appeared to be ultraviolet—the subject, Sven, suffused in cool purple-gray halftones. Alan was speaking to him—speaking *and* listening—as if embroiled in a heated conversation with the chimp. Despite Alan's adversarial posture and a laundry list of wild accusations including paranoia, deceit and wild talk of a conspiracy among his colleagues—*for god's sake, Alan, he's a chimp!*—Sven merely stared emotionlessly into the eye of the camcorder. The one-sided conversation was as chilling a moment as Ethan had ever witnessed. Leonelli's bloody homecoming was a sure candidate for the Goosebumps Hall of Fame, but that had a kind of slasher film gaudiness to it. This, on the other hand, was quiet and psychological. Pure lunatic soliloquy.

At first he believed that Alan had simply cracked. Solitude, isolation, boredom—stronger men had crumbled under less. After a dozen subsequent viewings, however, the missing half of the dialogue had begun to take shape in Ethan's mind. Soon, he was ad-libbing for Sven the words Alan had hallucinated. Sven's treachery did not end with his thieving of Ethan's Kirk Gibson jersey; it went much deeper. The little shit-disturber was fucking with Alan's mind, pushing his buttons. Ethan could see it in Sven's beady black, ill-omened eyes. He was up to something. Trouble was inscribed in the deep wrinkles lining his ugly little face.

Fast forward: A crash course in relativity proved to Ethan that no matter how bad things seemed at any given moment they could always get worse. For Alan and the rest of the first expeditionary team. *For himself.* Of the two men sprawled on the floor of the common room entangled in one another's grasp, only Schmidt still clung to life. His graying hair was matted with blood that gushed from a ragged crater where his left ear should have been. Although severe by any standard Ethan imagined it was not this particular injury, nor was it at least a dozen other cuts and welts marring Schmidt's face and neck—*bite marks?*—that gave rise to his pitiful moans. In fact every last one of his fingers had been cleaved away at the first knuckle, leaving only his thumbs and more blood. Much, much more blood. And he was the lucky one.

Northcutt's fingers, too, had been hacked off but there was also a hole in his forehead centered just above the bridge of his nose. The hole was perhaps an inch in diameter—not particularly big, but obviously deep—and out of it burbled something mushy and wet that was almost certainly brains. Northcutt's eyes remained fixed on the hole—open, upward and crossed—the whites of which incandesced eerily in the dusky purplish light.

If there had been a speck of doubt about the one responsible for the murderous rampage, it was instantly dispatched when Leonelli pushed his way past Alan into the center of the frame and drove the pick end of the ice axe so forcefully through Schmidt's skull—in one side and out the other with a pulpy *thwack!*—that it lodged in the wood floor beneath. Only when Hamsun and Lim cantered into the picture did Alan let go of the camcorder.

But Ethan's lesson was far from over. Picking up the drama mid-frame, Leonelli recorded what amounted to the last moments of Alan's life. With Lim lying there broken Hamsun rumbled something absurd at Alan and came for him. The evil dimwit was chuckling, eyes blazing, his wild blonde beard clotted with food scraps as he scampered after Alan calling out to him in an unintelligible dialect like some sort of deranged horse whisperer. Alan tried talking sense into him, but reason no longer figured into Hamsun's system of behavioral checks and balances. For the first time, fear crept into Alan's eyes.

One of the last installments came on the heels of Alan's retreat. Leonelli followed Hamsun, egging him on, as Alan backpedaled around the room dodging the Norwegian's outstretched arms. Although inadvertent, the most telling detail of any file of footage was revealed as Alan circled behind the folding table where the team took its meals. The first time it was just a blur, a momentary slip of the camcorder as Leonelli panned across the surface of the table repositioning for a better angle on the action. But during one of the many dozen subsequent viewings when Ethan had plodded through the macabre reality show frame by frame looking for answers he was able to give the blur an identity: A frying pan . . . A frying pan full of human fingers. Crooked, shrimp-like, evenly browned. He'd been so horrified by what he had seen of Northcutt and Schmidt that he hadn't even considered the possibility that there was a reason behind the blunted hands of the two men. A method to the madness.

In his zeal to capture the moment Leonelli bowled over as Hamsun stalked after Alan. Good for Alan. Bad for Leonelli. The camcorder crashed to floor but kept recording—below the ankles mostly. The most significant details of the next few moments were captured primarily on audio—grunting, gasping, cursing—for the camcorder now lay on its side where it had been kicked beneath the table by one of the men. The subsequent video consisted of a horizontal image of scuffling feet. Then

Leonelli hit the floor and the deadly dance was over. The gourmet chef lay crumpled on his side, facing the camcorder, wide-eyed and basted red with his own blood.

Enter Sven. Summoned by the commotion, the chimp stole quietly into the common room. At first only his feet were visible beneath the hem of the Kirk Gibson jersey. When he reached Leonelli he bent over at the waist, cocked his head to one side and looked into the dead man's unblinking eyes. He then noticed the camcorder, and seeing that he was not being watched, made a beeline for it. Forbidden fruit. Apparently, it was one of a remaining few items in the station still off limits to him.

For several seconds Sven manipulated the curious device in his dexterous hairy-backed hands. At one point his face filled the screen—the auto-focus trying but failing to accommodate the super close-up—a warped humanoid image no less distinct than what Ethan had observed of the men he once knew. Sven then embarked on a mini-epic, imitating what he had observed of the camcorder's operation. He managed to capture only one image of any interest: the other two chimps Okum had intended as vessels for Ivan—unnamed and uninfected—still locked in their cages staring warily at Sven. After a few brief moments Sven toddled into the storeroom where he'd apparently been holed up for some time. He discarded the camcorder in favor of a half-eaten jar of peanut butter, smacking and pushing out his lips.

Another thirty-six hours had passed by the time the record button was again depressed. The explosion had already destroyed much of the station. Sven was now the subject, and one of the Russians was filming. They were still in the storeroom, Sven's nest now mucked up with pink fire-retardant foam. Zhenya and Georgiy were trying to calm the aggravated chimp, talking and cooing at him as if he were a scared child. Ethan could hear Shurik's low booming voice and guessed that he was the one operating the camcorder. Zhenya and Georgiy had cornered Sven and were gradually inching toward him. Sven jutted out his head and bared his teeth, but made no other move. He seemed run-down, lethargic. The fur about his arms and head was dull and matted, and Ethan's Kirk Gibson jersey looked as if it had been worn in a food fight. The Russians bickered among themselves while Sven eyed them suspiciously. A woman's voice—Alyona. She was there with them. Zhenya looked over his shoulder into the camcorder, said something and smiled. As he swiveled his head back to face Sven, the chimp sprang at him. Gunshots ripped through the storage room, knocking Sven off his feet and tumbling him backwards into the nest. Alyona moved cautiously into the frame of the picture, prodded Sven with the smoking barrel of an AK-47 and . . .

That was it. Shurik had stopped recording. What had happened to Sven after Alyona had shot him was anyone's guess. All Ethan knew was that the chimp was nowhere to be found when he and the others had arrived on the scene a couple of weeks ago. There was one more segment piggybacked onto the rest. Until now Ethan had only watched it once. It was of him and Alyona fucking: her biting him, him clubbing her in the head. *What the fuck*, he thought, allowing the segment to continue past the point at which he usually restarted the file at the beginning, *the bitch had it coming.*

Every time he watched it Ethan had tried to separate himself from the terrifying world captured in HD, but something kept him coming back for more. At first it was curiosity, the need to know what had happened to Alan and the other members of the first team. Then, wanting to be sure, he had run through every second of footage again and again looking for evidence of a culprit other than Ivan the Terrible. Somewhere along the way he'd gotten sucked in. The morbid, train wreck fascination of it was impossible to resist. When he wasn't watching, the footage called to him.

That was how it had started. Better them than him—this, of course, was the allure. Slowly, however, the realization that he was riding the same train compelled him to take a different kind of interest in the recording. Ethan was relatively certain that DeLuca and the current team were, at least so far, unaware of how fucked they all were. They hadn't seen what he had seen, and therefore couldn't possibly have known where and how their fates would intertwine with those they'd been sent to toe-tag. Information was power. Ethan would guard his secret until he figured out what his next move was going to be. If anyone learned that he was infected, game over. He thought about approaching Claire, but trust no longer figured into his reckoning of the world.

Even with the mounting body of evidence, Ivan still seemed farfetched, the stuff of science fiction. But then again so had the flesh-eating Ebola virus before some unfortunate dirt farmer in darkest Africa had unleashed it on the world. And now there were symptoms to consider. He was running a fever. He had borrowed a thermometer from the first-aid kit to make sure that it wasn't psychosomatic. No such luck: 103.4°. He was burning up. He hadn't slept well the last forty-eight hours, his muscles ached, and his throat hurt when he swallowed. The rescued footage was like a guided tour: *"Today you'll be experiencing this, tomorrow you'll be experiencing that, and the day after . . . Well, you'll either be dead or you'll wish you were."* Before long, he'd be reduced to a homicidal lunatic. Then it'd be too late—his brain too far gone—for him to wiggle his way out.

Whatever course of action he decided on, the logistics were going to be a bitch. This was Antarctica—he couldn't just dial up a cab. Even if it were that easy, some nasty winds had knocked out the relay dish, crippling their communications for the time being. At least that was the version DeLuca was selling. What did it really matter anyway? No doubt, Okum was listening in. Ethan's best and perhaps only hope lay with Kent, the only one among them who could fly the Osprey. If Ethan could get himself back to McMurdo there would be too many witnesses present for Okum to stick him in a cage. He could worry about the rest later.

From the moment his plan had first crystallized, Ethan knew that it would be easier handling Kent one on one than among the others. Divide and conquer. Fortunately, getting him alone wasn't going to be a problem. Every four hours he fired up the Osprey's engines to keep them from icing over. A simple hijacking—how difficult could it be? The problem was going to be getting inside the Osprey without alerting DeLuca and the others to his intentions.

A few days ago it would've been a piece of cake. Because he wasn't directly involved with JPAC, Ethan was more or less ignored by the others. He stayed out of their way, and they left him to do his own thing. But this was no longer the case. Although DeLuca and his guys carried on as if nothing had changed, Ethan knew better. It all started shortly after they had returned from the Russian station. Once Claire had run through her ordeal with Zhenya and Shurik, and had convinced DeLuca and the others that she was okay, their attention shifted to Ethan. They were far too interested in his cut lip. When questioned about it, Ethan explained that he had accidentally bitten himself during dinner with the Russians. Bishop had wanted to take a closer look, but Ethan wouldn't have anything to do with it. They had been watching him ever since. Not overtly, especially not since he had locked himself in his quarters, but watching him just the same.

He could hear them tiptoeing around in the corridor, keeping tabs. He'd seen shadows under the door, had even lain on the floor hoping to identify his watcher by the type of shoes he wore. He had even called out to them, but of course they didn't answer. Not a fucking peep, though usually the sound of his voice was enough to scare them away. It was as if they expected him to turn into a werewolf. How could they have known? Only Ethan had seen the footage. Only he knew that the Russians were infected, that Alyona, *fucking rattlesnake bitch of a whore*, had poisoned him with her saliva. He hadn't given much thought to how the Russians had become infected. He didn't know and didn't give a shit.

Even if he had wanted to help them it was too late. Obviously, Alyona and her comrades had made Ivan's acquaintance well in advance of Ethan's own memorable introduction. Poor schmucks had probably already settled down to the business of killing each other. He was guessing that they had been infected sometime in the past five or six days, maybe a week. During dinner they were bundled up like Eskimos. Infected. It also explained why Alyona had tried to make a Happy Meal out of him.

Ethan couldn't honestly say that he knew any of the Russians all that well, having interacted with them only briefly on a couple of occasions. Still, he'd observed nothing in their behavior to expect the sort of nascent savagery that had reared its head three nights ago. Where was he going with all of this? *Focus. Now's not the time to go off on some tangent. Oh, yes . . .* Why he believed that DeLuca and the others were still stumbling around in the dark. Simple: even Ethan had attributed the behavior of Shurik's gang to a case of cabin fever. In fact, if he hadn't tracked down the camcorder there would've been no reason for him to believe any different.

Why, then, had they been spying on him? He had asked himself this very question again and again but hadn't been able to come up with a plausible answer. When it finally came to him, he wished it hadn't. Alan's tooth . . . the unscrupulous bastards! If they wanted it, they'd have to pry it from Ethan's cold, dead hand. He would never let all that remained of his best friend end up rattling around in the bottom of a shoebox tucked away on a dusty shelf in a government forensics lab somewhere. He had been sleeping with the tooth under his pillow for safekeeping. Now that he was going mobile he needed to hide it. In an hour and ten minutes Kent would fire up the Osprey, regular as clockwork.

Kent usually let the engines run for about five minutes, just enough to get the bird's blood pumping. Fortunately for Ethan, the entire station was modular, the floor of which comprised a grid of interlocking panels. Once he had gotten his hands on the proper tools it was relatively easy removing the bolts that held the panels in place. He chose the panel directly beneath his bed so that he could camouflage his escape route should the need arise. He'd been out through the floor once already—a dry run to see that it could be done. The station sat on a raised foundation about eighteen inches above the ice. The crawl space was home to a network of heating conduits wrapped in insulating sheathing. Although it was a tight fit, Ethan had managed to belly his way to the overhang that deflected the wind around the base of the structure. He had loosened the bolts on one section of the wind skirt, and was confident that he could kick it out when the time came. If things went according to plan he'd be back at McMurdo and on his way to a Christchurch hospital before anyone realized he was gone . . . provided Kent could get the Osprey airborne in this wind.

Ethan had a plan, he had the camcorder and the memory cards, he had his persuader for Kent—the biggest cooking knife he could find in the kitchen was sheathed in the top of his boot. All he needed now was a place to hide Alan's tooth and a little patience. What better way to kill an hour than a virtual stroll down Memory Lane? *The Real Housewives of Antarctica*—one more time from the top!

He was at the part where Leonelli, drenched in blood and clutching the ice axe, threw open the station door . . . There was shouting, commotion, someone called Ethan's name in a stern voice, and it was as if that world became this world and this world became that world. He was confused, disoriented. The hazy distinction between Alan's reality and his own was more pronounced than ever and he was slow to react. Again, someone called his name. A trick! They were trying to confuse him. Catch him off guard. DeLuca must've figured out his plan. A gust of wind rattled the loose floor panel and Ethan expected Price to come storming out from under his bed, guns blazing. Without thinking, he popped Alan's tooth into his mouth and swallowed it. *They'll never find it now. Not unless, they cut you open.* There was more commotion—someone pounding on his door. His heart raced. He reached for the knife in his boot but stopped short when he realized the voice calling out to him belonged to Claire.

"Ethan? . . . We found someone in a crack in the ice not far from the station. A few hundred yards . . . He must be one of yours." She pounded on the door. "I know you can hear me!" she pleaded. "What's gotten into you?! This is really fucking important." Long pause. "I'm scared."

Ethan balked at the idea that anyone had survived the blast. He was having a hard time processing information. Then again, Ellis had never returned from his trip to the dry valley with Leonelli. It was possible that Leonelli had murdered him and dumped the body so the others wouldn't be able to prove what had really happened. The pieces fit—JPAC still hadn't located the remains of two of the team members. Ellis was one of them. The other . . .

"It's Lim," said Claire. "Come on, Hatcher, don't do this." Several moments elapsed before she spoke again. This time she was calm. "We're gonna bring him back to the station. I guess you can see him then."

But Ethan had stepped back inside the footage, was lost in its myriad convolutions, a prisoner of its dark direction. Alan was ordering Lim to get help from the Russians . . . So it wasn't a trick. DeLuca, Claire—none of them had seen the recording. They couldn't have known that Lim had made it out before the blast. Why hadn't Ethan thought of it? They were vacuuming up dust bunnies when they should have been searching the ice field. This changed everything.

"Hatcher," Claire called out again. "Who are you talking to?" She abandoned her earlier reserve and hammered on the door. "I can hear your voice . . . Ethan, please, you're freaking me out!"

Ethan wrenched himself away from the video and stashed the camcorder under his bed. He pulled his pant leg down over his boot, concealing the knife. "Okay," he said. "But you have to leave before I come out."

"Ethan, what's wrong with—"

"I mean it!" he shouted. "Or the door stays locked."

How, when and why the radical shift in the group dynamic had come about, Claire couldn't say. Undoubtedly the pieces were in place from the beginning. The *real* beginning—200,000 BC—when *Homo sapiens* had slaughtered his Neanderthal cousins in the push for Stone Age dominance. For her, the wake-up call coincided with the rape attempt—a timely reminder that man was little more than a creature of brutish habit and base instinct. Civility, morality—these were affectations, sugar coating, the sweet veneer of civilization. The other stuff—hunger and lust and aggression—was hard wired.

It took some coaxing but she eventually talked Hatcher out of his quarters. He smelled as if he'd been moonlighting as a stable boy—this wasn't nearly as bad as the fumes seeping out from under the door to his quarters—but she was grateful for his expertise at the controls. Finding the crevasse this time around was considerably more difficult than when gravity had swept Claire into it earlier, albeit less painful. Her bruised flesh recorded each bump as the tundra buggy bounced and lurched over the uncertain terrain. After searching for close to an hour they found themselves positioned along its fractured edge, a jagged laceration cutting deep into the hide of the frozen beast known to them as Antarctica. The buggy's enormous headlamps saturated the area with brilliant white light that spilled into the crevasse. The walls, a dizzying shade of Caribbean blue, opalesced so intensely that Claire's brain ached at the sight of it. She and the others stood shoulder to shoulder staring dumbly at the dead man fused to the icy ledge beneath them.

Bishop was the first to speak. He had to shout to be audible above the wind. "This is exactly why I haven't defrosted my freezer in the last five years. You never know what you'll dig up."

"I need a long stick or something," yelled Price. He was squatting on his haunches squinting into the crevasse.

"What are you gonna do?" asked Bishop. He was still staring at Lim. "Poke him and see if he moves?"

"Are you gonna go in there and get him?" Price asked.

"Last time I checked, bars beat stripes."

"That's what I thought," said Price.

A few seconds later Witz returned cradling a car jack.

"I asked for a stick."

"Where am I going to find a stick out here?" asked Witz. "It's not like we're in the middle of the forest."

Price snatched the jack from Witz's hands. "Just give it to me."

Price stood over the crevasse and hurled the jack at the base of the ledge where Lim held his gargoyle's vigil. The entire floor shattered like glass, the twinkling shards sucked into a bottomless black abyss. "We're gonna need some rope."

Price secured one end of the rope around his waist and looped the other end through a tow hook on the front of the tundra buggy. Meanwhile, Bishop and Witz were arguing about something. Lately, even petty disputes had become fertile ground for larger, more hotly contested matters of opinion into which reason and logic rarely figured. This led to that, and that became this, and before long they'd be lunging at each others' throats like dogs.

"Let it go, you two!" Price barked. "This is some serious shit . . . It's a long god-damn way down. Drop me, and I'll climb back out and kill the both of you."

Bishop began to pick up where he'd left off—something about eating 'pencil dicks' like Witz for breakfast—but Price thrust his index finger at Bishop's masked face. "Think I'm playin', you big dope? Try me!"

Claire had never seen Price like this. He was usually in control of his emotions, every bit as machine-like in mind as he was in body. But like he said, this was for real. One slip-up and he was as good as dead.

"This isn't over," Bishop informed Witz malevolently.

Once Price made his way over the edge of the crevasse it was only a matter of moments before he occupied a space on the icy ledge next to Lim. He then, very carefully, slipped out of the makeshift harness and secured it around Lim's torso. "Okay," he shouted. "He's all yours."

They hauled on the rope but Lim wouldn't budge. After a few attempts, it became clear that getting him out of the crevasse wasn't going to be as easy as they'd thought, especially with the ground being as slick as it was. Even with their combined effort, traction was hard to come by. None of them had bothered to wear crampons. To make matters worse, Lim was fused to the ledge, his broken arm and subsequent outpouring of blood like glue binding him in place.

"Ease up on the rope," said Price. "Let me see what I can do." A short time later he called, "Catch," and tossed something out of the crevasse.

Witz snatched the object from the air. It was Lim's arm, severed just below the tourniquet at the point of the fracture. When Witz realized what he was holding, he quickly passed it off to Bishop, who then proceeded to sing into the hand-end of the ragged limb as if it were a microphone. Doing his best Sinatra, he sang "If I make it here, I'll make it anywhere . . ."

Claire was impressed at how well Bishop sang. His voice, though muffled by the neoprene mask, was full and resonant. A classic nightclub tenor. The familiar lyrics swelled above the blast of the wind, and for a few beats in time she was strangely enchanted.

"What the hell?" Hatcher called into the crevasse.

"I guess I don't know my own strength," Price apologized.

Once Price had been pulled to safety they gathered in a half-circle around Lim's frozen corpse where it now lay near the edge of the crevasse. No one spoke. Somehow words didn't seem relevant. For that matter, nothing seemed relevant. In fact, Claire wasn't sure why she'd been so gung-ho to come back for Lim in the first place. She was cold and felt sick to her stomach.

DeLuca broke the spell. "Now what?"

"Don't look at me," said Bishop. "This wasn't my idea."

"We load him up and get him back to the station where it's warm," said Price. "Then we can figure out what to do with him."

"Amen," Bishop agreed.

"I'm not touching him," said Witz. He was staring into Lim's eyes, dead and milky white. "It's like he's looking at me."

"We'll all do this together," said Price. "On three . . ."

Witz shook his head no, his gaze still pinned on Lim.

"Either you help us get this oversized Popsicle into the buggy," said Bishop, "or you can walk back to the station."

"The guy's frozen to the core," said Price. "The only thing he's looking at is a trip to the morgue."

"I don't know," said Claire. "Witz might be on to something . . . I know a guy, a cryogenics expert at UC Berkeley, who swears that in the next few years it will possible to freeze human beings and then completely reanimate them given the right conditions. All it will take is finding the right spark."

"A spark, huh?" Bishop mimicked.

"A catalyst," Claire corrected. She was of course trying to get even with Witz for pretending to leave her out here, but that didn't mean there wasn't a kernel of truth to it. "Chemical, electrical, biological . . . Something to jumpstart the engine. Anyway, just because it hasn't happened yet doesn't mean it can't. When Mary Shelly wrote *Frankenstein* in the early 1800's no one believed that heart transplants were possible, and now surgeons are performing them every day."

There was a momentary pause as they pondered what she had said. Maybe it was the darkness or the dirge-like howl of the wind, but for a moment Claire almost believed herself.

"Stop messin' with his head, will ya?" said Price. "We've been out her long enough."

"Let's just get it over with," Witz huffed. He squatted and cupped his hands together under Lim's head.

As they were lifting the body—no more than a hundred pounds at best, but a hundred pounds of incredibly awkward deadweight—Bishop lashed out to scare Witz, grabbing at his ribs and growling fiercely. Witz recoiled as if snake bitten, throwing up his arms and falling backward. The sudden uneven distribution of weight caused Claire and the others to drop Lim. He struck the ice with a dull ceramic clank. Claire looked at the ground, half-expecting to find a pile of shattered remains.

"I'll kill you!" Witz growled, lunging at Bishop.

"Got you good, Pencil Dick!" Bishop howled, sidestepping Witz's attack. "I hope you brought clean diapers!"

But Witz was beyond reach of Bishop's taunts. Hatred as pure as any Claire had ever witnessed now guided his actions. Bishop had managed to avoid the first attack, but poor footing gave Witz, the lighter of the two men, the upper hand. Again, he lunged, this time catching Bishop off-balance and knocking him off his feet. Bishop was no longer amused as he brushed himself off and stood tall. He looked bigger now, the buggy's lights stretching his shadow and imbuing him with a bold theatrical presence that somehow made him seem more immediate, more real, as if acting out a scripted transformation that would advance the plot toward an inevitable conclusion. He was through playing. Just when Claire thought Witz would get the message and back down, he surprised her and assumed a defensive stance, egging Bishop on. Claire didn't know if it had anything to do with where Witz had grown up—northern Minnesota was covered in ice two-thirds of the year—but he moved with an uncanny elegance that beguiled Bishop's slip-sliding advance.

"Stand down!" Price shouted, but for one reason or another the signal wasn't getting through to Bishop.

Although the initial go-around had moved them away from the crevasse, Bishop and Witz were now dangerously close to its edge. Witz would feint one way, get Bishop turned around, and then come at him from another direction, striking out as he skated past. The blows he landed were largely ineffectual, the choreographed assault rich with potential comedy were it not for the crevasse looming dangerously near. Claire knew better than anyone just how slick the ice could be, that in this frozen frictionless world you were never more than one misstep away from a crash course in the physics of gravity.

Witz's very next pass taught him the lesson Claire had recently learned herself as he miscalculated and skated into Bishop's waiting arms. In one sweeping motion, Bishop seized him and flung him outward and away. Witz's arms shot out as his left leg kicked upward in a desperate bid for stability that was not without an involuntary grace. It all happened so fast, so fluidly—a natural extension of a well-executed routine—that even Witz marveled at the effortlessness of his accidental arabesque as it carried him over the edge of the crevasse and into the gaping abyss. Spotlighted in the cool burn of the headlamps, Bishop stood there dumbly grabbing at nothing like a figure skater whose partner was snatched out of the air mid-flight—a triple-axel or a salchow—by forces beyond mortal comprehension.

"Witz!" Claire shrieked, her voice pulled after him into the great void.

"What the hell did you do?" Price shouted, moving as quickly as the unsure footing allowed to the edge of the crevasse.

"It was an accident," Bishop replied inertly.

"An accident!" DeLuca echoed. He grabbed Bishop by the parka and shook him violently. "You crazy bastard, you killed him! You killed Witz!"

"I didn't mean . . . The ice . . ." Bishop stammered. "You saw him coming after me. It was self-defense."

"The relay—" DeLuca continued, his rage acquiring an edge of despair. "Witz was the only one who had any idea how to fix it. We're fucked!"

"We still have the Osprey," said Price.

"What if the weather doesn't hold, then what?"

Price shook his head and moved back towards them. "Standing here freezing our asses off isn't gonna bring Witz back. Let's just get back to the station and finish what we started. We can figure this mess out later. Hatcher, give us a hand."

Claire had been too stunned to keep tabs on everyone. First the fight, now this. She'd never thought that her fear of the dark could be so easily pushed aside, but here she'd been immersed in night for the better part of two hours, and other more prominent fears now occupied her senses. At one point or another, Hatcher had retreated into the shadows in back of the buggy. He now stood eyeing them warily, melting into blackness as paranoia consolidated around him.

"Stay the fuck away from me," he warned.

"You heard Bishop," Price responded in a carefully modulated voice. "It was an accident. Coulda happened to any one of us. Isn't that right, Bish?"

"Maybe . . ." Bishop muttered emptily, suddenly indecisive. "I don't know, I don't know!"

"Go fuck yourself, Price," Hatcher called back. "I'll drive us back to the station, but I'm not going anywhere near that hole. You're all fucking nuts."

With a little effort the three of them—Price, Bishop and Claire—managed to coax Lim into the passenger compartment. From his seat at the controls, Hatcher watched each of them very carefully, including Lim whose mocking expression unsettled them all just a bit.

Ethan didn't believe in destiny, but he was smart enough to make the best of a fucked-up situation. Lim's frozen corpse had forced him to push back his plan to hijack the Osprey, but it had also sweetened his insurance policy. All along he had planned to use the camcorder footage to keep Okum off his back. But what about a cure? Ivan was only getting stronger, digging in its heels. Ethan's best and perhaps only hope resided within the possibility that an effective antibody could be developed. Ethan was no immunologist but if he remembered correctly such antibodies were derived from weakened or dead specimens of the infectious agents they were designed to kill. Therefore, it made damn good sense to have plenty of Ivan on hand if and when he made it back to civilization. This had all occurred to him in a flash of inspiration as Claire had insisted that they defrost Lim in the interest of procuring blood and tissue samples for scientific analysis. With an ample supply of infected blood Ethan's doctors wouldn't have to tap into his own precious reservoir.

He would postpone his departure another twenty-four hours or so—however long it took Lim to defrost, and Ethan to siphon off a couple of pints. To speed things along they'd stripped Lim naked and immersed him in a makeshift bath that was really nothing more than a large waterproof skin supported by a collapsible metal framework. The bath was laced with wire conduits that supplied the unit with heat. A glorified electric blanket. The unit was specifically designed to treat extreme cases of hypothermia but what the hell no one was going to catch a chill with the heater inside the station cranked up like it was. Lim wasn't complaining. He was a pulse and a couple of tokes off a joint away from calling his new digs a Jacuzzi.

Twenty-four hours, give or take. That's what Ethan was guessing. Kent wasn't going anywhere—not with their communications out and the weather acting up like it was. But how does one pass the time when time is standing still? As far as Ethan was concerned it may as well have been twenty-four years. A prison term. Day bled into night, night into day. He'd been an idiot to sequester himself away from the others, locking himself in his quarters like that. Not only had the isolation made him a little stir-crazy, he had given his "colleagues" free run of the station. It was a miracle they hadn't left his ass stranded here. Probably the only thing that had kept them hanging around this long was their inability to communicate with the outside world. The moment Okum caught wind of Ethan's condition, he'd evacuate the rest of them.

High, dry and cold as Lim's frostbitten cock—that's exactly how they would have left him. The fact that Bishop had flung Witz to his death, whether accidentally or not, was a godsend. As long as the relay was down Okum would be kept out of the loop. And last but not least, it proved that Ethan wasn't the only one feeling the pressure. If DeLuca and his guys weren't rattled before, they sure as shit were now. They were afraid of him and it was turning them against each other.

Until now he'd let paranoia lead him around by the balls, but not anymore. He'd keep an eye on JPAC until the last possible moment—mingle, mix it up—before making his getaway. *Keep your friends close and your enemies even closer . . . Isn't that what they say?* He could tell from the way they acted toward him—the troubled looks they secreted between one another, the way they deflected his questions with brusque monosyllables and vague gestures—that they knew. He was a danger to them. A carrier. It was written all over their faces. They were climbing the walls to get away from him. *Typhoid-fucking-Hatcher!*

The disinterest they had expressed in the discovery of Lim was obviously part of the same pitiful act they'd been putting on for weeks. Only a moron would have bought such studied aloofness. They were amateurs, soulless hacks. It was all about getting Ethan to drop his guard, lulling him into a false sense of security so they could toss a net over him and stick him in a cage. Out there in the cold, standing over the crevasse that like a tear in the fabric of space had swallowed Witz whole, they had momentarily dropped the act. But back inside the station where it was warm, far removed from the flimsy backdrop of their transparent performance, they picked up where they had left off, braving Witz's loss like soldiers are supposed to.

"Glad to see that you've rejoined society," DeLuca remarked. He was reclined on the sofa watching Price and Claire duel it out on the treadmill. He was drinking something clumpy and yellowish from a plastic cup.

"Is that what you call this?" said Ethan. "If that's the case, I don't want any part of it."

DeLuca thought it over, his impassive brown eyes reflecting inward. "There is one great society alone on earth: the noble living and the noble dead."

"Lovely sentiment," said Ethan. "I'm sure Witz would appreciate it. But like I said, I don't want any part of it."

DeLuca sighed deeply and took another sip of his drink. "Bishop, hang up the microphone for a second and see if you can rustle me up some more of these powdered eggs. You're right, they're not half-bad like this."

"Pure protein," Bishop agreed. "But that's the last of them."

Lathered in sweat, Price stepped down from the treadmill and turned it over to Claire. She was like a quarter horse straining at the starting gate before a big race. This was a look Ethan hadn't seen before. Yes, it was a variation on a theme—Claire was fiercely determined in everything she did—but ordinarily she wasn't this animated. Always in control, she played her emotions close to the hip. If there was an ounce of bravado in her, it hadn't been evident until now. She glared at Price as he dismounted and flashed him a cocky smile.

"You're mine," she declared soundly. She then gathered her hair into a ponytail and secured it with a rubber band.

"Looks like you're in trouble, Price," said DeLuca.

"I'm in trouble?" Price responded calmly. "Look who's talking, Mr. It-was-an-accident."

Nonplused Bishop went on. "Care to make it interesting?"

"It's your money," said Price.

"Who said anything about money?" Bishop devoured the last strip of turkey jerky and cast aside the empty bag. "I didn't say anything about money."

"What'd you have in mind?"

"Pound of flesh?" said Bishop, gnashing his teeth for effect.

"Tell you what," said Price. "I'll buy you a juicy steak when we get back to civilization."

"And if we don't make it back?"

Price's tone suddenly became adversarial. "I plan on seeing to it that we do."

Bishop shrugged and resumed what he'd been doing for the good part of the last hour. It hadn't taken him long to recover in the wake of the alleged accident that had sent Witz plunging to his death. It was as if the heat that had thawed their bones on the ride back from the crevasse—the same heat that had imparted a fever-sheen of melted ice crystals to Lim's sallow flesh—had killed off any trace of remorse. He now wandered the station, crooning mindlessly into Lim's severed arm. From the old standards to dark musings spawned from a vocal tradition much older than civilization, he serenaded them with a mutant breed of song that somehow managed to capture the mood they were all feeling.

From the moment Claire stepped on the treadmill she knew that something was different. Maybe she was still riding the adrenaline high from her hell-bent toboggan ride across the ice. Or perhaps she was finally over the fallout of the vodka and whatever drugs Zhenya had slipped her the other night. Whatever the reason she couldn't have been more exhilarated with the feeling of unbridled power now surging through her veins. Price was a goner. Claire hadn't bothered with a warm-up and had programmed treadmill for twenty-five minutes at the maximum speed of twelve miles per hour. Thirty seconds into it and she was already feeling her stride. A week ago, a pace like this would've killed her. Now it was a walk in the park.

She had always been competitive, particularly when the competition involved men, but this, this feeling inside of her was unprecedented. She didn't just want to beat Price—she wanted to crush him. For the first couple of minutes she was bothered by a throbbing ache in her left butt cheek. The fall into the crevasse had marked her with a bruise the size of Texas and the color of blackberry jam. But it no longer hurt. In fact, she took a masochistic pleasure in aggravating the injury. It would make her victory over Price that much sweeter. Pain was no longer a physical sensation, but a state of mind. All that was left of her now was a heartbeat, working muscles, and a mission.

Price had agreed to accompany her to the Russian station provided she took the checkered flag. Nothing in the world was going to stand between her and the opportunity to identify the urge gnawing at her insides. Shortly after the incident . . . *Listen to yourself, will you? The son of a bitch tried to stick his dick in you without your permission. Stop being so Mary Poppinish about the whole thing and call it what it was! R-A-P-E.* The first day or so after Zhenya had tried to *rape* her—*Good, now we're getting somewhere*—Claire was too shell-shocked to make sense of what she was feeling. There was a lot going on inside her head, but it was all jumbled together.

Shame, embarrassment, stupidity—if it involved self-loathing, chances are she'd been down that road already. She could identify each like the back of her hand. As for what else Zhenya's assault had let out of its cage . . . So far all Claire could say for certain was that she was now dealing with a species of emotion she had never before crossed paths with. Although she wasn't quite sure what she hoped to accomplish by returning to the scene of the crime, she knew that Price wouldn't come along without a compelling reason. He could drive the tundra buggy; Claire couldn't. Otherwise, she would have gladly made the trip alone. She could take care of herself. Of this, she was now eminently certain.

To arouse Price's curiosity, she considered mentioning the gunshots she'd heard but resisted the impulse for fear that he'd exercise good judgment and decide to stay the hell away. One thing was certain, good judgment was not the guiding force behind Claire's desire to return to the Gulag. Instead, she convinced Price that she wanted to confront Zhenya for her own peace of mind. Otherwise, she would remain the helpless victim. To put it simply, she needed closure. It was a tired cliché, but there was some truth to it. Closure, she'd decided, could mean just about anything you wanted it to. As for her true intent—that was a little trickier to pin down. The feelings smoldered deep inside of her, powerfully familiar and yet unassailably dormant. Like the first stirrings of sexuality in an adolescent, she was compelled by an urge shrouded in the mystery and allure of biological imperative.

"That's a hell of a pace," said Price. "But you'll never be able to keep it up."

Claire was ten minutes into the program and running effortlessly. She rode atop a mighty swell of mind and body.

"What bothers you more, Price?" she asked. "The fact that I'm a woman, or that you didn't see it coming? Did you think I'd just let you go on winning indefinitely?"

"Save your breath," he answered confidently. "You got a long way to go."

Claire knocked out the remainder of the twenty-five minutes and stepped down from the treadmill. Although she was dripping sweat, her breath was coming easily. As her body temperature had risen so had her strength. Really, she was just getting going when it was suddenly over. She didn't know what to make of the expression on Price's face. It was an odd mix of approval and suspicion.

"You on steroids or something?" he asked, his gold eyes flickering curiously.

Apparently, victory—*or something*—was in the air. Only moments after Claire left the common room and seconds before Ethan could do the same, McKenzie shot up from his workstation and cried out jubilantly: "Salt and pepper!"

DeLuca polished off the remainder of his powdered egg smoothie and wiped his mouth on the sleeve of his parka. "What are you talking about?"

"The finger Bishop collected the other day . . ." McKenzie went on. "Those crystals we were wondering about . . . They're salt crystals. And the little black flecks are pepper."

DeLuca perked up slightly. "I thought you said we didn't have the equipment here necessary to make that determination."

"We do, but we don't," said McKenzie. "I don't know why I didn't think of it sooner."

"You didn't?" said Ethan, the mere idea of it flip-flopping around in his stomach like a live fish.

"You sly old bloodhound," said DeLuca. He appraised McKenzie with a shrewd look. "That's why you're the best in the business."

"You know," McKenzie explained immodestly, "before I got into this line of work, I thought about writing a food column for the *Chicago Tribune*."

"Remember your cholesterol, Doc," said Price. "We're a long way from the nearest cardiologist."

McKenzie chuckled and said, "There's barely any meat. It's not even worth the effort," turning the finger over in his hands.

DeLuca looked at Hatcher. "This may explain why we haven't been able to locate any of Ellis's remains."

Ethan didn't like where this was going, especially given the contents of the camcorder footage. Was it possible that DeLuca and the others knew what Leonelli had done to Northuctt and Schmidt? Of course it was possible—at this stage of the game anything was. But then why beat around the bush? Why not just come out and confront him with the truth? Maybe they were doing it to keep Ethan off-balance, prevent him from gaining the upper hand . . . Or maybe they were crafting an alibi, something to go front page with in case their dealings in Antarctica were ever leaked to the press. *Plausible deniability*—isn't that what Okum had said? Ethan could see it now—a twisted little yarn about a cult of scientists eating each other because their megalomaniacal leader had worked them too hard . . . It was a hell of a way for Okum to cover his ass if push came to shove. If Ethan ever went public with Ivan, the pieces would already be in place to have him discredited, maybe even committed. He was in a world of shit if anyone ever learned that he had swallowed Alan's tooth—evidence of his own participation in the macabre feast. Uncle Sam could claim the mission was strictly humanitarian, that they were saving the little piggies from the jaws of the Big Bad Wolf. A rescue op.

Fortunately, proof of Ethan's innocence was digitally encoded on the memory cards. But of course, this is what DeLuca and his henchmen were really getting at, wasn't it? Somehow they knew that Ethan had gotten his hands on the video. And what better way to claim it for themselves than to get him to offer it up as his only defense?

Bishop bent over at the waist and placed his ear to Ethan's belly. "Ellis?" he called. "You in there?"

"If he is," Ethan remarked casually, "that'd make him about the only thing you haven't eaten."

This last remark got Price on Bishop's case about the impending shortage of food. Ethan seized the opportunity to slip away. Although the signs were there he hadn't realized how profoundly they had been affected by stress until shortly after he had returned to his quarters. He was sitting on his bed listening to the wind howl when there was a knock at the door. It was Claire. Wearing nothing but a towel, she had apparently just come from the shower. Secured across the top of her breasts with a simple tuck, the scant covering fell to just below her crotch. Ethan tried not to stare but her long toned legs kept his eyes riveted. She glided towards him and it was as if the room experienced a sudden change in atmospheric pressure. Ethan's breath quickened as Claire loosened the towel and let it drop to the floor. He was sure it was a trick of some sort, a decoy, but he may as well have been attempting to deny gravity its hold on him so powerful was the allure of the furrowed wonderland between Claire's legs. Rational thought was subordinated to carnal desire as she looked purposefully into his eyes and stripped away his polar gear.

When Claire got to his boots, she paused to examine the kitchen knife tucked in alongside his right calf. She ran her finger along the edge of the blade before laying the knife on the floor. "Sharp," was all she said.

Ethan was still trying to figure out what he'd done to deserve this when Claire pulled him into her. It wasn't karma—that was for damn sure. Unlike Alyona, Claire took her time with him. She was determined and yet yielding, responsive to his touch though not afraid to do a little groping of her own. At one point he considered that she might be on some sort of drug, lost in the carefree realm of narcotic bliss. But this was Claire he was talking about. She was as wary of aspirin as were most people of heroin. Her nipples hardened to pebbles between his thumbs and forefingers as she heaved passionately beneath him. There had never been a time in Ethan's life when sex hadn't felt right, but this was different. It was somehow more significant, an immutable law of chemical interaction catalyzed by more than mere lust. It was elemental and real and vital.

With each thrust, Claire urged him deeper inside of her. The external world faded into the warm sweet oblivion of her cunt and he began to believe that he could spend the rest of his life right where he was without a single regret. He had always asserted that they fit well together, a perfect coupling of male and female sexual anatomy, but it was beyond that now. If anything, their bodies interfered with the realization of a greater truth. Ethan found himself straining desperately against Claire's inner thighs, every nerve in his body coiled around the possibility of release. With Alyona he had pussyfooted around. It had snowballed so damn fast that he'd hardly been able to get his bearings. *Wham, bam, thank you Sam, and don't let the door hit you in the ass on the way out!* Not this time, though. Claire wanted it, and he was sure as shit going to give it to her. But then her legs tensed, her body went rigid, and Ethan found himself in a crushing scissor lock.

"Get off of me!" Claire shouted.

"Like hell," he said. "I'm not done." He'd thought it had been a little too easy. Claire wasn't the sort of girl who gave it up without a fight. Truthfully, he welcomed the challenge. It would make his conquest that much sweeter.

"Now," Claire intoned forcefully.

"You want to be on top—is that it?" asked Ethan. "Always the control freak. Whatever—suit yourself."

And with that things quickly went south on him and Ethan suddenly found his balls in the vise of Claire's clenched fist.

"Now," she repeated.

Ethan rolled off of her, paralyzed by the pain shooting through his groin and causing his stomach to convulse mightily. Claire stood and released him from her grasp. She looked more disoriented than angry. She collected her towel from the floor and backed away from him, covering herself. Ethan had to fight back the swell of bile rising in his throat, equal parts nausea and rage.

"What the fuck's your problem!" he shouted.

"What the fuck do you think's my problem?" Claire shouted back. "I wasn't born with your dick in me."

"Oh, no . . ." said Ethan, sobering quickly to his plight. "Fuck that. That may have worked back at the Gulag but you can't pull that shit with me. Not here. No fucking way. No one will believe you."

Something near the foot of the bed caught Claire's eye. "What's the knife for, Ethan?" she asked accusingly. "How do you explain that?" She was shivering.

"Do you even know where you are? You're in *my* room. *You* came to me." Ethan sat up and leaned against the wall. "I don't know what you're after, but it won't work." And then it dawned on him. "You want a reason to lock me up, don't you? Get the fuck out of here!"

Claire did not move.

Ethan lunged for the knife, taking it in hand. "Get the fuck out of here! NOW!"

Claire opened the door and backed out of the room without taking her eyes off of him. Kent was standing in the hall, eavesdropping. He was nearly a full head shorter than Claire and looked more swollen than he did muscular in his one-size-too-small T-shirt.

"What are you looking at?" Ethan demanded. He slashed at the air with the knife to let Kent know that he meant business, and then locked himself in his room. One thing was certain: no one was going to force open the door. Once the lock was engaged, the room was like a bank vault.

"You sure about this?" asked Price. It had taken him a few minutes, but now that he had a feel for the controls he guided the tundra buggy across the ice like a pro.

"I'm sure," Claire replied frankly.

She couldn't say what specifically had led her to Hatcher's bed, but she had a pretty good idea that it had something to do with what Zhenya and Shurik had tried to do to her. For years Claire had repressed the truth about her mother's passive complicity in the abuse, both verbal and physical, she suffered at the hands of her husband. It was this willingness to turn the other cheek that had enabled Claire's father to abuse his wife without consequence for more than a decade. When such thoughts assailed her, Claire beat them back into hiding where they couldn't get at her so easily. But Antarctica had thrown open the gates on what she had harbored for so long, and no longer was Claire's mind granting asylum to the worst inside of her.

For the past couple of days her subconscious had been running wild, so much so that at times it governed her actions. She had been moving in a sort of trance, neither here nor there, then nor now. She may not have fully understood what it was she had to do, but she was sure that whatever path she took when it came time to deal with the two Russians would guide her to the promised land of emotional wellness. She was looking forward to becoming a more complete human being just as her mother had upon realizing that turning the other cheek was simply another way of asking to be hit again. Although Claire knew in her heart that her mother's actions were justified, she had never really accepted her father's death as an absolute necessity. Doubt was an ugly word, particularly given that her mother wasn't alive to defend herself. But Claire often wondered if there might have been another way. That is, until she too had been victimized. Claire wished her mother were here right now so she could tell her that she finally understood, that she applauded her mother for having the guts to do what had to be done.

Five years ago Hatcher had forced her into a decision that she'd never wanted to make. It was time to take back what was hers. Her entire life Claire had tried to downplay what it meant to be an only child. But as an evolutionary biologist it was only natural that she be reminded of the grim finality such a designation entailed. She marked the end of the Matthews family line. The final flicker of a genealogical flame on the verge of dying out forever. Another failed form. It was the aim of every species on the planet to make as many copies of itself as possible. Yet Claire had failed to make just one. The revelation had come to her in the shower as she basked in the glory of her victory over Price. And never before had she been filled with such utter hopelessness and resolve. Biology, maternal drive, human ego—call it what you will. Claire was suddenly determined to leave something behind, to make a copy of her. She wanted her child back. She wanted it with the same desperation as every creature on earth from simple protozoa to mud-skipper to man. If Hatcher wouldn't give it to her willingly, she'd take it from him. He owed her that much. By the time she was thinking rationally it was too late. She awoke as if from a trance to find herself in Hatcher's bed going at it like an estrous rabbit.

What had gotten into her? Why the sudden urge to get knocked up? She'd asked herself these and other questions as she showered for the second time in twenty minutes. A few weeks ago Claire was certain that she was pregnant, that a rogue sperm had slipped past Eric's knotted vas deferens and breached the defenses of her reproductive system. Then she had arrived in Antarctica, death had surrounded her, and the nagging worry that a life was growing inside her had been pushed to a remote corner of her mind. She still hadn't gotten her period, but there were now other things to worry about.

Unfortunately she couldn't take a scrub brush to her brain, but at least she could wash away any physical traces Hatcher had left behind. It was work showering. Every muscle in her body was sore. Maybe she wasn't sick at all, just exhausted. She'd been pushing herself especially hard both physically and mentally the past couple of weeks. All the exercise, the stress, the sleepless nights, the competition with Price—it was finally catching up with her. Even her breasts ached.

Claire rinsed off and toweled dry.

But there it was again. The burden of being a scientist. Logic and reason were only parts of the equation. Empirical data, proof—without this Claire would never be totally convinced of anything. Especially if it involved her. Not if the odds were a billion to one.

Eric had given her the do-it-yourself pregnancy test as a joke really. He knew that she wasn't pregnant, that her concerns were unfounded given the circumstances. But he had also known that allowing her the option of proving it to herself would put Claire's mind at ease. She had resisted this long because she didn't want to rub Eric's nose in the fact of his own infertility.

She wouldn't admit that she'd actually gone ahead and used it. She could tell him that she'd lost it. Or thrown it away. She could worry about the details later. In a matter of seconds the innocuous plastic stick was in her hands, awaiting a splash of her urine. *99.3% accurate. Scary number. Blue and you're good to go. Pink and you're a mama. Simple enough.*

Waiting for the tiny strip of chemically reactive paper to change color was longest five minutes of her life. She paced around the bathroom wondering how life might be different for her if she had a child: dirty diapers, late-night feedings, love so pure it was intoxicating. How would she ever get anything done? Add a baby to the mix and she wouldn't have time to breathe let alone be able to carry on with her research. But she was being ridiculous. There was just no way that she was pregnant. She was wasting time. After two minutes she gathered up the little plastic wand from the edge of the sink and dropped it in the trash. She'd been careful not to look.

"What the—Tell me I'm hallucinating." The sober pitch of Price's voice contrasted sharply with the look of disbelief transfiguring his face.

At first it was difficult to make out. The wind was blowing close to sixty miles an hour and the buggy's headlights could scarcely penetrate the aggravated curtain of ice clattering against the windshield like handfuls of rock salt. The reflection produced an eerie incandescence inside the passenger compartment, drenching them in hard silver-white light. They had only a few seconds to assimilate the outlandish specter bearing down on them at a veritable snail's pace before the impending head-on collision forced Price to veer sharply to the left.

So out of context was the old red tractor that Claire too would've believed she was hallucinating had she not remembered it from the Gulag. The decrepit vehicle was hardly the sort of thing you expect to find paying its due as polar transport, but here it was heading straight for them. What was left of the original paintjob was scabbed over with patches of rust. Metal primer had been sprayed on as a sort of unguent to soothe those places that were especially bad, but this too was now stricken with the same blight that was slowly reducing the tractor to oxidized dust.

The driver's seat and controls were positioned midway between its long steel engine housing and a pair of enormous rear wheels. The driver was fully exposed to the elements, lacking any shelter whatsoever from the wind or snow or fossilizing cold. In this case the unfortunate soul at the wheel was Georgiy, the cook. He was wearing a heavy wool army issue overcoat, the same orange, food-encrusted oven mitts from dinner the other night, and a tall fur-lined hat secured to his head by flaps that covered his ears and tied under his chin. Otherwise his face was no more protected than that of his companion who rode shotgun standing erect on a small platform fitted between the fender and the driver's seat. It was Shurik, his heavy black beard all but white with clinging ice crystals. With one arm he steadied himself on a long staff of some sort, bold and upright as a Hun warlord. He too wore a heavy wool overcoat, the shoulders of which were adorned with scraggly animal pelts. The facial expressions of both men were a mixed breed of amusement and menace. Frostbite was a foregone conclusion—and for Georgiy, possibly blindness. Only Shurik wore goggles and these were impractically dark—the kind welders use to guard their eyes against the blinding firelight of their trade. This may have explained why neither Georgiy nor Shurik appeared to notice the tundra buggy as the tractor trundled noisily past into the darkness. Or maybe they were already dead, clinging to their cadaverous grins as thousands of tiny ice pellets nibbled at their exposed flesh like maggots.

"Where the hell are they going?" Price asked.

"Beats me."

"Should we go after them? You might not get another chance to confront the dude."

"Forget it," said Claire. "Chances are, they're dead anyway."

"I don't like this."

"Look," said Claire. "Up ahead—a light."

Price cut the engine about a hundred feet from the entrance. It was suddenly quiet but for the wind lashing at the buggy. Price listened raptly for a few seconds and then dug into the front of his parka. He withdrew something shiny and black, and studied it in the frail glow of the light that had guided them to the Gulag's doorstep.

"A gun," observed Claire. "Good idea."

Price chambered a round and disengaged the safety. "Glad you approve."

Claire was surprised to hear herself speak the words. A pacifist by nature, she had never really liked guns. Most of her life she had absolutely hated anything associated with violence. Suddenly, she couldn't understand her aversion. It just seemed a little reactionary, that's all. *Guns don't kill people. People kill people.* Isn't that what they said?

Price thought the situation called for a delicate hand so the two of them weaved their way through the field of debris outlying the station's perimeter looking for an entrance a little less conspicuous than the front door. The junk was largely unrecognizable to her: farm equipment, modern sculpture, the greasy steel guts of a dismantled factory? Impossible to say because most of it was flocked with snow and ice. Only bits and pieces hadn't submitted to the downy white—a turn valve, a metal rod, a pronged appendage extended like a grasping hand. A winter garden of topiaries, any or all of which could have passed for homesteaders buried in a blizzard. Reason tried to convince her that it wasn't three generations of Donners lying beneath the glacial mantle, but at the moment her mind wasn't listening to reason. Warily, she eyed the humanoid forms, half-expecting one or all to shrug off its ivory cloak and come groping through the dark after her.

They found a side entrance and forced their way in behind Price's shoulder. They were in the kitchen, witnesses to a panoply of hygiene transgressions, any or all of which would have compelled the Board of Health to condemn the place on sight. The air reeked of dirty dishwater and spoiled meat. Claire gagged on the oily fug as she tore the neoprene mask from her face and breathed in the unfiltered stink. Poorly ventilated, the room was washed in cooking grease. A thick yellow-brown film streaked every square inch of wall space. Especially concentrated on the ceiling above the battered stove, greasy stalactites had begun to inch their way earthward a fraction of a millimeter at a time. The gluey medium acted like flypaper, hosting a variety of airborne detritus from single hairs to what were presumably food particles though could have been just about anything. The greasy appliqué was only outdone by the mountain of filthy pots and pans that erupted from the floor in the center of the kitchen. Although Antarctica was too cold to sustain most bacteria, many of the pots had been neglected for so long that decay was begrudgingly taking its course. Stagnating water and disintegrating organic debris conspired into a kind of moldering stew.

"No wonder I've been feeling like something the cat dragged in," said Price. He'd picked up a long metal serving spoon and was exploring the contents of a blue enamelware Dutch oven. It was the same pot from which Kesha had served them *pochlebka* stew the other night. Each turn of the spoon produced a lethargic upwelling of bones and clotted gray broth. "This is one recipe I can live without." Price looked at her. "You still up for this?"

Claire was antsy. Zhenya was close and she was itching to find out what she had in store for him. "Why wouldn't I be?"

"Just be ready, that's all I'm saying."

"For what?" Claire asked.

"Anything."

Price stirred the pot again, dragging the spoon along the bottom and turning it over in disgust. Clinging to the spoon was the skeletal remains of a hand, stripped almost entirely of flesh though bound loosely together by a web of ligaments and tendons. "Oink oink, my ass!" he scowled. "A hundred bucks says we just found out what happened to Ellis."

"Hold your horses," said Claire. "Just because it looks like pork and tastes like pork, doesn't mean that it is pork."

She should've had stronger feelings about Price's discovery. Indeed, there was a distinct possibility that she was now a practicing cannibal. But she'd discovered a beat-up roasting pan stashed beneath the bottom tier of a metal shelving unit and was anxious to identify the source of the strange odor emanating from it. The pan itself was shrouded by a badly soiled bath towel. Corsage-like whorls of diluted blood bloomed on the surface of the towel where it clung to the irregular contours beneath. Claire crouched on her haunches and casually pulled back the bloodied shroud. The gaseous stink that arose from the grisly cache of bones punched her in the nose. She had a feeling whose remains she was looking at—the quizzical black eyes and broad pithecoid nose. So maybe she wasn't a cannibal after all. She grabbed the disembodied head by a bloody hank of fur and plunked it on the stovetop next to where Price was busy playing Betty Crocker.

"Unless Ellis was a direct descendant of Java man," she announced, "this ain't him."

"Talk about a face only a mother could love."

Claire was suddenly overcome by a dizzy spell. She steadied herself against the stove to keep from falling over.

Price grabbed her by the arm. "You okay?"

"A little tired, that's all." The spell passed quickly and she continued. "The Russians must've thought they struck gold when they discovered this little guy hiding out in the wreckage."

"Pork is one thing," Price winced. "But this . . . I can almost guarantee you that Allah would not approve."

Claire studied the chimp head one last time. "Meat is meat," she remarked nonchalantly. "100,000 generations of incisors don't lie. Like it or not, man's a born carnivore."

Price was about to say something when a man strode casually into the kitchen. Claire had never seen him before—not at dinner the other night and certainly not like this. He'd been scalped to the bone just above the point where woolly auburn sideburns crawled onto his cheeks. To say that the underlying stratum looked raw and painful would have been to understate the truth in the worst way. Blood, seeming pints of it, had clotted about the egg-like hemisphere in a thick gelatinized layer so that at first glance Claire thought she was looking at the oblivious creature's brain. Unsupported and beaten down by the force of gravity, his orbital ridge had descended upon his eyes. The slumping flesh—though an effort had been made to correct it with a swath of shiny steel thumbtacks studding the ragged seam from ear to ear— had a primordializing effect on his entire face. Man circa 80,000 BC. One glimpse was all Claire needed to connect the missing crown of flesh with the collection of would-be animal pelts Shurik had been wearing about his shoulders. Scalps.

Other than an attempt to straighten his face—you would've thought he was adjusting a necktie so perfunctory and natural was the gesture—the man seemed totally without regard for the uninvited guests in his midst. However this was before he had readjusted his face—first pulling taut the skin over one eye and then the other, and retacking each with an upholsterer's deft hand—so that his drooping eyelids no longer interfered with his vision. Whether merely incidental or engendered by a new awareness of his surroundings, the *ad hoc* facelift had given him a hysterical look. Blood loss had imbued his skin with a sickly greenish-white tint, and his eyes were glazed over with slick silvery light.

And then he was on them. There wasn't time to figure out what had set him off, no less attempt to reason with him. Not now, not while the crazy fool was latched onto Price like a police dog. Although Price was considerably larger than his wild-eyed attacker, he was caught off guard. Somehow he managed to stay on his feet, but picked up another hitchhiker in the process. The Dutch oven was now stuck to his left foot as he stumbled errantly about knocking things over—a played-out slapstick gag but for the simple fact that he was engaged in a life or death struggle.

"Do something!" Price shouted. "Get this freak off of me!"

Claire reached for a cast-iron skillet but noticed something of much greater interest to her. During the fracas Price's gun had found its way onto the floor and was now camouflaged in with a scattering of kitchen utensils and dirty dishes. Claire concealed it in her waistband before using the skillet to dislodge the man from Price's back with a resounding blow to the back of the head.

"What was all that about?" Price asked.

Claire was laughing hysterically. Tears muddled her vision. She could hardly catch her breath. "You should've seen yourself," she gasped.

Price lifted his leg, the Dutch oven closed over his foot like a bear trap. "Ha-ha, very funny. Now help me get this thing off."

It was as if the Gulag had been left to the whim of a planetary catastrophe. Claire and Price were the only signs of life other than the man who had attacked them in the kitchen. The temperature alone was as good a reason as any to abandon ship. It was cold, much colder than it had been the other night. Each breath was like a exhaling a cloud of smoke. Claire was beginning to think that Zhenya wasn't worth the trouble. At this point it was a toss-up between returning to the station and a humane environment, and seeing whatever this was through to the end.

The room in which they had eaten dinner was utterly devoid of activity. Had there been a struggle of some sort? Anywhere else the signs would have been inescapable, but the place was already such a wreck that it was hard to say at first glance. And then they began to notice the bullet holes and shell casings strewn about the floor.

Price held one of the sofa cushions to his face and peered through a hole big enough pass his fist through. "Maybe that's where Shurik was going—to buy a new sofa. What a shame, this one really held the room together."

"Great," lamented Claire. "The heater's dead."

She fiddled with the controls for a few seconds in the hope that the gut-shot war surplus relic would miraculously come to life, but like its friend, the sofa, was mortally wounded.

"We'll give it a decent burial when we're done. Right now, let's worry about finding Zhenya. Last thing I need is DeLuca reporting me AWOL."

Upon finding herself in Hatcher's bed Claire hadn't known what to think, but the truth of the matter was now coming back to her one blurry frame at a time. She was beginning to realize that it had happened more or less like he said. One moment she was standing in the shower letting the hot water scald her naked flesh, the next she was throwing herself at him. There was no point trying to restrain herself. Her biological clock was ticking too loudly to be ignored. She was a slave to animal instinct. She couldn't say what had thrown the switch, only that it had incapacitated her ability to reason. She hoped it wouldn't be this way when she finally came face to face with Zhenya. She wanted to be there mind and body.

Claire was determined to get this over with but not so single-minded that her curiosity wasn't aroused when she and Price passed the nerve center of the Gulag en route to Zhenya's quarters. The other night the door to the weather room was secured with a heavy padlock. It was odd considering they were thousands of miles away from prying eyes, but it was hardly enough to arouse suspicion. The Russian government was notoriously paranoid. However, the padlock was now missing— shot off from the looks of the gaping hole in the door.

The room beyond was larger than she'd expected, about the size of one of the lecture halls at Los Caminos. Right away it was obvious that the space was not being used in the capacity the Russians had intimated. It looked more like a defunct automotive repair shop than a sophisticated weather tracking station. Machine parts similar to those cluttering the perimeter of the station lay about the room in neglectful slumber. Long steel rods, the thickness of a grown man's arm and fuzzed over with a velvety layer of rust, were bunched carelessly along one wall. It was apparent that no one had set foot inside the room in a very long time. A half-dozen pipe wrenches, the smallest being many times larger than any Claire had ever seen, dangled from hooks along the wall inside the door, each assigned a particular spot by a stencil outline rendered in flaking red spray paint. One of the wrenches, more than half as tall as Claire, was missing, its empty stencil all that remained.

So the Russians had lied about their reason for being in Antarctica. It wasn't as if they had been standing guard over a crashed UFO complete with little gray aliens trapped inside. Price suggested natural gas or oil exploration—not that Claire really cared one way or another. As far as she was concerned it was all pretty low on the interest spectrum. There was, however, one feature that caught her eye. While the majority of the floor consisted of rough wood planking, a large metal grate lay atop the floor in the center of the room. A rectangular section of the grate was hinged so that it formed a kind of trapdoor. The trapdoor was cocked open. The padlock that had once secured it had been shot off like the other. Claire stood atop the grate and gazed into a hole that was for all intents and purposes bottomless.

Her mind was slow to make the connections that were usually second nature to her, but she was not so altogether gone that a dead body had lost its power to fascinate. She recognized Kesha from the other night—pale and baby-faced—though he, too, had been scalped. Like the man in the kitchen, his strawberry blonde hair had been claimed as a souvenir for Shurik's homemade war robe. He was wedged into the hole about ten feet below the grate, his body folded brutally in half at the waist so that he could have worn his feet as earrings. Still apparent was the distorting agony he had experienced upon finding himself scalped, broken-backed and trapped, his expression a mixture of intense awe and suffering. His arms were extended above his head as if he had spent his last pinched breaths reaching out for help.

"We should leave," said Price. He, too, stood over the hole, astounded by the acute geometry of Kesha's final repose.

But Claire was already on her way out of the room, afraid that Price would pull the plug before her work here was complete.

Un-fucking-believable, thought Claire, as she poked her head in the door of Zhenya's quarters and discovered him reclined in a folding chair with his pants bunched up around his ankles. Alyona was kneeling between his open legs, her face buried in his crotch.

For a couple of days now Claire had wondered at the incalculable instinct urging her return to the Gulag. The behavioral patterns of many species of bird—migratory routes etched into every fiber of their being—were influenced by natural forces that until recently had defied the comprehension of ornithologists. But it was no magnetic field that had guided Claire back here, nor was it any less an irresistible force that now took control of her actions. She was thinking too clearly to hide behind an insanity plea.

Claire had spent the last twenty years manufacturing an illusion of security and self-reliance. Kickboxing, weightlifting, martial arts . . . If it was merely physical fitness she was after, weightlifting and running would have sufficed. It was a man's world—figuratively and literally. Evolution had seen to it. Might made right. Physical superiority had laid the foundation for 2.5 million years of male dominance. It may not have been as straightforward as the days when women were clubbed over the head and dragged back to the nearest cave for a savage romping, but things weren't going to change without a nudge in the right direction. Zhenya was bigger, but she was smarter. He was stronger, but she was more agile. He plodded through life with his dick in his hand. She carried evolution's torch. He was her Neanderthal. She was his *Homo sapiens.*

And now this . . . It wasn't the sex that bothered Claire. It was the fact that Alyona was *enjoying* it, giving it her all. It was the fact that Claire had fucked Hatcher with the same zeal less than two hours ago, and that she was now forced to re-visit her own actions. But what she found most offensive was Zhenya's lack of active participation; he simply sat there, head tilted back, dead to the world. The little shit hadn't even bothered to take off his hat, the earflaps tied in a decorative bow beneath his chin—God's gift to women.

"I'm telling Ethan," Claire interrupted. She had approached the lovers from behind. Until now, they were oblivious of her presence.

Alyona looked back over her shoulder, the lower half of her face sticky with blood. "*Awww,* no way!" Price groaned, stumbling backward toward the door.

But Claire had already imploded, her rational mind collapsing around the anonymous instinct that had led her here. In that instant, she could see only blood. And it was this, an unmistakable declaration of danger and distress that sparked something purely reactive inside of her. The gun was out of her waistband so quickly that it was as if she had been born with it in her hand. She fired three shots into Zhenya's chest, three successive thunderclaps before there was time to consider her actions. She marveled at the ease of the explosive deathbringer, man's ingenuity at all things destructive. And it was like pumping three bullets into a side of beef, Zhenya absorbing the slugs with little more than a quiver.

"What's wrong with you?" Price shouted, disarming Claire and ejecting the clip in a single nifty move.

Although it was Alyona, not Claire who knelt in a pool of blood smiling with guilty pleasure, Price wouldn't take his eyes off either of them. Zhenya's crotch had been eaten away, mutilated beyond recognition. Grieving Sioux women occasionally performed similar acts of ritual mutilation on the bodies of slain enemies to exact retribution for their braves lost in battle. Something to do with maintaining the equilibrium of the breeding pool between native peoples and their white invaders. But with cutting implements, not with their mouths. Not like this. Not the genitals.

"It was an accident," said Claire.

Price was incredulous. "You shot him three times!"

The odor of burnt gunpowder filled the air. "I guess my survival instinct took over."

"Closure—that's what you said! You didn't say anything about instinct. *Instinct . . .*" Price repeated bitterly. "You talk like you're Jesse James or some damn shit!"

Claire placed her hand on his shoulder. "Price," she explained, "he tried to rape me—or have you forgotten that?"

"Shut up!" Price barked. He leaned against the door jamb scratching his head with the gun barrel. "I can't think."

Alyona was now standing face-to-face with a cracked mirror someone had affixed to the wall in the interest of good grooming. There was an indefinable foreignness in the way she looked at herself that couldn't be explained by the blood alone. It was deeper than that, buried far beneath the surface, well below the dusky bruise that clouded the upper left side of her face. Again, it was something in the eyes, the same silvery gleam Claire had observed in the others. But Claire was now distracted by her own image. This was not the face of the woman she thought she knew. It was somehow out of sync with the rest of her, as if her face was a mask and the consciousness behind it was reacting to a different set of cues than the ones that ordinarily governed her behavior. Alyona had drifted away from the mirror, leaving Claire to gaze upon her distorted image alone.

"Hey, Price, have you noticed anything different about me lately?"

Price's face contorted angrily and he grabbed her by the arm. "We're done here."

As they were on their way out a single gunshot split the night. Claire and Price rushed into the adjacent quarters. There, amid the disconsolate clutter of a life in limbo, they found Alyona's body stretched out on the floor. She almost looked peaceful lying there, blood gurgling from a hole that like an idea too late in coming, passed neatly in one ear and out the other.

"Shurik," Claire remarked distantly. "We have to get back to the station!"

Enough was enough. Ethan couldn't wait any longer. Everything was going to shit. First Alyona, then Claire. *Crazy bitches.* Why was it that every woman he screwed ended up wanting to kill him? It was just one more thing for him to think about in a situation that was rapidly going from bad to totally fucked. If the writing wasn't already on the wall . . . But that's right it was. He'd nearly forgotten the discombobulated goodbye note finger-painted in pink goo on the wall over Lim's bed in the room he'd shared with Alan.

How long does it take to defrost a human body? A veteran of countless Thanksgiving dinners, his mother would probably know. Ethan vaguely remembered her calculating the time needed to defrost a frozen turkey—a formula based loosely on weight. But that was in the refrigerator . . . Or was it at room temperature? *Fuck!* The way Kent had looked at him when they had bumped into each other in the hall was all the convincing Ethan needed that he was running out of time. Lim had been soaking buck naked for close to six hours in water in excess of 120° Fahrenheit. If Ethan got his shit together he could catch the next flight out when Kent fired up the Osprey in another forty-five minutes. But for one key item—a pint or two of Lim's blood—he was packed and ready to go.

The air in the storeroom was humid enough to raise tropical plants. The walls sweated and the floor was slick with condensation. Ethan may have been a bit overzealous with the thermostat. He wasn't trying to boil Lim after all. *Dim sum. Lim sum. Funny.* He checked the thermometer and found that the water temperature had reached 131° and was still climbing. The color had returned to Lim's flesh, proof that the bath was working. The hot water had enticed his blood back into the surface capillaries bringing with it real hope for Ethan's plan.

It was almost a shame to disturb Lim. He looked so tranquil soaking there in the balmy spa-like atmosphere that it was easy to forget he was dead. His eyelids had relaxed in the heat and now lay closed. Water droplets congregated on his face and brow. Ethan had never thought about it before, but Lim bore an uncanny resemblance to the Dalai Lama. Oh well, too late for a career in the movies. He drew the knife from his boot, knotted his free hand in a tuft of Lim's hair and began sawing at his throat. The jugular—the Old Faithful of blood conduits. It was his best bet. He'd heard somewhere that even slightly nicked the vein could disgorge a fountain of blood more than eight feet into the air. A modest gurgle was all Ethan needed now. He planned on caching his oil-strike in a twenty-ounce commuter mug. Primitive, and not exactly sterile, but it had an airtight lid with a thumb-actuated the drinking spout. This wasn't about earning style points.

Goddamn dull piece of shit knife! Leave it to Uncle Sam to dump $100 million on an F-16, but skimp on cutlery. German was the way to go—Henckels or Wusthof. There was steel that held an edge. He'd never realized that cutting a man's throat could be so much work. And the lousy footing didn't help any. His heavy rubber-soled boots may have been a life-saver in the snow, but they were like ice skates on the wet floor. He got down on one knee and braced himself against the edge of the tub. Leaning in close, he realized that the pinkish hue he had mistaken for a healthy glow was actually a trick of the water in which Lim was soaking. Upon thawing, Lim's broken arm—that is, the portion above the tourniquet which Bishop had not appropriated for his karaoke jam—had begun to ooze blood. The bathwater was now tinted pink.

Now we're getting somewhere. Ethan had been sawing at Lim's jugular like a freaking lumberjack and only now had the leathery flesh begun to yield beneath the dull blade. But that's as far as he would ever get. A thin red line had opened and it was as if all the agony and suffering in the world was suddenly released. Lim revived as the blade bit into the sinewy connective tissue underlying his epidermis. He cried out, the sound emanating from his throat like a ton of gravel sluicing down a metal spillway, raw and grating and hard. The stricken cry knocked Ethan back reeling. *Impossible. No fucking way. I'm hallucinating.* But Lim was now sitting up, his eyes wide open and milky white. He groped for the lip of the tub with his severed arm, realizing only distantly that the limb was defunct, useless. He cried out again, the same gravelly, grating inhuman pitch. Ethan clamped his forearms over his ears so that the terrible noise—*a parasite, that's what it is, a voracious parasite that will eat your brain*—couldn't burrow any deeper inside his head.

And this was only the beginning. Wracked by whatever demons now assaulted his mind, Lim panicked. He must've felt as if he was being boiled *alive?* He flailed his limbs, thrashing and punching at the bloated membrane enwombing him in scalding water. The flimsy aluminum framework supporting the bath flexed and creaked in protest. It was designed for ease of transport, to accommodate someone who was near-dead and acting like it. But Lim's struggles were pushing the portable apparatus to its limit. Spasmodic contractions gripped the heaving sac. Then all at once it buckled. Lim spilled out at Ethan's feet in a cataract of steaming bathwater. Shivering, he uncurled from a fetal self-embrace and rose trembling to his knees. His milk-white eyes—whether or not they could see at all was impossible to say—snapped open and settled on the knife Ethan clenched in his hand. He threw back his head and let loose with a miserable croaking noise—a great big naked hatchling new to the world and the innumerable dangers it harbored.

"Hey, remember me?" Ethan tried feebly. "It's Hatcher."

Lim gathered himself off the floor in a fit of herky-jerky movements. His skin was the color and texture of raw bacon fat. He watched Ethan guardedly, his expression intimating a dawning distrust.

Ethan had no idea what to make of the marine biologist, so he laid the knife on the floor, making sure that it was in easy reach. He then held out his hands as evidence of his benign intentions. Lim's untimely resurrection had changed things up on him. It was going to take Ethan a few seconds to recalibrate his thoughts. "Friend," Ethan intoned stupidly, thumping himself on the chest.

He didn't have time for this bullshit. Problem was he hadn't planned on cutting the throat of a living human being, if indeed Lim qualified as such. He was still hopeful that this was some sort of autonomic response, nerves firing after the fact. Okum hadn't said anything about Ivan making zombies out of people. But hey, there was probably a lot Okum hadn't told him. Maybe whatever had reanimated Lim would wear off and he'd drop dead—this time for good. It wasn't sound scientific reasoning but Ethan was done trying to get the pieces to fit his old notion of the world and how it worked.

After allowing Lim to stare blankly at him for more than minute, he'd had enough. Kent would be firing up the engines soon. The involuntary twitches and jolts wracking Lim's body didn't mean he was ready to dance the lambada, but it convinced Ethan that his batteries were nowhere near running out of juice.

"Listen cowboy," said Ethan impatiently. "I can't wait all night for you to ask me to dance. If there's something on your mind spit it out."

Ethan wasn't sure what it was, but something he'd said had caused Lim's ears to prick. There was a new recognition in his expression. He seemed to be connecting with an idea or memory frozen deep beneath the surface of his iced-over eyes. A distant smile parted his lips.

"Giddy up, you wacko son of a bitch and die already! I've got a flight to catch."

So much for asking politely. Lim's expression suddenly acquired a new bent. A twisted look crossed his face and he began to bray like a wounded mule. The godawful noise raked over Ethan's nerves. If DeLuca, or anyone for that matter, heard the commotion . . .

"Will you shut up? I don't have time for this shit!"

Ethan grabbed the knife off the floor, stepped forward and thrust it into Lim. He had been aiming for the stomach—it would make things easier if Lim's heart was still pumping—but had sunk the blade deep into in the meaty part of Lim's right thigh. Lim howled in pain and Ethan stabbed again. This time the point of the knife struck Lim in the rib cage, glancing off bone. Lim rocked back on his feet and howled even louder.

"Relax," Ethan growled. "I'm not trying to kill you." He was sizzling with rage, could feel it boiling inside his veins. "I just want a little of your blood."

Lim spun about wildly, crashing into the walls, his feet becoming entangled in the wreckage of the bathtub. The purest form of terror imaginable stampeded over the permafrost of his brain. Predator versus prey. A maimed straggler cut off from the herd, alone and vulnerable. But Lim had somehow laid his only hand on a telescopic mountaineering staff and was now backed into a corner swinging blindly. Ethan feinted and jabbed with the knife, looking for an opening in Lim's careless but effective defense. He was nearly blinded himself when Lim swiped him across the forehead with the pole's pointed end, opening a shallow cut above his eyebrows.

Summoned by the noise, Kent was the first to arrive.

"Don't just stand there!" Ethan shouted. "Give me a hand! He can't handle both of us."

Kent's jaw dropped, his small close-set eyes wide with disbelief. "B-b-b-b-but, he's dead!"

"D-d-d-does he look dead?" Ethan mimicked. "Come on, before he hurts himself. I'll count to three and you rush him. One . . . two . . ."

On three, Kent bolted from the room. *Fucking pussy,* thought Ethan. *I'll do this myself.* He was slowly angling in toward Lim when a familiar noise caught his attention. It was the Osprey. A gust of panic blew into him. Lim was still swinging, however at this point Ethan was more concerned about hitching a ride with Kent than catching a homerun chop upside the head. Kent had probably blabbed to the others about Lim. By now they were piling into the Osprey, anxious to get the hell out of here before Ethan came after the rest of them.

As he went for the door, Ethan collided with Bishop. Stunned, they looked at one another and then back at Lim who was still swinging away. Something impossible to quantify passed between the two men—understanding perhaps, but it was hopelessly muddled by the malaise that was eating away at both of their minds. Or maybe it was the knife Ethan clutched in his hand. Suspicion. Distrust.

"I think he wants his arm back," Ethan blurted as he forced his way past Bishop.

There was no time for secrecy or stealth. Ethan blew by DeLuca and McKenzie in the narrow corridor leading to the common room. They called after him but by then he was out the door and into the raw gusty night.

He boarded the Osprey through a small door just aft of the wing. The noise from the engines was deafening, a low repetitive ebb that he felt somehow connected to. The flow of power. Invisible machinery at work. *Good,* Kent wouldn't hear him coming. Ethan closed the door after him and moved toward the cockpit, the knife fused to his hand. Deep rhythmical vibrations shook the troop compartment which was ablaze in lurid red light. His head was buzzing with adrenaline. Alan's tooth gnawed at his gut.

Kent was in the pilot's seat flipping switches and checking instruments. When he was done making the pre-flight preparations he removed a pair of night-vision goggles from a small plastic case and fitted them over his eyes. He looked like a pathetic little bug and Ethan felt powerful, gigantic. He was close enough to squash Kent when a jolt rocked the Osprey and he was knocked back on his heels.

Heavy gusts buffeted the craft as Kent fought to get them off the ground. Ethan dropped to his knees for balance. Scarcely had they risen five feet off the ground when they were slammed back to earth by the wind's heavy hand. Kent worked the controls feverishly, battling for a foothold on the uncompromising weather. Again, the Osprey began to rise, Kent gunning the engines so that they whined in protest. The aircraft shuddered violently, bucking this way and that, but they were airborne at last.

In his haste to skip town, Kent had forgotten one thing. The Osprey was still connected to the heavy electrical cable that kept her cylinder heads from freezing over in the sub-zero cold. No sooner had they begun to level out when the slack was taken up, the cable twanged tight, and the Osprey's nose pitched sharply upward. The nose then dipped abruptly and for a split-second Ethan was weightless, hovering above the floor of the troop compartment as if gliding on a powerful updraft. A split-second later an earth-rending shriek filled the cockpit. And then all was white.

Claire had been staring into the face of a blizzard for nearly an hour as they crept slowly back across the ice field. She was now seeing things. Her optic nerves must have gotten fried from the dizzying swirl of white raging inside the buggy's headlights. There was no other explanation for the blinding nebula of light coming straight at them out of the night sky.

Whatever far out conclusions Claire may have jumped to were instantly dispelled as the ghostly silhouette of the Osprey, their only way home, took shape in the windshield. A split second later it was so close that Claire could make out Kent's desperate smirk in the red-orange glow of the cockpit instrument panel. The Osprey's nose was angled sharply downward, its massive props buzzsawing through the glittering fabric of night. They were going to be chewed up and spit out in a red spray of propeller wash and mangled scrap metal. At the last possible moment Price gunned the engine and steered them sharply to the left.

An inconceivable din filled the passenger compartment as one of the churning rotors bit into the buggy's roof, peeling it back like the lid on a canned ham. One instant Claire was resplendent in a glory of sparks, the next she was being attacked by a swarm of ravenous ice crystals. But there was no time to take cover. She was nearly thrown from the buggy as their evasive maneuver sent them hurtling across the choppy terrain. She grabbed at anything she could get her hands on. Only luck kept the buggy from rolling over as it skidded and bucked down a sheer embankment. By the time they were on even ground again the engine had stalled. It was suddenly quiet but for the low, interminable wailing of the wind.

"You still in one piece?" Price shouted.

Claire nodded. "That's something you don't see every day." She scanned the passenger compartment for her mask and goggles. Moments earlier they were on the seat next to her, but had disappeared in all the excitement.

"I always wanted a convertible," said Price. He tilted his head back and watched the weather rage overhead.

"Now how do we get home?" Claire wondered aloud. "I guess driving back to McMurdo is out of the question."

"Be grateful we didn't fly."

"I can't find my goggles," said Claire.

She got down on her hands and knees and checked under the seats. It may have been nothing more than shock, but Claire felt as if her eyes were beginning to crystallize in their sockets. With a wind-chill factor of -80° it was better to err on behalf of caution than end up living the rest of her life in permanent darkness. Just the thought of it filled her with a crazy dread.

"Must've gotten sucked out by the wind when the roof was torn off." Price's goggles hung loosely around his neck. He slipped them over his head and handed them to Claire. "Take mine."

"You can't do that, your eyes will freeze."

"The station's not far," he assured her. "The GPS is useless without the receiver, but I think I can get us back anyway. You navigate, I'll drive."

"We don't even know if this heap will still go."

"Are you going to argue with me, woman? Or are you going to do as I say and put these on?"

Claire snatched the goggles from Price's hand and fitted them over her eyes. "We'll take turns."

The buggy was reluctant to start, but eventually the engine rumbled to life and they both breathed a sigh of relief. A moment later they were underway, Price retracing their path to the point at which they had been forced to veer off course. Although their tracks had almost been completely erased by the wind, enough remained that they were soon pointed in what was presumably the right direction.

Although it was less than fifty yards behind them, the wreckage of the Osprey was just barely visible beyond the rear window. Angry tongues of flame whipped into a frenzy by the wind played over sections of its crumpled fuselage. But even this brilliant illumination was unable to penetrate the snowbound night for long. Claire blinked once and then twice, and the funny-looking aircraft that was part plane part helicopter was gone.

"Maybe we should go back," said Claire. "Check for survivors."

"Bad idea," said Price. "We turn around now, we might never find the station."

Claire looked at him. He was shielding his eyes with his forearm. "I'm not sure finding it will make much of a difference."

"Just keep your eyes open."

"We're sick, Price."

"We're going be a lot worse than sick if you get us lost." Price squinted into the trackless void that lay ahead of them.

"I mean it," she said, grabbing him by the arm. "You saw the Russians. We've been exposed to whatever it is that's making them act that way."

"Cabin fever is what's making them act that way."

"I don't know how much Hatcher's told you about the previous expedition, but they had a monkey along with them."

"Why haven't we seen the station yet? It should be right in front of us."

"Don't you get it? *S. iroquoisii* needs a living host to survive. Live storage. It's a lot easier getting a lab animal through customs than a test tube full of a deadly pathogen."

"And how do you know all of this?"

"It's only a theory, but it makes sense . . . We were fine until the other night. Then we were fed contaminated meat and—"

"Not *we*," corrected Price. "I never touched the stuff, praise be to Allah."

"What about the juices you told Shurik were oh-so good? You were still getting trace amounts."

Price balked. "The heat—cooking would've killed whatever it was you think we're infected with."

"Wake up!" Claire implored. "The temperature of the water around the vents is hot, really hot. To *S. iroquoisii*, a pot of hot soup would feel like a lukewarm bath."

"I don't like this," said Price. "We should've at least seen a light by now."

"Don't change the subject—you feel it too."

"The only thing I feel is cold."

"Why do you think Kent tried to skip out on us? He's the only one who's not infected. He must've sensed something was wrong, something the rest of us couldn't see because of how we are."

Price threw off her arm. "It's hard enough driving in these conditions without you distracting me."

"Whenever my body temperature rises I start having these thoughts. Scary thoughts. You saw what happened to Witz."

Price slammed on the brakes and brought them to a sliding stop. "What happened to Witz was an accident," he declared firmly.

"Maybe," said Claire. "But would that same accident have happened a week ago?"

"You're nuts."

"Iroquoisii's responding to heat. Think about it. Even you said how hot we've been keeping the station. You think it's a coincidence?"

"No, I think it's cold."

"Twenty minutes ago I could hardly remember my own name. And now . . . The cold air is like smelling salts. When the temperature drops, the symptoms relax. The organism must be thermophilic. Deprive it of heat and it lapses into a hibernative state. That's why the Russians were keeping the Gulag so damn hot. Heat is one of the body's primary weapons against infection, but in this case it's just the opposite. The clever little fiend has been tricking us into making it stronger. We're its personal incubators. *S. iroquoisii* is using us just like it used the chimp. Now we're the lab animals."

Claire detested her own stupidity almost as much as she admired *S. iroquoisii's* genius. If only she had spotted it earlier things might have been different. She was now armed with information that wasn't much good to her. Their communications were out, their only way home was a flaming wreck, and she was shacked up with a bunch of would-be psychotics, any or all of whom could turn on her without warning. And this wasn't even the worst of it. As the cold pushed *S. iroquoisii* back down inside of her the night grew even darker.

"We need to get back now!" said Price. He released the brake and stomped on the accelerator. The buggy lurched forward.

Claire wasn't listening. Something else now had her attention. It was her father's voice—always searching, always moving—stalking after her on the claws of the wind as the wounded buggy limped back toward the station.

The pain was excruciating, on the verge of unknowable. Like childbirth, he imagined, it was an experience unto itself. *Claire would have thanked me if she had any idea.* But Ethan realized that it was he who should probably be thankful. He might never have regained consciousness if it wasn't for the agony in his ribs. Worse than a hangnail but not bad considering the crash had reduced the multi-million dollar Osprey to a flightless heap of junk. Blood, bone, oil and metal—not to mention various other fluids and parts—were now commingled in the same way, though to a lesser degree, as the grim remnants of men and machine that rescue workers encounter at the sites of commercial airline disasters. Too grotesque to stomach, too rich with drama and suspense to look away. *Survivors? Virtually every disaster has its fortunate few.* But it was still too early to tell. The pain in his side was no mere flesh wound. Death didn't always come at you head-on.

Ethan surveyed the wreckage around him with a degree of awe and wonder that bordered on the mystical. Kent's left arm still gripped the throttle control, both torn completely out of their respective sockets. Ethan had never noticed it before but Kent wore a simple gold band on his ring finger . . . *What do you know, Mr. Universe was married. Lucky girl.* What remained of the pilot was buried beneath the Osprey's caved-in nose section. Kent's lap was a mess of exposed wires, viscous lavender hydraulic fluid, and a tangle of clumpy yellowish cable that Ethan soon realized was intestines. The air was thick with the stink of blood and fuel and shit.

On impact, a large section of the Osprey's windshield had popped out of the fuselage leaving behind a big, black gaping hole. Snow and ice flooded through the opening like a plague of insects, clinging to everything in sight. Before long the cockpit resembled the inside of Ethan's freezer back home minus the empty ice trays, the half-drunk bottle of Absolut he'd bought to celebrate something or other, and a twist-tied bag of frozen vegetable medley that had been there for years. He tried to move but a fierce bolt of pain quickly changed his mind. He lay on his back until the worst of it had subsided before trying again. He took a deep breath and attempted to heave himself into a sitting position. This time the pain was so intense that he was nearly pulled completely under. Waves of white hot darkness crashed down on him. *No fucking way!* He'd rather deliver triplets than go through that again.

Broken ribs—it had to be. Each breath was like gulping fire. Gently, Ethan probed the area with his fingertips. It occurred to him that pain and life were now interdependent. The snake that feeds on its own tail. Again, he thought of childbirth. *Claire had been a fool to want this.* At first, he thought that one of his ribs had broken through the skin, the bone slick with blood. But it was too smooth and the angle was all wrong. *You fucking klutz, you stabbed yourself!* He raised his head and looked down the length of his body. Sure enough the knife handle jutted from his right side. The blade was lodged just beneath the ribs he thought he'd broken, nestled wickedly in amongst his internal organs. Blood soaked the torn fabric around the wound, the slick oxygenated red of slow death. He tried pulling out the knife, but his guts wouldn't let go of the blade. He'd end up like Kent if he pulled any harder.

How bad was it? *A Band-Aid sure as shit won't fix it.* He chuckled to himself but this, too, hurt so he shut it down. *Doesn't seem to be bleeding too badly. But don't go blowing yourself just yet . . . That coppery taste in your mouth—it's blood. You're bleeding internally. So, no survivors after all. Tough break, kid. No one here but the dead and the dying.* Ethan lay back and closed his eyes, hands folded across his stomach. Alan was in there somewhere—part of him at least. *One lousy tooth. I know, I know— I had it coming. But do you have to be so goddamned smug about it? Shut up, and let me die in peace.*

Hypothermia wasn't quick but at least it was relatively painless. Beat wrestling with the kitchen knife in his belly. *This, I can do.* He was already shivering. His fingers and toes were numb. The cold was working its magic. Drowsiness washed over him. His blood was beginning to thicken. Strawberry syrup oozed through his veins. *Close your eyes and go to sleep. Let it take you.* But something wouldn't let him. A revelation. *If Lim revived, then why not me? You might as well stuff an apple in your mouth and feed yourself to Okum on a silver platter. Thaw and serve guinea pig.* Ethan had no intention of regaining consciousness on the dissection table while a team of army doctors cut into him.

As things stood, he wasn't going anywhere. Not as long as he remained skewered. It hurt too fucking bad when he moved—like the knife was dicing up his insides. He wouldn't make it ten feet before blacking out. Getting the blade out was going to hurt, and there was a good chance that uncorking the wound would kill him. The knife might be the only thing keeping him from bleeding to death. But at least he'd go out swinging.

With a few good yanks he managed to open a tear in the fabric around the wound. He then removed as much of the insulation from the parka as he could, piling the white synthetic fluff on his stomach. Once the knife was out he was going to need something to plug the hole.

Ethan grabbed the handle, gritted his teeth and pulled.

It wasn't the pain that bothered him so much, it was the slow steady tug o' war with his guts he was now committed to. The sinewy tissue binding his internal organs to the smooth walls of his abdominal cavity strained against the retreating blade. Sickening, elastic—a rubber band stretched to the breaking point. The knife

was either going to give up and slip out quietly, or he was going to end up disembow-
eling himself. His heartbeat drummed in his ears. Darkness clouded his peripheral
vision. *Hang on, don't pass out!* He relaxed his grip and let the blackness subside. He
waited until his mind had cleared, tightened his grip on the knife, and pulled with
every ounce of strength he had left. The dull edge of the blade grated against the un-
derside of one of his ribs as he dragged the knife from its bloody hole. *I'm going to be
sick*, he thought. But the worst of it was already over. Ethan removed one of his gloves,
gathered up the insulation from his parka and stuffed it deep into the hole with his
bare fingertips. The wound was warm and sticky-wet. Burbling with life. He saw
why Ivan was so at home. Between the miserable cold and the savage wind howling
through the cavernous hulk of the Osprey, Ethan would have gladly crawled inside
himself to keep warm if it was possible.

Once on his feet Ethan took a few moments to get his balance before moving.
Darkness still pressed in around him, but he shook it off and shuffled into the cockpit. Kent occupied the pilot's seat like a stargazer, his head thrown back toward the
sky. The night-vision goggles rested cockeyed on his face but they were mercifully
intact. Ethan wasn't going to find his way back to the station with a white cane.

Price was now wearing the goggles and Claire had shrunk into the protective shell
of her hood, pulling tight the drawstring so that her face was sealed against the cold.
For some time, she'd been scanning the darkness for signs of the station. Despite the
generally poor visibility, they should have at least been able to make out something—
if not the structure itself then certainly the glow of its lights. Convinced that they
were hopelessly lost, she'd given up and turned sole responsibility for the search over
to Price. Tucking herself away like a turtle wasn't going to keep her from joining Lim
in the frozen foods section but without the goggles her mind was free to wander.
Within moments she was back at Eric's house, her senses awash in mellow Southern
California sunlight.

The front door was open and Eric stood in the kitchen preparing dinner. He was
talking to someone. A woman's voice, soft and lilting, mingled with the languid
hiss of running water, the even staccato of vegetables being chopped. Bright light
streamed through the windows, splashing the wood floors and smooth plaster walls
with a warm honeyed glow. A woman sat at the dining table—approximating words
in gentle musical tones, cooing softly to an infant latched onto her breast. Claire
knew instinctively that she was the woman, that it was her child nursing contentedly
in the wholesome light of the afternoon sun. And she was overcome by a warmth so
pure and penetrating that it hurt.

She'd given herself over entirely to the vision, hoping this would be her last stop
en route to wherever it was the cold was taking her, but then there was a crash and
Claire was thrown into the windshield so hard that the glass fractured beneath the

force of the impact. One kind of pain gave way to another as the luminous image of the infant at her breast withered and died.

Claire picked herself up off the floor of the tundra buggy and took a quick inventory of her body. She didn't feel half bad considering that she had survived two near-death experiences in the last twenty minutes. A few bumps and bruises but nothing a few Advil couldn't fix. Satisfied that she was still in one piece, she helped Price to his feet. The wind hurtled overhead and roared into the passenger compartment where the buggy's roof had been peeled back by the Osprey.

"What did we hit?" Claire asked.

"I won't tell if you don't," Price joked through clenched teeth.

She looked over his shoulder. There was a momentary break in the weather and she was able to make out the obstacle in their path. Cast in the fierce glow of the buggy's headlights was the intact portion of the derelict station's common room. They had driven right into it.

Claire couldn't imagine how Price had failed to see it even in near zero visibility. And then she got a good look at him in the glow of the instrument lights, the goggles askew in the aftermath of the collision that had opened a bloodless cut along one cheek. The cold was killing him, driving the blood from his face deep into the core of his body where it wouldn't freeze. At least not immediately. This, however, left his exposed skin especially vulnerable. Gone was the chocolate bronze luster she had known. A hoary layer of frost had taken its place. His eyes peered out of icy cracks. Panic gripped her as she wondered how long before her own face, exposed as it now was, succumbed to the cold.

"It's not polite to stare," Price mumbled.

Good, she thought, *he can still see me.* But Price was now having difficulty speaking, his face acquiring the stony rigidity of a plaster cast. It was her fault. He was freezing to death because she'd been careless with her own gear. She'd given him back his goggles, but only because she'd believed they were already dead, and by then it was too late. Mercifully, there was no time to dwell on her actions. She took off her parka and stripped out of the long-sleeved thermal undershirt she was wearing. She was naked beneath. The wind was like acid on her exposed flesh, millions of tiny capillaries constricting simultaneously as her blood sought refuge from the vicious assault. She got her parka back on as quickly as possible and snugged her hood down tightly over her head. By the time she got the zipper up her teeth were chattering like castanets and her flesh smoldered hotly.

"What are you doing?" Price asked sleepily. He was slowing down, hypothermia creeping over him.

"We're going to play follow the leader."

Claire pulled her shirt over Price's head and tied it firmly in place with the sleeves knotted over his eyes so that they were doubly insulated against the cold. A trained survivalist, he didn't resist. It was this or certain blindness.

Claire maneuvered him to the door of the tundra buggy and tried to get her bearings. Confronted with the terrifying reality of what she was about to do, she was hardly able to focus. Her plummeting body temperature had driven *S. iroquoisii* back into hiding. The courage she had mustered under his guiding hand had now abandoned her. Once again darkness ruled her mind. She was beginning to think that infection and the madness it caused were preferable to the omnipresent sense of doom and subsequent helplessness lucidity imparted. How long would it take her to freeze to death if she missed the station and went wandering off into the night? Definitely less than an hour, but an hour could feel like an eternity as anyone who's lived in the shadow of fear knows.

"What are you waiting for?" asked Price. "Let's do this."

"It's too dark," said Claire. "I'll get us lost."

"You've walked the same stretch a half-dozen times. Fifty yards—you can do it."

"I'll give you the goggles and—"

"Listen, I'm already half-blind. This is all you. Now get your ass in gear." Price's voice was firm but supportive. The shirt tied over his head made him look like a hostage.

Claire positioned herself in front of him and put his hands on her waist. "Hang on."

Fifty yards wasn't a long way to go—half a football field, a tiny fraction of the distance she ran four days a week—but ten yards into it and she was having trouble staying on course. The same wind that had knocked her off the mesa seemed once again determined to kill her. For every step she took forward it pushed her one step to the side so that the tendency was to advance diagonally rather than in a straight line. It didn't help that she had Price in tow. He shuffled along behind her like an old man, slow and uncertain. *Leave him. You have to. You won't make it back otherwise.* And she was suddenly gripped by a longing desire to see the results of the pregnancy test she had hastily discarded prior to their little outing. At the time, settling things with Zhenya and Shurik was all she had cared about . . . *All S. iroquoisii had cared about.* Now, faced with the likelihood that she was going die out here, she needed to be absolutely certain that she wasn't carrying a life inside of her.

"Price," Claire shouted above the wind. "I want you to stay right here." She tried to keep her voice upbeat, optimistic. It was as much for her as it was for him. "Don't move. I'm going to take a look around and see if I can figure out where we are."

"Don't forget about me," was all he said and it was almost as if he knew.

"I'll be right back," she replied hollowly.

Price released his grip on her waist, and Claire moved forward into the darkness. She took ten steps and then looked back over her shoulder. Price was gone, swallowed by the howling night. It then hit Claire that she was alone. She panicked. What had she done? *Price saved your life and this is how you repay him?* It was wrong, worse than wrong. It was murder. And Claire's father didn't waste any time letting her know it.

He was everywhere at once, a drunken voice coming at her out of the darkness. Low and guttural with bestial overtones, it was as if she was being stalked. An electric charge trickled down her spine and she had the distinct feeling that he was creeping up behind her. However each time that she wheeled to face him she was greeted by the same terrible emptiness. But he kept coming and she kept turning, and soon she was whirling round and round. Badly disoriented, she would never find her way back, and Price would freeze to death because of her, and her last moments on earth would be spent on her knees crying like a little girl into the face of a blizzard.

And like that the storm broke, leaving in its wake a thick white smoky fog. Made up of billions of microscopic particles of ice it wasn't like any fog she had ever seen. The powdery mist caught what scarce moonlight was available and distributed it evenly throughout the entirety of its mass, engulfing her in an eerie phosphorescent tide. In the absence of the wind the silence was now deafening. Claire's sobs were suddenly audible in the stillness, her father's voice reduced to a mocking whisper. She still had no idea where she was or in what direction she should head, but at least she had managed to get a harness on her nerves.

"Price," she called tentatively at first. "You out there? Price!" she shouted. But there was no answer. The fog acted like a baffle and Claire had no idea how far, if at all, her voice penetrated it. She called out again. Nothing.

She was trying to make sense of her footprints so that she could retrace them when the same electric charge trickled down her spine. An ominous figure coalesced from the fog directly in front of her. Faceless and mute, it advanced on her with greedy outstretched arms like a nightmare chasing down another hour of sleep. Frightened, Claire lurched backward and wound up flat on her ass. She turned and was clambering away on her hands and knees when someone hissed her name.

"Price?" Claire's heart was thudding in her chest. She exhaled deeply and stood.

"Can you see me?" he asked.

"You're standing right in front of me." Price's head was still covered by her shirt. "Why are you whispering?"

"I heard something. I think it was the tractor. Listen . . ."

Claire listened. "I don't hear anything."

"Maybe I imagined it." Price continued in his normal voice. "No way they could have made it this far on that old bucket. Not exposed like they were."

"I didn't forget about you," said Claire.

"I know."

Somehow they managed to find the station even though not a single light burned to guide their way. If anything, the fog had thickened; in fact, it was now so dense they could have passed within ten feet of the brooding black structure and missed it altogether. Luck was on their side though and they spotted it enfolded in the clinging vapor like a haunted house. They worked their way along the perimeter until they came to the entrance. Claire paused before opening the door.

"What is it?" asked Price.

"It's totally dark," she replied, unable to look past the irony. "They really abandoned us. We're stuck here."

"We can worry about that later. Right now, let's get inside where it's warm. I want to see if I'm going to have to trade in my stripes for a guide dog."

Price removed the shirt from his head the moment the door closed behind them. Some of the color had returned to his face, but it looked bad. The flesh on his cheeks and the tip of his nose was gray with frostbite. He rubbed his eyes and squinted hard, blinking several times so that tears might again flow from his frozen tear ducts.

"The shirt—" he offered bravely. "It was a good idea."

Claire passed her hand in front of his face but he didn't respond. "Oh god, Price, I'm sorry." This was her fault. She would confess everything . . .

But then Price's head snapped up, he looked her in the eye and said, "I'm just messin' with you, girl. You did good. Now let's see what we can do about getting some real light in here."

For some reason the station was now illuminated by the auxiliary lights. Each room was fitted with a single high-intensity unit. These ran on big ni-cad batteries that were continuously charged as long as the generator was supplying the station with power. The moment the generator stopped running, the auxiliary lights kicked on automatically. From that point on you could expect to get three, four hours tops, before the batteries ran out of juice. Of course, the bathroom was the only room in the station not so equipped. Claire tried to do the math, to figure out how long she had left before the lights went out, but really there was no point. She had no idea when the generator had breathed its last breath. Right now she could only hope that Price was able to get the thing up and running before her father came looking for her once again. She gave Price back his goggles and mask, and helped him find a flashlight.

"If I'm not back in twenty minutes . . ." said Price.

"I'll come get you."

Minus the warm bodies that had once occupied it, the common room was in no greater state of disarray than when she had raced Price on the treadmill a few scant hours ago. Other than the absence of real light there was no indication just how much things had changed since then. The truth was impossible to quantify, epochal in its enormity. *S. iroquoisii* had spoken, and its word was now recorded in the gospel of the flesh. Her flesh. Hatcher's flesh. In the flesh of DeLuca and the others. Alan had tasted the eons-old sacrament—no longer was there any doubt. But to what extent had he embraced this deadly covenant? Had things been as bad as they were at the Gulag? She dreaded to think what evolutionary mayhem Hatcher, DeLuca, Bishop and the others would have unleashed on the world if the Osprey hadn't crashed. A tragedy for the remaining expedition members, but a lucky break for humanity. At least it was warm—not warm like it had been when the generator was still pumping heat through the station, but a thousand times warmer than outside. Claire's mind was racing. She couldn't just sit here waiting for Price to return.

Pink. The same anemic hue as the fire-extinguishing foam that had mucked up the derelict station. And now it—*pink*—was mucking up her life. Claire sat on the floor of the bathroom and studied the little plastic wand in her hand. 99.3% accurate. She had never particularly liked pink. Even as a girl she had thought it too prissy, a tacit declaration of feminine helplessness. Now the only pink thing she owned was a pair of lacy thong panties Eric had given her. Pink—she read the instructions on the box again just to be sure though arguably she had known all along, known where it really mattered. Her body was already starting to adjust to the new life inside of her—nurture, accommodate, protect. She was ravenously hungry, her hormones were running wild, and . . . Despite the fact that her life was suddenly twice as complicated, she took a small measure of comfort in the possibility that *S. iroquoisii* wasn't entirely to blame for her condition. She hoped against reason that the organism wasn't trans-placental, that somehow her body's natural defenses would rise up and protect her unborn child.

Until now Claire had accepted that she was going to die out here. Somehow, some way—Antarctica wasn't going to let her leave. Too much had happened to allow her to believe otherwise. She'd been choked, drugged, fallen into a crevasse, nearly frozen to death, almost ripped to pieces by a crashing aircraft that was ferrying her back-stabbing colleagues to safety . . . Oh, and she'd almost forgotten . . . There was also the small fact of *S. iroquoisii* to consider. She was carrying a prehistoric organism of some kind inside of her, the effect of which had had a hand in each and every one of her near-death experiences. Not to mention the actual death of several others. So actually, she was living for three.

Pregnant. It wasn't fair. Not to her, and especially not to the life developing inside of her. If—and it was a big if—she got out of here alive she'd be faced with some mammoth decisions. In all likelihood, her baby would be infected just like she was. On the one hand, it would be that much better equipped to cope with the rigors of existence than the average human infant—stronger, more determined, a belly full of fire. But would she be bringing an Adolph Hitler into the world? A Mike Tyson? A Marquis de Sade? *Or worse?* Would Claire even live to have the chance?

She clutched the little plastic wand over her heart and closed her eyes. Her mind fast-forwarded through an unclouded pregnancy full of love and light. Eric rubbing her round belly, the fresh smell of roses blowing in through the windows of the El Segundo house, tiny shoes awaiting the pitter-patter of plump little feet. There was a newly decorated room—all teddy bears and bumble bees, soft colors and fuzzy fabrics. And of course a crib, baby's first habitat outside the womb. But then Claire thought of the cage she had found amidst the wreckage of the derelict station—*Lab-i-tat, the play on words was awful*—and the image of the rose-scented afternoons and warm amber light went hideously wrong on her.

Rewind: Claire had just been wheeled from the delivery room and sat upright in a sterile hospital bed. She was drenched in cold, bitter sweat. Matted and stringy and pasted to her forehead, her dark hair resembled clumps of sea grass. The light that filtered through the windows was the color of ash, a voided shade of life. Baby was at her breast—the celebrated first feeding—but she was taken by a strange feeling. No one had bothered to sever the umbilical cord. The pulsing conduit snaked out from beneath the bedcovers, wended its way across the liquid white floor, and disappeared out the door and into the hallway beyond. It was tough and sinewy and lively with current. Despite the fact that she could only see ten or so feet of it, Claire knew where the umbilical ended. Where it *began*. Somewhere further along the hallway, and much further still, it descended into a very dark and deep hole in the ice at the bottom of the world. She looked upon her newborn child where it continued to feed, greedily now, and it was blood not milk that flowed from her cracked nipple.

The blizzard had blown until it was hoarse from the effort, but it had let up now, at least for the time being, and the air had thickened into a swampy miasma that was colored green by the night-vision goggles Ethan had lifted off Kent's eviscerated corpse. And although the high-tech oculars were working just fine—gathering the scant light of the moon and concentrating it in a narrowed field—he could hardly see his hand in front of his face. Darkness was one thing, but this fog—about the only way you could hope to get a handle on it was with an ice cream scoop. He wished he hadn't left his own goggles on the floor of the Osprey, but there was no point kicking himself now. He was alive and that's more than Kent could say for himself. But hell if the sickly green light wasn't fucking with his head . . . And the pain in his side. *Fucking amateur, serves you right for stabbing yourself.*

He was singing what few verses he remembered from "Born on the Bayou"—actually it was one verse, the chorus—when a welcome sound caught his attention. For the past several minutes the only thing he'd heard was the off-key ramblings of his own voice. *The generator—what else could it be? You lucky ass son of a bitch!* Although he had started out from the Osprey with a pretty good idea where the station was, he had gotten turned around by the blizzard and had pretty much been wandering erratically through the drowsy green haze ever since. Faint, but there it was, the low repetitive *chug-chug-chug* of internal-combustion. Warmth, electric light, food. He did his best to pinpoint its source and headed in that direction.

Faster than he would've thought possible, he bore down on the generator. Or was it bearing down on him? Ethan scarcely had time to throw himself clear of the onrushing specter that rumbled out of the haze and nearly ran him down. *No fucking way! It can't*—But even distorted as it was in the staticky green field of the night-vision goggles, there was no mistaking the tractor. Seeing it like this was pretty fucking unlikely, but stranger still was the fact that no one was driving it. And then it was gone, eaten up by the fog. Ethan lay face down in the snow, the fall re-igniting the agony in his side. Getting back on his feet hurt like hell, but he gritted his teeth and picked himself up—first to his hands and knees. The synthetic down insulation he had used to stuff his wound was soaked all the way through. There was no way of knowing how much blood he had lost—what oozed surface-ward, and what washed into his peritoneal cavity.

Ethan was cursing his stupidity when a thin spot in the fog revealed a shadowy glimpse of the station, a great black spider lying in wait for an unsuspecting passer-by. A minute or two later he was at the door and free of the malingering green fog.

The common room was bound together by the splintered light of the emergency floods. He was just about to remove the night-vision goggles when the main lights snapped on, and it was like staring into the heart of a green supernova. Lightning bolts of pain shot through his optic nerves and straight into his brain. He ripped off the goggles and threw them to the floor. He was rubbing the fire out of his eyes when chaos erupted all around him. Shouting and the pounding of footsteps . . . They were coming for him. He'd known that he was going to have some explaining to do. After all, DeLuca and the others hadn't abandoned him as he'd originally suspected, it was he who had abandoned them. And now they wanted answers. Possibly more.

He was reaching for the knife in his boot when Bishop called out to him: "Grab him, Hatcher! Don't let the slippery bastard get away!"

Ethan looked up and was nearly bowled over by Lim. He was astounded to find that the little man was still alive though the naked wild-eyed creature carrying his snapped-off arm around like a relay race baton hardly constituted a living being in the conventional sense. Seeing that his escape route was blocked by DeLuca who had positioned himself in front of the door, Lim took refuge behind Ethan. Apparently he had no recollection of what Ethan had done to him less than an hour ago, even though the long narrow cut above his jugular and the stab wound in his right thigh still oozed gooey, red-black blood.

"Give me the arm," Bishop cooed, munching away at one of his protein bars. "And we'll let you go."

Lim looked confused. His partially defrosted mind was incapable of processing the rush of stimuli coming at him from every direction.

"Easy, now, we don't want to hurt you," said McKenzie, inching his way toward Lim. "We just want a few drops of your blood so we can help you."

As Lim turned to face McKenzie, Bishop made a move. It was only a quick jab-step to test Lim's wariness, but it was enough to convince them that the cornered marine biologist was a long way from throwing in the towel. Lim's head snapped back almost instantly and Bishop backed off.

"You idiots!" Ethan shouted. "Give the guy a break, he doesn't even know what planet he's on. Why don't you let him die in peace?"

"The crazy little fucker bit me!" Bishop explained incredulously.

"We can't just let him have free run of the place," said DeLuca. "Not in his condition."

"Then lock him outside." Ethan didn't have time for this shit. "Let the cold take care of him."

Bishop thought it over. "Bad idea. He'd find a way back in." He removed a protein bar from his pocket, unwrapped it and took a big bite. *"Mmmh . . ."* he groaned,
smacking his lips and waving the protein bar back and forth in the air. Lim's head
followed magnetically. "Lemon chiffon cheesecake with raspberry-flavored protein
nuggets." He took another bite. "Ooh, that's good," chewing loudly. "This is what
you want, isn't it?"

"Maybe Hatcher's right," said DeLuca. "Lock him outside. There's only one way in."

"You're forgetting the hole in the side of the station," Bishop snapped. "A goddamn elephant could wander through it."

"Hole?" Ethan wondered aloud.

"Kent tried to ditch us," explained McKenzie. "He must've forgotten to unplug
himself before takeoff. He almost tore the place in two."

Bishop ignored them and spoke to Lim. "Tell you what . . ." he said, producing
two more protein bars from his pocket. He studied the wrappers and made his pitch.
"I'll trade you one of these—Kona fudge chip or yogurt-dipped oatmeal, each packed
with 35 grams of pre-digested protein concentrate and . . . well, a bunch of other
shit—for your arm. What do you say? Hell of a deal . . ." There was now a malignant
edge to his voice though he was smiling broadly, a great big car salesman's grin.

Lim frowned contemplatively. It appeared as if he was ready to accept the terms
of the deal when DeLuca interrupted.

"You're sick," he said. "We can help you."

Bishop exploded into laughter. Tears clouded his blue eyes. *"Sick . . .* That's good.
I've seen dead people who were in better shape." He wiped the tears from his eyes and
caught his breath.

"What the hell's keeping Okum?" DeLuca asked, speaking to no one in particular.

"The blizzard . . ." said McKenzie. "Can't get off the ground."

"Fucking great," said Bishop. "We're stuck. Now what do we do?"

"I, for one, am going to rustle up something to eat," DeLuca suggested wearily.

Ethan could've sworn that he saw him wink at Bishop and McKenzie.

"Good idea," said McKenzie. "A little grub'll do me good. How 'bout you,
Bishop, hungry?"

Bishop's eyes widened and he nodded enthusiastically. "I could eat a horse!"

The three men passed a look between each other, a coded message written in their
eyes. They were up to something and Ethan didn't like it. Where exactly they were
going wasn't clear to him at first. What was clear though was that Okum figured into
all of this more prominently than anyone had let on. Ethan'd had his suspicions but
this confirmed that he was on the outside looking in. Not that it made a whole hell
of a lot of difference now. Too little, too late. But then he saw what Okum's three
stooges had planned for Lim and was reminded that this was a long way from over.

DeLuca, Bishop, McKenzie—they were slowly closing in on Lim, tightening the
noose, using their insipid chatter as a distraction. Primitive little men with point-

ed sticks circling their prey amid a din of birdcalls and glottal clicks. They hadn't washed or shaven in days. And then there was Lim. He danced around behind Ethan as his mind imploded in a firestorm of short-circuiting neurons and amped up survival instinct. Ethan, himself, was beginning to feel cornered, trapped. He was beat-up and bleeding internally. The lame beast at the end of a blood spoor. Any closer and they'd be on top of him. Every cell in his body was suddenly charged with adrenaline. "Don't come any closer!" he warned, whipping the knife out of his boot. "I mean it, stay back!" He slashed at the air in front of Bishop's face with the reddened blade and bared his teeth.

"Where the hell have you been anyway?" asked Bishop, tugging at the mossy growth on his chin. His eyes sparkled meanly.

"Kent was leaving without us so I tried to stop him."

"You tried to stop him?" Bishop echoed dubiously. "You were planning on ditching us just like you ditched your buddy, Alan, and left him to die."

"You don't know what you're talking about."

"Where's Kent now?" asked DeLuca.

"Dead," said Ethan.

"And the Osprey?"

"Scrap metal. We crashed."

"We're fucked," said Bishop. "Without power, we'll freeze to death."

"Okum will be here soon," DeLuca assured him. But it was clear that he was also trying to convince himself.

Bishop pointed at the chart they had used to keep track of the dead from the first team. "That's what Okum wanted—proof that everyone died in the explosion. Now that we've given him that, what else is there? We're all infected. He's not going to take the chance of allowing this thing to spread."

"Okum doesn't give a damn about what happened to the first team," said DeLuca. "This is what he's after." He looked at Lim. "A living specimen."

McKenzie nodded in agreement.

"We're living specimens!" Bishop exclaimed shrilly. "Or hadn't you noticed? What makes you think Okum's not going to stick all of us in a cage?"

"He gave me his word that . . ."

"His word?" Bishop was on the verge of losing it. "Okum gave you his *word*." A stricken look danced across his face. "I hate to break it to you Major but we're not getting out of here alive. Not like this," he said, his voice plateauing an octave or two above what was normal for him.

"Let's just keep our wits about us," said DeLuca. "Losing our heads isn't going to help matters."

Bishop wasn't listening. He muttered something under his breath and did this flailing thing with his arms as if fending off an invisible assailant.

"Lab rats," Ethan interrupted. "Bishop's right—Okum doesn't care who or how just as long as he's got fresh meat for the chopping block. You can forget what he told you. When Okum gets here—and he *will* get here—we're all fucked."

Ethan didn't know if Okum was coming. He knew as little or less than any of them. But he needed a diversion, something to buy himself time so he could figure things out. He still had the emergency transmitter Okum had given him—to be used under one condition and one condition only. *In case everything goes to shit . . .* Ethan remembered the words well. What choice did he have? He was out of options. He still had his bargaining chip. The camcorder footage. But how was he going to smuggle it out of here?

DeLuca turned to McKenzie. "What if Hatcher's right?" he asked. "What if Okum gets here and . . ."

Before DeLuca could finish his thought Lim was wracked by a series of violent convulsions. A deep visceral rumbling in his guts boiled over into a fit of peristaltic spasms that traveled up and down the entire length of his body. The last of these spasms culminated in a globular rattle in his throat. Lim was now doubled over, dry-heaving. A strand of saliva nearly a foot long dangled from his chin before breaking free and splashing to the floor. A second later he was vomiting fiercely, the contents of his stomach giving rise to a pungent cataract of partially-digested sludge and digestive juices. A final convulsion, more forceful than the rest, produced the only remnant of food not entirely broken down. An exclamation. What lay on the floor at their feet was really nothing more than a couple of knuckles bound together by a ragged covering of half-digested flesh. The nail was still intact.

Bishop and the others had retreated several paces in the face of the voluble discharge. They stood there dumbfounded as Lim bolted through the gap vacated by McKenzie and into the central corridor. Claire emerged from the same corridor a split-second later, her eyes fixed and distant. She was especially calm for someone who had nearly been run over by a dead man.

"Was that Lim?" she asked.

"In the flesh," Ethan confirmed.

Slowly, Claire came around. "Somebody tell me WHAT THE FUCK IS GOING ON!" she shouted.

Ethan brushed past her. "You might want to think about writing out your will."

He made it to the outer hallway where he came across Lim crouched on his heels like some half-formed thing prematurely spilled onto the delivery room floor. He was leaning into the wall, his back to Ethan, his bony shoulders knitting furtively over something. Although Lim was too far gone to pity, this didn't prevent Ethan from taking a personal interest in him. Ethan knew that he should go straight to his quarters and activate the transmitter, but he needed to know what terrors awaited him on the shore opposite sanity.

He approached with his hands outstretched—the knife now concealed in the sleeve of his parka—and announced himself with a warm "Don't be afraid." Lim glanced over his shoulder, his mouth working as though attempting to form words. Failing to produce a single syllable he resumed his earlier posture.

"Look," said Ethan, pulling up ten or so feet short of him. He still wasn't quite sure who or *what* he was dealing with. "I can help you if you'll just tell me what you're going through. If you can understand anything I'm saying . . . Anything at all."

Lim ignored him.

Just a simple answer—that's all Ethan wanted. He wasn't asking for a song and dance. A few measly fucking words. Of course he realized that no answer was in a sense an answer unto itself. But it definitely wasn't the answer he wanted, the answer he *needed*.

"Don't ignore me!" Ethan called. He was frustrated. "Hey, I'm talking to you." He strode angrily up behind Lim and rapped on his skull. "Anyone home?"

Lim spun about on his haunches and snarled. He was eating someth . . . *Fuck no!* Ethan fell back reeling, his legs like rubber. Not even Okum's nasty little bedtime story about the doomed crew of the *Annenkov* could have prepared him for this. He steadied himself against the corridor wall and puked his guts out, a corrosive mixture of blood and bile. Only the sharp pain in his abdomen kept him from blacking out completely as yellow waves of nausea crashed over him. So this is what he was becoming. And he thought he had imagined the worst. Lim looked at him blankly, his eyes seething with the strange smoky light of moonstones. He was eating his severed arm as if it was a turkey drumstick—*his own fucking arm!*—stripping away hunks of flesh, tearing hungrily into the mealy tissue until most of what remained was stuck in his teeth.

And the bad news kept coming. Everyone but Claire had known from the beginning. All of the details weren't yet clear to her, but one thing definitely was. She'd been used. But it was worse than that. She was an accomplice in this mess. Lim was about the only person who figured to be in deeper shit than she was. But even he had one up on her. Lim's brain, as DeLuca had so delicately put it, was mush. Right now he only cared about one thing . . . And then it struck Claire. It wasn't Euclidean geometry but the wisdom was perfectly linear, uninterrupted by superfluous tangents, inspired in its directness and simplicity. Lim was interested in one thing and one thing only: the variable continuum that fell between Point A and Point B known as *life*. There was survival and then there was everything else. Who knew that her tongue in cheek invocation of Frankenstein for Witz's benefit would come back to her like this?

Life on earth had had to begin somewhere. Maybe *S. iroquoisii* was even older than she had realized. Maybe he wasn't merely a performance booster, but the very spark that had ignited the primordial soup of a lifeless planet and given rise to every species on earth. This could explain why he proliferated in close proximity to hydrothermal vents. Located primarily along active subduction zones, these hotspots comprised the vestiges of earth's volcanic past—tectonic foundries where liquid rock boiled out of her superheated core to create the world's existing landmasses. Lim, alive? Perhaps only inasmuch as his body was still host to cellular activity. He was like a game piece from one of those old-school electric hockey rinks—unmitigated energy and nervous jitters. But truly alive? *You say tomato . . .*

When Claire had first realized that she was pregnant, she was angry. Not at anyone or anything in particular, but at the world, at time, at the mechanical universe for sticking her in the worst place imaginable, in the worst situation imaginable. *S. iroquoisii* had betrayed her. She'd sat on the floor of the bathroom pitying herself while the world ticked by. After ten minutes she finally picked herself up and shuffled into the common room. She didn't want to die alone. But seeing Lim, a naked brain-dead zombie with one arm fending off four able-bodied men, was like catching a whiff of smelling salts. What doesn't kill you makes you stronger—isn't that how it worked? A day, a year, millennia . . . No one said evolution was a stroll in the park. Survival was a lowdown dirty business. The weak need not apply. For every action there had to be a decisive reaction. Jungle law. If something bites you, bite it back. Claire was going to be a mother. It was time that she behaved like one and set an example for the little one she would soon be bringing into the world.

Claire watched and listened as DeLuca and the others concocted a plan to capture Lim. Their minds were no longer guided by necessity or reason but by a hunting instinct that was much older and more deeply embedded in the human genome. They were all set to put their plan into action when they were interrupted by three successive knocks at the door. DeLuca leapt at the door and barricaded it with his shoulder.

"It's Price," Claire explained. The three men regarded her strangely. It was as if they had no idea who she was or what she was doing there. "He's been trying to fix the generator."

The knock came again. This time it was louder, more insistent. They eyed the door suspiciously as Price tried to force it open. A couple of inches was all he got before DeLuca lowered his center of gravity and pushed the door closed again.

"Bishop!" DeLuca hissed. "Get your fat ass over here and help me. I can't do this alone."

Bishop smiled unsympathetically and unwrapped another protein bar.

"What are you doing?" asked Claire. "Aren't you going to let him in?"

The three men looked at each other and then at Claire. She was now moving towards them. Price had been outside for close to thirty minutes. He wouldn't last much longer especially considering what he had already been through.

Bishop was the first to speak up. "How do we know it's Price?" he asked.

"Who are you expecting?" Claire replied angrily. "The big bad wolf?" She parked herself directly in front of him and got in his face. Well, not exactly. At six-four, he towered over her.

"No one," Bishop replied flatly. He took a bite of the protein bar and chewed it noisily. "I'm expecting no one, that's the point."

"Well, it's not no one," said Claire. "It's Sergeant Price . . . *Your friend*. And if you don't let him in he'll freeze to death."

"If it's Price," asked Bishop, "why doesn't he say something?"

"Because his face is covered, you idiot. You know how cold it is out there."

Bishop's voice flatlined. There was foreboding in his pale blue eyes. "What did you call me?"

Claire's muscles tensed as she sized him up. A significant portion of her martial arts training had focused on ways to bring down an opponent bigger and stronger than herself. If she couldn't get in a good groin shot, she'd go for Bishop's bum knee. And if that failed, there was always the windpipe. Her instructor had warned the class away from employing the latter in any but the direst of situations because such a blow was potentially lethal. Claire didn't know if present circumstance qualified as dire or not, but she was done fucking around.

Sensing her resolve, Bishop seemed to swell before her eyes, acquiring additional mass the way many species of animals will when threatened. He straightened up and pushed back his shoulders so that the fabric of his parka drew tight across his bulging chest. A week ago Claire had been unable to imagine Bishop, a gentle giant, competing in a sport as brutal as college football. That, of course, was before *S. iroquoisii* had crashed the party. Now he looked as if he'd wandered out of the pages of Norse mythology—a blonde-bearded warrior king who wrestled sea monsters for sport. He was even bigger than Claire realized, easily double her own weight.

"Bishop's right," McKenzie interrupted, wedging himself between the two of them. "It could be the Russians. We just don't know."

Claire eased up a bit but did not let her guard down. "Trust me," she said. "It's not the Russians. They're all dead—Kesha, Zhenya, Shurik . . . I was there."

"Dead?" DeLuca remarked warily. "When? *How?*" His eyes widened and his face drained of color.

"What about the girl?" asked Bishop. "The one Hatcher was diddling?"

"Her, too."

"I should've seen it earlier," DeLuca muttered. He was still leaning against the door, but his legs were no longer braced for leverage. They were merely crutches, feeble little sticks keeping him upright.

"You should've seen *what* earlier?" Claire shouted.

"Ivan . . ." DeLuca whispered.

"Who's Ivan?" Claire demanded. "You mean *S. iroquoisii*? Is that what this is all about? That's why you needed me, isn't it? To confirm your discovery."

"I bet it was Okum," said Bishop. "Tying up loose ends. It's probably him on the other side of the door. Let him in and we're dead."

"It's her he wants," DeLuca blurted, pointing at Claire.

The door snapped open before Claire had time to digest what DeLuca had said. It was just four or five inches, but that's all it took for someone to get a hand inside between the latch and the frame. *Someone* because Claire had only to glimpse the stained orange oven mitt to be convinced that it *wasn't* Price they were keeping at bay. *Impossible* . . .

Bishop was slow to react as DeLuca was forced backward by a powerful thrust that sent him sprawling to the floor. The door flung open, admitting a blast of cold foul-smelling air. Shurik and Georgiy occupied the center of the rectangular void, their faces so badly frostbitten as to seem ravaged by fire. Chin, cheeks, and nose were enameled with shiny black frost blisters and flaking necrotic tissue. The flesh outlying the most severe damage looked as if it had been gnawed away by rats—raw and red and shredded. Both men had enough facial hair to limit the extent of the damage—particularly Shurik with his overgrown black beard—but at this point it was moot. Neither man would ever want to look in a mirror again. Shurik was still wearing the welder's goggles—a crisp pane of ice encrusting the lenses—but Georgiy was almost certainly blind. His eyes had crystallized in their sockets.

Shurik's lips had withdrawn from his teeth to such an extent that the damage appeared to be the work of a flesh-eating bacteria well on its way to consuming his entire face. Every tooth in his mouth, not to mention the whole of his gums was exposed in the broad predatory grin circumnavigating the lower half of his face. De-Luca, McKenzie and Bishop were mesmerized by the toothsome specter looming before them, his shoulders adorned with the scalps of his murdered comrades. An enormous pipe wrench perhaps five feet long, the one that had apparently occupied the empty stencil on the wall of the drilling room back at the Gulag, was cradled across his chest like a war club. A wicked looking carving knife, its handle fashioned from the spiked end of an antler, was tucked into a length of electrical cord knotted about his waist. Georgiy was armed with an AK-47 slung over his right shoulder; however, Claire doubted his ability to use the weapon effectively blind as he was.

No one moved. The two groups of men simply stood there, facing off like rival clans on opposite sides of an eons-wide gulf—*Homo erectus* meets Neanderthal. Then Shurik made a low rumbling noise in his throat and stepped over the threshold. Georgiy followed, clutching the fabric of Shurik's parka to guide him. And like that the gulf was bridged. Georgiy released Shurik and removed one of the oven mitts so that he could dig balls of wadded up cotton from each of his nostrils. He then cocked his head backwards and inhaled deeply through his nose. He took several whiffs until he picked up the scent he was searching for. His useless gaze panned over the three men and settled on Claire. For the first time she noticed the blood smeared over the front of her parka. Dimly, she realized that Hatcher had been clutching his stomach as he pushed past her moments earlier, but until now she hadn't made the connection.

Shurik must have also picked up on the alluring scent because he slowly swiveled his head in her direction. Claire was frightened but she was also exhilarated. She understood the ancient dynamic at work and it filled her with a sense of purpose that was heightened by the fact of her pregnancy.

The moment Shurik burst through the door *S. iroquoisii* had lit a fuse inside of her. This was the dirty stinking quasi human who had wanted to rape her. Claire remembered the Gulag with sudden revulsion. She had thought it a little gross at the time, but she had failed to notice what lay beneath all the filth and squalor. *S. iroquoisii* had given her sight beyond seeing. Zhenya, Shurik—every one of them living there like that—represented the worst of a tangential line of men. No wonder their own government had left them to rot down here. Evolution was brutal, but it was also wise. Shurik's clan marked a dead-end.

All of this occurred to her on an instinctive level as she moved toward Shurik and Georgiy with one thing in mind. The ideas inhabiting her head were unlike any she'd ever had before. Not thoughts exactly, not in the conventional sense, but directives encoded in the very fiber of her being. Her breath quickened as super-oxygenated blood flooded her brain and gorged her muscles. Her field of vision narrowed and became incredibly sharp. About three feet from Shurik she broke into a sort of loose-jointed boxer's dance. Then in a single fluid motion she transferred all of her body weight to her left leg and brought her right leg up into her chest so that it was cocked at the knee. A split-second later she uncoiled her leg with deadly force, planting her foot in the center of Shurik's torso just below his sternum.

The kick launched him backward through the open door and out into the night. A hoarse gasp rattled through his dead drawn lips, but he was still grinning even as the impetus planted him on his back on the ice. Claire reloaded and did the same to Georgiy. He never saw it coming. From that point on it was chaos.

"What the hell was that?" exclaimed Bishop. "Did you see them? It's like freakin' Halloween!"

"Don't just stand there!" shouted Claire. "Help me!" She was already pushing the sofa toward the door.

Bishop joined in and the two of them managed to barricade the door just moments before Shurik began hammering away with the wrench. "I told you it wasn't Price!"

"You were right, I was wrong," Claire admitted reproachfully. "Now move! De-Luca, McKenzie—grab anything you can! We can't let them inside!"

DeLuca was paralyzed with fright. He looked around blankly as the three of them barricaded the door with everything they could get their hands on. The television, chairs, workstations, pots and pans, laptop computers . . . Right now every ounce mattered. Books, DVDs, microscopes, the treadmill . . . Shurik's assault sent shockwaves reverberating out over the floor beneath them like ripples over the surface of standing water. Each blow released a current of energy that traveled up through Claire's legs and into her brain. Part of her wanted to let Shurik back in so she could finish what she had started, but she'd been cold for several hours and was still lucid enough to know better.

DeLuca was a different story. He responded to each metallic blow with a startled jolt. "We have to get out of here!" he croaked. He began tearing at the barricade, trying to make his way through to the door.

Claire grabbed him by the shoulders and shook him. "Out?" she echoed. "Think about it—*they're* out there. If we can hold them off long enough they'll freeze to death. You saw how bad they look. They're half-dead already."

Recognition worked its way into DeLuca's eyes and he slumped into Claire. "Okay," he said, "that's a good idea... That's a good idea."

"Good," said Claire, stroking his head. "Freaking out won't help. We've got to stay calm."

It was suddenly quiet. Shurik had given up battering the door. The still had a tranquilizing effect and DeLuca looked at Claire hopefully. For a moment, no one said a word. Then Bishop asked, "Has anyone seen McKenzie?"

They looked around and quickly discovered McKenzie sitting on the floor, his legs splayed awkwardly beneath him. The color was gone from his face and he was clutching his chest.

Bishop laid him out on his back and placed a sofa cushion under his head. "Bad heart. I guess he couldn't handle all the excitement."

Claire remembered her first conversation with McKenzie back in the Christchurch Airport bookstore. Although it had only been a couple of weeks, it seemed as if light years had passed since she'd stumbled across Alan's name in that morbid little piece in *The Times of London*. McKenzie had mentioned something about a bad heart, however with what Claire now knew of all the lies and deception, she was surprised to learn that it, too, wasn't all part of the act. She no longer knew what to believe, who to trust.

"We have to get him to a hospital," said DeLuca. "He'll die if we don't."

"What hospital?" Claire asked. "Have you forgotten where we are?"

"The first-aid kit—we can ..."

"He didn't cut himself shaving!" Claire shouted. "The man's had a heart attack!"

McKenzie's breathing was shallow. His cheeks were hollow. He looked dead lying there, hands folded across his chest. A stone effigy, drawn and gray.

Suddenly DeLuca looked old and haggard. "It wasn't supposed to be like this," he moaned.

And then the banging started again. This time with a greater sense of urgency. DeLuca nearly leapt out of his skin. "What do you want?" he shouted. "What do they want?" he whimpered.

"Us," Claire replied simply. "Meat."

The last thing Ethan wanted to do was activate the emergency transmitter. Literally, the last goddamn thing. Activating it meant that he was out of options, that he was royally fucked. Activating it meant that Okum would send in a crew ASAP to mop things up. Activating it meant that even his bargaining chip—the camcorder footage—might not be able to save his ass now. *Fuck it.* All bets were off. He pushed the button and hurled the little black box into the wall. A moment later he noticed a low, virtually imperceptible whirring and a random succession of clicking noises coming from the other side of the door. His first instinct was that somebody was trying to pick the lock. He checked however and was relieved to find that the door was secure.

Safe for the time being, Ethan threw back his head and howled at the top of his lungs. Defeated by the poor acoustics of the room his pathetic lament died without consequence, much as he was now dying from the self-inflicted wound in his side and the bug in his brain. Okum would be here soon . . . *When?* Five hours maybe. Less? All Ethan knew for sure was that this was as close as he would ever get to his modest villa in Ravello, and day trips by ferry to Capri, and all the exotic *signorinas* dripping gold Italian sunshine and warm wet welcome for the good-looking American who lived in the hills overlooking the sparkling Tyrrhenian Sea.

He lay on his bed and for a few blissful moments was able to imagine what it would've been like to be that man. To live a life of simple privilege, unfettered by responsibility and work. To eat bread and drink wine and wrestle between the sheets with a beautiful girl talking dirty to him in a language he didn't understand. But then he was jolted back to reality—the one so diametrically opposed to that of his dream—by the thunderous pounding that had stopped for a time and now shook the station once again.

He studied the zip-pack of memory cards. Too big to swallow, he could either destroy the evidence or simply let Okum have it. What did it matter? He was about to become the latest addition to some sort of Black Budget petting zoo, the only difference from the actual thing being that he would have a computer probe up his ass instead of some kid's filthy little hand. What he needed now was a postal drop box; somewhere he could deposit the disk and mail it to himself. That way Okum would have no choice but to work with him, to complete the deal they had started. That's how it was done in the movies—trust the smoking gun to the infamously unreliable hands of the US Postal Service. Keep the bargaining chip in limbo long enough to negotiate a deal that was mutually agreeable. A deal that didn't end with the hero grabbing his ankles . . . A drop box here, anywhere for that matter—good luck. The big blue steel containers that once stood watch over every neighborhood in America were now an endangered species thanks to the . . . *You stupid, beautiful, brilliant fuck!*

Internet. Email. His drop box had been right there in front of him all along. He'd download the raw footage and send it to himself as an attachment. Of course he'd forward the file to both his USC and personal web addresses. But he would also forward it to Alan and to Claire and to anyone else who wouldn't be around to open the attachment. *Yes!* And old Nosworthy. Even if the greasy bastard figured out how to open the file he'd have sense enough not to go shooting off his mouth. He and Ethan had an understanding, more than an understanding . . . A pact, really. They had enough dirt on each other to bury the other guy so deep that he'd need twenty feet of garden hose just to get a breath of fresh air.

All Ethan needed now was a signal. He wasn't buying into any of that bullshit about the relay dish being out of whack. Just like he didn't buy that Witz's death was an accident. Maybe Witz had gotten cold feet, maybe he'd given DeLuca reason to believe that he couldn't be trusted with whatever shit was going down. Witz may have known communications but he wasn't exactly Navy Seal material. Survival skills were not his forté. Sending him out to "repair" the relay dish here and in weather like this was like condemning him to death. And when he made it back alive . . . Suffice it to say that Bishop saw an opportunity and made the most of it. No, Ethan was sure the relay was working just fine.

It didn't take a genius to figure out that DeLuca was trying to control the flow of outgoing information. And why not? If any of what Okum had said was true, they were sitting on word of an apocalypse. They had probably password-protected outgoing signals to keep up appearances—and DeLuca's impassioned reaction to Witz's death was an inspired bit of theater, if not a bit melodramatic—but they weren't fooling anybody. Not by a long shot. Ethan hadn't gotten those three little letters that came after his name—PhD—by being an idiot. Even if there was a password, he was certain that he could look into DeLuca's cunning little eyes and see it there tattooed on his soul. And if not—well, he'd find away to get him alone and beat it out of him.

For the past couple of weeks JPAC had been accessing various databases via a wireless router located in the common room. Ethan had no idea what had been going on since he'd parted company with the others ten minutes ago . . . *Boom!* Another blow shook the floor beneath him. And another . . . *Boom!* Nor was he in a hurry to find out. There was also Okum to worry about. If he somehow managed to intercept the transmission Ethan was sunk. But what the hell, he was running out of options and, more importantly, blood. Shock was fast-becoming an issue.

There was another problem. Besides whatever schemes JPAC had brewing, he couldn't simply waltz his way into the common room, sit down at one of the computers and start punching away at the keyboard. One thing was certain—they were all wired directly into Okum. Just a whisper, that's all it would take, and he'd be screwed. He'd never even have the chance to see just how lucky he was. What Ethan needed now was a diversion, something to get the others out of the common room for five minutes give or take.

Lim. *Of course.* If Ethan told DeLuca and Bishop about what he'd seen—that the snarling, naked fool was actually eating his own arm—he might be able to rekindle their desire to capture him. If there was one thing Ivan had given them it was an acute and chronic susceptibility to the power of suggestion. The tiniest spark was all it would take to ignite a three-alarm blaze. Plant a seed of doubt in their minds and he could harvest all the paranoid fears he could imagine for them. Truth be known, it was only a matter of time before Lim's hunger exceeded his domestic supply of meat and he would be forced to pursue an alternate source of food.

Ethan disengaged the deadbolt but the door wouldn't budge. The knob was like a hunk of stone in his hand, useless and dead, connected to nothing. He tried the lock again, twisting it back and forth, the bolt sliding easily in and out of the faceplate, but with similar results. He didn't understand. There was no reason for the door not to open. Everything was working the way it was supposed to. He clutched the knob with both hands and heaved backward with all his strength, but it was useless. He may as well have been attempting to pull up a tree, roots that dug in for miles. Panic surged through him, setting off a rush of adrenaline that electrified his limbs and sent him scrambling around the room in search of a way out. There was still the hole in the floor but fear now stood in the way of reason. An intelligence, inanimate and cruel, lurked behind his imprisonment, and this alone was enough to scare the sense out of him.

And then he saw it, the transmitter lying on the floor in pieces. The clicking coming from within the door—no one had been trying to pick the lock. He was as paranoid as the rest of them. How could he have been so fucking ignorant? *The transmitter—Jesus Christ! You did this to yourself!* Activating it had triggered some sort of automatic locking mechanism and now Okum was on his way to collect his catch. Ensnared like a goddamn animal! Ethan would chew off his own leg before he gave himself up like a mangy, flea-bitten coyote. *Like a Ha Tinh pygmy rhinoceros. Like a common pig.* 'A nifty carrying case'—isn't that what Okum had called the Russian submarine's escape pod? And now Ethan found himself packaged nice and neat for express delivery. Narrative symmetry. A case of history repeating itself. *Inspired planning?* Call it whatever the fuck you want—Ethan wasn't about to end up like the Russian sailor whose own comrades had sent him to the bottom of the ocean in a steel tomb. If push came to shove he'd join Witz at the bottom of the crevasse. Let Okum try to get his hands on him then.

Ethan wasn't big on religion—he hadn't been anywhere near the inside of a church since his mother had forced Sunday school on him as a child—but he remembered enough of Sister Roberta's lessons to know that a plague of locusts was one of a handful of portents that foretold the end of the world. The buzzing was indistinct at first, distant—a low, oscillating pitch that set the air on edge and made his skin crawl. Within seconds, it grew into a tangible force that ripped apart the static night and sent waves of high-frequency vibrations scurrying ant-like over his flesh. In a matter of heartbeats, the buzzing grew into a thunderous roar that shook his tiny living quarters to the foundation and rattled the locked door in its frame. The vibrations yielded to a rumbling tremor that crescendoed in a sharp jolt and slammed him into the wall. This was no plague of locusts bent on stripping bare a field of wheat;

this was an earthquake, the badass, wrath of God type that had devoured Sodom and Gomorrah in a single yawing gasp. *Not an earthquake, an icequake! Of course . . .* Ellis had warned them that disturbing the ancient, icy strata could trigger a chain reaction and give rise to an isolated cataclysm. *Like a pebble striking a windshield . . .* Ethan remembered the words well. So that was it—the ice field was breaking apart! It truly was the end of the world.

Ethan's mind screamed at his legs to take action, to move, to get his ass in gear! The floor now heaved underfoot, listing badly one way, then another so that he staggered drunkenly from side to side. It was nearly impossible to keep his footing as he fought to move his bed so that he could access his escape hatch. The pain in his side was excruciating, but he ignored it and was finally able to expose the loose section of flooring. He used the knife to pry up one edge of the panel so that he could get his gloved fingers beneath it, but by then the world had fallen out from under him and his stomach shot upward into his throat like a helium-filled balloon. And then just as suddenly as the ice had come apart, the earth stabilized. The floor still rolled gently beneath him but he could stand without bracing himself.

Ethan's first thought was to get the hell out of there before the aftershocks hit. If he could make it off of the ice field he'd at least have a chance. The Russian station—he could email the footage from there. *Maybe even lay your hands on a gun—a last stand. See, no reason to lose your head. Get off the ice, get your feet on solid ground and skirt the edge of the basin . . . Fuck, you can do it! Just lie low and pick your way along the cracks and crevices fringing the base of the mountains . . . When Okum's welcome wagon shows up, keep your head down. Definitely do-able. Fuck frostbite. Fuck the blood-gushing hole in your side. Fuck Ivan. Fuck everything! Look how far you've already come. You're a goddamn survivor, top of the food chain just like Claire said, right? Tooth and fucking nail . . .*

One thing he'd learned over the past several weeks was that survival in Antarctica was performed incrementally, taken where it could be gotten, a nibble here, a nibble there. Until yesterday, he'd merely been going through the motions, bottom feeding, getting fat on whatever filtered down. But it was all a great big lie. He was a gingerbread man living in a gingerbread house. Sweet, soulless oblivion. But now the frosting was off, and dying had breathed life back into him.

With the worst of the quake behind him, it was easy to overlook the insensate drone still gripping the night sky. His mind was crowded with memories and ideas—some his own, others he couldn't place—static noise, psychic feedback, voices. The camcorder footage played on and on—Leonelli in his blood-mask, a fool's banquet of glowing question marks answered with unequivocal certainty, *Alan* . . . poor Alan arguing with a monkey in the cool lavender twilight of emotional wellness—the digitally-scored coda of a recorded history only he, Doctor Ethan Hatcher, of all the world would ever know. The wind had picked up; biting and gritty, it scraped over the exterior of his quarters, scouring away the paint one molecule at a time. *Incre-*

mentally . . . He threw back the loose floor panel, his escape hatch, and for the second time in as many moments the world dropped out from under him.

The station shrunk from sight—ten feet, twenty, then a hundred, until it was on the verge of disappearing altogether—as Ethan was carried up and away in the claws of a Sikorsky Skycrane. The fog that had cloaked the frozen earth half an hour earlier had begun to dissipate—swirls and wisps and clinging white webs—pulled apart by a rising breeze. Each of the seven remaining habitation modules was capped by a strobing beacon that bled arterial red into the gauzy veil of fog clinging to the earth. It all happened so suddenly that he hardly knew what to make of it—up and up and into the night—plucked from the ground as if by some great predatory bird.

He would've jumped but by the time the impulse identified itself suicide seemed redundant. Wherever they were taking him, death was a foregone conclusion. A done deal. Deep down, part of him had known this all along—that really it was the only way out of the shit he had gotten himself into—from way back when Okum had first told him about the Russian geologists who'd come to Antarctica in search of a fabled oil gold mine and had tapped into a glut of blood that had fueled two and a half decades of mayhem and death.

As the Skycrane leveled out three hundred feet above the earth, the derelict station coalesced beneath him, fading in and then out again. Still wrapped in fog, it was only partly visible against the moon-illumined sea of ice. Although holding together elsewhere, her smashed fore section admitted a rolling surge of mist that swamped the floor of the common room, tumbled through her passageways and flooded the gloomy living quarters where now only death called home. Ethan could see his team standing there amid her splintered beams and ragged walls—his *crew*—sailing into the province of nothingness. Northcutt, Ellis, Lim, Leonelli, Hamsun, Schmidt, even Sven, their monkey mascot dressed to throw out the first pitch on Legends of the Game Day at Dodger Stadium, but most especially Alan—eyes twinkling stoically in the singular solitude of abandonment, awaiting the return of their captain so that the ship might finally go down in peace.

Once DeLuca faced the facts—he was a dead man, they were all as good as dead—it hadn't taken much coaxing to get him to spill his guts. Hatcher had known from the beginning. Claire wasn't so much surprised as she was ashamed of herself for being sucked into this. She was not only their expert, she was their prize specimen. A pregnant female—but how could anyone have known? She had only just learned herself. Hatcher, of course—he was up to his old tricks. He'd never forgiven her for switching the Ha Tinh and now he was determined to see that she take its place. The recovery operation was secondary, really nothing more than an elaborate smokescreen. Something to show the DOD oversight committees in DC, but that was as far as Claire had wanted to take it. DeLuca had gone into greater detail, muddled though it was by his growing dementia, but this was already more than she could stomach. The details didn't matter—they, whoever *they* was, wanted her unborn child.

Claire thought about going after Hatcher—this was her first instinct. To hunt him down and kill him like a gazelle cut off from the herd. He was wounded, hobbled by injury. She was strong and highly motivated. The blood trail was still fresh. Easy prey for the expecting lioness, the sustenance her cub would need to ensure his own coronation as king of the beasts. But there was something else, a different directive, and this interrupted one instinct and subordinated it to another that was even more urgent.

At first the noise was little more than a far off vibration that set her bones thrumming like a tuning fork. But in a matter of seconds it grew into a rumbling force and convinced her to leave the hunt for another day. The walls shook and the sky overhead stormed in protest as if it was being ripped apart by massive claws. Claire crouched over McKenzie and assumed a defensive posture. Every muscle in her body was coiled about a single purpose. She was alert but calm, poised and ready for whatever came her way. She recognized the noise tearing at the sky and yet couldn't quite place it because part of her was no longer connected to the world of men. She was now more aware than she had ever been in her life, yet it was a different kind of awareness. She knew, for example, that McKenzie was dead. Even without laying a hand on him, checking for a pulse, placing an ear to his chest—she knew. She could sense death—not by the obvious vehicles of decay or decomposition, but in the same way a vulture circling hundreds of feet above the earth knows in its bones that dinner is there waiting for it. She knew also that Price was not coming back. He had been gone too long and the cold would have overtaken him by now.

She wasn't sure how she felt about any of it—alone, isolated, outnumbered—but she knew what she didn't feel. She had liked McKenzie, trusted him, but he had lied to her like the others. Price had saved her life, however it would have never come to that if . . . To hell with them all. Sadness, regret, anger—these words no longer figured into her vocabulary. They were as useless to her as *what if*—indulgences for the weak. She saw that now. Emotion no longer factored into the equation. Survival was the sum of everything. Perfect, absolute. Nothing else mattered.

The noise had become deafening. It was everywhere at once, a parasite that had worked its way inside of Claire and now occupied the remotest corners of her being. It continued like this for some time—an eternity compressed into the space of a minute—when a powerful jolt rocked the station. Claire was thrown off balance as the floor beneath her shifted violently. An abrupt *thunk* punctuated the din like a pair of mechanical jaws locking onto the throat of something warm and alive. The floodlights flickered briefly but continued to bathe her surroundings in osseous halftones. By the time Claire realized what was happening, what was really happening, the volume and intensity of the commotion had reached a terminal pitch.

She took off running and had nearly made it to Hatcher's quarters when another jolt rocked the station, slamming her into the corridor wall. Cold air laced with fuel exhaust flooded the narrow passageway. The acrid fumes stung her nostrils and brought tears to her eyes. And then she saw it—in fact, she might have continued running straight into the darkness if Bishop and DeLuca were not blocking her path. The two men stood where seconds earlier the door to Hatcher's quarters had barred them from entering. Now there was nothing—no door, no quarters, no Hatcher. Just a hole looking out on the bottomless pit of night. Severed wires dangled about the neck of the opening like the aftermath of a beheading. Claire squeezed between the two men in time to catch a shadowy glimpse of habitation module ONE as it was carried up and away in the clutches of the tummy-tuck helicopter she remembered from the tarmac at Williams Field.

"After the disappearing act Hatcher pulled with the first group of schmucks, I was pretty sure he'd find a way to leave us high and dry," remarked Bishop. "But I sure didn't see that coming."

"Are you sure he was in there?" asked Claire. It just didn't seem possible. Ten minutes ago he'd bled all over her. And now . . . Gone.

DeLuca nodded and held out his left arm. "Our wristbands—when one of us enters our quarters, the door automatically locks. You saw what comes next." He did this thing with his hand: up, up and away.

Claire knew he was telling the truth, but she couldn't accept it, *wouldn't* accept it. It was way too scary—the idea that a group of transport helicopters had taken up a holding pattern somewhere off in the night and was waiting for the signal to whisk each of them away. "You're full of shit."

But Bishop's expression confirmed the worst of her fears. "The whole thing is remote-operated," he said. "Slicker than snot, if you ask me." He ran his hand around the perimeter of the opening. "Okum really outdid himself. The whole place snaps together like Tinker Toys."

"Bastards." Claire had gotten so used to wearing the wristband that she'd nearly forgotten about it. She went to rip it off but resisted the impulse. She couldn't afford to be reckless now that she was thinking for two. "So, this Okum character is the one pushing the buttons?"

"A flick of the switch," Bishop affirmed, "and it's *bon* fucking *voyage. Arrive*-goddamn-*derci.*"

Then his head imploded.

Bishop scarcely twitched as his jaw was turned inside-out and pushed through the back of his skull by the force of the blow. Less than an arm's length away, Claire was greeted by a bloody mosaic of mishmashed teeth and bone that now only vaguely resembled the humorless smirk he'd worn as Hatcher was spirited away in the belly of the Skycrane. She had only a second to contemplate Bishop's rearranged grin before it was ripped away in a mighty backswing that left a gaping hole

210 ~ Fade to Black

once occupied by the lower half of his face. He crumpled where he stood, every ounce of tensile strength in his body going slack with instant death. A second later Georgiy bounded doglike through the opening left by the capsule, sampling the air with his nose. The AK-47 was still slung across his back, but he was far more interested in luxuriating in the scent of the kill provided by his master, Shurik. De-Luca staggered backward into the wall, bracing himself for support as he watched Georgiy plunge his face into the steaming pot of gore that had once been a man's skull. Time slowed, was captured in milliseconds, Claire's optic nerves sizzling like lit fuses. She was an adrenaline bomb set to go off.

Shurik appeared on Georgiy's heels a moment later, the wrench, his war club, wreaking a tornado swath of destruction with each swing. Claire's head was nearly piñata'ed as the wrench's blood and brain caked jaws whistled past her nose. She dropped and rolled to her left as Shurik swung again, this time in a hell bound arc that punched a ragged hole in the floor only inches from her face. He reared back to take another swing, but the wrench was stuck, gripped in fangs of splintered wood.

Glowering down on her, Shurik paused—emotionless, imposing, mechanical—a radio tower that was now receiver to a rogue signal. Claire tried to get through to him, to disrupt the scrambled flow of information, but it was useless. He was now operating on a different frequency, dull and as impenetrable as lead, and she got the feeling that the eyes of a dead man hid beneath the black welder's goggles. Ice crystals as plump and plentiful as maggots festered in the carrion that was once a round fully-fleshed face. She was entranced, hypnotized by his cadaverous smile, lost in the dark and foreboding woods of his beard. By the time Claire broke free of his demoniac hold on her, the rogue signal had reasserted itself and Shurik had nearly worked the wrench free.

Leveraging herself on her left arm Claire cocked her right leg and snapped it forward, catching Shurik just below the left kneecap. His leg buckled to the sound of splitting wood and he pitched over. A massive thud shook the floor.

Claire clambered to her feet but Shurik seized her by the ankle and pulled her legs out from under her. He clicked his teeth evilly, gnashing them together like the claw-blades of a garden mulcher as he pulled her into him. Claire groped for something to hold on to, a weapon, anything she could use to defend herself, but it was pointless. She was dragged past where Georgiy lapped at Bishop's bashed-in face, too caught up in his own canine fervor to give her a second thought. She was strong, stronger than ever before in her life, but she was still no match for the enormous Russian. She kicked him again, this time connecting with his mouth. Shurik's head snapped backward, his teeth awash in new blood, but he did not let go. He drew her toward him until they were laying head to foot. He then spun her around and rolled on top of her, pinning her to the floor.

He worked his bloody, frostbite-blackened fingers into her hair closest the scalp and forced her face to within inches of his own. Emanating from deep inside of him, a subterranean rumble gathered force behind his teeth and swelled into a low, pealing, thunderous burp.

Claire nearly vomited.

"I guess this means the honeymoon is over," she gasped, trying not to inhale the gurgling release of digestive gases.

But Shurik kept on smiling devilishly and reached for the carving knife. Coming up empty-handed, he took his eyes off Claire to pinpoint the knife's location. A moment earlier it had been secured around his waist; now it was gone. He was slow to connect the dots and it cost him. Claire slashed out with her left arm—her right arm was still crippled from the wrench blow—and succeeded in lopping of his ear. Shurik grabbed the side of his head and rose up howling. Claire then kneed him viciously in the groin. The belching fiend stiffened and she was able to roll him off of her and scramble out of his clutches.

Some mother she'd turned out to be. Look at the company she was keeping: rapists, murderers, cannibals. Maybe the kid was better off not being born. The decision, however, was not in her hands. It was in her genes—fortified, unassailable. Millions of years of evolution united toward a single cause. Survival. The life inside of her was the only life that mattered.

Claire held onto the knife and bolted into the central corridor, putting some distance between Shurik and herself. She wasn't hiding; she was buying time. She was going to need every second available to her if she wanted to get out of this alive. History had proven that brains and resourcefulness invariably won out over brawn. Just ask Cro-Magnon—a relatively successful substratum of Goliaths wiped out by puny *Homo erectus*. Muscles were nice, but a plan was better.

She had one of two choices. She could either commit herself to the wintry darkness—take her chances in the elements and hope against reason that she would be able to overcome her fear—a fear that had reasserted itself with a vengeance. But even then she was only choosing the manner of her death—freezing versus being scalped or eaten, possibly both. Or she could stand and fight, take what *S. iroquoisii* had given her and go out swinging. At least inside she could see her enemy—that is as long as the emergency floodlights remained operational. But out there . . . Monsters really did inhabit the dark. The proof was in hot pursuit.

The station was one big mousetrap—she knew that now. And therein lay the crux of her plan. By this time it was pretty damn obvious that some government shadow agency wanted living specimens. The what and the how of it had already been laid out for her. The why—that was a different story and one she was absolutely certain she could do without. If it was living specimens they wanted, then that's what she'd give them. Only it wasn't going to be her. Who knows, they might even have a change of heart after tangling with Shurik and Georgiy?

Bait and switch. It was one of the oldest cons in the book, not to mention the only one Claire knew. It had worked for her once before so why not try it again? Grad school flashback. It was only fitting that one of the darkest chapters in her life would come full circle on what seemed to be the darkest night in the history of the world. It was like the expedition to Vietnam all over again. Only this time it wasn't the Ha Tinh pygmy rhino's life on the line, it was her own. She was beginning to think that the wristband might be of some use to her after all.

In this land of bitter extremes, Shurik was only just warming to the occasion. The first of it rattled out of his throat like a handful of stones cast into a rusted downspout. This was followed by a grating howl that chased after Claire through the floodlit corridor. A low, guttural condemnation that in the world of men and beasts meant only one thing. He intended to kill her. It was time for him to prove that he was still the Alpha male. Now before the hyenas and vultures came poking around. The hairs on the back of Claire's neck bristled. Shurik had served notice. He was coming after her. With the bulk of his weight now carried along on one good leg, the other dragging lamely behind him, the floor shuddered beneath each cantilevered step.

Boom-scrape! Boom-scrape!

Only once in her life had Claire been in such desperate need of a hiding place. It was as if she had spent the last twenty years running from a ghost only to arrive back where she had started. Adolescence. The headwaters of the stygian current she'd been drowning in since the night her father had made a game of scaring her to death.

Hide and seek.

Her quarters, a modular capsule identical to the one Hatcher was carried away in, might well be secure enough to keep Shurik at bay. The door was strong, the walls thick, but there was no way she was setting foot anywhere near it. She had been to Africa, seen the wildebeests poised along the water's edge drinking tentatively from the river that spelled the terrible midday thirst. Not even a ripple . . . And then just like that an explosion of teeth and blood. Kicking and bleating. Dragged to their death in the jaws of a crocodile that had been lying in wait. It all happened so suddenly that in the first furious turns of the death roll, the poor stupid animals must have thought that it was the water killing them. No, Claire wouldn't go near her quarters. Not a chance. She was too close to the river's edge as it was already.

Claire wound her way around the outer corridor until she had nearly circled the entire station. *Fucking great—trapped on a merry-go-round!* She pulled up just short of where she had stood moments earlier and very carefully peeked around the corner. Georgiy must have followed after Shurik because Bishop's body now lay cold and unmolested. Steam no longer climbed out of the bloody crater in his face. A layer of frost had taken hold, fuzzing over the site of the impact with pink crystalline spikes. DeLuca was still there pressed against the wall—eyes fixed, mouth ajar. Despite everything, she needed him now. He was as close to an ally as she was going to find now that Price was gone.

She called out to DeLuca in a whisper, but she wasn't sure if he had heard her. So devoid was he of any outward signs of life that he may as well have been made of wax.

Until he blinked she was under the impression that he had somehow died—of fright, strangulation, *S. iroquoisii* . . . Maybe he had frozen to death. The station was hemorrhaging heat through the gigantic hole in its side opened when the Skycrane had plucked Hatcher from the earth. Who could say? None of this was by the numbers. She was inclined to forget about DeLuca, to figure things out by herself. From what she could see, he had all the getup and go of a bookend. But if there was a chance that he could help her . . .

She called out again, waving her arms, but it was impossible to say if he'd seen her or not. Time was something she didn't have. Shurik was probably lost in the concentric maze of corridors, but sooner or later he would stumble across her and she'd be forced to confront him. It was either that or run forever. By all rights the guy should have been long dead. His battery, however, was still fully charged. She had written him off once before. She wasn't going to make the same mistake twice.

"Psst, DeLuca!" she hissed. "Snap out of it."

DeLuca's head swiveled toward her, the sound of her voice softening his waxen cast. He tried to speak, but nothing came out. Right now, the last thing Claire wanted was to announce her whereabouts to the world. Calmly, she held her forefinger to her lips and hushed him.

"Wait a second," she whispered. "They'll hear you. I'll come closer."

But DeLuca had already reloaded the thought and pulled the trigger a second time. Pure horror—there was no other way to describe it—grated over every note of the pathetic aria that passed through his lips. "MY HAIR . . . HE STROKED MY HAIR!" he crooned, the blood wrung from his face by the sheer force of his anguish. "HE STROKED MY HAIR!" he shrieked again. And again and again and again, each repetition bringing him closer to a reality he didn't want any part of. There was no point explaining that his scalp was safe as long as she had Shurik's knife. DeLuca had already made up his mind. This was how he was going to die.

As for herself, Claire still wasn't sure but she didn't even need to look to know that it was Georgiy spying on them from the end of the corridor. Suddenly, she could smell him very clearly, yet another of her muted senses brought to life by *S. iroquoisii*. Anointed in the sickening mélange of a scavenger, he eyed her with a hunger that bordered on the pornographic. He was a freak and a cannibal, but mostly he was a nuisance. A bloodhound, a birddog subsisting on the prowess of its master. But also pointing the way, initiating the kill. And it was this aspect of his nature that Claire both detested and feared.

"DeLuca . . ." she tried again. "You have to pull it together, or we're both going to die!"

DeLuca just hugged himself and rocked back and forth.

Already she could hear—no, *feel*—Shurik approaching, his lopsided gait sending out ripples through the floor of the station and up into her legs. With a few brisk strides she narrowed the distance between DeLuca and herself and grabbed him by the front of his parka. The burn in her veins was like the sensation of the chemo-

214 ~ Fade to Black

therapy drugs her mother had described, hot and ubiquitous, but it was not enervating like the drugs. Those were thick and deadening. Sleep-inducing. Life-stealing. But this—it was combustible, 190 proof hemoglobin. Her victory over Price on the treadmill was nothing. Right now, she could run with the whole goddamned contraption strapped to her back if she wanted.

"Come on, snap out of it!" she demanded, slamming DeLuca into the wall. "We've got to get out of here!"

Frustration, anger, rage—Claire's head was so mixed up that it could've been any of a dozen emotions that directed her hands around his windpipe. Before she realized what she was doing, she was choking the life out of him. And then DeLuca's eyes went wide. Claire relaxed her grip just in time to hear him wheeze, "Behind you . . ." before he slumped to the floor.

Claire barely managed to deflect the shaft of the wrench with her right forearm, otherwise it would have taken off her head. Her entire right side was engulfed by a paralyzing numbness that left her half-crippled. If the knife was still in her hand, she couldn't feel it. No, she had dropped it . . . But where? Shurik took another swing—amazing that he could wield the wrench so easily with one arm—but Claire avoided the blow by ducking under it and throwing herself into his chest. Her kickboxing instructor had once demonstrated for the class how proximity could be used to one's advantage in close quarters combat. The idea behind such a move was to negate the effectiveness of an opponent with a longer reach and turn what was ordinarily an advantage into a disadvantage. Shurik however was not your average opponent. True, the tactic had spared her another blow from the wrench but his free arm, the one that now swung her around by the hair, was every bit as unyielding. He slammed her into the wall so hard that it knocked the wind out of her and left her reeling. Much more of this and Shurik wouldn't need the carving knife to scalp her—he'd rip it off of her with brute force. She tried to struggle free, but he had her hair knotted tightly about his fist. This time he wasn't letting go.

She looked to DeLuca for help, but he had long since bolted into the night. If only she hadn't dropped the knife . . . And then she saw it lying on the floor at her feet. But Shurik saw it too and savagely reigned back on her hair before as she could pick it up. Claire kicked the knife away for no other reason than to postpone what was clearly inevitable. It skittered across the floor, stopping just short of the junction of the central corridor. The next thing Claire knew she was being dragged along by the hair toward the knife. Shurik carried the wrench on his opposite shoulder caveman-style.

Not since the night she had buried herself beneath the towels in the linen closet had Claire felt so helpless. She could practically feel the knife blade grating over her skull, separating flesh from bone as Shurik peeled back her scalp. The junction—it would be Claire's last chance to save herself. Shurik, however, must have also realized this for no sooner had they come upon the knife than he laid down the wrench and cuffed her on the side of the head. She was conscious, but a groggy haze engulfed her brain. Shurik planted his knee in the center of her chest, bearing down on her sternum with all his weight until she thought it would crack. As the air was compressed from her lungs, the edges of her vision succumbed to inky darkness. She felt as Shurik, almost tenderly, lifted her head off the floor with one hand and laid the blade of the carving knife against the base of her skull. Then sawing—quick decisive strokes back and forth that bit into the flesh below her occipital bone.

There was pain but she was strangely disconnected from it, drifting. Overcome by a sensation of out-of-bodiness she had never before experienced, Claire was witness to the scene as it unfolded as if looking down on herself from above. Shurik attended to her with the practiced hand of an expert, his shoulder blades knitting industriously over her prone form. Every now and then he would give her hair a good stiff yank to urge the process along, and a jolt of pain would threaten to reign in the tether that allowed her to drift peacefully above. But she wasn't ready to die. Not here, not like this. She gritted her teeth against the ripping noise that echoed in her skull and crowded the narrow passageway as layer upon layer of consciousness was stripped away. She was restless like never before, a pitiful reflection of the life inside her that would never be born. She was struggling—her arms flopping weakly at her sides—but it was as if a truck was parked on top of her.

She was just about gone when an explosion penetrated the fog consolidating around her brain. Shurik lurched forward, his right shoulder coming apart in a spray of blood and tissue. He raised up and Claire could breathe again, the sudden rush of oxygen speeding life to her dimming senses.

"Get off of her or I put the next one in your head!"

Claire recognized the voice. It was Price. Back from the dead. He had entered the station through the hole once plugged by Hatcher's living capsule, and stood with his gun trained on Shurik.

The hulking Russian was not impressed. He turned away from Price and was prepared to resume his macabre ritual when another shot rang out. This time it was his left shoulder that caught a 9mm slug, a veritable mosquito bite when pitted against the tidal bore of adrenaline surging through his veins. But it was enough to get him to lay aside the knife so that he might dispatch with the irritating pest. He left Claire where she lay, gripping the wrench as if it was a flyswatter.

A rush of cold air scalded Claire's lungs as she inhaled deeply. Weakened from the lack of oxygen, she was barely able to lift her head, her muscles limp and rubbery. Price stood about ten paces back from Shurik, staring down the barrel of the semi-automatic. He was straddling Bishop's mutilated corpse. His goggles dangled loosely about his neck—not that it mattered. His eyes were in worse shape than Claire had first thought. A mucousy crust had formed around the lids, the intelligent glint usurped by a rheumy haze.

"That's close enough!" Price warned, drawing a bead on Shurik's forehead. He blinked repeatedly to keep his vision in focus.

Shurik now stood with his hulking back to Claire where she lay on the floor choking on the sudden abundance of air. Although seemingly impervious to injury, he seemed unsure of the situation. Maybe Price had actually gotten through to him, the bullets opening a pathway for rational thought, a reawakening of his own mortality. But then he let loose with a piercing blast—at first it was nothing really, a shrill exhalation that exploded in a teakettle summons—that was as spine-tingling as the clenched grin from which it emanated.

Neither Claire nor Price knew what to think until Georgiy scrambled full-tilt out of the central corridor—laughing, shrieking, it was impossible to say in the moment. He bounded over Claire in a sort of half-erect ape scamper and blew past Shurik. Price saw him coming but was unable to keep the caterwauling freak in his sights. He squeezed off three rounds before Georgiy closed the gap. The second shot bit into the flesh of Georgiy's left upper thigh, altering his trajectory enough that Price avoided the brunt of the impact. The gun, however, was knocked from his hand as he exploited Georgiy's momentum and steered him into the wall with a bruising thud, stunning him.

Price blinked hard to clear his vision and when he opened his eyes Shurik was in face. Before he could make a move Shurik pinned him to wall beneath the wrench. Price tried to squirm free but Shurik was too strong, the wrench braced tightly across his chest, crushing the life out of him.

Claire rolled onto her hands and knees and picked up the carving knife Shurik had left behind. The blade was wet with her blood. She was woozy and disoriented, but managed to rise to her feet. She ran her hand along the base of her scalp, exploring the flap of skin bleeding warmly down the back of her neck. The wound was deep, but it wouldn't kill her. No major arteries had been cut and already the extreme cold was stanching the flow of blood. She rushed Shurik and plunged the knife into the back of his neck. She hoped to sever his spinal cord—breaking the circuit that granted him mobility was the only way she could think of to stop him—but the blade glanced off one of the vertebrae and lodged in the thick strap of muscle upholstering his scapula.

Shurik wheeled on her, allowing Price to slump to the floor. He planted Claire on her back with a hockey check across the chest. This time he wasn't after souvenirs. He spun the wrench around so that its head was angled downward directly over her face and prepared to plunge it into her skull.

Head ringing from any of a half-dozen concussions she had suffered in the past twenty minutes, Claire mistook the churning ebb of the helicopter's rotors as a by-product of her misfiring nervous system. It wasn't until the corridor was flooded with blinding white light from the helicopter's underbelly that she realized they were on stage. A second later a red, pencil-thin beam cut through the brightness and a shot was fired. Shurik dropped the wrench and fell to the floor in the grip of an inexplicable spasm.

"Get out of here!" yelled Price. "Go!" He was doubled-over rubbing his eyes.

"Why did you save me?" Claire shouted back. "Why, if you knew I was dead?" Now wasn't the time or the place, but she wanted answers. Part of her, the part she remembered—the scientist—still lingered somewhere inside her.

"Because they want you alive," he confessed miserably. Price reached for his gun, but Claire stomped on his hand before he could get his fingers around it. He winced in pain. "I was following orders."

"I'm pregnant, you son-of-a-bitch!"

"I know."

"You couldn't . . . I didn't . . ." she stammered. "Eric was the only one . . ."

"I know," Price said again.

Claire was on the verge of losing it. Her mind wasn't working rationally enough to make absolute sense of what Price was saying, but a half-formed truth was beginning to take shape much as the life inside of her was rapidly moving from concept to reality. "LIAR!" she shouted, cuffing him on the side of the head with the barrel of the 9mm. "STOP FUCKING WITH ME!" She was shaking, equal parts fear and rage.

Price stroked his cut cheek and dabbed his bloodied fingertips with the tip of his tongue. "Go now. They're here for *you*."

"No . . ." said Claire. "I don't believe you."

The helicopter had moved on, leaving them in relative darkness, though it hadn't gone far. Claire could still hear its rotors hacking at the frozen night on the opposite side of the station. Suddenly, she felt as if it was stalking her, waiting for an opening, waiting for her guard to come down. That there were men inside of it didn't even occur to her. It was an entity unto itself armed with freewill, menace, hunger.

Price calmly reached for the gun.

Claire's hand tensed, her finger pressed against the trigger. She had stopped shaking. "I'll kill you," she said.

Price nudged Shurik with his toe. "Do it now before Sleeping Beauty wakes up."

Shurik's massive chest heaved and a slow, decay-laden breath gurgled in his throat.

"He's not dead?" Claire asked, incredulous.

"You don't get it," said Price. "Dead is no good to them. Living specimens . . . Vessels for the organism. He's stunned, that's all."

Shurik moaned and rolled his head to one side. His fingers twitched. Price crabbed away from him, still too weak to stand.

"Close your eyes," said Claire.

"What?" Price moaned.

Claire leveled the gun at his face. "Close your eyes or I won't do it."

Price obliged and Claire fired a single shot into his left kneecap. A hideous snarl contorted his face as he roared in agony. Rage had rekindled the fire in his eyes and it now shone on Claire with white-hot intensity.

"What the fuck?" he bellowed, clutching his leg.

"I can't kill you," said Claire. "You saved my life. It wouldn't be right." She shrugged apologetically and backed into the corridor. "I bet if you ask nicely, he'll do it for you."

Shurik was now sitting up. His face looked as if it had been pieced together from butcher scraps. Price attempted to drag himself away, but Shurik's hand was locked onto his good leg like a bear trap. "Claire!" he shouted after her. "Cla—" But by then she had turned the corner and the only life she cared about saving was the one inside of her.

Claire's life was a jigsaw puzzle. She was holding all of the pieces but it was impossible to make them fit. Too many lies. Too much deception. Layer upon layer of subterfuge had pushed her past the point of reason and left her grabbing for the truth. Guesses—these were all she had left. And right now she couldn't afford to guess. She didn't know why she'd believed Price when he said that they—whoever the fuck *they* were—were here for her. Paranoia probably—hell if she wasn't being assaulted by every fear, phobia, and delusion she'd ever experienced—but right about now when all hope seemed lost she was predisposed to believe the worst. Besides, who else was left? Witz was lost down a hole, McKenzie's heart had sold out on him, *they* had Hatcher, and the others were dead, except for maybe Price. But probably him too because his screams had dwindled and the corridor was mostly quiet now but for the mechanical drone of the helicopter.

If it was her they wanted . . . Well, chances are they weren't going to give up, not after all of this, this elaborate setup, so many dead already, until they got what they were after. Claire collapsed into the corridor wall outside her quarters and cried for the first time in as long as she could remember. Even when her mother had drifted into morphine-induced death she'd clamped down on her emotions and had never shed a single tear. Her mother, the real victim, hadn't cried once through the entire ordeal—not the diagnosis, chemo, hair loss, the pain, terrible pain—so Claire had followed suit and sucked it up. She had to be at least as strong as her mother. But this, it was unfair, unconscionable, cruel—she didn't know *them* and worse yet, *they* didn't know her. A vessel—that's what Price had said. Like goddamn fucking Tupperware, that's all she was to them. And her developing child—a vessel within a vessel.

She was cornered, trapped; there was no way out of it. She could hear the helicopter, a giant bird of prey, holding its position above the station while she cowered within the quaking walls like a field mouse. She wanted them to fly back to wherever it was they came from, to leave her to freeze to death. Anything was better than the death they had planned for her. She threw back her head and shouted, "GO AWAY!" But it was pointless. Either they weren't listening, or didn't care. Her plea was really nothing more than a squeak, a pathetic little mouse cry, an admission of vulnerability and defeat. No, they weren't going anywhere. Not without what they had come for.

Not without her.

Claire still had Price's gun. She could kill herself and end all of this right here, right now. It wasn't victory, but it wasn't defeat either. Her will, her terms. It was easy pressing the muzzle to her temple, easy lining up a shot that would splatter her brains, easy telling herself that this was the only solution. But it was impossible to pull the trigger. She believed in life, its stubborn hold, good or bad, on all things it inhabited. Its chemistry, its magic, was simply too strong. "WHAT ARE YOU WAITING FOR?" Claire shouted. But of course she knew the answer.

She tucked the gun into her pants and fingered the wristband. It was her only way out of here—this or a body bag. And only one of these ensured the survival of her child. She wasn't thinking long-term now, but incrementally. Minute to minute, buying time. Nine months was a long way off, but each second brought her a step closer to bringing something good into the world. What if she played along with them, wandered into their trap deliberately, let them carry her away? She could reason with them, make a deal, at the very least beg for the life of her child, give herself up as collateral. Behave herself—be the best, most cooperative damn guinea pig in the history of animal experimentation. Or maybe she could escape from wherever it was they would take her. It was worth a shot. The heater was no longer blowing and the station was getting cold. Death was close by. She needed to do this now.

She'd hoped to get pregnant, if ever at all, *after* she was carried across the threshold of the honeymoon suite in the arms of the man she married . . . If ever at all. *C'est la vie.* Maybe the next time around she'd get it right. But she was a realist, and nothing in her life to this point had suggested that things would work out any differently. It was only fitting that Georgiy came scampering along at that very moment, not on a majestic white horse as Claire, when she was much younger of course, had been misled into believing, but on his own two hands and feet. A white jackal at best. Her Prince Charming, face lathered in scavenger's blood, though not beneath making a kill himself if the opportunity presented itself. And as much as she detested him, his feral lunacy and dumb allegiance to the organism thriving in his veins and guiding his actions, she admired the purity of his instinct. He was an example to live by; if that is, he didn't succeed in killing her first.

She turned to run but Georgiy was on her in a few lopsided strides, a tornado whirl of reckless fury that sent both of them sprawling to the floor. He was smaller and much less powerful than Shurik though made up for it with quickness and agility. Like a dog, he went straight for her neck, the carotid and jugular, panting and gnashing after the warm red river that flowed beneath the surface. She tucked in her chin to protect herself from his champing jaws, so he bit her on the cheek, tearing away a strip of flesh and choking it down before diving in again. Claire pummeled him in the face with her fists but the injuries she inflicted were superficial, his nerve endings deadened by adrenaline and frostbite and bloodlust. He plunged for her neck again, and this time she pressed her thumbs into his eye sockets, hooking them deep behind the dull dusky orbs and wrenching his head savagely to one side with all her surging strength. She must have snapped his neck because he shuddered and went completely limp.

Claire rolled Georgiy off of her and rose to her feet. Her blood was pumping furiously now and her earlier plan of surrender seemed like a joke. Suicide wasn't any way for a mother to take care of her child. If there was one thing she wanted to instill in her offspring it was the need, the obligation to keep fighting no matter the odds or likely outcome. Evolution wasn't inevitable. The only guarantee was that each success story was built atop a foundation of innumerable failures. She would teach her child this simple fact.

She removed her wristband and looped it over Georgiy's wrist. "I do," she uttered defiantly as she carried him in her arms to the entrance of her quarters and heaved him across the threshold. *Always a bridesmaid* . . . She closed the door and waited as the room automatically sealed itself off. Once the trap was sprung the helicopter throttled into position. Moments later, Claire watched as the habitation module detached like a rocket stage and was carried off into the polar night.

This left her and Shurik. She couldn't take him head to head but if she used her cunning and was careful she might just be able to manage the Russian Neanderthal. As long as the auxiliary floodlights remained on she could keep it together. She was considering her options when any semblance of a plan she may have had evaporated in a whirlwind of slashing rotor blades. The helicopter—different from the others, a troop transport from the looks of it—hacked its way over the ice field and touched down less than fifty feet from where Claire stood in the opening only just now vacated by her quarters. Maybe her little ruse hadn't fooled them, or maybe they were here for Shurik—whatever the case, she was screwed. Hiding from Shurik was one thing; hiding from the ghostly specters that swarmed out of the transport's side was another. There were five or six of them, each sheathed in insulated white polar shells that in nearly every respect but color resembled the blue Smurf suits Claire and the others had worn on their initial forays into the derelict station. Not an inch of skin was exposed, and their identities were concealed beneath the sinister glint of mirrored face shields that captured the blazing chrome-white intensity of the helicopter's running lights. All but one was armed with heavy white rifles. They were fanning out, communicating with hand gestures, circling the station, moving toward it, guns shouldered in anticipation of trouble. This was bad, very bad. Two of the six—yes, six, she'd counted them—broke off from the others and entered the generator shack. Power—they wanted real light, serious candlepower, not these pale little floods that couldn't excite a firefly. But then they emerged, rocking a drum of fuel out the door and easing it onto its side.

Before Claire realized what they were doing, a not-so-distant explosion shattered the night, hurling an enormous fireball into the sky. A split-second later a concussive wave came gusting across the ice field, an invisible hand that urged Claire back into the shadows. *The Russian station*, she realized immediately, *they blew it up . . . They're destroying the evidence! So much for hiding out until the sun comes up.*

Although her obituary was already as good as written, she was more determined than ever to do this on her own terms. It wasn't logical and it certainly wasn't going to change things, but she needed to know who had done this to her. She needed to unmask her executioner, to look him in the eye and, if possible, kill him. It was simple. Of course there was only one of her and six of them, but she had *S. iroquoisii* on her side and enough adrenaline coursing through her veins to bring her to the verge of spontaneous combustion. She could hear them, sense the vibrations of their footsteps traveling up through the soles of her feet, the faceless white ghosts, gliding through the station, checking for survivors. *No, not survivors. Subjects. Not me*, thought Claire, moving toward them through the main corridor faster than was rational. She was through running, through hiding. If this was to be her Alamo, she'd take as many of them as she could with her to the grave. She was going hunting.

She arrived at the junction just beyond the entrance to the bathroom and positioned herself so that the first ghost to turn the corner would get the surprise of his life. This time, she wouldn't try to reason. She wouldn't beg. And she sure as hell wouldn't hesitate. She'd strike without warning and plunge Shurik's carving knife into any part of him that would accept her blade. She'd stab and stab and keep stabbing until there was so little white left of his suit that when his companions finally stumbled across his corpse they'd mistake him for Santa Claus. Red, dead and anything but jolly.

How it had come to this, she couldn't quite say. She'd lived a lifetime in the past two . . . Or was it three weeks? All of this, from the very beginning—Hatcher's offer, the blind eye she had turned either willfully or subconsciously to the whole fucking charade in this laboratory turned burial ground, to the man whose blood she'd soon bathe herself in—was a great big blur. At best she'd been seeking a desperate solution to a hopeless situation. At worst, euthanasia. Assisted suicide. No happy endings here. And then it struck her—history was repeating itself. It was here that the maternal bloodline thickened and converged, Claire's destiny intermingled with that of her mother. She'd often wondered at her mother's state of mind on that fateful night when resolve had overtaken restraint and turned a life-giver into a life-taker.

The situation was nothing like this, and yet it was in many ways identical. Claire had always believed that her fear of the dark had grown out of the twisted game of hide and seek her father had forced upon her so many years ago. But it was now clear to her that it had also grown out of that image of her mother, spattered in blood, glowering over her father's dead body like a wild woman. Because here too was darkness—the haunting image sprocketing noisily in the theater of her mind each time the lights went out.

Despite her incredible strength, the knife in her hand was suddenly very heavy. Torn between who she once was and what she had become, Claire could barely support the weight of the blade, no less wield it against another human being. He was within ten feet of her when her grip gave out and the knife clattered to the floor. He stopped dead in his tracks, stiffening as she withdrew into the shadows, holding her breath. Claire waited, her pulse racing, muscles tensed. She thought about picking up the knife but couldn't move. A sickening paralysis had taken hold of her and would not let go. In a moment of weakness she had betrayed her location and had lost her only chance at making a fight of it. If this was the best she could muster, then she deserved to die.

A few days ago McKenzie had described one of the crime scenes he'd investigated before retiring from the Chicago PD: an unidentified prostitute shot in the face with a 12-gauge at point blank range. Claire hadn't given the grim reckoning a second thought until now, but suddenly she couldn't get the image out of her mind. It wasn't so much the incident she found memorable, it was the manner in which the woman had died. Guided by instinct, Jane Doe had thrown up her arms in a final defensive posture, the buckshot shredding her hands and fingers before obliterating her face. It was textbook, McKenzie had explained, right down to the tissue samples forensics had collected from beneath her long painted fingernails. Not that the evidence mattered—the shooter had never been identified. Without a suspect, without a witness, the case was closed almost immediately. For months, McKenzie had been tormented by the same image—Jane Doe pleading for her life in those last interminable seconds before the hammer dropped. With all that had happened Claire wasn't sure if she believed McKenzie, but he'd claimed that it was one of the main reasons he'd come over to JPAC. No answers, no sense of closure, no way of putting a faceless prostitute to rest. Not with the scant resources that had been at his disposal as a member of the Windy City's finest. But it really didn't matter what Claire believed. Like it or not, she was on the verge of becoming that Jane Doe, another anonymous victim the world would never hear about. And it was all over but for the . . .

Shouting. Claire couldn't believe her luck, but there it was—a man's voice, calling urgently to anyone who'd listen, booming through the corridor at the speed of sound. Trouble of some sort. More shouting, other voices thrown into the mix. Shurik! Her stalker broke off the hunt and bolted back the way he had come. Claire waited until his footsteps had subsided and peeked around the corner.

She was alone again. *Now what?* The wind was picking up and she was cold. She didn't want to die here—whether on her terms or at the whim of a total stranger. Not here, not like Alan and all the others, not like Jane Doe. Hatcher's plan to ride the Osprey out of town may have failed in the worst possible way, but at least he'd been willing to die trying. She gathered the knife off the floor and followed the sounds of the commotion to its source in the common room.

Just as she had thought, a handful of the ghostly white specters were embroiled in a life or death struggle with Shurik. They had laid down their guns in favor of less lethal means of subduing the Russian brute. Two of them wielded chairs like lion-tamers—circling and prodding at Shurik as he swung on them with the massive wrench—while another worked at looping a noose about his neck. The noose was at the end of a long rigid shaft, perhaps eight feet from tip to tip, of the sort used by Animal Control to restrain vicious dogs and such. The one handling the noose was having a hell of a time getting it over Shurik's head as it was nearly impossible to keep him in any one place long enough to get a bead on him. There was a loud metallic gong and the clatter of steel as Shurik's wrench connected with a collapsible chair and ripped it from the grasp of one of his assailants. The chair flew across the room and knocked the chart bearing the names of Alan and the other dead members of the first research team off the wall. Spun about by the force of the impact, the one who'd been holding the chair regained his balance only to be caught in the head with a colossal blow that fractured his mirrored face shield and almost certainly his skull. He fell where he'd stood, the life gone out of him without any indication that a living human being had only a split-second earlier occupied the white polar suit lying at Shurik's feet like a readymade body bag.

Without missing a beat, two others took up the cause of subduing Shurik, jabbing at him with their rifle butts in a coordinated attack, delivering stiff blows to his torso, both front and back. A third remained well out of range of the wrench's deadly radius, steadied himself on one knee and took aim with a tranquilizer gun. Shurik dropped the wrench and his hand jumped to his throat just above the mantle of human scalps. The hypodermic dart startled him, causing him to pause long enough so that the noose could be looped over his head. Once in place, the noose—it looked like a fan belt—drew tight, restricting the flow of blood through the carotid artery and cutting his strength in half. In a last desperate bid for survival, Shurik seized the long metal shaft with both hands and flung its handler through the air. A second later, the powerful sedative began to take effect and in a matter of moments Shurik slumped into a fitful state of unconsciousness.

Dumbstruck, Claire watched as Shurik was first bound and then strapped to a long spine board like those used by EMT's to transport car accident victims. The team worked as one—a single word was never uttered between them—as they claimed their specimen and gathered up their dead. Only one did not participate and it was he who looked Claire's way as she stood in the mouth of the central corridor gaping stupidly. In all the mayhem she had unwittingly edged out of the shadows, exposing herself. Rather than remaining still and possibly avoiding detection, she'd instinctively jumped back, diving into the dishwater gloom of the corridor floodlights. If anything, it was her panicked retreat that had caught his eye. Okay, maybe he hadn't seen her. *There's a chance—Fuck, he's coming this way!* But why hadn't he alerted the others?

By the time Claire got her ass in gear, he could've practically reached out and grabbed her by the hood of her parka. It had to be her guy, the one she'd been lying in wait for just minutes earlier. But if it was him, why was he no longer carrying a gun? Claire ducked left at the junction of the outer corridor and pinned her back to the wall.

Why are you running? He's unarmed and you've got the knife. What happened to going down fighting? You saw what they did with Shurik. You're next. Claire gripped the knife tightly and peered around the corner. He was no longer coming after her, but had stopped just inside the corridor entrance and was fiddling with the floodlights. First one, and then the other, he very methodically removed the bulbs from their sockets. The light dimmed. He proceeded further into the corridor and did the same thing with the only other set of floodlights in that section. Now more ghost-like than ever, he moved through the darkness he'd created with a sureness and sense of purpose more terrifying than any gun.

Whoever was after her had done his homework. He was using Claire's fear of the dark as his weapon. It was she who was suddenly unarmed. Her mouth went dry and her throat shriveled inward so that it was as if she was breathing through a drinking straw. This time she did not let go of the knife, but instead white-knuckled it until her hand was numb. Mild shivers gave way to fierce tremors that wracked her body. Entirely certain that he was after her—not just anyone, but her specifically, Claire Elizabeth Matthews, with all her childish fears and emotional baggage—she ran.

She was right back where it had all started, her father's voice rising up inside her head—a ghoulish tenor syncopated to the drumming of her heart and the frantic beat of her footsteps—every bit as terrifying as it had been nearly two decades ago. She ran, but like before there was nowhere to run. She waited at the next junction, one of eight equidistant from one another the octagonal structure comprised, and tried to calm herself. The sadistic bastard strode purposefully after her, pausing again to disable the floodlights, effectively barring her passage were she to consider doubling back. The way he seemed to create darkness was almost supernatural to her, an ability no more comprehensible than the way in which the bioluminescing creatures of the deep ocean created light. Because of the cold, the strength *S. iroquoisii* had imparted to her had dwindled to next to nothing, though in its absence her senses had retained an acuity that was intolerable. Each turn of the bulb in its socket grated over Claire's spine.

She forced herself out from behind the wall and approached him, knife clutched in front of her, though at that moment she would have gladly traded it for a flashlight. She inched slowly forward, not because she thought she could take him by surprise, but because her legs were like stone. And then he stopped what he was doing to look at her, his gloved hand still wrapped around the bulb.

"I'll kill you," she stammered.

Although he was taller than she was, she could see herself in his convex face shield, stretched to the breaking point and willow-thin, as he appraised her with a slight inclination of his head.

Ignoring the knife in her hand, he looked away and finished unscrewing the first bulb. He then held it out in front of her and let it fall to the floor. There was a hollow pop as the pressurized gas within was released in a spray of broken glass.

"Stop!" Claire commanded as he began to unscrew the lone remaining bulb. She summoned what little remained of her ebbing strength and slashed at the air with the knife. "Don't!" she growled unconvincingly. "I'm not afraid of you."

Another turn of the screw, the light flickered, contact was broken and darkness's black tide rushed in. He turned to face her, the slow synthetic crinkle of his suit enveloping her like a static charge of pure fear as he extended his arm and dropped the bulb.

Claire wasn't sure how she made it to the supply room—where the will had come from, how she'd gotten her legs moving—only that it was no better than a tomb to her now. He was using the darkness, herding her with it, and she had responded like a scared little bunny trying to outrun a prairie fire. It had been her idea to thaw Lim so that she could check his blood for . . . *What? Signs of infection, disease, antibodies* . . . If only she'd checked out Hatcher's offer a little better . . . *If only* . . . *What else did you tell them about me, you son of a bitch? I hope you suffer.*

The floor was now slicked with frozen bath water, the rubberized fabric bath in which Lim had revived was deflated, placental. Like every other move Claire had made in the past couple of weeks, she'd blundered through the door and nearly broken her neck as she skated wildly across the room and onto her back. She scarcely had time to collect herself and dive behind a stack of shipping crates before the door swung open.

She watched through a narrow slot between the crates as he closed the door after him and disabled the room's only source of light. The pursuit had taken her only halfway around the station's circumference, but because the habitation modules were booby-trapped the supply room was her best option.

"Come out, come out, wherever you are . . ."

Muffled by the suit, his words rippled over her, a toneless refrain that arrived on the tail end of an echo that had terrorized her since childhood. No longer was he an anonymous menace terrorizing her with second-hand information. By invoking her darkest hour he'd crossed over and become the one demon she'd never been able to outrun.

It wasn't the darkness Claire had feared all these years, it was what lived inside it. She'd been too young, and then her father had been too dead for her to ever confront him, and this alone had prevented her from moving on, evolving. Ever since, she'd been waging a war against a foe she couldn't confront. But now he was real, resurrected like Lim. Possibility was no longer bound by the laws of science she'd once known and understood. This life inside of her—it was an immaculate conception of sorts—so far removed from the plausible that its existence implied miraculous intervention. Suddenly, the darkness wasn't so dark, her path illuminated by promise.

He must have heard her coming because he deflected the knife with his left forearm as Claire rushed at him out of the blackness. Avoiding the kill-shot was dumb luck on his part—she'd been aiming for his heart—but she'd managed to draw blood, its oily-sweet perfume sparking a fire inside her. It was as though a hibernating sense, one that was buried inside her all along, had been awakened by the scent of blood and she was now somehow able to see through the blackness. All at once darkness had texture, hue, layers. It wasn't high-resolution, but instinct operated on its own wavelength. She rushed him again—he was like a Rorschach blotch spilled onto black construction paper, distinctly familiar in his alienness—but again he was ready for her. This time he caught her by the arm with both hands and slammed her wrist down on the hard edge of a shipping crate—once, twice, three times, until the knife was knocked from her grasp and clattered to the floor.

Claire twisted free and dropped to her hands and knees. De-fanged, she searched for the knife frantically. It was her only shot against an opponent who despite the impossible visibility seemed to know her every move. Tangling with Shurik had emptied her tank and she was now running on fumes. The hand-sawn scalp wound at the base of her skull throbbed plaintively with each rush of blood called to the aid of her failing muscles. And then just as she got her hands on the knife, her head whipped violently back and another shade of black, deeper than the others, was added to this new palette of hers.

He kicked me in the head. This was the first thought that managed to penetrate the syrupy blackness oozing through Claire's synapses like motor oil. Why then was he cradling her head in his lap, stroking her face? She again found herself imagining her father inside the suit, but this time it was atonement guiding his hand—it was how she wanted to remember him. But, no—though her night-sight, along with her other senses, had been knocked out of whack by the blow to her head, the delirium was wiped away by the glove's sterile touch, negating any trace of humanity the cryptic gesture may have otherwise imparted. Every move he made was now amplified by the darkness—the crinkle of his suit, the hollow scrape of his breath against the face shield, even the visceral gurgle of his digestive tract—small reminders that this was a man and not a nightmare masquerading inside a white hazmat suit.

Claire remembered how strange, how totally unreal it felt eavesdropping on the inner workings of her own body the first time she had donned the Smurf suit. She had been alive for nearly thirty years, but until that moment had never really connected with life, at least not in a way that was relevant. And now she was pregnant and she couldn't have escape life's relevance if she tried.

He went on cradling her head in his lap, his stomach turning over like a garbage disposal growling at capacity. *Something he'd eaten? Stress—his conscience repaying him with ulcers?* Claire was too tired to care. She had reached a place she'd never thought possible and was only interested in sleep. It wasn't until she caught a whiff of his irreconcilable scent—a pungent distillate of fear, frostbite and decay—that she even considered the stomach noises belonged to someone other than the person stroking her hair. Maybe she'd forgotten about Lim because she'd assumed that he was dead like the others. But still he clung to life—self-preservation, hunger—and it was the latter of these triumphing over its cousin that brought him out of hiding in search of food.

Claire knew what Mr. Rubber Jammies couldn't possibly know isolated as he was from his environment. The technology he wore around him like a security blanket cut him off from all but the most blatant markers of the sensual world. Although the scent announced itself with the subtlety of a cavalry charge, he was totally oblivious of the thundering cascade of stomach acid and cannibalized remains, a peril so close that Claire could smell it on Lim's breath. Nor did he catch the foggy star-shine of the ravenous eyes cutting through the darkness toward him.

Claire no longer knew which category of beast she fell into—predator, prey, scavenger—she had been, and was all three in a sense. A creature of opportunity like her ancestors, she pushed aside forethought and gave free reign to her instincts. *H. erectus* hadn't triumphed over his physically dominant cousin, *Neanderthalensis*, by fighting fairly. Individually, neither Claire nor Lim was a match for the ghost. Fatigue and injury had left them vulnerable. But together, liberated of the civilizing influence *S. iroquoisii* had all but extinguished in them, they were a force capable of driving their foe into early extinction.

The fight was savage and desperate. Claire and Lim were connected by an organized hunting instinct, the same inborn frequency that had guided Shurik and Georgiy. They were a wolf pack of two—circling, lunging, timing their assault so that their prey remained hopelessly off-balance. The coordinated attack was taking its toll. Pitted against the two of them, he was expending much of his energy just staying on his feet. His arms were growing heavy. Claire could see it in the way he kept dropping his guard. Soon, his strength would fail completely and they'd be on him. Lim's occluded eyes blazed dimly as he sensed feeding time drawing near.

It was all over but for the vultures when Claire was caught off-guard by a flailing blow to the chin that spun her around and planted her on her knees. Blood filled her mouth, but if anything her senses were sharpened by the warm metallic rush of liquid coating her teeth and exciting her taste buds. Then, as if she knew exactly where to find it amidst the frantic scuffle of feet, her hand closed around the knife handle—there were no accidents anymore, only awareness and instinct. She had her fangs back.

Lim had fastened himself to the ghost's back like an overgrown parasite and was hanging on with his one arm. Claire coiled her legs under her and sprang, leading with the knife, driving it in and upward beneath the sternum into his heart. And just like that he stiffened, fell flat on his face and died. She crouched at his side and slowly ran her hand over the length of his body. Killing a man wasn't at all what she'd expected. She tried for a moment to label her feelings but it seemed pointless because what she had done was no less automatic, no less vital to her continued survival than drawing a breath. In another context, she may have given her actions more thought but right now it was cold and she was shivering. Lim squatted next to her, rocking on his heels and whimpering softly.

Claire wasted no time skinning her quarry. One long zip and the suit opened up releasing a perfumed scent that was instantly familiar to her—*bath soap*—though was so out of context she dismissed it as her imagination. He was tall and rangy though hardly frail. She was surprised that he hadn't injured her worse. It was almost as if he'd been holding back, going easy on her. She didn't know how long it would take rigor mortis to set in, but worked quickly to get him out of the suit. Handling him so closely like this the familiar scent announced itself with even greater insistence until it was like a fist hammering on her olfactory receptors. *Just because he smells like . . .* She was being ridiculous of course, ignoring the law of probability. Half the men in America used the same bath soap. It didn't mean a thing. First his legs, then his upper body—good, now she was getting somewhere. Though naked but for a pair of boxer shorts, his skin was still warm. Claire ran her hands over his torso and touched his face however she was like a blind woman attempting to read Braille for the first time. Like the scent, the pieces were familiar but she could not make them fit. Not unless she was willing to abandon reason altogether and surrender herself completely to paranoia as Hatcher had done.

Claire snapped out of it as voices crackled over a tiny headset located in the suit's hood. She was reminded of her situation as the transport helicopter throttled up outside the station, giving rise to a maelstrom of cold and wind and ice. Everything was happening fast now. It was time to go. Soon, the other men in white hazmat suits would come looking for their missing comrade.

The suit wasn't exactly a perfect fit but neither was Claire's new persona—*not yet*—and she was adjusting to this easily enough. She was now armed with the certainty that whatever the situation, she could and would adapt. It was warm inside the suit—the ghost's life residue, the instant warmth of a built-in heating unit—a thousand times warmer than the clothes she'd shed to become him. First the left sleeve, then the right . . . *God, it feels good to be warm again. So fucking good.* Her body temperature already on the rise, and she was once again plugged into *S. iroquoisii's* energizing current. Last on was the hood, and *zip* . . . She now saw the world through the eyes of another. Rose-colored glass, it was not.

One picture was worth how many words? In this case ten million wouldn't have been enough to describe what she was feeling at that moment. It made no difference that the man laying at her feet, the man whose long athletic muscles Lim was cannibalizing with carnivorous zeal, was rendered entirely in the aqueous green halftones of night-vision optics. Nothing—not full color, not words, not Grand Jury testimony, not even beautiful daylight itself could make things any clearer to her.

Eric.

Other than her mother, he was the one person in the world Claire had trusted fully. She now saw that paranoia lived in the shadow of truth, not to mislead but to protect. That desire—thirst in the case of wildebeests, the need for love in her own—was what compelled them to the river's edge despite the dangers they knew lurked beneath the surface. But at least thirst was understandable, absolutely necessary to survival, and the wildebeest could not be blamed. Love, however, the quintessential human desire, was weakness, an impediment to survival. Illogical, messy, manipulative—it clouded instinct, impaired judgment, made one vulnerable to hurt much deeper than a crocodile's jaws. Claire had drunk from that river and now she was feeling the fangs.

Of all Eric's deceits—convincing her that she *had* to put aside her misgivings about Hatcher and do Antarctica, his counterfeit goodness and integrity, his alleged vasectomy . . . Of all these and countless others, she was bothered most by the pregnancy test because with this he had blinded her to the one instinct that mattered most. She had doubted the life inside of her and for this reason she had done nothing to protect it. Claire's mother hadn't killed her own husband to protect herself. She had done so to protect Claire. But in killing the man she loved, she had killed a part of herself. Cancer hadn't taken her mother's life—shame and guilt were the agents of her suffering and demise. The illness whose origin the doctors had traced to her mother's ovaries had actually developed in the cracks of a broken heart. Cancer was simply the vile manifestation of two decades of grief.

Her mother had spent the last twenty years of her life apologizing for what Claire had never truly believed was absolutely necessary until now. But there it was, an epiphany she had been carrying inside of her from the moment of her own conception. Nowhere was the human survival instinct more deeply ingrained than in the contract of the maternal bond. Self-preservation was only about the self inasmuch as it was biologically incumbent upon every species on earth to survive long enough to produce and raise viable offspring. Simple perpetuation. Ultimately, self-preservation, the grand-daddy of all the biological directives, was about sacrifice. No matter the cost—them or you—the means of getting there were justified, *necessary*, as long as it ensured that one's DNA lived on.

Lim was too busy satisfying his own needs to see it coming. Claire used a chokehold to interrupt the supply of oxygen to his brain until he flopped around like a fish and passed out. She then took him by the ankle, dragged him out of the hole in the station's side and across the ice to where the last ghosts were piling onboard the helicopter. She was greeted without suspicion at the door to the troop compartment by a man shorter than herself. His voice, inflected with the slight syrupy drawl of an educated southerner, crackled over the headset. He was barely audible above the slashing rotors and howling wind.

"Well, I'll be damned," he said. "Look what the cat dragged in. If he ain't a sight all dressed up in his birthday suit with nowhere to go."

Claire didn't respond.

"There's blood on you," the voice continued incidentally. "He give you any trouble?"

Considering it was Eric's blood the ghost was talking about, there were a million ways she could have answered, but she held her tongue and simply shook her head no. She then patted the hood where it covered her ear to indicate that her headset was malfunctioning.

"We can put a man on the moon . . ." he began, only to interrupt himself. "Never mind that now, you can fill me in on the way back to base."

Flaming ruins marked the spot where the Russian station had once stood. Red and orange tongues of fire whipped into a frenzy by the wind feasted on the scattered debris, driving the long polar night into temporary remission. Claire sat wedged among a row of men, each wearing a white hazmat suit identical to her own, a mirror image of the quiet specters sitting across from them on the other side of the troop compartment. She had banked on this—that the ghosts would remain suited up until they returned to "base" and underwent some sort of decontamination procedure to ensure they weren't carrying any unwanted hitchhikers. As for Claire, there was no reason to suspect that it was her camouflaged among them. As far as anyone but Eric knew, she was locked inside the belly of a Skycrane on her way to wherever it was that men did terrible things in the name of science. Had the ghosts known that Georgiy was the living capsule's sole occupant, they would in all probability still be combing the station looking for her. But just like Hatcher had been back in Vietnam, they were so smug certain about the infallibility of their plan that no one had bothered to check. She'd give almost anything to see the looks on their faces when they threw open the door to her quarters and Georgiy, drenched in blood and foaming at the mouth, came bounding out like Cujo.

No one spoke for nearly an hour as the helicopter plowed ahead through the unstable air, jolting and shuddering violently. The powerful turbines moaned in protest but somehow the pilot was managing to keep the bird aloft. If the other passengers were at all concerned they didn't show it. She wondered about the faces behind the masks. What kind of men treated a death-defying flight over an insurvivable wasteland onboard an aircraft whose primary cargo was a drugged and bound cannibal as all in a day's work? Dangerous men. Men, in almost any other situation, to be afraid of. But not now. Not this Claire.

She had killed Eric in virtually the same way her mother had killed her father. The irony, of course, was not lost on her. Nor was it especially relevant given her new outlook on life. Whether or not she had seen the real thing, Eric was who he was. Like so many species in the animal kingdom, his outward appearance—handsome, alluring—belied his true nature. The vibrant dorsal fins used by lionfish to attract mates can also inflict great pain, even death on the unwary. But second-guessing herself was a waste of time. Still, she couldn't help but wonder when and how it had begun. Was Eric's treachery inborn or was it adaptive? It was frustrating that she would never know for certain, but as a scientist she knew better than to expect tidy, neatly-wrapped answers. Rarely did the pieces just fall into place. You had to make them fit. Maybe one day she would take the time.

Claire tried to sit still, remain focused, to distract herself from the chaos creeping into her mind. But it was hot inside the suit—hotter, she was sure, for her than the others—and she could feel the carbonated sizzle returning to her bloodstream with an urgency impossible to ignore. The suit's filtration unit did a good job of providing her with clean breathable air, but it also prevented heat from escaping. And it was this, the heat, as mysterious and compelling as any drug that was beginning to wreak havoc on the outward display of indifference she had manufactured out of civilized self-restraint. The universe's greatest catalyst—from the Big Bang to the solar radiation that warmed earth's atmosphere to man's harnessing of fire—heat changed everything. It was changing her.

Another rocky hour passed, and then another, and Claire began to suspect that her headset was truly defective. At first it was little more than a murmur that tugged on her ear to come closer, to listen. Without being too obvious, she looked over the immobile forms around her, but could tell nothing from the expressionless hoods. Maybe they were on to her—this was all a game to them—an encore performance. Drive Claire mad, trick her into revealing herself. The whisper, however, continued to grow until, as if picking up a radio broadcast in one of her fillings, it filled her head with static feedback.

For the past couple of hours, she hadn't given Shurik much thought even though he lay at her feet strapped to the long spine board. No one had bothered to remove the welder's goggles, but Claire didn't have to see his eyes to know that the sedative had worn off. She realized this at precisely the moment she also realized that the radio broadcast in her head was coming from him. Though of significantly greater amplitude, it was part of the same closed frequency transmission that had guided the coordinated attack with which she and Lim had conquered Eric. Migratory birds, schools of sardines numbering in the hundreds of thousands, even insect swarms relied on similar modes of communication to instruct and organize—phenomena beyond the definitive grasp of science—but this was no simple command to fly south for the winter. Teased from the static tapestry like a loose thread that bound all the others together, came a single word, an evocation really, that ranked foremost in the unspoken lexicon of all species on earth . . .

Feed!

Delivered with the force of a commandment from God, the utterance imprinted itself on the circuitry of Claire's mind and began repeating at regular intervals. She tried to shut out the ancient impulse, but it quickly bypassed reason and intellect, the neocortex. Instead, it targeted her archipallium, the primitive reptilian brain and seat of animal instinct as if it had known all along the path of least resistance.

As her hand passed into the bloody tear in the front of her suit, Claire couldn't help but feel that she was reaching deeper inside herself than ever before. Somewhere in there her baby was cannibalizing her to live and grow—stealing calcium from her bones, iron from her blood, water from her tissue—driven by the same requirement that guided the carving knife Claire withdrew. The strange feeling gnawing at her insides wasn't doubt or misgiving. It was hunger. She was eating for two now.

Before any of them knew what was happening Claire slashed the broad nylon restraints immobilizing Shurik's torso. As she attempted to cut free his legs, someone tackled her. But it didn't matter. Shurik sat up, grabbed one of the ghosts by the throat and nearly twisted off his head. Two others went after him but he mashed their skulls together as if breaking eggs for an omelet. All at once, Claire's head was filled with chaotic chatter. It was impossible to differentiate between Shurik's insurgent broadcast and the sudden din of voices blaring over the headset.

Wriggling and larval-white, the ghosts piled on Shurik like maggots, but they were still no match for him. Sensing that the entire mission was about to go down in flames, and with it himself, one of the ghosts jockeyed for an opening so that he could fire a kill shot into Shurik's brain. It was the one with the slow, syrupy drawl. Claire knew this because his was the only voice not vying for a piece of the scrambled airwaves inside her head. Formidable in his vestal whites, he resembled some sort of avenging angel sent from the distant future. Off-balance and rather than take a chance, he angled his way in through the tangle of thrashing limbs and pressed the muzzle of a snow white .45 to Shurik's forehead. Buried under the same avalanche of bodies as Shurik, Claire jab-kicked the ghost behind the knee as he squeezed the trigger, buckling his leg. He let out a very un-angelic cry, the gun jolted upward, and the stray bullet punched a hole the size of a quarter through the top of the troop compartment before shattering one of the rotor blades.

"MAYDAY! MAYDAY! MAY—"

Claire was brought back to consciousness by a pain that was on the verge of plunging her into shock. She felt as if every bone in her body had been smashed. The voices in her head were gone, but these had been replaced by other voices. Soon, she realized that someone was talking to her although she couldn't make out what they were saying above the icy blast of the wind and the clacking of her teeth.

She tried to remember what had been going through her mind in the moments leading up to the crash, yet couldn't locate the catalyst behind her suicidal actions. That is, not until a man's voice penetrated the waves of murk lapping at her brain and she was hauled from the crushed troop compartment by her ankles. Someone removed her hood and shined a flashlight in her face. It was pitch black and the blazing light stung her eyes. Her head flopped to one side and she saw two men in red parkas examining something at the end of a broad stripe of blood leading away from the wreckage. It was Shurik—half of him anyway, frozen solid as he'd dragged his guts across the ice.

The light was back in Claire's face and her cheek was suddenly warm . . . A man's hand—he had removed his glove to check her body temperature. Her body devoured the stingy little crumb of heat and it was like a taste of a drug whose habit she'd only recently kicked. Just a tease, but it was enough. *More,* she wanted to cry out. *More!* But the words were still too distant, far off echoes in her head.

"This one's hypothermic," the man who was touching her called to another. "But she can be moved." He then took his warm hand from her cheek and the cold bit into her once again.

Claire's baby, the hunger growing deep inside her—it returned with an urgency and sense of purpose that silenced her clacking teeth and lifted her from the abyss. "No!" she roared, but was gently forced down as she attempted to stand.

"Relax," came the man's voice. It was firm and reassuring. "I'm a medic," he said. "You're going to be all right."

Claire locked onto the medic's wrist and pressed his bare hand to her cheek. She thought of Father Terrero, both a scientist and dedicated man of God, setting fire to the *Mission Nuestra Señora de la Candelaria,* the mission he had brought up from the barren earth with only blood and sweat and the strength of his conviction to guide him. He had endured eight years of blistering Arizona summers and stinging cold winters, Yankee and Confederate raiders from the north, Mexican *banditos* from the south, smallpox, cholera, drought, starvation . . . He'd even been forced to watch as one of his nuns was raped by a twelve year-old boy, but had shown divine forgiveness in caring for the boy's father—the same man who'd held a knife to his throat while Sister Beatrice had lain prone in the dust praying for merciful death— as he urinated blood all over one of the mission beds while dying of syphilis less than six months later. Yet throughout it all Father Terrero's devotion to the word of God had remained steadfast, his faith in the wisdom of the Holy Father unshaken. Claire could see him performing the Sign of the Cross, sanctifying the ground with holy water, reciting the twenty-third Psalm as he touched the torch to *Nuestra Señora's* thatched roof, but knowing that prayer alone could not exorcise the demons—demons only he had seen under his microscope—from the dead Iroquois braves now rotting in the mission beds. But the Catholic Church had seen things differently and had branded Father Terrero a heretic, too righteous for his own good, guided not by the Bishop's decree but by his own conscience. The man who had sacrificed so much of himself for the good of mankind was excommunicated. Alienated from his peers and from his calling, Father Terrero was dragged to death behind an Indian hunter's horse for conspiring with . . . *A Ha Tinh pygmy rhino.*

But Claire would not let that happen to her. Not again. Not this time around. She would hide among them, wear the skin wisely, would look after herself and her own interests. She would fear the dark no longer. She would use it to her advantage. She would hunt quietly and she would feed furiously. She would lie in wait for the dumb and desirous to come to her. A crocodile in wildebeest's clothing—it was all going to be so easy now. By the time they saw the fire in her eyes blazing just beneath the surface she would have them in a death roll.

"You're going to be fine," came the medic's voice again. "I promise." And his hand on her bare cheek was like Father Terrero's torch, the fire spreading quickly through her, obliterating the past and lighting the future. "Right now, we need to get you warm again."

Biographical Note

An avid outdoorsman and naturalist, Dr. Josh Pryor divides his time between Southern California, where he lives and teaches English at Saddleback College, and anywhere that has yet to be "civilized." A kinder, less psychotic version of Joseph Conrad's Kurtz, he is more at home in a bug-infested swamp, jungle, or forest than in the lavish comforts of the big city. In 2001, Dr. Pryor, an aspiring recluse and visionary, spent seventy-seven consecutive days living in an ancient sandstone hermitage in Turkey's historic Cappadocia region. His diet consisted largely of bread, water, cashews, and dried apricots. Dr. Pryor is an exhaustive researcher in alternative theories of history, cryptozoology, science, and human evolution. His passion for knowledge and discovery has led him to the remote mountain highlands of Laos, the turbulent shores of Indonesia's infamous island volcano, Anak Krakatau (Son of Krakatoa), and most recently to the "Lost World" of Papua New Guinea's Mount Bosavi crater. In December of 2011, Dr. Pryor will accompany a group of scientists and researchers to coastal Venezuela to catalogue endemic species of the great tepuis, massive stone "islands in the sky" that are home to some of the most unusual and elusive creatures on earth, including the legendary veinticuatro ant whose bite is said to induce twenty-four hours of intense pain. Currently, Dr. Pryor is researching a book of historical fiction chronicling the life and work of famed occultist, Aleister Crowley, of whom he is a direct descendant. Fascinated by extinct languages and arcane texts, Dr. Pryor has worked extensively with a group of fellow scholars and paleolinguists at deciphering the enigmatic 15th century Voynich Manuscript. A dedicated conservationist and advocate of human rights, Dr. Pryor is a supporter of Trout Unlimited and Amnesty International. To date, Dr. Pryor has authored two masterpieces: his young sons, Josh Jr. and Luke.

CPSIA information can be obtained
at www.ICGtesting.com
Printed in the USA
FSOW01n1045140916
24945FS